A Stable Life

Maria V. Badin

To my husband and my brother—who believed I could be a writer long before I dared to believe it myself—and to my animals who, with every breath and hoofbeat, taught me the true meaning of A Stable Life.

CONTENTS

VALLEY VISTA RANCH

E arly morning in the submontane valleys of the San Gabriel Mountains, in a sleepy town of California, sits Valley Vista Ranch. Valley Vista Ranch holds in its hands a celebrated equestrian history passed down through generations of horsemen and women who inhabited its domain. Its roots are based in the time-honored Western homestead, producing not only exceptional horses but also remarkable horse people. Stories of strength in breeding, training, teaching, and most notably competing lie on the earth of this ranch with more stories to come.

The sun rises radiating iridescent hues of red, yellow, and orange over the wandering hills and valleys where Miller's Pond glistens in the distance, decorated with oak trees filled with memories of days past. A mare and its foal walk up to the pond and partake in its richness. She lowers her head and gently nuzzles her foal, her soft muzzle brushing over its neck and shoulders in a tender greeting. The foal, still a little wobbly on its legs, leans into the touch with a quiet whicker, comforted by the familiar warmth of its mother. The foal, eyes closed, drops his head down to the water. A hawk makes its presence known with a loud billowing squawk over the valley as he hunts for his breakfast. The mare and foal's ears perk up to the sound, but continue their idyllic morning. More horses, a rainbow display of geldings, wander to the other side of Miller's Pond and drink. The mare lifts her head, swishes her tail, establishing the time-honored matriarchal pecking order. The geldings acknowledge her presence, but otherwise leave her and her foal alone.

Miller's Pond. It holds the secrets and dreams of generations. A proposal. A ruggedly handsome barely twenty-year-old man, dressed in tattered overalls, his blonde hair slicked underneath a cowboy hat, Hank Miller, after five years of courtship, finally elicits the courage to ask Mirabella (his eighteen-year-old girlfriend) for her hand in marriage. The memory of Hank on bended knee and Mirabella's gentle, whimsical smile and nod of affirmation still lingers in the leaves of grass.

"We can make a glorious life here." Hank gestures towards an untamed valley.

"I see a breeding barn, arenas, pastures, you name it. All natural. We'll do it the right way." He hurriedly exclaims. Mirabella, an exotic dark haired beauty of Argentinian decent, flickers her emerald green eyes and softly asks.

"Children?"

"Oh yeah. Lots of them. An entire herd of 'em. Can you see it, Mirabella? Horses will come to this pond. We'll be the envy of the horse world. Horse people from around the globe will be waiting in line for our horses. We'll breed race horses, rodeo horses, show jumpers. You name it."

"Dressage?" She asks, already knowing the answer.

"The sky's the limit. We can bring the best mares from your family's ranch and breed 'em with my stallions. We'll keep track of all the bloodlines. Nobody will have the quality that we bring to the table."

He points to a clearing that over looks a row of bushes, tall grass, and maple trees.

"I'll build you a dressage court over there with the landscape behind you. " He hugs her close to him and kisses her forehead. And with that, he set the course for the Millers. Miller's Pond became the harbinger of all their plans and dreams.

In the distance, a grey 1986 K20 Chevy pickup truck, with one hubcap missing, slowly, with little semblance of shocks, approaches the gate. A grey mist hovers over the grass as Missy Harrison drives through the gate under a sign reading "Valley Vista Ranch". Missy, twenty, a senior in college, with long blond hair tied in a tight single braid under a blue faded baseball cap, smiles in the rear-view mirror revealing a sun-burnt face covered with light brown freckles and bright sea-colored eyes. She pulls down the baseball cap emblazoned with the logo, "WEG SHOW JUMPING 2019." A row of international flags lines the bill of the cap. She stares off to the distance out of her window, daydreaming of her day to come.

Missy stands on the podium with a gold medal draped around her neck, laying brilliantly between the lapels of her red show jacket. She grasps the medal with her ungloved hand and brings it to her lips - kisses it - and places it back on her chest. Her other hand, carrying a ring of flowers, waves to the crowd. Tears flow down her face, her legs shake in her white breaches as the American anthem plays over the loudspeakers. She looks over to her coach, Tegan Miller, smiling back at her. Missy giggles when she sees Tegan mouth the words, "Way to go, kiddo," and looks at her with the adoration of a mother who's sharing this moment they've been working towards since she was a child. She then looks forward to the American flag, lifts her chest and proudly sings the anthem with the rest of the audience.

Missy looks at her dog, a tuxedo black with white chest and white nip on her chin, Staffordshire Bull Terrier, affectionately named Bentley, and taps her baseball cap;

"That's going to be me someday, Bentley." Bentley barks. Missy scratches her dog's head between its ears and continues down the road lined with a white piped gate. Large Sycamore trees behind the pipe gate create an umbrella of leaves and branches over the road. Rays of light peer through the leaves and bounce off of Missy's dust and fly-infested windshield. Missy turns on the windshield wipers, attempting to clean the windows, but only makes it worse.

"Dammit," she mutters to herself. Bentley places her head on Missy's lap. Missy affectionately looks down to Bentley, smiles, pats the steering wheel.

"At least it drives." She laughs.

Missy passes a row of paddocks inhabited by a myriad of bay, gray, and chestnut-colored horses. She rolls down her mud stained window, clicks her lips.

"Good morning, my beauties." She sings. The horses' ears perk up, they look up in unison, and whinny a good morning to her. She continues down the road and parks next to a sign reading "Valley Vista Ranch Riding Club Office" with an arrow pointing to the right. Missy gets out of the truck with Bentley following closely behind. She heads towards the office, smiles, and, like most young adults, instantly changes her mind.

Missy hurries toward the stall, muttering under her breath. "She'll *definitely* be pissed." Gravel crunches under her boots as she glances at her watch, her stomach sinking. Five minutes. Maybe ten, if she's lucky. But there's no way she's leaving without seeing him.

She lets out a sharp whistle, and almost immediately, Remington's glossy black face appears over the stall door, his striking white blaze catching the light. His warm whinny cuts through the morning stillness, his ears flicking forward at the sound of her voice.

"Remi!" she calls, her pace quickening, heart pounding in a way it always does when she sees him. The rush of affection feels as fresh as it did the first time she laid eyes on him.

Sliding the latch open, she steps into the stall and shuts the door behind her. "Good morning, buddy," she whispers, her arms wrapping around his neck like she hasn't seen him in weeks, even though she gave him a full spa bath and infrared treatment just last night. His warm coat smells of hay and leather, and she presses her cheek against him, soaking in the moment.

"How's my Mr. Grand Prix, Gold Medal-Winning Beast? Did you sleep well?" she asks, pulling back to meet his eyes. Remington snorts in reply and nudges her pocket with his nose, clearly on a mission.

Missy laughs, shaking her head. "Impatient, huh? Alright, alright." She digs into her pocket and pulls out a molasses cookie, holding it flat in her palm. Remington takes it delicately, his soft muzzle brushing against her hand.

"Listen, Rem," she starts, her voice dropping to a whisper, as if sharing a secret. "You and me? We're going all the way. First stop: Grand Prix. And after that? The Olympics. Can you see it? Gold medals, flowers, ribbons everywhere. It's gonna be huge."

Remi tosses his head, as if he's in on the plan, and Missy grins. "That's right. You get it. We'll be unstoppable." She strokes his sleek neck, her fingers playing with his mane. "You're my ticket, Remi. You're my big shot. All I have to do is keep you happy and healthy. I'll take care of the rest."

He nips at her sleeve, clearly more interested in treats than grand ambitions.

"Alright, you greedy beast. One more," she says with mock sternness, pulling out another cookie. She holds it teasingly for a moment before letting him take it, then kisses his muzzle. "But that's it for now. Keep this up and you won't fit over the jumps."

She gives his neck a last pat and steps back toward the door. "Okay, I gotta run. Momma Bear's already on a rampage, and I'm not trying to get grounded from riding."

She hesitates, one hand resting on the door, and looks back at him. Her heart swells, a mix of love and determination.

"We're gonna have an epic ride later. Just you wait."

With one last glance, full of adoration, she steps out of the stall and latches the door. As she hurries toward the office, she feels a renewed sense of purpose. Remington watches her go, his tail swishing and his eyes bright, as if he knows exactly how far they're going to go together.

The office is a converted barn stall, potted red, yellow, white, and pink flowers decorate either side. Above the office door, a blue and white wooden sign hangs reading, "Tegan Miller Performance Horses" with a professional graphic logo of a horse jumping over a fence below the words. Missy motions Bentley to the dog bed just outside the door. Bentley wags her tail and rolls into a little ball on the bed. Missy opens a squeaky screen door and enters.

Missy looks at the wall covered with horse show photos. Her gaze centers on a photo of a young woman dressed in a red show jacket with royal blue lapels, white show breeches, a determined look on her face, flying over a 1.5 meter oxer with her bay horse. Underneath the framed photograph, a plaque reads:

2012 Gold Medal Showjumping
US Olympian - Tegan Miller and Paratrooper

Missy smiles to herself and walks over to a case filled with trophies and medals. She lingers at the case. Her gaze moves to the picture of her in show regalia (white breeches, navy show coat, helmet, and tall boots) astride Paratrooper with a blue ribbon on his bridle and blue and white sash around his neck; Tegan smiling holding the reins and silver plate at the 2017 Junior Jumper Nationals. The shriek from the protesting door opening shakes her out of her revelries. She turns as Tegan rushes into the room, nose buried in her iPad.

Tegan sighs and slumps into her chair behind the desk, too drained to acknowledge Missy's presence. She tucks wild strands of dark brown hair into a long French braid covered with a beaten up dark blue baseball cap inscribed in white letters with the word "Paratrooper." Her hair cascades down a white polo shirt with a blue collar, "Tegan Miller, Head Trainer", with the graphic horse logo embroidered on the chest in blue, tucked into a pair of khaki breeches. She removes a piece of hay out of her hair, tosses it to the floor. She gazes at her sunburnt arms, rubs the dust off her skin, and then rubs her tired, thinly lined, emerald green eyes. No make up, Tegan is an exotic beauty just like her mother, with a hint of her father on her lips and stoic chin. In her mid-thirties, tall and slender, years of riding registered on her body as she subconsciously rubs her left shoulder, stretches, and yawns. She unclips a radio attached to her belted breeches, places it on the desk, and continues scanning her iPad as Missy approaches.

"Hey, Tegan, it's a great day for a ride. Remington—" Missy says hopefully. Tegan looks up from her iPad. "Not gonna happen." She replies.

"Oh, come on. You promised." Missy pleads. Tegan points to a bench across from the desk with a stained coffee maker and a tray of bagels.

"Grab me a coffee, will ya? And a bagel." Tegan looks back at her iPad. Missy grudgingly fills Tegan's coffee cup inscribed with the saying "Go Big or Go home...United States Show Jumping Team" and decorated with a horse jumping over an American Flag, and grabs a bagel. She hands it to Tegan. Tegan looks up at Missy's crestfallen face, chuckles.

"Okay, okay. I'll get Oscar to lunge Remi. If he's not too crazy, we'll work on him after lessons. My schedule is crazy today, but I should have some time around four," Tegan says.

"Really? You mean it?" Missy's face brightens. Tegan cocks an eyebrow.

"Only if you get the horses ready for lessons, muck the stalls, and do whatever Oscar needs. No dillydallying."

Missy squeezes Tegan's shoulders.

"Yes! Thank you, thank you, thank you!" She heads to the door and looks at Tegan like she would look at her mother. Their eyes meet. Tegan stands up and waves her hands at her.

"Go... Before I change my mind." Missy rushes out of the door. Tegan winces, massaging her shoulder. She shrugs her shoulders and rolls them back and down.

"Come, Bentley!" Missy calls. Bentley barks and trots after her. Tegan smiles, sits back in her chair.

She swivels her chair away from her desk, the weight of the morning's decisions pressing down on her. Her gaze falls on the wall behind her, lined with memories, and her breath catches as her eyes land on a faded black-and-white photo. She stands and crosses the room, her steps slowing as she approaches the portrait.

It's a young girl with pigtails, perched confidently atop a golden palomino pony. Beside her, a middle-aged man grins proudly, one hand resting on the lead rope. The warmth of the image feels like a time capsule, pulling her back to simpler days. Her fingers tremble as she brushes the glass.

"Hey, Dad," she whispers, her voice cracking. Tears well up in her eyes, and she blinks hard to keep them from spilling over. "It's been a while. But... I'm still here. The place has changed a lot since you left. I think you'd like it. Made some improvements. Fully automated. State-of-the art. The works."

She pauses, her lips curving into a small, rueful smile. "Who am I kidding? You'd hate it. You'd probably set fire to the Eurocizer the second I turned my back." Her voice drops into a gravelly imitation of his. "'You're not doing it right, kiddo!'"

A sad chuckle escapes her, but it fades quickly. She straightens the frame, her fingertips brushing against the wood before stepping back to take it all in. The silence presses in as she wraps her arms around herself.

"We're importing now," she admits quietly, as if confessing to the photo. "Jake and I set it all up. Top bloodlines from Europe. Cutting-edge training. The complete package. It's what we had to do, Dad. The breeding program just... it took too long to yield anything worthwhile, and the bills—God, the bills were endless."

She wipes her face, forcing herself to breathe evenly. "No one wants homebred horses anymore, not like they used to. They all want imported stock—flashy, proven, and ready to win." Her voice lowers, a hint of frustration creeping in. "Times are changing, Dad. Valley Vista has to change with them. If we don't keep up with the competition, we'll get left behind."

Her eyes flicker back to the photo, the guilt and uncertainty evident in her expression. "I know this isn't what you would have done. You believed in building from scratch, in taking the time to get it right. But I couldn't wait anymore. It's not like it used to be."

She presses her lips together, trying to keep the emotion from bubbling over. "I just... I hope I'm doing the right thing. I hope you'd understand."

Her throat tightens, and she exhales sharply, brushing her fingers once more over the frame. "I hope I'm making you proud, even if it's not your way," she whispers under her breath.

She straightens her shoulders, giving herself a moment before turning back toward her desk. There's work to do—and she's determined to make sure all of this, every hard decision, every sacrifice, will be worth it in the end.

The radio clicks. Oscar's voice resonates with a thick Mexican accent.

"Señora Tegan? You there?" Tegan turns around and grabs the radio.

"Here, Oscar." She replies.

"The 7 a.m. ladies are getting restless. Demanding to know-" Oscar's voice crackles over the radio.

"Where's Jake?" She asks, annoyed. "Never mind, I'll be there in five." She clips the radio back onto her belt, shoves the iPad down the back of her breaches, grabs her coffee and bagel, and dashes out the door.

Tegan rushes to an arena decked with brightly colored jumps, world class synthetic footing, and muck buckets and rakes next to the jump standards. Tegan looks up to a sign reading, "Hank Miller Oval," and smiles. She enters a cemented walkway, covered with a blue and white awning, and adorned with tables. She sits at a desk, picks up a microphone, turns it on. Feed back goes through the speakers. She looks out to the arena where a four horse and rider combination patiently waits for their lesson.

"Good morning, everyone." Tegan fakes a smile and speaks into the mic. Cathy trots her grey gelding, appropriately named Maserati X, up to the rail. Her horse swishes his tail in annoyance as she pulls aggressively on the reins to halt him. The horse shakes its head and stumbles under the pressure of the bit. Cathy harshly kicks her horse with her spurs; he kicks out, and Cathy almost falls off.

Cathy Turner, a blonde, buxom socialite in her late forties, with more money than sense, has been a part of Valley Vista since the Hank Miller era. She let everyone know of her financial commitment to the ranch and to the sport. Impeccable riding clothes from Europe, she's one of those riders that looks better than they ride. She always wears too much makeup to conceal her age, with a hair in a tight bun covered with a jeweled hair net under a gem encrusted helmet that glitters in the sun every time she turns her head - which she does often, curses under her breath.

Tegan, frustrated, turns off the mic, places it down on the table, and steps into the arena. Tegan gently scratches the horse's neck at the withers and takes the reins as Cathy straightens herself. The horse relaxes and nuzzles Tegan. A muffled laughter comes from the other riders.

"You okay, Cathy?" Tegan softly asks. Tegan straightens the brow band on the bridle.

"Maserati never does what I tell him to do. I can't believe he's an ex-Grand Prix show jumping horse. I mean really, Tegan, he's impossible." Cathy says, upset. Tegan hands Cathy the reins.

"Why don't we try to relax your hands on the reins and take these spurs off?" Tegan smiles as she attempts to undo the spurs. Cathy jerks her foot away.

"Jake told me that the spurs would help me get him in front of my leg. I'm tired of having to kick him forward all the time. Where is Jake? He was supposed to help me get ready for the show. I'm going to do the point, ninety's." Cathy raises her voice so the others can hear her.

Tegan ignores Cathy's question and continues to remove the spurs. She adjusts Cathy's leg to be under her hip and walks over to the other riders. Cathy reluctantly follows. Tegan checks and adjusts the students' tack and riding positions, and then heads to the middle of the ring.

"Today, we are going to work on your riding position and eye." Groans from the students meet Tegan's words.

Tegan points at the jumps that are set 0.90 meters.

"Before you can effectively jump those, you must guide your equine partner with a precise position, path, and pace. So... poles, ladies. Pick up a trot." More groans again meet her words, but the ladies pick up the trot as Tegan sets up poles in the arena.

A red 2002 BMW 330Ci convertible races into the parking lot next to the Hank Miller arena. Dust flies everywhere as Jake exits his car. He lights a cigarette and slicks his dark brown hair peppered with grey. Wearing ragged army green cargo shorts, grey t-shirt, and tennis shoes, Jake looks down at his watch with his bloodshot, wrinkled eyes as he hastens to the arena. He looks into the arena where Tegan finishes coaching his student, Cathy, over a line of poles and three jump fences (a typical grid exercise for jumpers). Cathy easily clears the final fence (a 0.9 meter oxer) in the line in a perfect jump position with a big smile on her face. Tegan glares at Jake, then quickly returns her full attention to the students.

"That was wonderful, Cathy. Notice that if you maintain your position, the horse can do what you ask him to." She explains. Cathy hugs her horse.

"I knew he could do it. He understood everything I asked him. I love you, Maserati!" Cathy exclaims. She hugs her horse and kisses him on the neck.

"You see... You don't need these." Tegan hands Cathy her spurs and winks.

"You're right. Thanks, Tegan." Cathy says and takes her spurs.

The other riders approach Tegan as Jake walks up to Tegan's side.

"Ladies, you all rode brilliantly. Today we covered some basics, most notably your position, but I can't express it enough; the basics get you over the fence, especially during a mishap. Remember the three 'P's' of jumping - Position, Path, and Pace and you will answer any question a course asks you. Get it?" Tegan asks. The ladies nod their heads in unison.

"Thanks, Tegan." The ladies say in unison as they walk their horses back to the barn, gossiping all the way.

Jake rolls his eyes and says sarcastically under his breath.

"Yeah, that horse does what she asks because I found her that packer ex-Grand Prix Jumper. Cost her a pretty penny, I might add."

Tegan clenches her fist in anger, turns to Jake and in a hushed voice, teeth clenched, she says.

"You're late. My office after morning lessons." She turns her back to him and storms out of the arena as another group of riders approach. Jake shakes his head, walks out of the arena and sits at the desk. He turns on the microphone as another set of riders enter the arena.

He takes a drag from his cigarette, lifts the mic to his lips.

"Good morning, ladies. Pick up a trot."

Up and Over Ranch

White clouds pillow the sky above a clear blue lake draped next to a railroad track. Two deer (doe and stag) walk up to the calm lake; it creates a perfect mirror image of their likenesses drinking in perfect harmony with the earth. The stag nestles the doe's pregnant belly, continues drinking. God's county. Life continues in a slow rhythm of animal and land. The serenity of the deer permeates a simple truth - life is life. A breeze ruffles their coats. They raise their heads in unison, aware of another presence. A yellow locomotive from this foreign species emits a whistle ending the one moment of tranquility, scattering the deer from the lake. The train nonchalantly passes, erupting another whistle as it hurries to its destination.

Beside the railroad track, a horse and rider gallop behind the train. The rider smiles, scratches his horse's neck as they gain momentum. He urges the horse to increase his speed with a press of his legs and a light flick of his reins on the horse's haunches. The horse grunts, flicks one ear back on his rider, flares his nostrils for more air, and pursues his target. Dust kicks up. They easily overtake the train, jump the tracks, and head to a barn over the hill nestled in a wild grass-covered valley in the distance.

Up and Over Ranch. A patchwork quilt of sand arenas with hand built jumps, paddocks, and barn which houses twelve horses. A U-shaped barn, with an out-door coral connected to its stalls, stables four horses on each side. The rider, Carson Peterson, owner and trainer, trots his trusty horse, Rusty, down the dirt road towards the main office.

Rusty is a horseman's horse, the kind that makes even seasoned equestrians stop and take notice. A striking blend of Quarter Horse and Thoroughbred, he's a paint stallion with a coat the color of sunlit rust, his haunches flecked with a constellation of white dots. His flaxen mane and tail seem to shimmer in the sunlight, and his intelligent, dark eyes hold a depth that hints at a soul wise beyond his years.

Rusty came into Carson's life when he was five years old, and the two have been inseparable ever since. Their bond runs deeper than horse and rider; it's as though they share an unspoken language. Rusty isn't just a horse to Carson—he's a partner, a confidant, and a best friend. The stallion, while willing to train with anyone, always seems happiest when Carson is in the saddle. Together, they've navigated trails, worked tirelessly in the arena, and even competed, but their favorite moments are the quiet ones.

Late at night, long after the barn has quieted and the last light has flickered out, Carson often slips out with Rusty to the dimly lit arena. The air is still, broken only by the rhythmic sound of hooves brushing against the sand. Carson unclips the lead rope, and Rusty springs forward, muscles rippling beneath his paint coat, his mane streaming behind him like a banner.

Carson stands in the center, barely moving, his presence alone anchoring the moment. He lets out a sharp whistle, then a low, drawn-out call. Instantly, Rusty circles back, eyes bright and ears pricked, reading Carson's voice like a familiar melody. Carson raises a hand, and Rusty slows, turns, trots toward him in tight spirals, as if tethered by an invisible thread.

They move together—Carson walking, then jogging, turning, stopping—all matched by Rusty in perfect sync. There is no halter, no whip, no need. Only trust. Only joy. The stallion responds to each subtle cue as if the man's thoughts are his own, their bond built from countless hours, quiet patience, and the pure delight of companionship. In the moonlit hush of the arena, they become a single rhythm—man and horse, playing, learning, listening. Moving as one.

On cooler nights, Carson sets up a small fire by the pasture, strumming his guitar while Rusty grazes nearby, his ears flicking toward the soft chords. Occasionally, Rusty will lift his head and amble closer, as if drawn to the music, standing quietly beside Carson as though listening to every note.

Rusty's personality is larger than life. Known around the barn as "the great escape artist," he has an uncanny knack for getting out of stalls, pens, or any other enclosure meant to contain him. There isn't a latch he can't figure out or a barrier he won't test. The barn staff has long since stopped trying to confine him completely, knowing he'll roam the aisles, inspecting his "herd." Rusty takes his self-assigned role as barn patriarch seriously, often stopping by each stall to check on the other horses, his calm presence a comfort to all.

Despite his mischievous streak, everyone adores Rusty. His human-like qualities—his ability to assess a situation, his curiosity, and his almost telepathic connection with Carson—make him a legend anywhere. But for all his fame and antics, Rusty's heart belongs to Carson. Together, they are a testament to the bond that every horseman dreams of—a partnership built on mutual respect, endless trust, and a shared understanding that words could never capture.

A wood plank with the barely visible words "Up and Over Barn, Carson Peterson, Trainer" lies next to the office door. Carson gently halts his trusted partner, Rusty, and dismounts. Carson removes his cowboy hat and dusts the dirt from his jeans. Rugged, and weathered good looks, in his early forties, black hair speckled with grey, blue eyes, Carson is a horse person's horseman. A modern day horse whisperer, he's a relic of today's equestrian world. He could find a homemade remedy for most horse ailments and jump a horse over a meter twenty fence bareback one day and rope cattle the following day. He hands Rusty a sugar cube from his pocket and pats him on the neck. Rusty nuzzles Carson and then gently pulls on his pocket with his teeth.

"Want more?" He says as he reaches into his pocket. Rusty paws the ground in affirmation.

"Well, I guess you deserve it." Carson says as he hands him another cube. Carson looks over to the barn and sheepishly smiles as Manuel, his groom, approaches, a disapproving look on his face. He shakes his head as Carson loosens Rusty's cinch. Carson hands him the reins. Manuel inspects Rusty's soaked coat. He rubs his hands down Rusty's four legs.

"Been racing the train again." Manuel grunts.

"Beat it by a mile. Right, Rusty?" He looks at Rusty. Rusty shakes his head up and down. Carson motions his head to the arena.

"She here yet?" He asks.

"You've got a couple of minutes." Manuel replies.

"Thanks." He looks at Rusty, scratches his cheek. "Catch you later, Buddy." He says.

Rusty snorts as Carson walks towards the arena. Manuel guides Rusty to the wash rack, pads down his legs, looks up at Rusty.

"Cold hosing for you, my friend."

Carson enters the arena and smiles to himself; he watches his young working student, Bethany, set up a grid of jumps. Sweat pours down her face as she moves the make shift standard and sets the poles for an oxer. Bethany, sixteen and determined, light brown hair streaked with purple highlights tied into a low ponytail underneath her baseball cap, looks up at Carson and waves him over.

"What ya think?" Bethany gestures towards the grid. Carson inspects the grid.

"Who's this for?" He replies with a fatherly reproach. Bethany looks down, hesitates and then blurts out.

"He's ready. I know he is. He's young but... I've been doing poles for months. He can do it."

"Yes... But. What's the first rule of training a young horse?" Carson grabs a pole and places it on the sand.

"Instill confidence with repetition. A confident horse will take you all the way. Slow progress is better than no progress. I'll take the grid down." She says in a monotone voice, her shoulders shrugged in defeat. Carson chuckles to himself and places his hand on her shoulder.

"How about we see how Winston does with the poles? If he looks good, we'll do your grid." He pulls down her baseball cap.

"Cool color." Carson motions to Bethany's hair. She swats him away, grinning ear to ear.

"Stop it. You know, Car, you could do with some color. Purple is the way to go. Grey is so yesterday." She covers her mouth in mock embarrassment. Carson laughs out loud and says.

"I'll stick with yesterday's grey." He walks over to the grid. "Great job on the grid, by the way." Carson says with pride.

"Really? Thanks!" Bethany jumps up and down with excitement.

"Now get Othello ready for Caroline. She'll be here any minute." He says.

"Yes, sir!" Bethany replies with a mock salute.

Carson watches as Bethany scampers off to the stables. Carson shakes his head and walks toward his office. A black Mercedes Benz sedan pulls up. A heavy set man in an ill-fitted suit and tie, late fifties, sweat pouring down his face, quickly gets out of the vehicle and approaches Carson before he enters the office.

"I've been trying to get a hold of you. Ringing your phone daily. No voicemail. No answering machine. I'm surprised it's still connected!" He says, exasperated. He takes a handkerchief out and wipes his forehead. Carson shrugs his shoulders.

"Wanna come inside, Benny? I have a couple of minutes before my first lesson." Carson opens the screen door. It's squeaks in disapproval.

Benny wipes off an old dusty leather chair with his handkerchief, looks up at Carson as he hangs his cowboy hat on a rusty nail on a wall covered with horse bits of every style and size. The office is a converted tack room. Bridles hang on make shift nails in the shape of a horseshoe and saddles on saddle racks hang on an opposite wall. A glass cabinet filled with over two decades of pictures, trophies, books, and belt buckles from both Western and English riding disciplines gathers dust in a lonely corner of the room. The cabinet pays homage to all riding disciplines and years of horse training. The cabinet is also a subtle reminder of Carson's horsemanship, however; its placement in the room suggests a humility in the owner. Carson casually sits across from Benny in front of an uneven, dilapidated desk. He scratches his chin, looks directly at Benny, smiles.

"What's up, Benny?" He says.

"Don't what's up, me, Carson. You know what's up." Benny scowls in frustration. "I can't hold off the bank any longer. You either sell or we foreclose. Your choice." He says as he wipes his forehead again with his handkerchief.

"I'll get you the money next week. I have a..." Carson opens a desk drawer.

"It's too late for that, Carson. I've told you time and time again. You can't keep missing payments. Even if you had the money which I know you don't, the bank is done with you and to be honest as much as I like you, so am I." He replies. Carson's eyes widen at the change in his friend's tone.

"Benny?" Carson asks.

"Yes?" Benny, still frustrated, replies.

"How long have we known each other?" He asks.

"Twenty years." Benny's voice softens, but he quickly stiffens and blurts out.

"That's not the point, Carson, and you know it. I've been stalling the bank for as long as I could out of my friendship to you." Benny stands up, hands shaking, hands Carson foreclosure papers, shakes his head in disappointment, and quickly mutters.

"If you would just do what I tell you and charge your clients more, spruce up this place, and work with the 'right people'. But no. You have 'principles, integrity'."

Benny points his finger at Carson.

"Well, those principles and integrity have lost you your barn. There's nothing more I can do. Have your things out by the end of next month." Benny turns away from Carson and hastily walks out the office door, slamming the screen door behind him.

Carson picks up the papers, looks out at Benny with a smirk on his face, and calls after him.

"We're still having drinks tonight?" Carson gently asks. Benny stops in his tracks, turns and faces Carson, shrugs his shoulders, with a saddened look in his eyes, and says.

"Sure, Car. First round on me." Carson smiles at Benny, shrugs his shoulders and replies.

"Sounds good. See you around seven. And, Benny, all rounds are on you."
They give each other a knowing nod from their many years of friendship and both laugh. Benny drops his head in defeat, eyes gazing into the dirt.

"Sorry I couldn't do more, Car." Benny says.

"It's ok, Ben. It's on me," Carson replies.

Benny sheepishly smiles back at Carson, waves, gets in his car, and drives off. Carson looks at the papers, sets them down on the desk, grabs his cowboy hat, and heads out the door to teach his first lesson of the day, just like any other day.

REMINGTON

Tegan slams the door as she enters, disrupting Jake's slumber on the vintage black, well-worn leather couch next to the door. He jerks up, wipes the sleep off his face, reaches for a cigarette. Tegan glares at him. He puts the cigarette back in his pocket. He glares back at Tegan. An awkward silence fills the air.

"I can't take this. Late all the time. Twenty-minute lessons. Not resetting jumps. Clients are complaining. This...is not working." She barely maintains her calm as she looks at him. Jake rolls his eyes, grabs a stale bagel from the desk, slumps back on the couch, and takes a bite.

"Are we doing this again?" Jake grins and brings on the charm. "C'mon, Tegan, we're the top riding facility in the state. We can do anything we want, and those clients of yours wouldn't even notice. Those ladies don't care. They ride to look interesting to their friends. Something to talk about at their dinner parties." Jake takes another bite of the bagel, scowls, throws it at the wastepaper basket, misses. He gets up, starts walking to the door.

"I've got a lesson to teach." He says.

"Jake, I'm serious. I'm tired of cleaning up your messes. I need someone who's dedicated to the lesson program so that I can work on the prospects. That was the deal and you're reneging. Stop phoning it in and get with the program." Tegan says, exasperated. Jake smirks and laughs.

"The program? There would be no 'program' without me. I built this place. You were just another barn, bleeding money, with a talented rider until I came. All those client horses out there, I chose. I got the contacts, darling. Your prospects are a waste of time and money. Daddy's little girl chasing that stupid dream of breeding and training five star horses. We agreed to shutter the breeding program. That's not where the money's at and you know it."

"How dare you? You were a washed up wannabe actor when I plucked you up from obscurity. I'm the reason you have those contacts. They wouldn't even talk to you until you worked with me. I'm done, Jake." Tegan takes a step towards Jake.

"Now get your things..." She's interrupted by a loud bang. Missy bolts through the door, big smile, with a singsong voice.

"It's 4:30. All the barn chores are done. You promised..." Missy stops in her tracks as she senses the tension in the room. Missy sees Jake and Tegan frozen like sculptures in a garden.

"Did I miss something?" Missy cautiously says.

Jake shrugs his shoulders and says in a mocking tone.

"Ask Queen B, here. I've got a lesson to teach." He sarcastically bows to Tegan and walks out the door. Tegan blinks back the tears from her eyes, looks at Missy's concerned face, places her arm around Missy's shoulder, and says.

"Let's go see how Oscar is doing with Remi." Missy puts her head on Tegan's shoulder.

"Thanks, Tegan. I've been waiting all day for this," Missy says.

"I know, kiddo. Remi is your dream horse. I know all about dream horses." Missy giggles. Tegan knowingly smiles at Missy.

Remington comes from a long line of racehorses, home bred from Hank Miller's super star thoroughbred, Royal Winter. He was the last horse foaled while Hank was alive and holds a special place in Tegan's heart. A stallion, his dark bay shiny coat with four white socks, a white blaze down his face, and a thick neck, was always a head turner at the barn. Majestic, like his father, he's a beautiful mover with a lofty trot, intended for the racetrack, just as fast as his sire, but he would never break away from the other horses. He had seven starts, but no places. His racing career was over before it began. They put Remington out to pasture after his last race, but the pasture fence could never hold him.

Each time Oscar turned him out, he would jump the six-foot fence and gallop back to the barn with Oscar running cursing in Spanish, halter in hand, after him.

A natural show jumper, which was not expected from an off the track thoroughbred; at age four, Tegan began training him to jump. Most people loved Remington's looks, but feared getting close to him, while Missy adored him. To Missy, Remington was her horse. She would never leave his side, sometimes sleeping on a cot next to his stall whenever she could. Remington hated to be groomed, often kicking out when Oscar attempted to get him ready for Tegan.

But Missy had the magic touch, the magic whisper, and the magic cookie. She knew exactly how to touch him, how to talk to him, and what treat would appease him anytime he became anxious. Missy was the only "groom" that Remington would tolerate.

But to Oscar, Remi was just another crazy horse on the opposite end of his lunge line. Sweat pouring down his face, Oscar holds on as Remington, in a full gallop, gives another huge buck.

"Whoa, caballo! Whoa!" Oscar exclaims as he jerks on the lunge line, bringing Remington down to a trot. Tegan walks into the round pen while Missy waits outside, impatiently tapping her foot. Oscar slows Remington to a walk and looks at Tegan, concerned.

"He's really hot, Señora." Oscar hands the lunge line to Tegan. Tegan pats Remington on the neck.

"Hey, Remi. How are you doing today?" She says as she kisses him on the cheek. Remington bows his head and knickers at her.

"What ya think, Teegs?" Missy shouts from outside the pen.

"I should get on him first to make sure he's okay." Tegan responds.

"C'mon, Tegan. I've ridden him a lot hotter than this. Plenty of times. My boy will be fine. Won't you, Remi." Missy kisses at Remington. Remington ears perk up in recognition of Missy's voice, and he paws the ground.

"I don't know, Missy. Oscar thinks..." Tegan says, concerned.

"You promised." Missy looks pleadingly at Tegan and pouts. Tegan smiles.

"Okay. But if he gets..." Tegan leads Remington towards Missy. Missy rushes in, grabs the lunge line, gently rubs Remington on his favorite spot behind his ear, and leads Remington to the crossties in full conversation about her day. She calls back to Tegan.

"You worry too much. I'll meet ya in the arena. I've already set up some poles and jumps. It'll be great." She marches off with Remington, leaving Oscar and Tegan in the round pen.

Missy pulls out his favorite treat out of her breaches. "Ya ready to have some fun, Remi?" He greedily swipes the treat out of her fingertips, nuzzles her shoulder, and nickers.

Tegan walks to the center of the arena as Missy, astride Remington, trots in. Missy checks her girth. Remington snorts and gives her a sizable buck, sending her slightly forward. She adjusts herself and smacks Remington with the crop. Agitated, he shakes his head and kicks out his hind legs and high steps in place. Tegan calmly walks up to Missy and Remington and says.

"Hand me your crop." She reaches out her hand.

"But..." Missy exclaims, slightly scared but defiant.

"Non-negotiable," Tegan sternly says. Missy hands her the crop as Tegan gently strokes Remington's neck and withers. Remington snorts and nods his head to Tegan. Tegan rubs his forehead and looks into his eyes. He pushes her back with his muzzle in protest. She backs up a few paces and looks up at Missy.

"He's anxious. For this to work, I need you to do everything I say. Got it?" She says. Missy nods in the affirmative.

"Okay. Lower your hands and send him forward in a posting trot. Keep him in a circle around me until he settles down." She draws a circle around her with the crop. Missy begrudgingly complies. Remington rears, but then trots forward.

"Good. Now widen your hands and keep pushing him forward into your contact. You want to make sure that he's connected to you and understands what you want," Tegan says as she turns to keep facing Missy and Remington. Missy complies. Remington tries to resist, but Missy gently coaxes him forward. Remington licks his lips as he lowers his head in compliance. Missy pats him on the neck and gives Tegan a huge smile.

"That's it, Missy. Widen your circle another five meters each time you circle, and then let's get him over some poles." She smiles as Missy completes the second circle around Tegan and heads to a line of poles.

Jake, saddle over his right arm, marches in anger towards his car. He opens his trunk, shoves his saddle in, closes the trunk, and takes out a cigarette and lights it.

"I don't need this crap." He mutters to himself. "I was on my way. I'm done. You know you can do your own thing. You don't need that bitch."

He looks up and slightly stumbles as he notices Cathy Turner standing next to his car, blond hair flowing perfectly down her perfectly fitted riding attire. Cathy smiles beguilingly at him, raises an eyebrow and says with a purr. "You get fired again, Jake?" He grunts his response, walks around her towards the driver's side door, and pulls out his keys. She snatches his keys away from him and giggles.

"Come on Jake, let's get a drink and we can talk about big bad Tegan." She laughs. He reaches for his keys and she playfully draws her arm back.

"Uh, uh, uh. Not until you buy me a drink." She grins at him like the snake in the garden of eden. Annoyed, Jake runs his hand through his hair. This hasn't been their first encounter and it won't be their last.

"Cathy, I gotta go. I have this audition that I have to prep for and..." He rambles. She shakes her head in defiance and yawns.

"Now take me for a drink and we can talk about your future here at Valley Vista." She purrs back at him. She places her hands behind her back and grins at Jake. Jake looks over to the Hank Miller arena and notices Missy trotting into a grid of fences. He rolls his eyes in disapproval. "That damn stallion again. It's always that stallion."

He walks over to Cathy and reaches around her back and grabs her hands and squeezes, trying to get her to release her grip on his keys. She tightens her grip in defiance and the car alarm goes off. BEEP! BEEP! BEEP! Alarmed, she drops the keys to the ground. Jake, with a scared look on his face, glances toward the Hank Miller arena.

"Oh God." He whispers. He runs toward the arena, leaving Cathy in shock at his car.

Missy gathers the reins with a steady hand, her eyes fixed on the line of jumps ahead. Determination sharpens her features, and her posture straightens in the saddle as she gives Remington a light squeeze with her legs. He responds instantly, surging into a forward trot, his ears flicked forward, already reading the challenge before them.

The grid stretches out in a clean, straight line: a ground pole first, then a low cross rail, followed by a vertical, and finally an oxer—the tallest of the set, just under three feet, its width adding to the test. Each fence climbs in height, demanding precision, balance, and trust.

Remington's hooves clip lightly over the pole, never breaking rhythm. As they approach the cross rail, Missy shifts her weight slightly forward. The gelding coils and springs upward, clearing it with effortless grace. His takeoff is smooth, and he lands lightly, transitioning seamlessly into a canter.

Missy steadies him with a half-halt, counting quietly under her breath. One... two... They meet the vertical in perfect stride. Remington lifts off powerfully, his knees tight to his chest, clearing the jump with textbook form. He lands balanced, and his canter strengthens and becomes more collected.

BEEP! BEEP! BEEP! The car alarm bursts into a cacophonic sound. Both Missy's and Remington's eyes widen in fear. Remington wildly shakes his head, rears, and crashes into the remaining oxer. Missy tries to hang on but ends on the side of the saddle as her shoulder slams into the standard of the jump. Missy screams out in agony, sending Remington into a maddening bolt. Tegan drops the crop and desperately runs after them. In a blind run, Remington gallops around the arena with Missy hanging on for life, her left arm limp from the impact on the standard.

"Pull up, Missy. Pull up!" Tegan yells. Through an act of sheer will and determination, Missy pulls herself back upright in the saddle, tears streaming down her face. Remington continues his manic bolt.

"Turn him towards the rail, Missy!" Missy, frightened, shakes her head "no".

"I can't. I can't!" She cries. Tegan, still running after them, takes a deep breath, becomes the rider on Remington and says calmly in a voice reminiscent of her father.

"Do it now, kiddo." Missy instantly grabs the reins with her right hand and pulls Remington towards the fence. He slides, then immediately stops. Missy slumps forward and rolls off the other side. Alarmed again, Remington steps on Missy's rib cage. Crack. A loud scream. Remington rears and bolts toward the end of the arena, jumps over the seven foot piped rail smacking his right front hoof and gallops away from the arena towards the pasture, snorting, bucking and squealing in fear with his tail straight like an arrow up towards the sky.

"Oh God." Tegan exclaims as she finally catches up to Missy lying face down crumpled in a ball of agony on the ground, convulsing. Jake, with a sickened look on his face, kneels next to Missy and looks up at Tegan.

"Should I go after Remington?" He stammers. "I told you we should've gelded him." Tegan glares at Jake, shakes her head, and steadies her voice. Her only concern is Missy.

"No. Oscar will take care of Remington. He knows what to do. What I need you to do is call the ambulance and then leave." Jake, embarrassed, looks at Tegan and sheepishly says.

"I'm sorry, Teegs. It was a mistake. Cathy wouldn't give me back my keys. I didn't mean—"

"Just do it." Tegan turns her back on Jake and focuses her attention on Missy.

FORECLOSURE

The Up and Over barn stands in twilight, its silhouette a bittersweet reminder of days gone by. Half the stalls sit empty, their occupants have moved on to new homes, while the remaining horses shuffle in their bedding, their soft nickers echoing faintly in the quiet. Dust motes swirl in the last rays of the setting sun, which cast a golden hue over the barn's wooden beams. Outside, the air is heavy with the scent of hay and the faint tang of approaching evening, the horizon ablaze in hues of orange and pink as the sun dips behind the distant line of trees.

They sold the barn. It's a fact that hangs in the air like an unspoken truth, weighing heavily on everyone's hearts.

From the main aisle, Bethany emerges, her face streaked with tears. In her hands is a cake, its intricate design a near-perfect replica of Carson's prized stallion, Rusty. The horse-head cake, adorned with flickering candles, glows faintly in the dim light, a poignant centerpiece for the gathering. Behind her, a solemn line of students follows—boys and girls of all ages, still dressed in their breeches and collared shirts, their expressions a mixture of sadness and reverence.

The group moves silently across the barnyard, their boots crunching against the gravel. A few steps ahead, a picnic table waits, draped with a checkered cloth and adorned with horse-themed plates and napkins. It's surrounded by platters of food: vegetable trays, chips, salsa, fried chicken, and coleslaw. The table's festive appearance, complete with a string of white lights hanging from the rafters above, feels almost jarring against the somber mood.

Bethany gently sets the cake on the table, her hands lingering for a moment on its edge as she exhales shakily. She steps back, wiping her face with the sleeve of her jacket, her gaze drifting toward the barn and the fading light beyond it.

The students settle on makeshift benches and hay bales scattered around the yard. Some sit in silence, their gazes fixed on the ground, while others glance toward Carson, their unspoken questions and emotions written plainly on their faces. The gentle hum of the lights above and the distant rustling of leaves in the trees are the only sounds breaking the stillness.

The cake's candles flicker and dance in the cool evening breeze, their tiny flames a fragile yet persistent light in the gathering darkness. The setting sun casts long shadows over the gathering, as if the world itself is mourning the end of an era at Up and Over barn.

Carson stands behind the picnic table and fidgets uncomfortably at all the attention. He looks up at Bethany with a questioning glance.

"Blow out the candles, Car." Bethany whispers, frustrated. Some of the younger students giggle in the background.

"Oh... yeah." Carson walks over to the cake and blows out the candles all at once. He looks up and awkwardly grins. The students applaud in unison.

"Speech. Speech!" They call out. Carson looks at everyone, noting all the people he will miss. He pulls down his cowboy hat to cover his emotions.

"You know, when I came to this place, I didn't know what it would become. I just wanted to find a piece of dirt where me and Rusty could share our love of the stable life with anyone who was open to horses, nature, and just being together. I don't know. I guess what I'm trying to say is that thanks to you guys, these past five years have been some of the happiest days of my life. I wish you all many days of big jumps and happy horses." Carson raises his bottle of 805 beer.

"Here's to the best students a lonely old cowboy could ask for." He takes a drink from his beer, a timid smiles crosses his face. Bethany, on cue, runs over to Carson and hugs him.

"We love you, Car." She softly sobs into his shirt. Carson looks up at the guests and they grab plates and dig into the refreshments. He tiptoes Bethany to a bench in the corner and sits her next to him. He pulls her fierce grip away from him, wipes her tears away, and playfully pulls on her purple ponytail. She characteristically pushes him away from her, laughs, and wipes the remaining tears from her face.

"You're gonna have a lot on your plate at West Haven Ranch." Carson says.

"Huh? What do you mean, Car?"

"Spoke to Frank Turner and he's real excited about you working for him. And Winston is going to need all your help to get settled there."

"Winston? But he's your horse."

"Just sold him to you for that horse's head cake. Great likeness, by the way." He points to the cake, pats her on her thigh. "I think I got the better deal." Carson gets up and heads over to the cake, leaving Bethany shocked and, for the first time in her life, speechless. Carson chuckles to himself as he cuts himself a piece of cake.

Janet, a petite firecracker, in her thirties, with bright orange-red short hair tucked underneath a cowboy hat, plaid shirt, wrangler jeans accented by well worn bright red cowboy boots, struts towards Carson. She looks around the room, grunts under her breath.

"Well, this sucks. This was the only place worthy of my time. But I guess all great things must end." She extends her hand out. Carson places his cake on the picnic table and gives Janet a bear hug. She pushes him away and playfully punches him on the shoulder.

"Ow, Janet! What was that for?"

"For not coming clean. You should have told me, Carson. I could have helped. I could have—"

"It wouldn't have mattered. This place was beyond saving. I wish I would have been better about the finances, but I wouldn't have done anything different. Next time, I'll make sure you run the facility." He winks at her and drinks his beer.

"So, what's next for you?"

"Oh, I don't know. Maybe go back into construction, do some farrier work on the side. Find a little place for me and Rusty to hang our hooves. Me and Rusty will figure it out."

"You know, Car, there's this ranch in need of some help. The trainer is an old friend of mine from back in the day when I used to be a show jumper. I trained with her for a bit. She's the real thing. Olympics. Gold medalist. Grand Prix wins all over the world. Tegan Miller's her name. There's a breeding facility. Fully automated. Her place is real swanky. Could be a nice change for you and Rusty. I could make a call..."

"Swanky?" Carson shakes his head and walks from the festivities to the arena. Janet chases him, her petite legs trying to match his long-legged stride. He enters the arena, heads toward his homemade jumps. Janet finally catches up to him, steps in front of him, and gestures for him to stop raising her hand in front of him.

"What do ya got to lose, Car? You've already lost your barn," Janet, almost out of breath, says defiantly. Carson grunts, tries to go around her. She heads him off again. She places her hands on her hips and kicks dirt at him. His eyes widen, but he acquiesces.

"I know you like to do your own thing, but this could get you back on your feet. You don't have to be there forever. Two months, six months tops." Carson looks out at his arena and barn. Sighs. Janet places her hand on his forearm. She squeezes his arm, tears in her eyes.

"You've been like a brother to me, Car. I wouldn't have been able to go professional in barrel racing if it wasn't for you. You can't go back to construction. Let me do this for you. Okay?"

Carson closes his eyes, imagining his life at the new ranch. He opens his eyes and looks at Janet.

"Name of the ranch?"

"Valley Vista Ranch. Tegan's father, Hank Miller, built it." Carson brightens up and a small smile crosses his face.

"Old Hank Miller's ranch? I haven't seen him in ages. Amazing horseman. Great horses. Won one of his foals in a rodeo. How's he doing?"

"He passed away. I believe a couple years back, and now Tegan's running his place. There was an accident with one of her riders and it's been mayhem and drama since. I heard— "

"Janet." Carson sternly says.

"Sorry, Carson. So... Do ya want me to make the call or what?" She says, annoyed. Carson turns away from her and heads to the barn.

"Carson!" Janet stomps the ground in frustration. "Why do you have to make everything so difficult?"

Carson, several steps away, turns and faces her, winks, and shrugs his shoulders.

"Make the call. Gonna have a talk with Rusty. Thanks, Janet. You're the best." He tips his hat, walks into the barn aisle and disappears around the corner. Janet knowingly shakes her head and says under her breath.

"Car, you sure are set in your ways. You crazy, cowboy." She chuckles to herself and heads back to the party.

The lights of the party disappear behind Carson as he heads towards the barn aisles. He turns the corner and notices Rusty making his rounds. Like a doctor, Rusty pokes his head into every stall, making sure all is well with his herd. Carson whistles. Rusty's ears perk up and he turns on his haunches, faces Carson and nickers. He trots towards him and stops. He nudges Carson's pant leg. Carson takes out a sugar cube, feeds him, and affectionately rubs his forehead. Rusty looks at Carson's face, quickly picks up his head in full alert and head butts Carson. Carson sadly chuckles to himself and pulls up a box and sits next to Rusty.

"Can't put anything past you, can I, buddy?" He strokes Rusty's neck.

"Well... I messed up again and we're gonna have to leave this place." He looks up at Rusty with a guilty look. Rusty snorts in annoyance and stomps his hoof.

"I know. I know. I thought this would be our forever home, too. But, I think I gotta better place. Much bigger. You'll love it. More horses for you to look after. More fields to roam. Real swanky." He sheepishly says. Rusty pins back his ears, snorts again.

"Sorry, Rusty. I love this place too. But, we'll adjust. We always have." Carson reaches up to his neck and Rusty backs up and shakes his head.

"C'mon, Rusty. I promise this time we'll make it work." Carson pulls out another sugar cube and presents it to Rusty. Rusty snorts, quickly spins on his haunches, and trots away, passing Janet as she approaches Carson. She sits next to Carson and looks back where Rusty trotted away.

"You told Rusty?" She says.

"Yep. Not happy about it."

"Really? I didn't notice." She says sarcastically. "Don't worry, Car, that horse loves you more than I've ever seen a horse love a human. He'll come around." She slaps him on the knee and smiles.

"Good news. Just got off the phone with Tegan Miller. She's real excited about you joining the team. The sooner you can get there, the better. They need help something fierce."

"Well, I guess there's no reason for me to stay here any longer." He takes his cowboy hat off and runs his fingers through his hair to cover up his sadness.

"Don't think I don't know how much this is tearing you up inside. You built a stable life here and now you're wondering if you'll ever get it back." She looks at him and continues. "But, Car, I believe things happen for a reason. Maybe you'll find something even better out there at Valley Vista Ranch." Carson looks at her defiantly. She shrugs her shoulder and says,

"I don't know. But what I know is that they could use someone like you to remind them of the true nature of horses. You have a gift and they're going to love you over there just as much as we do." She smiles at him with tears in her eyes. She quickly nudges him with her shoulder.

"Don't forget about us. Okay." She gets up, wipes the tears from her eyes and walks down the aisle. Carson stands up and heads towards her.

"Never." He says. She turns and gives him a big bear hug, shoves him away, and leaves him alone in the barn aisle. Carson looks around the barn aisle and kicks the dirt in front of him in frustration. A loud whinny in the distance. Carson smiles and runs toward the arena.

He looks at the open gate of the arena and chuckles to himself. In the center, Rusty stands in all his majestic glory, pawing the ground. Carson stops just outside the arena, closes the gate, leans on the rail, and whistles. Rusty trots over to Carson, stops in front of him, and nuzzles him with his muzzle. Carson rubs his forehead. Rusty playfully moves his head to the side and head butts Carson's shoulder and canters away, shaking his head in the air.

"Cheater! So that's how you're gonna play it!" Carson yells after him and jumps over the rail and chases after him. Rusty drag stops in the middle of the arena behind one of the jump fences, nimbly turns on his haunches and faces his playmate. Carson shuffles side to side; Rusty playfully mirrors him. The partygoers gather outside the arena and start chanting.

"Rusty! Rusty! Rusty!" Rusty dances around Carson, crossing his legs as he trots sideways. The crowd claps to his movements, encouraging him to do more. Rusty obliges the crowd by trotting in place and then turning in a 360-degree circle, lifting his front legs high into the air. The crowd cheers. Rusty canters sideways and then gallops towards the partygoers. He halts a foot in front of the crowd, spraying sand everywhere. The crowd hoots and hollers. Rusty, with his chest puffed out, bows. Carson catches up to Rusty, pats him on the neck and whispers in his ear.

"Show off. How about a ride?" Rusty responds with a nicker, maintaining his low bow. Carson swings his leg over Rusty's back and mounts him. Rusty stands with Carson on his back, holding his mane. Carson clicks at Rusty and they canter off towards a two-foot fence. Carson lets go of Rusty's mane, throws his arms out like an airplane as they sore over the fence. They canter towards the crowd. Carson swings his legs backward and pushes himself to a standing position on Rusty's back. They continue to canter as the crowd roars in approval. Carson clicks at Rusty again and slows down to a walk and then stops. Carson sits back down and whistles. Rusty spins on his haunches nine times, then immediately halts. Rusty raises his right front leg in unison to Carson, taking off his cowboy hat and raising it to the sky. The crowd cheers, and Rusty and Carson bow. Carson swings his leg over Rusty's shoulder and dismounts off the side. He pats Rusty on the neck and feeds him a sugar cube. Rusty wraps his head around Carson's torso and Carson hugs Rusty. Rusty unfolds his head from Carson's torso and they both walk towards the gate of the arena. With Carson at his side, Rusty unlatches the gate, pushes it open with his muzzle, and walks out as the crowd separates. The party goers follow Rusty and Carson singing "For He's a Jolly Good Horse." The party continues through the night.

Broken Body, Broken Heart

T egan curls up in a white cushioned chair, her legs draped over the armrest, a thin blue hospital blanket barely warding off the chill of the sterile room. The steady rhythm of the heart monitor stirs her awake, the soft beeping mirroring the unconscious tempo of Missy's heart. She rubs her eyes with balled fists, her body stiff and aching from a night spent in the contorted confines of the chair.

She sits upright, her gaze landing on Missy, still asleep. Missy's blonde hair clings to her face, damp with sweat that glistens like dew in the faint light. Her expression twists, eyes wrinkling as she groans softly in a restless, drug-induced slumber. The sight stings Tegan's heart, and tears prick her eyes. She quickly looks away, exhaling sharply to suppress the sob rising in her throat.

After a moment, she wipes her face, stands, and moves to Missy's bedside. She leans down and presses a soft kiss on her friend's forehead.

"I'll be right back," she whispers. Missy groans in response, her eyes fluttering but not opening.

The hospital room is small but filled with life, a stark contrast to its usual sterile atmosphere. Plush horses of all sizes, flower arrangements, and hand-drawn cards from the barn kids decorate every surface. Tack—bridles, halters, even Missy's favorite saddle pad—hangs on the wall alongside a massive sign reading, *"Get well soon! We love you, Missy!"* Despite the cheer, the beeping monitors and antiseptic smell keep the room grounded in the harsh reality of where they are.

Tegan steps out into the hallway, pulling the blanket tighter around her shoulders. She makes her way to the lobby, where a clunky coffee dispenser sits humming in the corner. Sliding a few quarters into the machine, she watches as a

Styrofoam cup drops and the coffee gurgles out in a mess, splashing more onto the machine's walls than into the cup.

"Damn it," she mutters, lifting the cup to inspect its meager contents. "I guess it's a cup-is-half-full kind of day," she adds with a wry, bitter smile.

She sinks into a hard plastic chair nearby, takes a tentative sip of the lukewarm coffee, and leans her head back against the wall. Closing her eyes, she lets her thoughts wander.

Suddenly, she's eleven years old again, her hair in pigtails flying behind her as she gallops bareback on Goldie Pony, her palomino with a flaxen mane. The pony's hooves pound the arena sand as they approach a two-foot cross rail. Hank's voice booms from the gate, full of panic.

"You stop that pony right now, kiddo!"

But Tegan doesn't stop, not until the jump looms before her. Goldie's head shoots up in hesitation, her wide eyes filled with fear. The pony plants her front hooves in the dirt, skidding to a halt, and Tegan flies forward, landing hard on her shoulder with a sickening *pop*.

Goldie bolts, leaving a trail of dust. Hank curses under his breath and sprints to his daughter.

He kneels beside her, his rugged face creased with worry. "You okay, kiddo?"

Tegan, tears streaming down her face, cradles her shoulder. "It hurts, Daddy," she whimpers.

Hank's eyes soften as he inspects her arm. "It's dislocated," he says gently. "Give me your hand, kiddo."

Tegan hesitates but complies, her trust in him unshakable. He grips her hand, places his boot against her shoulder, and with a quick, firm motion, pulls her arm back into place. The *pop* makes Tegan scream, and she collapses into her father's arms, sobbing into his plaid cowboy shirt.

Hank holds her tightly, his voice soft but steady. "I'm sorry, kiddo. I know it hurts. But you're okay now."

Through her tears, Tegan mumbles, "I wish Mommy were here."

Hank flinches, the weight of her words a punch to the gut. He strokes her hair, his own voice trembling. "So do I, kiddo. So do I."

After a moment, he pulls back and wipes her tears. "Now, about this pony..."

"She's mine," Tegan insists, her voice still shaky but resolute. "That kid doesn't deserve her. I'm training her to be a Grand Prix show jumper!"

Hank cocks an eyebrow, intrigued despite himself. "Really? I bred that pony to be a barrel racer for one of our client's kids. You know that."

"Well, they don't deserve her! She'll do anything I ask her. She's mine," Tegan says defiantly, her emerald eyes blazing.

Hank chuckles, shaking his head. "You've got guts, I'll give you that. But if you're serious about this jumper thing, you've got to do it right. No more shenanigans. Got it?"

Tegan nods eagerly. "Got it."

Hank stands, brushing the dirt off her overalls, then looks toward his old red-and-white Chevy C20 parked outside the arena. His boyish grin spreads across his face. "Your arm good enough to get some ice cream before we have the docs check you out?"

"Vanilla and chocolate swirl with caramel topping?"

"You bet ya!"

"Twist my arm, Dad," she teases, wincing as she rubs her shoulder.

"Good try, kiddo," Hank laughs, scooping her up and carrying her toward the truck. As he opens the passenger door, Tegan pokes her head out the window.

"Love you to the moon and back, Dad."

"You too, kiddo," he replies, resting his forehead against hers for a brief, tender moment.

That day was the first of many visits to the hospital. Injuries became an unspoken reality of equestrian life, but the hospital didn't just remind Tegan of falls and fractures. It reminded her of her mother's battle with illness, of long nights spent at her bedside, and of the hollow ache when her father, Hank, passed away suddenly years later. Hospitals were places of waiting, loss, and helplessness—places she had grown to hate.

"Ms. Miller? Ms. Miller?" The nurse's gentle voice pulls Tegan back to the present. She blinks up at the woman, startled.

"How long—?"

The nurse gives her a reassuring smile, squeezing her hand. "No need to worry. Missy is awake and asking for you."

Tegan bolts upright, rushing toward the room but stops abruptly to turn back. "Thank you. For everything," she says before hurrying on.

Inside Missy's room, the scene is as familiar as it is heartbreaking. The cards, the tack, the flowers—they're all reminders of how much they love Missy. But they're also reminders of how fragile life in the saddle can be.

Tegan sets the blanket on the chair and sits next to Missy. Her friend gives her a brave smile, but her eyes betray the pain she's trying to hide. Tegan knows that look all too well. She reaches for Missy's hand, her fingers warm and steady.

"Do you want me to get the nurse?" Tegan asks softly.

"No, I'm fine. It'll pass," Missy gasps, wincing as she shifts. "How bad is it?"

Tegan pauses, unsure of how to respond. "Maybe we should wait for the doctor..."

Missy's gaze hardens, her determination unshaken. "Teegs, please."

Tegan exhales and meets Missy's eyes. "You shattered your collarbone, so they put in a plate and screws to fix it. Rehab will be necessary, but you should recover within three to four months. You broke three ribs, but they'll heal on their own. You've got a slight concussion, but no brain swelling." She forces a smile. "Helmets. Gotta love them."

Missy stares at the heart monitor, her voice barely above a whisper. "Lower," she murmurs, willing it to calm.

"Missy?" Tegan asks, leaning closer. "You okay?"

"I just want to go home," Missy replies.

"I thought you'd stay with me while you recover. The doctor says you can leave tomorrow, and your mom agrees it's best—"

"No, Teegs. I want to go *home*. Please call my mom."

Tegan hesitates, swallowing hard. "I'll take care of everything. You just rest."

She pats Missy's thigh and steps out into the hall, her calm façade crumbling as she makes her way to the bathroom. Inside, sobs rack her body as she clutches the sink, cold water splashing her face over and over as if it could drown her sorrow.

When she finally lifts her head, her tear-streaked reflection stares back at her, emerald eyes filled with exhaustion and grief. She brushes her disheveled hair with trembling hands and forces herself to stand tall.

"You can do this," she whispers.

With a deep breath, she steps back into the hallway, walking toward a new reality—a reality where Missy's recovery is just beginning, and Tegan must once again shoulder the burden of holding it all together alone.

PARATROOPER

M ist blankets the hills surrounding Miller's Pond. Bird song echos from the trees as a fireball of sun emerges over the horizon as the new dawn approaches the fields of gold below. The tall grass and flowers rustle from the movement of life. Movement creates a serene stillness in time. The sun's rays peer through the branches, burning away the mist, revealing glistening rays which dance like diamonds off the pond in harmony with the flies. A frog croaks as it peers its head out of the shallow waters and leaps out of the pond, snatching a fly with its whip like tongue as it disappears into the grass.

Tegan drinks from her coffee mug on a nearby hill and closes her eyes as the orchestra of life plays a melodious reverie on her mind. She smiles as she feels the breath of her beloved horse, Paratrooper, on her cheek.

"Hey, Chewy." She says as she opens her eyes and looks up at him. He nickers and then nuzzles the top of her head. She reaches into her pocket and pulls out a cookie. Paratrooper quickly swipes the cookie out her hand.

"Chewy, manners!" She mockingly berates him. He playfully trots a few feet away from her and buries his head in the thick, tall grass and resumes his morning grazing ritual. Paratrooper. Her father bred Tegan's star stallion, who not only took her to the London Olympics but also won the Gold medal to everyone's shock, except Hank Miller. Affectionately known in the barn as Chewy, he stands at a glorious 17 hands. His color is a mixture of chestnut and bay, making him a blood bay with a white stripe down the front of his face and two white socks. His sire was the famous Oldenburg, Parabol, and his dam was Hank's own Thoroughbred mare, Why Guess?. Everyone in the horse community thought Hank was foolish to breed such an amazing award winning Oldenburg with an unknown and unproven thoroughbred. But Hank had a hunch, and it paid off in spades for Tegan. Chewy was Tegan's ticket to her first Grand Prix win, and from there, nothing could stop them.

Tegan reaches into the bag beside her and pulls out a bagel and blissfully partakes in the morning breakfast with Chewy. All her problems always seemed to vanish when she was with Chewy, and today was no different. She stands and walks over to Chewy and gently strokes his neck and shoulders. He raises his head and nuzzles her. He nips at her pocket.

"Another one? You are definitely the Cookie Monster." She laughs as she pulls out another cookie and feeds Chewy. He again snaps the cookie out of Tegan's hand and buries his head back into the grass. Tegan leans against Chewy and resumes her bagel breakfast.

She closes her eyes and images of her and her dad walking Grenwich Park arena filled with fans from every country invade her mind. Tegan, with a concerned look on her face, gazes around the filled arena and fidgets in her red show coat.

"Stop fidgeting." Hank says.

"There's so many people here." She replies.

"Doesn't matter. Remember, it's just you and Chewy out there."

"Got it." She says, trying to sound confident. Hank points to a 1.6 meter bright yellow vertical jump with three poles and struts to the fence, leaving Tegan at the end of the arena.

"Dad?" Tegan quickly follows behind him. He stops at the jump, folds his arms and smiles to himself.

"I know how we're going to win this."

"What? I thought you said to play it safe and place. Chewy seemed tired in warm up this morning."

"Change of plans. We've come so far. No one will expect it. All bets are on the Canadian. They won't see us coming. They're still shaking their heads that we made it to the finals."

"But Dad..."

Hank grasps Tegan's shoulders.

"You see the roll back to the yellow?" She nods her head 'yes'.

"Well, I want you to roll back tighter and slice the fence in this angle and gallop to the final oxer. Should shave a second or two from your time." Tegan looks at the sharp angle that Hank is making with his arm.

"You're insane. Chewy can't make that turn. We'll crash into the standards."

"Kiddo, God built you two for this. You can do it." Tegan shakes her head 'no.'

"I'm scared."

"I know, but this is your time. Your dream. I can only guide you. You're the one that has to grab it. What you say, kiddo?" Hank taps the bill of Tegan's helmet. She looks around the arena at all the jumps, closes her eyes, takes a deep breath, and visualizes her course. She opens her eyes and blinks, taking her father's hand and smiles.

"I'm ready." She smiles.

"Well, then let's go jump some sticks, kiddo." He squeezes her hand and they leave the arena together.

Tegan opens her eyes and looks at Chewy peacefully grazing in the field. She strokes his neck.

"I wish I could stay here forever." She sighs. "But life is not that simple, is it, Chewy? Especially my life. All this." She waves her arms in the sky. "All this takes money. Money... Gotta do silly things for money. Deal with silly people, instead of just hanging here with you." She wraps her hands around Chewy's neck and places her head on his shoulder. Chewy wraps his head around her torso and nickers. They share a deep breath of connection with one another.

He quickly lifts his head in high alert and snorts, his ears pricked forward at the sound of a golf cart heading in their direction. Tegan lets go of Chewy, watching him trot away before turning her gaze downhill. The sight of the golf cart coming up the path, Jake in the driver's seat with a cigarette dangling from his lips, makes her stomach churn.

"Dammit," she mutters under her breath. She kisses at Chewy, sending him running in the opposite direction as Jake slows the cart to a stop, climbs out, and walks toward her.

"What the hell are you doing here? In *my* golf cart! Smoking!" she yells, her voice cutting through the still morning air.

Jake hastily stubs out the cigarette and shoves it into his pocket, his face a mix of guilt and deflection. "Teegs, please. I'm sorry. Can we just talk?"

"No." Her voice is sharp, final. She steps past him, climbs into the cart.

"Teegs!" Jake calls after her, running as she takes off down the hill. "Stop! Please, just stop!"

Tegan clenches her jaw, her knuckles white on the wheel. "Dammit," she mutters again, reluctantly hitting the brakes. The cart skids to a stop, and Jake stumbles up to her, panting for breath.

"Get in," she snaps, not even looking at him.

Jake doesn't hesitate. He hops in, and before he can gather himself, she takes off again, dust flying in their wake. They hurtle down the hill; the cart bouncing over the uneven dirt path, the office and parking lot coming into view. Tegan rounds a corner sharply and slams on the brakes next to Jake's car, sending him lurching forward.

"Jesus, Tegan! You trying to kill me?" he exclaims, gripping the frame to steady himself.

"Maybe." Her voice is icy as she turns to him. "What are you doing here, Jake? You're fired. Or are you having a hard time grasping that concept?"

"I'm sorry, okay? How many times do I have to say it?"

"Not enough," she bites back, her emerald eyes narrowing. "I can't do this anymore. I don't want this. Don't you get it? You'll never change."

Jake exhales, running a hand through his hair. "I get it, Teegs. I promise. Please don't throw away everything we've built together."

Tegan scoffs, her laugh bitter and humorless. "Everything *we've* built? Seriously?"

"Tegan, please," he pleads, lowering his voice as if softening would win her over. "I just want to help. You need the help."

"Actually, I don't. I just hired a new trainer. She starts next week."

Jake's jaw tightens, his face twitching between shock and anger. "What? You've got to be kidding me. Come on, Teegs. Do you honestly believe someone new can just come in and replace me?"

"Yep." She flashes a wintry smile.

Jake leans forward, his tone turning desperate. "What about me and Missy?"

Tegan's confidence falters, her gaze shifting to the arena in the distance. "She'll come back," she says, though her voice lacks conviction.

"Teegs," Jake says, his tone softening further, almost paternal. "You don't really believe that, do you? She might come back for Bentley, sure. But you and I both know she's done with this. With *you*." He lets the weight of his words hang in the air before adding, "But I'm still here. Just give me another chance. I promise things will be different."

He places his hand over hers, giving it a gentle squeeze.

Tegan jerks her hand away, turning to face him fully, fire blazing in her eyes. "One slip, Jake. One. I mean it. Now go teach the morning sessions before I change my mind."

"Great. Will do." He pauses, his tone shifting to something almost casual. "Oh, by the way, I've got some leads—real buyers—interested in the homebred prospects. They've been asking for those classic Miller lines your dad worked so hard to establish. I told them I'd bring it to you first."

Tegan freezes, her stomach tightening. The mention of her father's breeding business is like a knife twisting in an old wound. She knows better than to trust Jake, but the idea of breathing life back into her dad's legacy tugs at her heart.

"Serious buyers?" she asks cautiously, her voice wavering.

Jake nods enthusiastically. "Serious as a heart attack. These folks know what they're looking for, and they know quality when they see it. I think we could finally turn this thing around, Teegs. Together."

Tegan looks away, her eyes fixed on the arena again, her heart torn between hope and doubt. Deep down, she knows Jake is spinning her a story, playing on her nostalgia and desperation. But with Missy gone and the weight of everything else pressing down on her, she wants to believe him.

"Fine," she says quietly, more to herself than to him. Then, louder, "But one slip, Jake. I mean it."

Jake grins, leaning back. "You won't regret this, boss. We'll make it happen."

"Go teach," Tegan snaps, turning the key.

Jake hops out, brushing the dust from his shirt as she speeds off, leaving him in a cloud of dirt. He slaps at the dust on his plaid shirt, lights another cigarette, and smirks to himself as he heads toward the Hank Miller Arena. Whatever game he's playing, he clearly thinks he's winning.

A New Adventure

C arson taps on his steering wheel to the sound of Lynyrd Skynyrd's classic, 'Sweet Home Alabama', blaring through the stereo speakers of his silver 1997 Dodge 3500 Laramie Cummins. He looks into his rear-view mirror at his four horse live-a-board gooseneck trailer. He knowingly smiles - Rusty must be tapping his hooves to their favorite song in concert with him. A lone passenger in the four horse trailer, Rusty loves traveling to music. Years back, after their fourth rodeo win, Carson outfitted his trailer with speakers in the back to keep his beloved horse company during their many cross-country adventures.

"Wonder what this new adventure will bring us, Rusty." He says.

He glances back at the breathtaking scene—umbrella trees arching overhead like nature's vaulted ceiling, sheltering the winding road that weaves through the rolling hills of Valley Vista Ranch.

"Real swanky, Hank Miller." Carson whispers to himself as he passes colts paired with their mothers grazing at Miller's pond. He continues down the road and turns and parks at the sign 'Valley Vista Ranch Riding Club Office'. He exits the vehicle, as Oscar scampers towards him with a harried look on his face. Oscar cocks his head at Carson, confused at his appearance - cowboy hat, wrangler jeans, weathered western button down plaid shirt over a white t-shirt, and well-worn cowboy boots.

"Hola, Señor. Welcome to Valley Vista Ranch. Are you here for lessons? We don't offer ranch lessons. There's a ranch down the road that I could show you how to get to. I have a horse there. You'll like it—" Oscar says. His radio clicks. The sound of a female voice resonates over the speaker.

"Oscar? Where are you?" Oscar unclips his radio.

"At the office, Señora. There's a cowboy here with a trailer who seems lost. I'm about to give him directions." He says. There is a long pause and then the radio clicks again.

"Okay, but get back here as soon as possible. I need you. Morning sessions are about to begin."

"Si, Señora. I'll be right there." Oscar clips his radio back onto his belt, wipes his forehead with his bandana, and fakes a smile. "The ranch is—"

Carson tips his cowboy hat down in respect, offers his hand to Oscar.

"Hi, I'm Carson Peterson. Tegan Miller hired me. I'm the new trainer." They shake hands and Oscar relaxes.

"Gracias a Dios! I'm so glad you're here. Forgive my mistake. I thought you were going to be here next week and you don't look like a trainer for the riding done here. Let me help you with the horses."

"Just one horse and he should be fine." Carson walks to the back of the trailer and unlatches the doors. Rusty walks out, heads directly towards Carson and nuzzles his pocket. Carson reaches into his pocket and feeds him a sugar cube and pats him on the neck.

"We're here, Buddy." He looks at Oscar. "This is Rusty. And you are—"

Oscar slaps his thigh and chuckles to himself.

"Sorry, Señor. I'm Oscar, Señora Miller's barn manager and head groom. He points to Rusty. I haven't seen a horse like that since - never mind. Hey Rusty, nice to meet you." Rusty paws the ground with his hoof in response. Oscar looks at Carson. Carson nods his head, 'yes.' He heads over to Rusty and pats his neck.

"Welcome to Valley Vista Ranch, Rusty. I can't wait to see what mischief you get into here. You're used to keeping everyone on their toes, aren't you, boy?" He looks at Carson.

"Where do you want to put him?" Oscar continues petting Rusty. Rusty nuzzles his hip pocket. "Sorry, amigo. I'll come more prepared next time." Rusty turns to Carson. Carson feeds him another sugar cube.

"Do you have any paddocks available?" Carson asks.

"Sure. Just past the stables, there is a row of paddocks." Oscar points to a row of paddocks enveloped by large leaves of grass and purple and orange wild flowers.

"Perfect... Rusty, I need you to go to the paddocks over there and relax while our new friend Oscar shows me around our new home. I'll come for you later and we'll explore. Okay?" Carson pats him on his haunches and clicks his lips. Rusty gallops towards the paddocks. Oscar, concerned, runs after Rusty.

"Wait! I need to open the gate." He says. Oscar quickly stops in his tracks and stares in disbelief, as though he's seen a Christmas miracle. Rusty approaches the gate, slows down to walk, casually unlatches and opens the gate, walks into the paddock, and begins grazing. Rusty whinnies back to Carson and Oscar. Oscar shakes his head and says sarcastically.

"You two should fit in perfectly here. Park your truck and trailer behind the stables. I have a few things to take care of for the Señora and then I'll take you to her."

"Sounds good. I'll see you in a few." Carson walks back to his truck and heads to the stables.

Oscar pulls up with an enclosed Mercedes style golf cart decorated with 'Tegan Miller Sport Horses' and a logo of a horse jumping over a fence in the front. He smiles as he stops the cart and steps out. Carson finishes unhitching his trailer from the truck, stabilizing the front hitch with blocks. He hands Oscar chock blocks and they both place the blocks in front and behind the wheels.

"Thanks, Oscar. Ready to go when you are," Carson says. Oscar perambulates to the truck, gently caressing the exterior as if he's just entered the sacred altar of St. Peter's cathedral.

"Last of the 12 valve Cummins." He whispers in reverence. He taps his fingers on the hood. Carson obligingly pops the hood, revealing the engine.

"¡Mira eso!" He tips his cowboy hat to Carson. "I haven't seen an original 12 valve Cummins in years. Everything stock?"

"Yep. Except I beefed up the transmission with a triple disc converter and the front end features the best of the best suspension parts, so I wouldn't have that infamous Dodge death wobble during my cross-country trips with the horses. It rides better now than when I got it years ago." He proudly says as he closes the hood.

"Bueno." Oscar says, standing still in admiration. Click. Click. Click.

"Oscar. Where are you?" Tegan exclaims. Oscar quickly picks up his radio.

"Coming, Señora. With the new trainer."

"What? She's not supposed to be here until next week. Never mind. Just bring her with you."

"Okay, Señora." Oscar clips the radio back onto his belt, shrugs his shoulders, and heads to the cart, leaving Carson dumbfounded. He enters the cart and turns back to Carson.

"You coming, Señor?" Oscar asks. Carson shakes his head as he gets in the cart.

"Just bring 'her' with you?" Carson asks.

"Don't worry, Señor. We'll sort this out." Oscar replies.

"Call me Carson."

"Well, Señor Carson. I'm glad your here. Señora Tegan will be glad as well. Trust me."

"I guess I have no choice." Carson looks out to the stables and sighs.

Oscar leads Carson up the wide wooden staircase to the Hank Miller Oval, the rhythmic creak of their boots on the planks blending with the soft rustle of wind through the nearby trees. As they crest the final step, the arena comes into full view, its sheer grandeur commanding attention.

The Grand Prix-level arena spans an impressive 150 by 250 feet, its pristine GGT footing glinting faintly under the mid-morning sun. The meticulously groomed surface, a blend of sand and synthetic fibers, appears almost velvet-like, promising stability and shock absorption for the horses that would soon glide across it.

Twelve show-jump fences stand at attention, each one a masterpiece of equestrian artistry. Brightly painted poles in shades of blue, red, yellow, and green rest perfectly atop standards decorated with intricate details—some bearing logos of past sponsors, others adorned with patterns of vines or checkerboards. Each fence tells a story, from simple verticals to elaborate combinations with narrow planks and airy oxers that demand precision.

By every other standard, staff position muck buckets and rakes with military precision, showcasing the arena's impeccable upkeep. The faint scent of freshly watered footing mingles with the earthy aroma of the nearby pastures, completing the setting.

White railings gleam against the sweeping backdrop of rolling hills, framing the arena like a polished picture frame. The judges' booth rises on the far side, perched beneath a wooden overhang, its wide windows commanding a clear view of every corner. Just beyond, stadium-style seats stretch along the perimeter, their weatherworn green cushions whispering stories of competitions long past.

Carson halts at the top of the stairs, struck by the scene. His gaze sweeps the oval—its clean lines, vibrant contrast, and meticulous prep—each element landing with precision. "Wow," he breathes, the word barely audible but loaded with awe. Oscar, a step ahead, glances back with a knowing grin. "Impressive, isn't it? Every detail's accounted for. Señora Tegan doesn't miss a thing."

Oscar and Carson step into the arena, their boots pressing into the pristine GGT footing as they take in the scene before them. The late morning sun filters through the rafters, casting long shadows across the arena, illuminating the graceful figure of Tegan astride a breathtaking white mare.

The horse is unlike any Carson has ever seen—her luminous coat dappled with grey star-shaped markings, as if an artist had delicately painted a fresco across her body. Her mane and tail shimmer like spun gold, cascading down her elegant frame. **Mirabella Mia.** A name that holds weight, history, and intention.

They watch as Tegan and Mia approach a blue-and-white 1.20 meter oxer. The mare's ears flick forward, her powerful frame coiling beneath her as she gathers herself. In one fluid motion, she launches into the air, her knees snapping perfectly underneath her chin, effortlessly clearing the jump with the grace of a horse meant for the heavens rather than the ground.

Carson barely registers the way his breath hitches. His eyes remain fixed on Tegan, the sheer precision in her posture, the quiet confidence in the way she lets the mare stretch through the landing. Even from a distance, he can see the way she and the horse move as one—an unbreakable partnership built on trust, patience, and something unspoken.

Tegan smiles as she brings Mia back to a rhythmic trot, then gently halts her in perfect balance. She reaches into a leather treat pouch clipped to her belt and offers the mare a sugar cube. "Good girl," she murmurs, her voice carrying just enough for them to hear. "I knew you could do it." She presses her forehead against Mia's elegant neck, invoking a silent promise between them.

Oscar chuckles, shaking his head. "Never seen a horse so determined to pick its own career path."

Carson glances at him, brow raised.

"Señor Hank bred Mia for dressage," Oscar explains. "With her effortless movement and beauty, Tegan was going to use her to break into the high-stakes dressage world—carry on her mom's legacy. But turns out Mia had other ideas."

Carson watches as Tegan straightens in the saddle, running a hand through the mare's mane before gathering the reins again.

Oscar presses on. "Every time Tegan led her into this arena—even in a dressage saddle—Mia locked onto the jumps like they were calling her. No matter what they tried, she chased the air. In the end, Tegan gave in and shifted her training to Grand Prix show jumping."

Carson's gaze lingers on Tegan as she trots toward them, her posture easy, commanding, yet undeniably elegant. She belongs here. The thought comes unbidden, a quiet acknowledgment of something he isn't quite ready to put into words.

She swings her leg over and dismounts smoothly, landing with practiced ease. As she hands the reins to Oscar, Carson quickly schools his expression, forcing away the admiration threatening to surface. Stay professional, he reminds himself.

"How was she, Señora?" Oscar asks.

"She was amazing. A real trier. She's gonna be something special. Is Maserati X ready? Ms. Turner will not be gracing us with her presence today and she wants him "tuned" up for her tomorrow." Tegan mockingly says with an English accent lilt in her voice. Oscar chuckles. Tegan turns her attention towards Carson, blinks and stares. Confusion covers her face like a mask hiding a secret.

"Hello. Have me met?" She asks. Carson walks over to her and holds out his hand.

"Hello. I'm Carson Peterson. Nice to meet you." Tegan begrudgingly shakes his hand and looks over to Oscar, still confused.

"I'm your new trainer. Janet called you last week—"

"Yes, Janet. But..." She looks him up and down. "I'm not sure if you noticed we don't do western riding here." She folds her arms in anger.

"That's fine. Riding is riding."

"Really? So jumping a four/five foot oxer is just riding?"

"Yep. Riding with some sticks in front of you." He says with a casual smirk. Tegan blinks again. Her eyes widen with memories.

"What did you say?"

"Shouldn't be a problem. Just point me to a horse and I'll get it done." He says matter-o-factly. Tegan shakes her head and laughs.

"Janet sure has a sense of humor. For now, you'll work for Oscar. I don't have time to train you on how to work with Grand Prix prospects. Maybe in a couple of months—"

Carson tips his cowboy hat. "Sorry to have wasted your time. I'll get my horse and—"

Bam! Bam! Bam! A scared look crosses Tegan's face. She looks to Oscar. "He's still in the stall? Did you at least tranq him?"

"Señora, I've been—"

"Never mind. Take Mirabella Mia back to her stall. Dammit!" She bolts toward the stables. Carson looks at Oscar, who shrugs his shoulders in complete dismay. Oscar kicks the dirt, swears under his breath, and hastily follows Tegan.

Remington snorts and rears with a wild look in his eyes. Tegan rushes to the stall, syringe in her pocket.

"Remi, it's okay. It's me. I'm here." She calmly says. Remington settles down and Tegan slowly approaches him. She pulls out the syringe and, like a viper,

Remington bares his teeth and snaps at her face. Carson instinctively pushes Tegan away as Remington's teeth crush down on his shoulder. Carson places his fist on Remington's neck and shoves him away. Remington incensed rams his body into the stall door.

"Remi!" Tegan scrambles back towards him.

"Stay back!" Carson says. He grabs the halter next to the stall door and puts it over his good shoulder. With a composed stance, he faces Remington at an angle and bows his head. Remington, ears pinned back, paws the ground and snorts again.

"It's okay, boy. No one is gonna hurt you." Carson softly says. Remington's ears prick forward and his eyes soften a little, but his head held high, still on high alert. Carson takes a slow step towards him and pauses. An eternity seems to pass as Carson gently waits for Remington. Remington licks his lips and nickers. Carson takes another step.

"What do you need, Buddy?" He softly asks. Remington looks out to the pasture, then moves his body towards Carson. This human won't hurt him. Carson opens the stall door, gently places the halter over Remington's ears, and leads him out of the stall. Tegan, in shock, says, "What are you—"

Carson raises his hand.

"Not now. I'm taking this horse out to pasture. He doesn't want to be here." Carson defiantly says.

"But he'll attack the other horses." Tegan responds.

"No. He won't." Carson says. He turns and walks away with Remington, leaving Tegan shocked, with her jaw dropped.

Carson opens the gate, leads Remington inside, and releases him into the pasture. Remington gallops off, stops in the middle of tall grass, and rolls. He stands up and begins grazing like nothing happened. Remington, like any other horse, lives in the moment; past fear has vanished as he becomes one with nature. Tegan pulls up with the golf cart and gets out fuming.

"You idiot. Don't you think we didn't try that? Now we can't turn out any other horses. He attacks them." Tegan says, frustrated.

"Patience." He replies. He looks over at the paddocks and whistles. Rusty lifts his head from grazing, goes to the paddock gate, opens it, gallops toward Carson, and halts right next to him.

"A quarter horse? You've got to be kidding me." Tegan says..

"Yes. And I'm not kidding." Carson replies. Carson pats Rusty on his neck.

"Rusty, I need you to help this horse. Can you do that for me?" Rusty looks up at Carson and nickers. Rusty walks toward the gate, opens it, and heads in.

"He's going to kill him." She says. Carson looks back to Tegan's angst ridden face and gently smiles. She crosses her arms in anger and looks away from Carson towards the pasture.

Remington threatened, bares his teeth, and charges at Rusty. Rusty stands his ground and right before Remington bares down on him, nimbly darts to the side. Remington shakes his head in anger and stomps his hoof on the ground. He turns and charges at Rusty. Rusty again holds his ground, and this time quickly darts to the left. Before Remington can turn around to charge at him, Rusty clocks Remington in the head with his head. He then grabs Remington's withers with his teeth and they canter in a circle until Remington relents. The fight is over, and Rusty establishes his alpha status. He grooms Remington in reassurance and Remington licks his lips, bows his head and grazes. Rusty looks up at Carson and nickers.

Carson removes his cowboy hat and wipes his dusted and sweat infused face with a handkerchief from his pocket. He places his good hand on his bloodied shoulder and assesses the damage. He walks over to the golf cart, gets in, and looks at Tegan.

"I'm gonna need some stitches." He says. Tegan looks back at him, tears in her eyes. Tegan, stunned, looks over to Rusty. She cocks her head and runs her eyes over Rusty's conformation. She blinks, shakes her head, and looks directly at Carson.

"I'll take care of it." She replies.

Tegan and Carson enter the office, and Tegan promptly proceeds to her desk and grabs the first aid kit.

She motions to her office chair. "Sit." Carson obliges.

"Shirt, please." Carson removes his shirt, winces. Tegan moves the shoulder strap of his tank top to better assess the wound. She pours water over the wound to remove the debris and blood gently oozes from the laceration. Tegan reaches into her first aid kit and removes some gauze. She hands it to Carson.

"Put some pressure on the wound to stop the bleeding while I get the sutures ready." She says. He places the gauze on his shoulder and patiently waits as Tegan prepares the utensils. She's amazed by his stoicism.

"Ready?" she asks. He shakes his head affirmative. She shakes her head and smiles to herself, remembering the same response from her father when she attended his many lesions. She applies the sutures like a practiced doctor. Silence fills the room as she continues her work. Tegan finishes the last stitch. Carson grimaces as Tegan dabs a cotton ball saturated with alcohol on his shoulder. She removes another piece of gauze and tapes it over his shoulder, then reaches for his plaid buttoned down shirt lying on the desk and hands it to him, gazing at his muscular body inadequately masked by his white tank top and quickly averts her eyes as he puts his shirt back on.

"Thanks." He looks around her office and pauses at the pictures on the back wall. He looks back at her, his eye contact unrelenting.

"Where did you learn how to do that?" He asks.

"Vet tech. Horse husbandry. Farrier. My father believed that a true horseman should be a jack of all equestrian trades. So. I became the local vet of the ranch before I could walk, so to say. Bandaging someone up at a moment's notice, especially my father. He had a knack for getting himself into fixes. A walking medical case until..." She looks away.

Carson stands and walks across the room. "About the horse trainer position?" He asks.

"Yeah. Right." She looks back at him with a determined expression. "You seem to know your way around horses. But... we have a certain way of doing things here and I'm not sure—"

"I'll tell you what... You let me work on that stallion out there and I'll follow your certain way of doing things." He walks toward her and sticks his hand out. "Deal?"

Tegan hesitates and takes a long look at Carson, measuring him up. She then looks at the wall of pictures and smirks.

"Sure. Why not? Deal." She shakes his hand with a tight horseman's grip. Their hands linger in a solid embrace, like old friends who don't want to say goodbye. Embarrassed, she loosens her grip and steps away.

"Why don't you get settled in and into some proper riding attire and meet me at the Hank Miller Oval? I have a couple more horses to ride and then I can show you around. You do have proper riding attire. Don't you?" She asks. Carson chuckles to himself.

"Sure. I'll meet you out there later." He tips his cowboy hat and exits the office.

Carson returns to the Hank Miller Oval and is barely recognizable in his tan breaches with a black woven belt, a white polo shirt with a blue collar, tall black riding boots, and a black riding helmet tucked under his elbow. He stops at the edge of the arena and intently watches Tegan train a baby horse. Tegan strokes the horse's neck and feeds it a sugar cube.

"Good boy, Lucky. Let's do it again. Okay?" She whispers. Lucky nickers. Tegan leads Lucky with a lead rope to a line of poles and a simple cross rail fence. Lucky, a stunning golden chestnut Oldenburg gelding already standing over 16 hands at the tender age of four, playfully shakes his head and trips like Bambi when he first learned to walk. She gently jerks the lead rope to gain his attention and jogs to the first pole. Lucky easily trots over and proceeds to the next poles. As they approach the cross rail, Lucky hesitates and trips. Tegan clicks at Lucky. He continues and over jumps the cross rail by three feet. Tegan giggles to herself, pats Lucky on the shoulder, and feeds him a sugar cube.

She leads Lucky to the mounting block, lowers the stirrups, and mounts. She scratches his withers and gently presses her legs on his girth. He surges forward and stumbles. She laughs to herself and urges him forward. Tegan turns Lucky around and trots him to the line of poles. He manages the poles and continues to the cross rail. Again, he over jumps the cross rail, and she stays with him as he bolts away. She halts him, bringing him down to trot in a circle, patting him on the shoulders as she slows him down to walk.

"I knew you could do it!" She exclaims. And like a schoolgirl with her first baby doll, she hugs his neck. She dismounts.

"I think that's enough for today. Don't you?" She says as she feeds him a sugar cube. She looks up at Carson, smiles, and waves for him to enter. He enters the arena and heads towards her.

"You clean up pretty nice. Almost didn't recognize you." She chuckles. He ignores the dig at his outfit and places his full attention on the horse.

"Nice horse. What's his name?" Carson asks.

"This is Lucky." She replies. She leads Lucky toward the gate.

"Lucky? Interesting name." He says.

"Yep. This horse has a way of getting into trouble all the time. He's a mess. A real life Bambi. But he never gets a scratch. So... " She shrugs her shoulders and smiles.

"Lucky." He finishes her sentence and they both laugh. He pats Lucky's neck. "Good name. Are you done?"

"Almost." She looks up and Oscar escorts a bay thoroughbred into the arena. She hands Oscar Lucky's reins.

"How was he, Señora?" He asks.

"He's still a klutz, but he's getting better. Hopefully, he'll find his feet in a couple of months."

"Thank you, Oscar." Oscar nods and escorts Lucky to the stalls. Tegan leads the lithe bay thoroughbred to Carson. The thoroughbred prances sideways and canters in place. A playful little devil disguised in the angelic face of an Arabian mare, a white blaze down the front of the face, with human like eyes, the thoroughbred snaps at Tegan like a viper. She pushes his head away and taps him with the crop.

47

"Settle. Settle." She says to the horse. She looks over at Carson.

"This is Veuve Clicquot, aka Bubbles." She hands him the reins. He looks at her, confused.

"I know you can handle a stallion on the ground, but can you ride? Indulge me?" She cocks her eyebrow and looks directly at him, as if to challenge him to a duel.

Carson takes the reins and looks out the arena to the crowd of stablemen and groomsmen gathering outside. Jake saunters up to the gate, lights a cigarette, smirks, and tips his baseball hat to Carson. Carson pauses his gaze at Jake for a moment and then looks directly back at Tegan.

"Sure, why not?" He confidently says.

"Need a leg up?" She says with a giggle. Carson ignores her, puts on his helmet, and leads a rambunctious Bubbles to the mounting block. Bubbles kicks out at him. Carson tunes out Bubbles' antics and mounts him. Bubbles jumps up and down in place, kicks the mounting block away, spooks himself, and canters sideways, snorting and contorting his body in ways not thought possible on a horse. Bubbles pins his ears back and spins like a top. Carson pulls on the outside rein, immediately halts him, reins him back five steps, and halts again. He makes Bubbles stand in a perfect square halt for what seems an eternity. Bubbles shakes his head up and down. Carson scratches his withers and softly whispers to him. Bubbles drops his head, exhales and chews on his bit like it's a pacifier. Carson pats him on the neck and urges him off to a long rein trot, nose barely an inch from the ground. He continues trotting Bubbles in a circle. Bubbles' eyes soften and, in a trancelike state, relaxes his shoulders and back.

"Did I miss anything? He still on?" Oscar rushes up to Jake's side.

"Yep." Jake shakes his head in disbelief.

"What's the pot at?" Oscar asks.

"Two hundred for Bubbles." Jake replies. Oscar reaches into his back pocket and pulls out his wallet.

"Twenty dollars on the Gringo cowboy." Oscar exclaims with pride. The men gasp in shock and whisper to each other. Jake stares at Oscar.

"I can't believe you..." Jake says.

"He's lasted longer than you did, Jake. You... Not even five minutos." Oscar smiles and continues looking into the arena. Jake smacks the rail in anger and pulls out his wallet.

"Fifty dollars on Bubbles!" He exclaims. He shoves the wallet back into his jeans. The men laugh and murmur to one another. Oscar pulls out his wallet again, takes out thirty dollars, and hands it to Jake.

"Match. Now shut up and let me watch." Oscar retorts. He rubs his hands together like a man on a mission and looks back out to the arena.

Carson gathers the reins with quiet confidence and sends Bubbles forward into a canter. The gelding flings his head with dramatic flair, nostrils flaring, and slams his front hooves into the ground like a challenge. His hindquarters coil and spring into the air, launching him upward with the power of a rearing stallion. He bucks again, twisting mid-air, tail snapping like a whip. His muscles ripple beneath his glossy coat as he leaps sideways with a sharp hop, then snaps back into forward motion as if nothing happened.

Carson moves with him, every joint fluid, every cue precise. He rides through the chaos without hesitation, guiding the energy instead of resisting it. Bubbles breathes deep, settles into the bit, and flows into a balanced, rhythmic canter—his strides long, his body elastic, his focus sharpening with each step.

Tegan walks into the arena and places a small cross rail in the center. Carson guides Bubbles into a bending line toward the jump. As they approach, Bubbles flings his head again, flinging a strand of sweat into the sunlight, and flutters his ears with wild indecision. He changes leads with every stride—right, left, right, left—as if testing every option before settling on one. His feet strike the sand with deliberate exaggeration, and his tail flicks with a touch of attitude. Ten feet from the jump, his body compresses like a loaded spring and launches upward. He clears the rail with a dramatic arc, soaring four feet above it and landing with a ten-foot gap, neck stretched forward and eyes proud.

The men by the fence release a chorus of sharp breaths. Carson keeps his seat, eyes ahead, hands steady. He gathers the reins just enough to offer support, then releases again into a loose trot. His fingers run gently along Bubbles' neck in praise, and the gelding stretches toward the contact with satisfaction.

"He wants more," Carson says to Tegan, voice steady. "Raise it."

Tegan jogs to the fence and lifts the rail to a full meter vertical. Carson shortens Bubbles' stride, feeling the electricity build beneath the saddle. Bubbles locks on to the fence, ears pricked, legs light beneath him. At just the right moment, he lifts into the air with perfect timing—neck arched, knees tucked, hooves clearing the top with grace. The bascule forms naturally, and he lands in perfect balance.

Without breaking rhythm, Carson turns him toward a challenging line—two strides to one, three fences: a vertical, another vertical, and a wide oxer. Each stands over a meter high. Bubbles approaches with precision, reading the distances as if he built the course himself. He clears the first fence cleanly, shifts into two powerful strides, sails over the second, and folds his legs tightly to meet the final oxer. After clearing the last, he kicks out with a happy buck and lands with a snort of satisfaction, ears flicking back to Carson as if waiting for approval.

Carson leans forward and pats his neck with a wide smile. He eases him into a trot, then a walk, letting the reins stretch long. Bubbles breathes deeply, his body loose and gleaming with effort.

Cheers rise from the rail. Carson halts in the center of the arena. Bubbles turns his head, gently nibbles at Carson's boot, and lingers with affectionate curiosity.

Oscar throws his fist in the air. "¡Sí! I knew he could do it! That gringo rides with legs like steel! No one has ridden a horse like that since..." He trails off, slaps Jake on the back. "Hand it over."

Jake scowls and slaps a wad of bills into Oscar's hand.

"Gracias," Oscar declares, holding the cash up like a trophy. "Drinks are on me tonight, amigos!"

The men cheer. Oscar waves them off. "Now get back to work!"

They groan but scatter. Jake huffs, throws Carson a glare, and storms off.

Oscar chuckles. "Gringos," he mutters, and heads into the arena.

Carson dismounts, unclips his helmet, and loosens the girth. Bubbles noses his pocket, lips twitching. Carson fishes out a sugar cube and feeds it to him. The gelding crunches it loudly, eyes half-lidded in bliss.

Tegan approaches, her face unreadable but her eyes blazing with emotion—anger, amazement, and something else tangled behind it.

She stops. Stares. Blinks hard once.

"I've got work. Oscar will show you around," she says, voice clipped. She passes him with purpose. "We'll go over tomorrow's schedule later."

Oscar raises his brows. "Señora, what about—"

"Please, Oscar." Her voice shakes, just a little, but she keeps walking.

Oscar shrugs and looks at Carson.

Carson hands him the reins. "Nice horse. Guess it's you and me, Oscar."

Oscar grins. "Sí, Señor Carson. Follow me."

They walk out together, Bubbles snorting between them, still buzzing from the ride.

TECHNOLOGY

O scar taps the iPad mounted on the barn wall. The screen glows to life, casting a soft bluish hue over the polished wood. A sleek digital interface loads instantly, revealing a comprehensive 3D map of the entire facility. Stalls appear in sharp resolution—each box labeled with the horse's name, breed, and a color-coded status bar. Green means fed, blue means turned out, red flag is a medical note. Next to each name, icons flash with up-to-the-minute alerts: farrier visits due, vaccine updates, temperature logs, turnout rotations, riding notes.

Oscar swipes through the stalls with practiced speed. He taps on Bubbles' profile, and a complete health and performance record fills the screen—deworming history, grain ratios, exercise logs, hoof X-rays, even a stress-level score based on biometrics captured by a wearable halter monitor.

"Here, Señor," Oscar says, tapping through tabs without missing a beat. "We track everything—vaccinations, feedings, turnout, rider sessions, owner preferences, shoeing schedules, vet visits, massage therapy, PEMF treatments, saddle fit reports, show records. Every detail logs itself in real time."

He flicks to a full-screen calendar. Bright boxes crowd every day. "You can see the upcoming shows, training clinics, vet days, and rider scheduling here. All of it syncs automatically to the app."

Carson crosses his arms and narrows his eyes at the screen. His body stiffens. The sheer efficiency unsettles him.

Oscar pulls out his phone and holds it up with a grin. "We've got an app, too. Download it, and you can check your horse list, update ride notes, get alerts, message clients, or even review slow-motion jump footage straight from the arena cams. One tap does it all."

Carson runs a hand over the back of his neck. His fingers linger there, tension climbing his spine. "Yeah, about that..."

Oscar's grin falters. He squints at Carson. "You don't use a phone, do you?"

Carson shakes his head once. "I don't carry one."

Oscar blinks, stunned. "You're a rare breed." He lets out a soft laugh, adjusts his belt, and tries to reset. "Okay. That's no problem. Check the physical board outside the tack room each morning. I'll print your schedule, list your horses, and flag anything urgent."

Carson scowls slightly, his eyes still locked on the screen. "Why not just tell me? This whole setup—" he motions toward the tablet, the blinking lights, the tidy color-coded chaos "—this isn't how barns are supposed to work."

Oscar rests a hand on his hip, unfazed. "This barn runs like a clock. Señora Tegan insists on it. Every detail matters. We manage over fifty horses, multiple trainers, over two dozen clients, and a dozen grooms. Without the system, it all collapses."

Carson glares at the display again. Horses don't belong on a screen. Reading the horse matters more than reading data. Hoofbeats speak louder than heart-rate graphs. A swishing tail or tightened lip reveals more than any blinking alert.

He huffs under his breath, jaw clenched. "Fine. I'll make it work."

Oscar claps him on the shoulder, his face lighting up again. "Good man."

Carson exhales through his nose. "That everything?"

Oscar nods. "For now. But the day's done. We're heading to Morrison's. You should come. Meet the crew. I'm buying."

He pats his pocket and flashes a thick roll of bills—today's winnings from the Bubbles betting pool.

Carson hesitates. He prefers quiet over crowds, but he doesn't mind Oscar. And after today, a drink doesn't sound half bad.

"Maybe I'll swing by later."

Oscar studies his face, reading the noncommittal tone. He raises an eyebrow. "Just the guys. Señora Tegan never joins us. She stays busy. But don't let that be you. Life needs sabor, Señor Carson."

Carson chuckles faintly, taps Oscar's shoulder. "I'll be there. Just need a minute."

Oscar gives a skeptical nod, then heads off down the aisle.

Carson turns on his heel and walks toward the pasture, his boots striking the concrete with a steady rhythm. Behind him, automated feeders kick on with a low mechanical hum. A blue arm releases a scoop of grain into a stainless steel bucket with a precise clatter.

He doesn't turn back. Technology buzzes and pings behind him, but his eyes stay forward. He heads for what still makes sense in his world—the rhythm of hooves, the weight of leather, the breath of horses in the early dark.

Tegan closes her iPad, sits back in her chair and undoes her single braid allowing her hair to cascade down her shoulders past her chest. She raises her arms, yawns, and runs her hands through her hair. She reaches into her pocket and pulls out her cell phone. On the screen is a picture of Missy smiling ear to ear, dressed in riding clothes, holding a lead rope attached to a black and white leather halter, standing next to Remington. She caresses the picture, tears in her eyes, taps the screen, and places the phone next to her ear.

"Missy here, well, not really leave a message or don't. Later." The phone beeps.

"Hey Missy. It's me. Tegan. Just wanted to say hi. Checkin' in. Hope you're doing well. I'm well. We're all well. Really well... Bentley and Remi miss you. We all miss you. There's a new trainer, but... Anyway, you're always welcome at Vista Valley Ranch... I guess what I'm trying to say is that Valley Vista is not Valley Vista without you. Would love to see you... Bentley's waiting for you. We all are. Take your time. Take care... Bye." She hangs up the phone, flings it on the desk, buries her head in her hands, and closes her eyes.

Paratrooper—young, fiery, and barely broken—rears high onto his hind legs at the end of Oscar's lunge line, his muscles rippling beneath a gleaming bay coat. His hooves slice through the air as his wild eyes roll white, his ears pinned back in defiance. Oscar, drenched in sweat, grits his teeth and yanks firmly on the lunge line, trying to bring the four-year-old back down to earth.

Instead, Paratrooper slams his front hooves to the ground and immediately rockets backward, dragging Oscar with him. The sand kicks up in thick clouds as Oscar stumbles forward, his boots digging deep as he fights to regain control. He plants his feet, grits his teeth, and yanks hard, bringing the stallion to a jerking halt.

Paratrooper snorts loudly, shaking his head in frustration before pawing at the ground in irritation. His tail flicks like an annoyed cat's, his nostrils flaring in challenge.

Hank Miller, standing just beyond the lunge circle, watches with an amused grin.

"That's good, Oscar," he says with a slow nod. "He should be fine."

Oscar turns and glares at him as if he's lost his damn mind. He wipes sweat from his forehead, then looks over to Tegan, who stands frozen outside the arena with wide, horrified eyes. He exhales sharply, shaking his head as he reels Paratrooper in, shortening the lunge line.

"Okay, Señor Miller," Oscar mutters, still glaring at the barely contained force of nature at the end of his line. He cautiously leads Paratrooper toward Hank and Tegan, the stallion still tossing his head, tail flicking in irritation.

"Thank you, Oscar. That'll be all today," Hank says, reaching for the reins.

Oscar mutters something in Spanish under his breath, unclipping the lunge line and carefully unraveling the reins from the throat latch before handing them over.

"See you tonight at Morrison's?" he asks, shaking out his shoulders like he just wrestled a bear.

Hank chuckles. "Sounds good. First round's on me."

Oscar tips his hat. "Good night, Señor. Señorita." With one last glance at Paratrooper, he walks off, clearly relieved to be putting some distance between himself and the unpredictable stallion.

Hank steps forward and caresses Paratrooper's forehead, his touch calm and confident. Instantly, the stallion exhales sharply, his body losing a fraction of its tension. He lowers his massive head and nuzzles into Hank's coat pocket, snuffling around with searching lips.

Hank chuckles. "Oh, I see how it is. You're nothing but a big ol' cookie monster, huh?" He pulls out a sugar cube and offers it to the stallion, who eagerly snaps it up, crunching loudly.

Hank turns to Tegan, grinning. "What do you think, Kiddo? Isn't Chewy perfect?"

Tegan takes a step back, shaking her head in disbelief. "Perfect? Dad, I am *not* getting on that horse." Her voice is sharp, her pulse still racing from the chaos she just witnessed. "He's still unridable, even after Oscar lunged him. I can't believe you actually think this is my next ride." She crosses her arms, frustration bubbling over. "We should've bought that horse in Europe. I *begged* you, but no—'*Home-grown is where it's at, kiddo.*'" She gestures at Paratrooper—*Chewy*—like he's the most ridiculous idea Hank has ever had.

Her voice wavers, but she pushes on. "Now I have nothing. My last ride is laid up for at least nine months. We're laughingstocks, Dad. I'm never going to make it to the Olympics at this rate. This—this is a *waste!*"

With that, she spins on her heel and storms out of the arena, the lump in her throat threatening to choke her.

"Tegan Miller!" Hank's voice booms after her.

She stops in her tracks but doesn't turn around. Her shoulders are stiff, her hands curled into fists.

Hank doesn't say another word. Instead, he takes a deep breath, tightens the reins, and steps toward the mounting block. With the effortless ease of a man who's spent his entire life in the saddle, he swings onto Chewy's back.

The stallion freezes for half a second, his ears twitching—then all hell breaks loose.

Chewy explodes into a full-bodied bronc-worthy buck, his back arching as he launches into the air. His hind legs kick out violently, his powerful muscles snapping like coiled springs. He lands, then bucks again, harder this time, twisting midair like he's determined to send his rider flying.

Tegan's breath catches. "Dad!"

She moves to rush forward, but Hank doesn't even flinch.

He leans back, sits deep, and keeps his hands steady on the reins. His movements are impossibly calm, completely unbothered by the chaos beneath him. Every time Chewy tries to rip the reins from his hands, Hank gently resists. Every time the stallion leaps sideways, he follows, never losing balance, never panicking.

Chewy pins his ears, slams his head down, and bolts toward the gate in a wild sprint, bucking every few strides.

Hank simply shifts his weight back, gathers the reins, and says, "*Whoa.*"

Just like that, Chewy stops dead.

Panting, the stallion's sides heave as he stands there, processing what just happened. Hank doesn't push him, doesn't punish him—he just sits quietly, giving the young horse a moment to figure it out. Slowly, Chewy lowers his head, his ears flicking forward.

Hank rubs his neck. "There you go, big guy."

He gently urges Chewy into a trot, guiding him into a large, steady circle. The stallion is still tense, still uncertain, but he listens. With every passing stride, his movements become more fluid, his ears locked onto Hank's quiet cues.

After a few minutes, Hank lifts his gaze to his daughter and smiles. Then, without a word, he nudges Chewy into a canter and guides him straight toward Tegan. As they reach her, Hank sits deep, squeezes lightly with his legs, and Chewy halts in a perfect square.

"That's my boy," Hank murmurs, patting Chewy's neck before looking straight at Tegan. His blue eyes gleam with warmth, affection—and just a hint of mischief. "If he can buck, he can jump. Isn't Chewy perfect, kiddo?"

Tegan stares, her mouth slightly open, her brain still struggling to process what she just witnessed.

For a moment, she hates how easy he makes it look.

Then she exhales, shaking her head with a sigh. "Yeah, Dad. He is." She finally admits, her voice softer now. "Can't wait to ride him."

Hank grins as he swings off the saddle, landing lightly on his feet. "The sky's the limit with this one. I can feel it." He hands her the reins and squeezes her shoulder. "We'll start tomorrow. Why don't you cool him off, kiddo? I'll meet you at Morrison's."

With that, he walks off, leaving her alone with the stallion who nearly killed Oscar minutes ago.

Chewy, apparently unbothered by his earlier tantrum, reaches for her breeches pocket, chewing at the fabric like a playful puppy.

Tegan chuckles despite herself and fishes out a cookie. "I guess it's gonna be you and me, Chewy."

She strokes his neck, feeling the power and potential beneath his shimmering coat, and leads him out of the arena.

Chewy nibbles at her shoulder, and for the first time since her last horse went lame, she feels something close to hope.

Knock. Knock. Knock. Tegan jolts upright, the past dissolving like steam. She shakes off the haze, runs her hands through her hair, and pushes it back from her face.

"Come in." She says. Oscar enters, sits on the couch. She clicks on her iPad.

"Yes. I'll start first thing with the Grand Prix prospects before morning lessons. I'm planning on showing Mirabella Mia in her first Grand Prix, so I'll need more time with her for the next couple of weeks leading up to the show. There are some other horses that might be ready as well. Be sure to tell Jake that this week's sessions need to focus on getting everyone prepped for the show. Qualifiers-"

"Señora, Jake says he'll be late tomorrow."

"What?"

"He has a family emergency."

"Yeah, right? Who is it now? His uncle Gin and Tonic?" She says sarcastically.

"I knew he wouldn't change. I guess I'll have to take care of everything as usual."

"What about Señor Carson? He could—"

"The clients don't know him. It's too close to the show, anyway." She adamantly replies.

"Señora, he can help—just ask. You hired him for a reason. I haven't seen riding like that since your father. With respect." Oscar stands firmly in front of her and matches her glaring green eyes. Tegan blinks.

"Very well, Oscar. I'll talk to him. Put him on the schedule. But if the clients complain—"

"I know. I know. I'll fix it." Oscar looks behind Tegan to the photos on the wall.

"You coming?" He asks, hopeful for a different answer.

"I'd love to, but I still have to check on the horses, and you know. Maybe some other time." She replies. She knowingly looks at her old friend and sheepishly smiles. Disappointed, Oscar opens the door. He turns and smiles back.

"By the way, Señor Carson does not have a cell phone." He shakes his head, laughs to himself, remembering a fond memory, and heads out the door.

"Good night, Señora." He says.

"Good night, Oscar." She replies. She turns off the iPad and heads out the door.

A quiet rhythm takes hold as Carson guides the two horses into motion, his seat steady, his cues subtle and sure. Rusty leads with calm authority, Remington shadowing his every step, both stallions lifting their legs with precision as they glide over the trot poles scattered like stepping stones across the sand. Their bodies move in near-perfect unison, each stride a mirror of the other—a pas de deux forged in instinct, trust, and gentle correction. The dance unfolds without fanfare, just the soft thuds of hooves, the faint jingle of tack, and the low hum of breath shared between them.

At the far end of the arena, Tegan leans into the top rail, elbows planted, her eyes locked on the scene with something just shy of wonder. She shifts her cap, adjusting it low against the fading light, and smooths her long ebony hair behind her ears. The breeze catches a few loose strands, and she tucks them away, unwilling to miss a single beat of the moment.

Carson, unaware of her watchful gaze, urges the horses forward with a gentle squeeze of his calves. Rusty stretches into a lopey canter, and Remington follows, lighter now, his frame more relaxed. Carson rides in sync with both, balancing the tension between their leads, holding them steady like a conductor guiding two instruments through a shared melody. The three move as one—unrushed, fluid, and entirely in tune—as they float down the length of the arena.

Carson looks towards the gate and notices Tegan leaning against the railing. He drops the horses down to a walk and halts. He dismounts Rusty, loosens his cinch, and ties the reins around the horn of the saddle. Rusty heads over to Tegan and nuzzles her. Tegan, surprised by Rusty's attention, backs away from the fence. Rusty paws the ground, frustrated.

"Sorry, Rusty. Didn't expect you to... Never mind." Tegan smiles and climbs over the fence. She pats him on the neck. Rusty wraps his head and neck around her waist. She giggles and hugs him back. Rusty pulls her closer like a long-lost friend.

"You're such a Casanova, Rusty." Carson playfully says. Rusty unwraps his head and neck from Tegan's torso and heads over to Carson and Remington. Carson leads Remington towards Tegan. Remington wide eyed jerks back his head and shuffles backward in a panic. Rusty quickly moves beside Remington and stops him with his hind quarters before he's able to drag Carson. Carson walks over to Remington and stands still beside him. Carson looks at Tegan. She gently raises her hand and whispers to Remington.

"It's okay, Remi. I'm sorry, boy. I didn't mean to hurt you with the needle. I just thought ..." She steps back to give Remington space. She reaches into her pocket and pulls out a cookie, and shows it to Remington. Rusty nudges Remington forward. Remington pricks his ears forward and glares back at Tegan like a betrayed child.

"Sorry Remi. I'm so sorry." She says as she turns away from Remington and climbs over the fence, stands patiently, hand extended, offering the cookie. Remington nickers and cautiously walks towards Tegan, with Carson and Rusty acting as a calmative alongside him. He accepts the cookie from Tegan's hand and drops his head. She smiles and caresses his forehead and cheeks.

"Good boy. Good boy, Remington." She says. She looks over at Carson.

"Thank you. You don't know what this means to me. This horse—"

"I get it. We're done for the evening, and this is just a bonus. Remington needs to regain his confidence, and this is the first step." He replies. Tegan unlatches the gate and they head out towards the stables. An awkward silence envelops the air. Rusty nudges Tegan. She looks at him and giggles and pushes him back.

"Rusty. You're such a troublemaker, aren't you? But effective. So Carson, I was hoping to talk to you about tomorrow."

"Yes?"

"Jake has a family emergency. We only have a couple weeks left leading up to the horse show, and it's the season qualifier and I need help. I was wondering if you could work with some students." She blurts out at record speed.

"Sure. Just let me know what you need."

"It'll be on the schedule. Just click— "

She shows him the iPad and clicks on the calendar button. He grimaces.

"Yea. About that. I'm not too comfortable with the technology mumbo jumbo. Can you just write it down for me?" He responds stiffly.

Tegan stops, shoves the iPad into the back of her breaches, and fiercely glares at him.

"That technology mumbo jumbo, as you call it, keeps this place running like clockwork. I thought Oscar showed you how to use the iPad. Everyone uses the iPad - all the groomsmen. Even our vet, and he's much older than you. If this is too much for you, Carson, I need to know right now. I can't start relying on you and have you flake out on me like Jake. I can't do everything." Hot tears brightly shine in her eyes. Rusty, annoyed, head butts Carson and whacks him with his tail. Tegan looks at Rusty and laughs.

"Thanks, Rusty. You with me, Carson?" She asks, challenging Carson. Carson leads the horses into the stalls, closes the stall doors, and faces her with a smirk on his face.

"I'm with you, Tegan." He says.

"Good. Lessons start at eight. Your schedule will be posted by midnight. Good night, Carson." She pats Remington on the neck, then turns and leaves him standing with the horses before he can respond.

"Good night, Tegan." He whispers to himself.

MORRISON'S

M orrison's had been the local watering hole for decades, a beacon of camaraderie for Valley Vista Ranch and the tight-knit equestrian community.
Whether it was a victory toast, a hard-earned paycheck, or just an excuse to kick
back after a grueling day, this was where they came to celebrate, to commiserate,
and to let loose.

The old pub was a blend of rustic charm and Celtic pride, its dark wooden
beams adorned with horse tack, old photographs, and championship ribbons
won by Valley Vista riders over the years. A massive stone fireplace crackled at the
far end, its flickering light casting warm shadows over the oak tables and leather
barstools. Morrison's always had a theme—tonight, an unapologetic homage to
St. Patrick's Day.

The room is a riot of green, white, and orange. Shamrocks, pots of gold, and
leprechaun cutouts cover the wood-paneled walls, and strings of twinkling green
lights dangle from the ceiling. Balloons cluster in the corners, their festive colors
bobbing with each burst of laughter. The scent of frying oil, fresh bread, and
spiced whiskey drifts through the air, mingling with the distinct aroma of old
wood and beer-soaked floors.

Behind the bar, William McDougall Morrison, the pub's proprietor, commands his domain. Dressed in faded jeans, a crisp button-down, and a towering
green top hat adorned with a gold four-leaf clover, he pours frothy mugs of green
ale with the effortless grace of a man who has done this a thousand times.

He reaches for the rusted brass bell hanging above the counter and gives it a
sharp ring. The crowd erupts, raising their glasses in unison, voices overlapping
in drunken cheer.

The lights dim, and a hush falls over the room as Paddy's Revenge, the pub's resident band, takes the small stage in the corner. A fiddle sings out a mournful opening note, followed by the steady strum of a banjo. Then, the unmistakable melody of "The Fields of Athenry" fills the pub, the song's haunting beauty wrapping itself around every soul in the room. As the chorus swells, the entire pub sings as one:

Low lie, the Fields of Athenry
Where once we watched the small free birds fly
Our love was on the wing
We had dreams and songs to sing
It's so lonely round the Fields of Athenry

At that moment, Carson steps through the pub doors. The music wraps around him like an embrace, the warm glow of the pub contrasting with the cool night air at his back. He hesitates for only a moment before stepping inside, his sharp gaze sweeping over the room, taking in the familiarity of drunken camaraderie, Irish folk ballads, and the distinct smell of wood, leather, and ale.

A blur of red curls appears in front of him.

"Here, cowboy. You're not fully dressed without it."

Jenny McDougall Morrison, the owner's sixteen-year-old daughter, grins up at him, dressed in a playful Irish wench costume—corset, layered skirt, and all. She shoves a tall green top hat into his hands, eyes twinkling with mischief.

Carson arches a brow but doesn't hesitate. He jams the ridiculous hat onto his head and joins in the chorus, his deep voice blending into the sea of voices that fill the pub. Jenny beams, clearly delighted, and grabs his hand, pulling him toward the long wooden table where the Valley Vista Ranch crew has gathered.

At the head of the table, Oscar sits like a king, one hand gripping a pitcher of green ale, the other already halfway through a plate of chicken wings. Pitchers of beer crowd the table alongside steaming plates of wings, thick-cut slices of soda bread, and baskets overflowing with golden, crispy chips. Oscar's face lights up when he spots Carson.

"Señor Carson!" he calls, his voice booming over the music. He motions for him to sit, elbowing Pedro to slide over. Pedro nudges his chair back, grinning. "Make room for the tamer of Bubbles!" Carson settles into the empty chair, and almost immediately, Oscar shoves a mug of green ale into his hand.

"Drink!" Oscar commands, clapping him on the back.

Carson barely has the chance to lift his mug before William rings the bell again. The room erupts into cheers, and as is tradition, every patron raises their glass and drinks. Carson takes a sip of the bitter ale, letting the warm burn settle in his stomach as he takes in the scene.

"You made it!" He says with bravado, confident in his new friend. "Amigos, this is Señor Carson, new trainer, tamer of the mighty Bubbles, and bringer of cervezas to all."

"Bien echo, Señor, Carson. I'm Pedro. We didn't think you'd last five minutes on that crazy horse. But you did and we all have cervezas because of it. So, gracias and bienvenido a Valley Vista Ranch." Pedro clicks Carson's glass and drinks. Oscar hands Carson a plate of wing dings.

"Coma. You must be hungry from the day."

"Thanks. I take it you guys come here all the time." He replies. Oscar nods his head.

"There is a long history between Valley Vista Ranch and Morrison's. This table has lots of memories from back when Hank Miller first purchased Valley Vista Ranch. He and William go way back. Best friends. Hank even loaned William money to build out this place. So you could say this place is our home. Family." Oscar says.

Carson looks around, taking in the camaraderie, the warmth. A genuine family. Something he's never really had. He pushes that thought aside and takes another sip.

"Let me introduce you to the Valley Vista Ranch family." He gestures toward the men. "You already met Pedro. Over here is Samuel. He's our farrier. There isn't a horse he can't shod. By him is Enrique. He manages all the ground maintenance. Over here is Raymundo, and there is Jacob, Miguel, Mundo, Alex, and Honario. Dr. White, our vet, usually stops by, but he had an emergency he had to see to. And there's the other trainer, Jake. He's well. He's Jake. It's better that he's not here. Trouble, that one is. But Señora Tegan always lets him come back." He sighs and shakes his head in disproval and then points to the men. "But this is the backbone of Valley Vista Ranch, Señor, and we are happy you're here."

Oscar, half drunk from the merriment, raises his mug; "To Señor Carson, the tamer of Señor Bubbles!" They all raise their glasses and say in unison. "Salud!" Carson self- consciously drinks with them. He faces Oscar.

"So what's the deal with Bubbles?" He asks. Oscar chuckles to himself.

"He's a test Señora Tegan gives to the new trainers. She's the only one who can tame that beast until you. So… You've become somewhat a legend with the groomsmen and you put that arrogant Jake in his place. I never thought I would live to see the day that someone would come and ride Bubbles the way you did. For that, I'm in your debt, Señor." Oscar places his hand on his chest and bows his head with respect.

"So, Carson, where are you from?" Samuel asks. Everyone leans forward in anticipation.

"Here and there. No where special. Home is where I hang my hat," Carson responds. He takes a drink from his mug.

"Well then, where did you first learn to ride?" Samuel counters. He knowingly winks at Oscar.

"Kentucky. Had my first shot on a horse as an exercise rider in the racing world. It was a rush. Some of the most amazing horses I've ever ridden. But I just couldn't get in line with the training. Wanted something different, so I became sort of a horse gypsy. Learning anywhere and from anyone I could. Met Rusty in Montana and the rest is history. Rusty has been my best teacher." He replies.

"Great Horse. Can't wait till you meet him, Sam. He reminds me of Hank's old quarter horse, Bob. Remember that horse?" Oscar asks.

"How could I forget him. He would just walk out from pasture to my rig, lift up his hoof for me to work on him. Never could figure out how he knew when he needed to be shod. Real special horse, that one. Nobody rode him but Hank. Not even Tegan. Hank named him Bob just because." Samuel replies.

"There was one time when I tried to get on Bob, and he would have none of that. He just lied down and rolled. I had to jump off!" Pedro exclaims. Everyone laughs.

"Serves you right. I had to talk Hank out of firing you." Oscar sarcastically says pointing and shaking his finger at Pedro.

"Yeah. I had to stay away from him for a month. Luckily, Tegan took pity on me and showed me the ropes. I was so green and cocky back then, but Hank always knew how to put you in your place. I learned everything I know from Hank, Oscar, and Valley Vista Ranch." Pedro wistfully says. He looks over at Carson and smiles.

"Wish you had met him. He meant everything to me—like a father, not just to me, but to most of the groomsmen here. He worked harder than anyone I've ever known and still found time to teach us, to guide us. Losing him hit us hard." Pedro crosses himself, and the rest of the table quietly follows.

"I did." He casually says as he takes a bite from a chicken wing. Oscar whips his head towards Carson.

"What? How? I've been at Valley Vista Ranch most of my life. I would have known if you were there." He exclaims.

"Montana. Rodeo. Won one of his quarter horses - The Duke. We were both interested in Rusty. A heated discussion and coin flip later, Rusty was mine. I remember Hank being quite beside himself to lose out on Rusty. He made me promise over and over again that I would take good care of him. He also forced me to ride for him. It was the first time in my life that I felt intimidated and nervous to ride in front of anyone. I could feel his eyes bore through my body."

"Did you say Montana?" Oscar asks staring into his beer.

"Yea. Why?"

"Was Rusty known by another name?" Oscar asks with a saddened look on his face.

"Back then, folks on the circuit called Rusty 'Bob's Mystery,'" Carson says.

"Should've known. The past always comes back to haunt you." Oscar says, with tears in his eyes. He takes a long drink from his mug.

"What do you mean, Oscar?" Carson asks, concerned.

"Back then, I got into some trouble with the law. I was in a bad way. Divorce. Drinking. Señor Hank could have let me rot in jail. Would've served me right. But he came up with the money to bail me out and got me a lawyer. I later found out that he sold Bob's foal to a ranch in Montana. Really broke him up to do it. But he did it for me. That's the type of man Hank was. I didn't know that he went back there to buy him back." Oscar looks knowingly at Carson.

"Rusty is Bob's foal. Hmm... Explains everything." Carson says. Oscar pats Carson on the shoulder.

"I'm glad that he went to a good home. To a person who truly understands and is worthy of him." Oscar raises his glass.

"To Señor, Carson. The tamer of Bubbles and the bringer of Bob's Mystery. Salud!" Everyone raises their beer mugs and shouts out "Salud!" and drinks their beers. Oscar leans over to Carson and whispers.

"Don't tell Señora Tegan. Too much too soon. Comprende?" Carson nods his head. Carson finishes his beer, takes off his top hat, and stands.

"I better get going. Early morning. Gotta work on some horses before classes start."

"But you just got here." Oscar protests. He stands and glares drunkenly at Carson. "Sit down, Señor Carson." Carson looks at Samuel and Pedro. They both motion him to sit down. Carson obligingly sits. Oscar grunts and mutters Spanish expletives to himself, then plops himself into his seat, almost falling off to the side. Pedro laughs. Oscar rights himself and glares at Pedro. Pedro guzzles his beer. Oscar looks back at Carson.

"So where are you staying?" He asks.

"My trailer. I have a live-a-board. It works."

"Unacceptable. You will stay with me and my family." Oscar adamantly says. Pedro's eyes widen.

"Tio, Don't you think he'd be more comfortable in his own place?" Pedro suggests.

"Si. Si. There's a cabin north of Miller's pond. I'll take you there." Oscar tries to stand up, but loses his balance and stumbles. Carson, worried, looks at Pedro. Pedro shrugs his shoulders. Carson grabs Oscar's forearm, steadies him and offers him his chair.

"Great idea, Oscar. Why don't you show me after work tomorrow?" Carson asks. Oscar nods his head and sits back down.

"Ok, Señor Carson. Mañana, I will show you. It'll be mucho better than your live-a-board trailer." Oscar smiles and takes another drink from his beer. He looks over at the entrance and frowns. Jake enters and hugs Jenny. She hands him a top hat and guides him towards the table.

"Mierde!" Oscar exclaims. They all turn their heads as Jake approaches the table. Jake grabs a chicken wing and takes a big bite. He extends his hand to Samuel.

"Hey Samuel, it's good to see you. Been a long time." Samuel reluctantly shakes his hand and looks over at Oscar. Oscar glares at Jake and slowly says.

"I thought you had a family emergency, Jake."

"Yea. Well...Been drinking much, Señor Oscar? How's that working for ya?" He sarcastically retorts. Samuel places his hand on Oscar's forearm, shakes his head 'no'. Jake smirks at Oscar. He looks over to Carson, fidgets under Carson's dispassionate gaze and silence.

"You're a half decent rider. Bubbles is kinda tricky, isn't he? You know me and Tegan go way back. Been with her for over ten years. Helped her build Valley Vista Ranch to where it's at today. So... If you need any tips, just let me know." He blurts out. Carson continues his calm, indifferent gaze and silence. Jake grabs more chicken wings, stuffs them into his pockets.

"Catch you gentlemen later." He turns on his heel and exits the establishment.

"Pendejo, Gringo. He's done nothing but take from Señora Tegan." Oscar tries to stand and wobbles. Pedro quickly rushes to his uncle's side.

"Time to go, Tío." Pedro slips an arm around Oscar's waist, steadying him. Oscar stiffens, pride flaring for a breath, then softens with a weary sigh and leans into his nephew's support.

"Si. The horses will need all of us. Señor Carson, Hasta mañana. So glad you're here. You will fix Valley Vista Ranch. No?" Oscar stumbles. Carson stands and proceeds to his other side. He looks over at Pedro and nods. They both guide Oscar to the exit.

"Adios amigos. Bright and early, mañana!" Oscar calls back to the men still at the table.

"Adios, Oscar." They respond and all knowingly look at one another. This hasn't been the first time Oscar has over indulged and they all know there's no use trying to stop him. Some things never change. Carson lets go of Oscar and opens the door.

"I got him. Don't worry, Señor Carson. I'll take him home." Pedro says as he drags Oscar to his car.

"It was nice meeting you. See you tomorrow." Carson says.

"Thank you for your help," Pedro replies. Pedro folds Oscar into the passenger seat of his car and waves to Carson. Carson waves back and climbs into his truck. He turns on the radio. The familiar sounds of country music fill the air. He turns the music up, shakes his head, and drives off into the night, wondering if this new adventure would be more than he bargained for.

THE MISFIT HORSE BRIGADE

The morning light shines through a window in Rusty's stall, bouncing off the bedding like fireflies dancing in the night. Rusty lying on his belly with his front and hind legs tucked underneath him rocks side to side, rises from his carefree slumber, and undergoes a ritualistic pandiculation of his body to greet the new day. He looks out of his stall and snorts. Remington and Carson are not in their stalls. Rusty whinnies, unlatches his stall door, and heads out on his quest to find his beloved new herd. He trots down the aisle towards the cross ties where Pedro is finishing up tacking Mirabella Mia. Rusty pauses and nickers at Mirabella Mia. She nickers back at Rusty. Pedro looks over at Rusty and smiles.

"Buenos Dias, Rusty." He says. Rusty nickers and nuzzles Pedro's jean pocket. Pedro pulls out a sugar cube and feeds Rusty and pats him on his forehead. Pedro sings to himself as he brushes oil on Mirabella Mia's hooves. Rusty taps his hoof on the barn floor, aware that his hooves need of care and oil.

"Perdón, Señor Rusty. We must not forget you. Must we?" Pedro laughs and starts applying the oil to Rusty's hooves as well.

Rusty's ears perk up towards the sound of Tegan's tall boots striking the barn floor in a military rhythm. He heads over to Tegan and wraps his head around her torso. Tegan knowingly, briskly massages behind both of Rusty's ears and feeds him a sugar cube. She hugs his head and looks over at Pedro.

"Where's Carson?" She asks. Rusty unwraps his head and the two look expectantly at Pedro.

"He's out with Remington, Señora. Wanted to ride before morning sessions—he's in the dressage arena," He replies.

"Perfect. I wanted to do some flat work on Mirabella Mia." She looks over at Rusty.

"Let's go check on Remi." She takes Mirabella's reins from Pedro and heads out to the dressage arena with Mirabella Mia on one side and Rusty dutifully on the other.

Remington's mouth foams as Carson leg yields to the right with both the front and hind legs crossing each other in a perfect syncopated trot. Carson turns down center-line and trots him forward in a straight line down to the center of the arena. He halts Remington in a square halt with both front and hind legs in perfect alignment, creating a square shape with the hooves. He pats Remington on his neck and gives him a long rein, and walks him around the arena. Rusty trots in with Tegan and Mirabella Mia following closely behind. Carson halts and Rusty nuzzles Remington and nickers at Carson.

"I thought you'd appreciate some sleep after yesterday." Carson says. Rusty paws the ground in disapproval. Carson chuckles.

"Okay, buddy. I'll get to you before I start my day." Carson pats Rusty on the neck.

"Do you mind if we join you?" Tegan asks.

"Sure. I'm just cooling Remington down before I start lessons. It's so beautiful here, especially in the morning. The dressage arena is perfect for connecting with Remington. I hope to get him over some poles sometime this week. He'll let me know when he's ready. "

"That's wonderful progress. I'd love to get on him when you think he's ready." He raises his eyebrow in surprise at her confidence in him. They walk together both on a long rein with Rusty in the lead guiding the way. She gently gazes at Carson. Enthralled by her intoxicating emerald eyes, Carson looks away and distracts himself by massaging Remington's neck. A calm silence fills the morning air as birds chirp in the distance.

"You know, my father built this dressage arena for my mom years ago. A Grand Prix rider in her time, she believed every horse and rider needed strong fundamentals, no matter their discipline. She gave me my first riding lesson—passionate, patient, completely in her element." Tegan gazes out toward Miller's Pond.

"She loved it here." She whispers. Carson silently gazes at her, allowing the moment to envelop them both. They walk together in perfect harmony.

"Oscar was pretty green this morning. Must have been a rowdy party at Morrison's. He's trying to hide last night, but I always know when Oscar partakes a little too much of the sauce." She sighs. "He'll never change, but he's been a part of this family since I was a child. We kinda grew up together. He's what's remaining of

Valley Vista Ranch. So, if he needs to celebrate, that's fine by me as long as the work gets done. And with Oscar, no matter what, the work always gets done."

"He's an impressive man. I love working with him." Carson responds. They turn down the long side and head towards the gate.

"Oscar says you're interested in the cabin. I can show you it after today's sessions. We could go over details of the show."

"Oscar said—"

"Trust me. He won't mind. By the looks of him, I'm doing him a favor." She says. They both laugh at Oscar's predicament.

"Sounds great. Well, I better get Remington back and set up for morning sessions." He nods and continues with Remington and Rusty out of the arena. Tegan keeps her reins long and gently urges Mirabella Mia to trot.

Carson leaves Remington and Rusty to graze and frolic out in the pasture. He latches the gate and heads to the Hank Miller Oval.

"Wish me luck." He says to his four-legged friends. They both look up, nicker at him, and continue with their morning graze. He heads to the arena and over the speakers is - Jake. Jake, cup of coffee and cigarette in one hand and microphone in the other, he looks over to the end of the arena at Carson and smirks. He pretends to ignore Carson's presence and looks over to his students, dressed perfectly in their riding attire, lined up at attention.

"Ladies, are you ready for the show?" He yells like a DJ at a concert. The women raise their crops and "Woo Woo" in unison to his chant and the horses prance around, disrupted by the cacophony.

"Let's pick up a trot and perform a twenty meter circle at each corner of the arena. Make sure you watch one another and time your circles. Make it perfect like I know you can. You know, 'Perfect practice makes perfect riders'." The women disperse to each corner and begin their drills. Carson walks up the covered cement walkway towards the table. Jake, with his feet up on the table, continues the lesson.

"Everyone, continue the twenty meter circle exercise in the canter. Remember to keep a consistent pace and path. Imagine each circle is a rollback to a jump. Timing is critical." He says. He covers up the mike and with a bored look stares at Carson.

"What?" He asks.

"Tegan wanted me to prep the students for the show." Carson replies. Jake rolls his eyes and coughs to cover up his sarcastic laugh. He points with the microphone to ring two.

"Your misfits, I mean students, are over there. Now, do you mind? I have a lesson to teach." Jake chuckles and turns away from Carson and raises the mic to his mouth.

"Very good, ladies. Now canter the poles in the center of the arena in six strides, then seven, then five. One at a time. Got it." The ladies nod their heads and Cathy on Maserati heads to the poles. Jake takes a drag from his cigarette, blows the smoke at Carson, and waves him away. Carson looks at him with pity and exits the arena.

Carson steps into Ring Two and stops dead in his tracks, arms crossing over his chest as he surveys the chaos in front of him.

Four riders drift aimlessly, their horses moving without direction, without purpose. A boy on a chestnut mare sits too stiffly, gripping the reins with rigid tension while his horse prances uneasily beneath him. A blonde girl in an oversized Pink Floyd t-shirt lets her gray pony wander along the rail, reins slack, his ears flopping in boredom. Another girl, her slight frame nearly swallowed by a big-barreled paint pony, kicks furiously at his sides, her legs barely clearing the edge of her saddle pad. The fourth rider, a tall teenage girl with immaculate posture, snaps selfies with her impeccably groomed Hanoverian while she scrolls through her phone, thumbing past posts with effortless detachment.

Carson inhales deeply, exhaling through his nose. This is going to be a long day.

"Everyone, bring your horses to the center." His voice cuts through the morning air.

Three riders begrudgingly comply, nudging their horses forward, but the girl kicking her pony in frustration remains where she is, her face red with irritation as the stubborn gelding plants his feet, ignoring her entirely.

Carson sighs and strides over, his steps calm and deliberate. Without a word, he takes the reins and gives the pony a gentle tug. The moment Carson touches him, the gelding snorts and moves forward, as if relieved that someone competent has finally intervened.

The girl huffs loudly, crossing her arms over her chest. Carson leads them to the center before addressing the group.

"Good morning, everyone. I'm Carson. I'll be getting you ready for the show," he says, his sharp gaze sweeping over them. "Before we get started, let's get to know each other. Tell me your name, age, your horse's name, breed, and what you hope to accomplish at this show. Sound good?"

The kids exchange skeptical glances, shifting uncomfortably in their saddles. A few mutter under their breath, clearly unimpressed. Carson ignores the lack of enthusiasm and strides over to the boy first.

The boy, a little portly and clearly uncomfortable in his too-stiff collared shirt, breeches, and tall boots, swings his legs back and forth, his glasses crooked on his nose. His chestnut mare tosses her head, prancing anxiously beneath him. Carson places a firm hand on the boy's calf, stilling his leg. Instantly, the mare sighs and drops her head.

The boy looks up, startled.

"Let's start with you."

He adjusts his glasses and clears his throat.

"I'm Nate. I'm twelve. This is Cinnamon. I don't know how old she is. I think she's a Warmblood." He shrugs. "I hate horse shows."

Carson raises an eyebrow. "Why?"

Nate scowls. "My coat and tie itch, my horse always runs away from me, and I never get a ribbon." He swings his leg again. Cinnamon snorts and kicks out. Carson presses a steady hand back on his leg. The horse settles instantly.

"You know what, Nate? I bet if you keep your leg still for Cinnamon, she'll be a lot happier—and maybe you'll get that ribbon."

Nate's eyes widen. "Really? I didn't think she cared about anything."

Carson smiles. "Horses care more than you think. If you care back, you'd be surprised at what they'll do for you." He pats Cinnamon's shoulder. "So today, I want you to focus on keeping your leg still. How's that sound?"

Nate nods eagerly. "Okay, I'll try."

"Good. That's all I ask."

Carson moves down the line to the blonde girl in the Pink Floyd t-shirt. She twists the end of her reins in her fingers, chewing her lip.

"Hi, my name is Cameron. I'm ten. This is Robbie. He's a Welsh pony. He's ten, just like me." She sighs heavily. "I hate horse shows, too."

Carson tilts his head. "Why's that?"

She shrugs. "I never remember my course. All the jumps look the same. I get nervous, forget where to go, and then I just leave the ring. Disqualified."

Carson nods. "We can fix that."

Her eyes widen. "Really? Robbie would love a ribbon. I just want to finish a course."

"Let's start with finishing a course. One step at a time."

Cameron grins. "Okay!"

Carson glances at the group. "Does anyone here actually like horse shows?"

All but one rider shake their heads. The exception sits perfectly upright, phone in hand, taking selfies with her gleaming Hanoverian. She types furiously, her fingers flying over the screen. Carson walks over and extends his hand.

"Would you like to join us?" he asks, staring directly at her phone.

With an exaggerated sigh, the girl rolls her eyes and hands it over. "Whatever."

Carson pockets the phone. She glares at him like he's committed a personal offense. "I'm Olivia. Sixteen. This is Max. Nine-year-old Hanoverian from Germany. You might've seen him in the Dove commercial. It went national."

Carson stays silent.

"I'm a brand ambassador for Ariat. They send me whatever I want." She flips her perfectly braided brown hair over her shoulder. "Won Junior Nationals last year at the meter. Got stuck here with these losers because apparently you're not supposed to tell your trainer to 'F-off.'"

She examines her nails. "I have over a hundred thousand Instagram followers. Don't care about horse shows, but my agent says if I do well enough, I might land a series regular spot on an equestrian show."

She stares at him expectantly. "So, what's your story?"

Carson ignores the question.

"I'm glad you're here, Olivia. You're gonna be a great help to me. Looking forward to working with you. Maybe Nationals at the meter ten, meter twenty? Sounds like a solid goal."

Before she can answer, he moves to the last rider. A tiny girl with brown braided pigtails, blue ribbons peeking out from under her helmet, shyly raises her hand.

Carson smiles slightly. "Yes?"

She whispers. "Hi, Mr. Carson. I'm Alexa. I'm seven."

She gestures toward her horse—a big, sleepy bay Quarter Horse. "This is Wally. I don't think he likes me. He never goes when I ask him. He just stares at the judges. Then my mom comes in and takes me out."

Her freckled face scrunches up. "Do I have to show?"

Carson smiles. "Not if you don't want to. But if we work hard together, I think you'll like horse shows. Deal?"

Alexa bites her lip, thinking. Then she nods. "Sure. If you say so, Mr. Carson."

Carson stands, scanning the group.

One boy. Three girls. Four distinct challenges.

For the first time, he looks forward to the lesson.

Nate rounds the corner in a rhythmical canter with Cinnamon and heads to a line of two vertical fences two feet three inches in height and six strides apart. He keeps his leg completely still as he approaches the first fence. Cinnamon's ears perk forward, and she easily manages the first fence and heads to the second fence. She clears the second fence and Nate pilots her to a perfect twenty meter circle and slows her down to a trot. He halts her and throws his arms around her in elation.

"Well done, Nate. You see, if you are mindful of your horse and work with them instead of against them, they'll be there for you. Your swinging leg was confusing and frustrating Cinnamon and she didn't know how to be there for you with all that noise. Now, she's trusting you. Keep up that solid communication, Nate. You can finish on that. Give her a long reign and walk her around to cool her down." Carson says.

"The grooms normally put her on the Eurociser when I'm done, Carson." He says, confused.

"Why don't you spend more time with her and then, if you still want to, you can put her on the walker? Also, you learn as much from watching others. Sounds good?"

"Okay." Nate replies in a huff. Carson walks up to the same line, raises both jumps to a meter, and turns the second jump into an oxer. He walks over to a third fence and raises that one to a meter as well.

"Okay, Olivia. You're up. Do the line in five and then rollback to this vertical. Make sure that you don't cut the turn after the oxer or the rollback won't work. Got it?" Carson smiles reassuringly. Olivia rolls her eyes at him.

"Whatever." She trots Max in a circle, then picks up a canter. She heads to the first fence and Max easily clears it. He lands and gets strong towards the oxer. Olivia panics and pulls back on the reins too hard mid way through the line and almost brings him to a halt. Frustrated, she cow-kicks him and he bolts, jumping the oxer off stride, knocking down the front and back polls. Afraid and annoyed, Max bucks and bolts on the landing side. Olivia halts him at the gate and throws her reins at him in disgust.

"You stupid effing horse!" She yells. She violently smacks him with her crop. He bucks, and she stays on by grabbing his mane. She grabs the reins and smacks him over and over. Cameron's and Alexa's eyes widen and they both cry. Carson stoically walks to Olivia and quickly removes the crop from her hand.

"Get off, now." He says, eyes glaring at her.

"But it was his fault." She says defiantly.

"Now." Carson stares her down and tears flow down her face as she dismounts Max. Carson gently walks Max to the mounting block, adjusts the stirrups and mounts Max. Max, still frightened, bolts away from the mounting block, his body convulsing. Carson quickly halts him, caresses his neck, and waits for Max to stop shaking.

"You're okay, boy." Carson says. Max settles and Carson canters him to the line and easily clears both jumps. He leads him to a perfect roll back to the third fence and calmly lands on the other side. He halts him, pats him on the neck, and feeds him a sugar cube. Max nibbles on his boot. Carson dismounts and walks Max to a crestfallen Olivia.

"You do that again; you're off the team."

"I don't care." She says, choking on her words.

"Yes. You do. I bet this horse is the only thing that matters to you. All that other stuff, 'Insta what ever', is meaningless."

"I hate you." She retorts.

"Fine. But from now on, you're my working student and you'll do what I say or we're done. Apologize to the team or leave."

"Apologize to these misfits. I'd rather eat dirt." Olivia sobs and runs out of the arena, leaving Carson with Max. Carson shakes his head and walks with Max towards Alexa and Cameron. He looks up at their tear-stained faces.

"Wanna go on a trail ride?" He asks. They both wipe their tears, look at each other, and giggle.

"All of us?" They ask in unison.

"Sure. Let me get on Max and get Nate." He looks over at Nate, who's cautiously walking in the far corner, avoiding the drama.

Carson leads the misfit horse brigade out the arena into the open pasture. He whistles, and Rusty gallops towards them. Carson halts Max as Rusty trots up next to him. Carson pats Rusty on the neck and looks at his students. Rusty nickers a "hello." The kids giggle.

"Everyone. This is Rusty. He's going to lead us on our trail ride." He clicks his lips and Rusty trots. Everyone, including Alexa, trots down the hill. Alexa giggles with delight.

"Mr. Carson. Wally's trotting!" She exclaims.

"Yep. You wanna try a canter?" He asks. Alexa grits her teeth determined.

"Ready. Mr. Carson." She replies. Carson kisses at Rusty and he canters. The horses follow Rusty and canter towards Miller's pond. In the distance, Alexa's voice rings out.

"Wally's cantering, Mr. Carson!"

"Yep," he says. Nate, Cameron, and Alexa burst into laughter, their earlier tension already swept away by the joy of the ride.

MAX

They bred Maximillian Roulette—Max—for greatness. A striking black Hanoverian gelding with four pristine white socks and a bold white star on his forehead, he carried himself with the effortless power and elegance of his German lineage. He came from one of the top breeding barns in Germany, his pedigree dripping with international champions.

When he was four years old, Jake had him imported to Valley Vista Ranch, one of the first imports under Valley Vista's new expansion. He stepped off the trailer—sleek, leggy, his coat shimmering like a raven's wing, catching flashes of blue in the sunlight—and Olivia locked on him, captivated.

Back then, she was just a horse-crazy girl, wide-eyed and filled with dreams. The second she laid eyes on Max, she knew he was the one.

She had begged, pleaded, bargained.

"Dad, please." Olivia had gripped his arm, her voice high with desperation. "I'll work for it—I'll do anything. There's never going to be another horse like him."

But Max wasn't just any horse. He was an expensive, unproven investment, and her family—already stretched thin—couldn't afford such an extravagant purchase.

A second mortgage, a signed contract, and a whispered promise that she'd contribute to his expenses—and Max was hers.

For a while, it was everything she had dreamed of.

Like any other horse-obsessed little girl, Olivia showered Max with unwavering love and devotion. She spent hours in his stall, reading to him, whispering secrets into his silky mane.

She braided his forelock and tail with ribbons of every color, hosting tea parties in the barn aisle where Max, ever patient, would nuzzle at her imaginary guests.

She turned his stall into an art gallery, taping up every crayon-drawn masterpiece, each picture more elaborate than the last. Every contest—stall decorating, costume competitions—she won them all.

And Halloween? It was their crowning moment.

Dressed as Daenerys Targaryen from Game of Thrones, Olivia transformed Max into Drogon, his black dragon wings—crafted from fabric, wire, and fierce determination—unfurling in a dramatic wingspan. The spectacle caused a stir at Valley Vista; the barn buzzing with admiration and awe.

Max stood at the center of her world, more than just a horse—he was her confidant, her anchor, the steady heartbeat behind every dream. With him, she shared secrets no one else knew, victories that felt bigger, and failures that stung a little less. His soft eyes listened when no one else did, and his breath against her shoulder calmed storms she couldn't name.

But the years passed, and childhood wonder turned into reality.

Max, once her dream horse, became an anchor—a responsibility, a debt, a career.

Olivia's family wasn't wealthy. Unlike the other trust-fund kids and heiresses who graced the Grand Prix rings, Olivia's spot at the top had to be earned.

She was talented—undeniably so. Sponsors noticed her. Ariat picked her up. Other brands followed. Suddenly, Olivia had contracts, obligations, expectations.

Riding wasn't about tea parties and glitter anymore. It was about rankings. Prize money. Social media engagements. The once wildly affectionate girl who kissed Max's velvety nose and called him her prince grew distant. Ribbons vanished from his mane. Doodles of her "perfect horse" stopped showing up on his stall wall.

Now, Max was just a means to an end. A job. A stepping stone toward something bigger.

And Olivia?

She stopped being that horse-crazy girl with a head full of dreams.

Now, she was just another rider in the circuit—climbing, clawing, pushing forward.

Max was no longer her fairy tale. He was her reality.

And reality was a lot heavier than dreams.

Olivia, with her long hair covered by an Ariat baseball cap, anxiously approaches the cross tie where Max is standing with his head hanging low in a tranquil half slumber, ice boots on all four legs - Carson grooming and massaging his back.

Carson whistles, and Rusty stands guard in front of Max. Olivia tries to walk around Rusty, but he turns sideways and blocks her progress. Tears flow down Olivia's face.

"Is he okay?" She asks.

"I thought you didn't care." Carson replies.

"I have a right to see him." She says defiantly. She approaches Max. Rusty turns to face her, paws the ground and nudges her away.

"I wouldn't mess with Rusty. Apologize for your behavior earlier and he might let you pass." He says. She crosses her arms and glares at him in defiance.

"I'm going to tell Tegan Miller about this. I could get you fired." She retorts. He looks up at her with sadness in his eyes.

"Go ahead. You're still not seeing Max until you apologize." He calmly says. As if on cue, Tegan rounds the corner and stands by Rusty. She feeds him a cookie and glares at Olivia.

"We have an absolute zero tolerance policy on horse abuse at Valley Vista Ranch. The only reason you're still on this property is because of Carson. If you don't want to work with him, then leave. I will make sure that Max goes to a more suitable home. Do we understand each other?" Tegan doesn't wait for an answer. She looks over at Carson.

"Let me know what's decided. I'll see you later. I have horses to take care of. Olivia, you're better than this." Tegan pauses and stares at Olivia. Olivia backs away and drops her head in shame. Tegan strokes Rusty's neck.

"Let's give these two some privacy. C'mon, Rusty." She walks out with Rusty right by her as if he was hooked to her hip. Carson places a blanket with ultraviolet coils on Max's back and walks towards Olivia. Ashamed, she looks up at him with her tear stained brown eyes.

"I'm sorry." She says, barely above a whisper. "I do love Max."

"I know you do, Olivia," he whispers, his voice warm with understanding.

"I'm just so tired. So much pressure to keep up. Some days, I don't even know where I am half the time. I worked so hard to pay for Max and now its turned into my life. I have no time for my friends. No time for anything." Tears flow down her face as she bites her lip in pain. Carson gently takes her hand and leads her to Max. Olivia gently massages Max's neck. He nickers back in gratitude. She wraps her arms around his neck and kisses his cheek.

"I'm sorry, Max. I promise I will never hurt you again. Okay?" She says. Max nuzzles Olivia. She looks up at Carson with a child-like smile.

"You know, Olivia. Max doesn't care about Instagram or Ariat. He only cares about you. A horse's world revolves around the present. They have a lot to teach us about being in the moment. With your talent, you could go real far with Max. You just have to learn to be in the moment with him. All the other stuff doesn't matter. So from now on, we'll work together to bring your partnership to the next level. But it's your choice, Olivia. You can walk away right now." Carson brings over a wheelbarrow and muck rake.

"What's that?" She asks, confused.

"You ready to work with me?" He asks.

"I thought we were good." She says stubbornly.

"We are, but you need to earn my trust, your horses's trust, and the team's trust." He hands her the muck rake.

"I had plans." She pouts.

"Plans change. Horses are not just about getting on their backs and riding. To be a true horseman or woman, you need to be committed to your horse's care and go beyond just riding."

"Seriously? We have grooms for that." She says. He pulls back the rake and points towards the exit.

"I guess you're not ready then. And to think, Tegan was ready to cut your board for your work. I guess I'll tell her..." He responds.

"No—please. I'm ready. I'll do whatever you say, anything. Just don't let Tegan take Max. He's all I have," Olivia pleads, her voice cracking as she clutches the stall door. Carson hides a smile and hands her the muck rake.

"So here's the deal. You're gonna work with me before and after school during the week and all day during the weekend. You will be the team leader and provide support and an example to the younger members of the team. They all look up to you, Olivia." He pushes the wheelbarrow towards her.

"When you're done with Max's stall, put Max away. Oh, and Olivia, welcome to the misfit horse brigade. I'm so glad that you're on the team." He says sincerely.

"Right. What does this have to do with horses?" She mumbles under her breath. He shakes his head, realizing that Olivia is going to be a hard cookie to crack.

"Take this as your first lesson on being in the moment." He pats her on the back, chuckles to himself, and walks away.

THE CABIN

Hunter arena Ring Two radiates polished perfection. Pristine footing—a blend of high-end fiber and sand—supports the floating gaits and precision of top hunters. Immaculate jumps line the course: rich wooden rails, crisp white gates, and lush green hedges echo the elegance of classic show venues. Before Carson stands a beautifully adorned wooden hunter fence, its base wrapped in cascading greenery over a stone-painted wall.

Carson, astride Ranger, a towering 17-hand dapple gray Westphalian warm blood, gathers his reins, settles his weight, and urges the gelding forward. Ranger approaches the fence in perfect rhythm, his powerful stride eating up the distance. With an effortless jump, they clear the obstacle, his knees snapping up tight, his landing soft as silk.

Outside the arena, a gaggle of women leans against the rail, whispering and giggling behind manicured hands, eyes glued to the new trainer. They swoon, they sigh, they murmur admiration.

Olivia, mounted on Wally, a stocky bay Quarter Horse gelding with a shaggy mane, catches the display and rolls her eyes so hard it nearly hurts.

"Unbelievable," she mutters under her breath.

Then, like a storm barreling in from nowhere, Shelly Windham bursts into the arena.

At fifty, she still commands attention—slim and petite, with an hourglass figure she dresses to highlight. Her tan breeches, tailored to perfection, hug her like a second skin, while her beige riding shirt, trimmed with gold horse-bit embroidery, opens just enough to hint at flirtation without inviting it.

"Olivia! Olivia!" Shelly hisses, half-shouting, half-whispering.

Olivia groans, halts Wally, and turns to face her.

"What?" she snaps.

Shelly's gaze flicks to Carson before her lips curl into a smug smirk. "Who's the new trainer on my horse? Nice mount, by the way." Her tone is dripping with condescension.

Olivia glances at Carson, then back at Shelly. "That's my trainer, Carson. I work for him now. This is Wally. Carson wants me to train him for Alexa."

She turns Wally away from Shelly, done with the conversation.

But Shelly lunges forward, gripping Wally's reins.

"Wait."

Olivia stares at her, incredulous. "Seriously? You're married, Shelly. Doesn't your sugar daddy give you enough?"

Wally snorts and flicks an ear back, sensing the tension. Olivia tries to move forward, but Shelly, playing innocent, subtly keeps pressure on the reins.

Shelly's eyes flash. "Shut up, Olivia."

Before Olivia can bite back, Carson trots over on Ranger, halting beside them.

"Everything okay, Olivia?" His tone is casual, but there's a flicker of awareness in his gaze.

Olivia shrugs dramatically, then rolls her eyes for good measure.

Shelly moves faster than a show jumper in a jump-off, stepping between Carson and Olivia.

With the skill of a professional basketball player boxing out her opponent, Shelly blocks Olivia's view, sticks out her hand, and—not so subtly—lifts her chest.

"Hello there, handsome. I'm Shelly Windham, and you're on my horse, Ranger. I love how you ride him." Her voice drops into a low, sultry tone, practically dripping seduction.

Carson smiles to himself, amused. He pats Ranger's neck, completely unfazed.

"He's a nice horse. He was a little backed off from the fences because of his bit, so I changed it. Hope you don't mind."

Shelly's lashes flutter. "Oh, no, no. Not at all." She steps closer. "Jake imported him for me—from Germany or France. I don't remember. But it cost me a pretty penny. Worth every cent." She tilts her head, eyes narrowing. "New bit, huh?"

Carson nods. "Yeah. The other one was too strong. It threw his balance and rhythm off."

Shelly lets out a fake gasp. "Oh, Jake thought it would help me manage him."

Carson tilts his head. "I can change it back if you'd like."

Shelly's eyes widen. "No, no. Actually... could you show me how to ride him with the new bit?"

From behind her, Olivia groans loudly.

"You've got to be kidding me."

Shelly gives Olivia a sharp glare. Olivia responds by dramatically miming vomiting, making a gagging sound.

Carson cocks his head, giving Olivia a warning look.

"Olivia, warm up Wally. I'll show you how to vocal train him in a second. Sound good?"

"Whatever." Olivia rolls her eyes again and kisses at Wally, trotting off.

Carson dismounts her horse and hands Ranger's reins to Shelly.

"Clear it with Jake and Tegan, and I'd be happy to show you how to ride Ranger with the new bit." His expression is unreadable, his gaze unwavering.

Shelly falters for a moment, clearly not expecting resistance. "Oh... okay. Carson, is it? I'll talk to Tegan and Jake." She spins on her heel, nearly tripping over her own feet as she leads Ranger out.

The gaggle of women watching from the rail snicker at her misstep.

Carson walks over to Olivia, who is watching the entire thing like it's a reality TV show.

"You dodged a bullet with that one. Don't worry, she won't talk to Jake and Tegan." Olivia smirks.

Carson chuckles. "I know. I don't think she's the type that does much riding."

They both laugh, Olivia grinning like they're best friends.

"You know, Carson, this might be the beginning of a beautiful friendship."

Carson raises a brow. "Nice movie reference. Casablanca is one of my favorites."

Olivia shrugs. "Never heard of it. Googled famous movie quotes and liked it. Now, are we gonna do this or not? I have people waiting."

Carson sighs. "Alright. Alexa's legs aren't long enough to reach Wally's girth line, so I want you to teach him vocal cues. That way, she can use them at the show. Start with the crop just behind your leg, give the verbal cue for 'walk,' and build from there. Got it?"

Olivia rolls her eyes. "Whatever. Let's get this horse trained."

Carson grins. "Why, Miss Olivia, your attitude is greatly improving. By this time next year, you might even have enthusiasm for horsemanship. Oh, and every time you say 'whatever' or roll your eyes at me—twenty-five push-ups."

Olivia's jaw drops. "What?!"

"Now, Olivia." Carson points to the ground.

She glares at him, throws her crop to the ground, and jumps off Wally. "Jesus. Now I have to do push-ups? This is so stupid."

Carson shrugs. "Now."

Muttering curses, Olivia drops to the ground and starts counting.

Carson mounts Wally and starts working on vocal training.

"At least you'll be stronger. That's one good thing about your crappy attitude. I can't hear you, Olivia."

"Ugh! You jerk. Whatever! Dammit!"

Carson grins. "That's twenty-five more."

Olivia's groans echo across the arena.

The sun sets like a ball of fire over the hill, casting brilliant orange and red lucent rays painting the sky above. Tegan enters the arena on Paratrooper (aka Chewy), bareback with a backpack over her shoulders. Carson dressed in his western attire with his cowboy hat drawn low over his brow, in a meditative zen-like trance canters Rusty around the arena. Rusty tacked up in a hackamore and a hand carved and silver-plated western saddle matches his rider's trance with his head hanging low, nose almost touching the footing. Olivia, annoyed, marches into the arena to confront Carson regarding her long, arduous work hours. She immediately halts beside Tegan and Chewy to bear witness to the magical bond between horse and rider.

Carson halts Rusty with the lightest whisper of rein, and the stallion, tuned to his every breath, pivots beneath him like a storm caught in a bottle. They spin—once, twice—nine full revolutions, each tighter and more precise than the last, until they settle into a square halt so still it could hang in a painting. For a heartbeat, silence reigns.

Then, with a soft shift of weight, Carson sends Rusty into a canter in the opposite direction. They spin again—same motion, mirrored with grace—two souls in a silent conversation, their rhythm unbroken, their trust absolute.

With a flick of the leg, Carson sends Rusty into a full gallop. The stallion explodes down the arena's long side, mane flying like wildfire, hooves devouring the ground. As they reach the final stride, Carson sits deep—Rusty reads the cue instantly—and they slide to a dramatic stop, dust erupting around them in golden arcs.

Rusty lifts his head and looks back at his rider, eyes soft, content. He noses Carson's boot, nibbles at the leather with playful affection. Carson laughs under his breath, pulls a sugar cube from his pocket, and offers it with a quiet pat to Rusty's neck—their dance finished, their bond wordless, unbreakable.

Olivia, tears in her eyes, mouth open in shock, looks up to Tegan.

"I had no idea." She says in a child-like voice. Tegan looks down at her warmly.

"I know. None of us did. He's a rarity. I would learn as much as I could from him if I were you. Good night, Olivia." She winks at Olivia and walks Chewy towards Carson and Rusty.

"Good night." Olivia sheepishly responds. She takes one last look at Carson and exits the arena.

Carson looks up at Tegan and Chewy and smiles. Still in her riding attire, her hair in a long loose braid down her back, and Chewy in a hackamore, they stand next to Carson and Rusty. Chewy turns and faces Rusty - snorts. He shakes his head and backs up Rusty. Tegan halts Chewy.

"Chewy, stop it. Sorry, Rusty. Chewy's used to being alpha." She says. Rusty nickers and drops his head in submission. Carson scratches Rusty's withers.

"Good boy, Rusty." He looks up at Tegan. "Rusty gets it. But don't let anyone know. Rusty's used to being the patriarch of the herd. This is the first time he's conceded his alpha status to any horse. Chewy must be something special." Carson replies. She looks at Carson in disbelief that he doesn't recognize her prized once-in-a-lifetime Olympic mount. She catches herself and smiles softly as she massages Chewy's neck.

"He is... Don't worry, Rusty. Your secret's safe with me." She laughs. She turns Chewy towards the gate. "You ready?" She asks. Carson adjusts his hat on his head.

"Sure. Lead the way." They canter off, chasing the glowing sunset as they head towards the cabin.

The cabin stands stoically atop a gentle rise, weathered by time but still strong, a testament to Hank Miller's craftsmanship. Built by his own two hands when he first purchased the land, it was the Miller family's first true home—a simple yet sturdy refuge nestled amidst the sprawling Valley Vista Ranch.

The exterior is rich with history. The log walls, once honey-gold, have aged into deep russet, their surfaces smoothed by decades of wind and rain. A wraparound porch, its floorboards worn and creaky, embraces the structure like a protective arm, offering a panoramic view of the rolling pastures and dense tree lines. The splintered wooden steps leading to the entrance bow slightly in the center, evidence of generations of boots climbing up and down.

A rustic love seat rocking chair sits just to the right of the heavy wooden front door, its burnt-red cushions faded and tattered from years of exposure. It was once Hank's favorite seat, where he'd sip his morning coffee, whittle pieces of wood, and watch the sunrise over his land.

Two iron black lantern-shaped lights flank the entrance, casting soft golden glows at night. The door itself is solid oak, its surface carved with intricate patterns—horses, wheat stalks, and the swirling initials "H.M." etched carefully by Hank himself. Large single-pane windows, their glass old and wavy, stretch along the front, framing the ranch in breathtaking detail.

Tegan and Carson halt their horses just outside the cabin.

Carson swings down from Rusty's back, loosening the gelding's cinch and removing his hackamore with practiced ease. He sets the tack on the weathered hitching post, where it joins Tegan's, her own hackamore placed neatly beside his.

Chewy nudges Tegan playfully, his soft breath warm against her cheek, before trotting off toward the pasture. Rusty follows, his copper coat glowing in the waning sunlight, his tail flicking lazily as he disappears over the hill.

Tegan leads Carson up the porch steps, her boots making the old wood groan beneath their weight. She kneels, lifting a carefully placed field stone at the base of the doorframe and pulling out a hand-forged iron key.

Carson's brows lift in amusement. "Nice key."

Tegan lifts it high, the antique metal catching the last rays of sunlight and throwing them in golden streaks across her palm. The handle curves into the shape of a horse's head, nostrils flared, ears alert, every line of the mane sculpted in fluid motion as it sweeps seamlessly into the shaft. The piece breathes with quiet reverence, an unmistakable tribute to the life Hank cherished.

"Yeah, my dad always had a flair for the dramatic," she says, a soft smirk tugging at her lips.

She fits the key into the heavy lock, turning it with a familiar click.

The moment Tegan pushes open the door, the scent of aged wood, dust, and faint remnants of smoke and leather greets them.

She flips on the light, casting a soft amber glow over the interior.

The living room is a time capsule, frozen in quiet abandonment. White bed sheets cover the furniture, ghostly outlines of the life that once filled the space. A stone fireplace dominates the far wall, its once-vibrant fieldstone now darkened by years of smoke.

Tegan crosses the room and yanks the sheet off the couch. A cloud of dust explodes into the air, swirling in the light like tiny fireflies.

Carson waves a hand in front of his face, coughing. "Guess it's been a while since anyone's been here."

Tegan smirks. "Yeah. Not exactly prime real estate."

The cabin is modest but filled with Hank's craftsmanship.

A rugged wooden coffee table, its surface etched with old knife marks and boot scuffs, sits before the well-worn couch, its brown leather cracked but inviting. An overstuffed armchair, its arms worn smooth from years of Hank's reading habits, rests near the hearth.

To the side, a small wooden dining table with two chairs—both carved with horse motifs—sits tucked into the corner.

A rocking chair sits just beside the fireplace, its seat perfectly molded from years of Hank's weight resting there. Carson imagines him sitting there, a whiskey glass in hand, staring into the flames.

Tegan moves toward the mantle, running her fingers over an old silver belt buckle resting there—the same one Hank had won in his younger rodeo days.

"This place was home before the ranch had barns, before it had arenas." She exhales softly. "Dad built this place with his own hands. Every beam, every nail."

Carson studies the space, taking it all in—the sturdy craftsmanship, the handmade details, the love Hank had poured into every inch.

"It's got good bones," he finally says, his voice quieter than before.

Tegan nods, a bittersweet smile tugging at the corner of her lips.

"Yeah. It does."

He walks over to the fireplace and caresses it with his hand. His hand wanders towards the mantle and picks up a framed picture of a stunning dark-haired woman with emerald green eyes dressed in a blue shad belly show coat, top hat, and white breeches astride a stunning white Pura Raza Espinola (PRE) stallion. He looks over towards Tegan with a questioning gaze. She walks over, and he hands her the picture. She smiles wistfully and caresses the picture.

"My mom and her mount, Zaragoza. Seems like a lifetime ago." Tegan gazes off into the distance, held by memories of the cabin. She blinks and shakes her head.

"I can remove these pictures if you'd like." She says.

"Not necessary. Only if you want to." He replies. She places the picture back on the mantle next to a picture of her on Paratrooper at the Olympics. She presses two fingers to her lips and then kisses the picture of her and Chewy. He looks at her with acknowledgment.

"Chewy is your Olympic mount. Sorry, should have known. Rusty obviously knew who he was in the presence of." They both laugh as he shakes his head in embarrassment.

"Don't worry. I don't expect you to know every horse on the property. Yet." She smiles back at him. She walks towards the hallway.

"There's two bedrooms and one bathroom. The kitchen is just down the hall. I could give you the grand tour if you'd like." She gestures toward the hallway leading to the kitchen.

"I can figure it out. How about you let me know what you need for the horse show?"

"Sure. Pizza?"

"They deliver here?" He says, surprised.

"Yep. Me and Joe go way back."

"Of course you do. Sounds like a plan." He smiles as he leads her to the table with two chairs. He removes the sheet, dusts off the table with his cowboy hat, and pulls out the chair for Tegan.

"Why thank you, Carson. Such chivalry. Thought it was dead." She says sarcastically as she sits. She pulls out her iPad from her backpack and sets it on the table. He joins her across the table. She focuses on the screen in front of her as she taps on the horse show application. Unbeknownst to Tegan, Carson leans back in his chair and stares at her, enthralled.

"We have twenty-five horses entered in the horse show. The lower divisions are in the morning with the advanced and professional classes in the afternoon and evening. I'll be showing two horses each night in the Grand Prix - Mirabella Mia and Luke 631. I can't cover all the morning sessions. So... if you could work with the kids and adult amateurs in the morning, I could focus on the more advanced students and get my horses ready. Missy and I would always..." She stops, places her hands next to the iPad, and looks at him with tears in his eyes.

"This is going to be my first show without Missy. I don't know how I'm going to get through this. Sorry. I didn't mean—"

"I get it." Carson leans forward and places his hand on hers and gently squeezes it.

"You had this system in place with Missy and now you feel like you're barely getting by." He lets go of her hand. Tears stream down her face. She quickly wipes them away.

"Yes. Missy was like a daughter to me. We did everything together and now she won't even return my calls or my texts. She hates me."

"She doesn't hate you. She just needs to process what's happened to her in her own time. Why don't you invite her to the show as a guest? You could appeal to her sense of being a part of the barn family. The kids won't stop talking about her. Especially Cameron."

"She loves those kids something fierce. Even when Jake made fun of them by calling them the Misfit Horse Brigade, she wore it as a badge of honor. It could work." She looks at him with hopeful eyes.

"Don't worry about the show. We'll find our own system. And I would be honored to help you get ready for the Grand Prix." He moves his chair to be right next to hers and looks at the screen of her iPad.

"The morning classes run in the Allen East and West arenas," she says, her voice brisk but focused. "Afternoons shift to the Large Oval and the Equidome. The Grand Prix rides take place in the Equidome." She taps the schedule on the screen and turns to him. "We can split the morning—I'll take West, you cover East. Then if you handle the Oval and Equidome later, I'll bounce between clients and check on the Grand Prix horses."

She looks up and studies him—his square jawline shadowed by stubble, the sharp angle of his cheekbone catching the light. He meets her gaze without flinching, his eyes steady, unreadable.

Their eyes lock, a quiet current building between them.

She leans forward slightly, exhales; the air shifting just enough to stir a strand of hair against her cheek. The moment stretches, dense and electric.

Color blooms across her cheeks. She blinks hard, then turns back to the computer, fingers clicking over the keyboard with renewed purpose.

"Do you think Remi would be ready for any of these classes?" She asks.

"No. But I could trailer both him and Rusty to the show and get him used to the energy. Rusty is an old pro at shows." He confidently says.

"Yes. I knew Bob's foal would take after his father. Bob's Mystery was never a mystery to me." She says raising an eyebrow and smiling back at him.

"You knew? When?" He asked astonished at her revelation.

"The moment Rusty galloped towards the paddocks and unlatched the gate. I could never forget Bob's Mystery. I foaled him after all." She nonchalantly responds. She looks at her computer and says.

"Remi will do well under Rusty's—"

"Bob's Mystery, I mean. Rusty is your horse?" He asks eyes widened in disbelief. He leans back in his chair.

"That's why he follows you the way he does. He's never done that with anyone but me. That's why your dad..." His voice trails off.

"Yes. It was hard to see him go. Broke my heart. But, I've never seen a horse so happy. So devoted. Carson, you don't have to be a horse person to see that you and Rusty are meant to be together. Like me and Chewy. I guess things just happen for a reason. And it's come full circle. Right?" She looks back at him with an uncanny home grown wisdom backed by a lifetime of lessons from her parents.

Carson, completely drawn in, completely captivated, leans forward, his fingers brushing against Tegan's hand. Before she can think, react, or retreat, his lips press against the back of her hand—gentle but firm.

"I never thought I would meet someone like you," he murmurs, his voice raw, unguarded, cracking slightly with emotion.

Tegan freezes.

Her pulse hammers against her ribcage. She can feel the warmth of his breath still lingering on her skin, the way his touch sends an unfamiliar, terrifying warmth curling in her stomach.

She should pull away. She should say something sharp, something cold, something to remind him (and herself) that she's his boss.

But she doesn't.

Instead, she leans in.

"Neither did I," she whispers, her voice softer than she intended.

Their eyes lock.

For a fleeting moment, the weight of responsibility, the rules, the rigid walls she keeps around herself—they waver.

Then—

Knock. Knock. Knock.

"You in there, Tegan?"

Joe's voice shatters everything.

Tegan jolts upright as if electrocuted, nearly knocking over her chair.

What the hell was she doing?!

Her heart slams against her ribs as she scrambles to recover, to shove the moment back into the box where it belongs. She grabs her iPad, stuffs it into her backpack with frantic energy, swings the strap over her shoulders, and practically lunges for the door.

She yanks it open.

"Hey, Joe! Thanks for bringing the pizza." The words tumble out of her in a rush, too loud, too fast. She gestures toward Carson like she's giving a PowerPoint presentation. "This is Carson. He's going to be living in the cabin."

Joe blinks at her.

Tegan snatches the pizza box from his hands, spins on her heel, and slaps it onto the table as if it personally offended her. She digs into her back pocket, pulls out a ten-dollar bill, and shoves it at Joe like he's an unwanted door-to-door salesman.

"Keep the change, Joe."

Joe stares at the money, then at her, confused.

Tegan plows forward. "Carson, we'll go over the details of the show tomorrow at the office, okay? Gotta run. Gotta do night check."

Her words pile over each other, messy and desperate.

"Joe, you're taking me to the office, right?"

Joe raises a brow. "Uh... what?"

Tegan widens her eyes at him, practically telepathically screaming at him to play along.

Joe just stares.

She mouths one word. "Now."

Joe sighs, shaking his head in exasperation. "Okay, fine. Nice to meet you, Carson."

Carson, still reeling from the abrupt shift in energy, barely gets out, "Nice to—"

SLAM.

The cabin door shuts so fast, the wooden frame rattles.

Tegan lets out a strangled sound, somewhere between a groan and a sigh.

Without another word, she grabs her hackamore and stomps toward Joe's truck.

Joe follows, bewildered.

"What the hell was that?" he finally asks as he watches her all but hurl herself into the passenger seat.

She yanks the door shut, stares ahead, and exhales through her nose.

"Just take me home, Joe."

Joe runs a hand through his jet-black Italian hair, mutters something in Italian under his breath, then gets in and starts the engine.

As the truck rumbles down the dirt road, leaving the cabin behind, Carson steps out onto the porch, pizza in hand.

He watches the truck's taillights fade into the darkness, disappearing down the road.

With a slow shake of his head, he plops down on the steps, chewing thoughtfully.

A familiar whistle cuts through the night air.

Rusty and Chewy gallop up from the pasture, hooves barely making a sound in the soft dirt. They halt in front of him, ears pricked forward.

Carson tears off pieces from his second slice of pizza and holds them out.

Rusty takes his first, chewing with the dignified patience only an old soul like him possesses. Chewy snatches his greedily, nipping at Carson's sleeve in demand for more.

Carson chuckles, shaking his head.

"She's just like a thoroughbred, isn't she, Chewy?"

Chewy nickers, tossing his head as if in agreement.

Carson leans back on his elbows, staring up at the moon-drenched sky.

He takes another bite of pizza, then mutters to himself, half amused, half intrigued.

"Just like a thoroughbred."

IT'S SHOW TIME

F airfield Horse Park buzzes with the unrelenting energy of a show day in full swing. The air hums with the clip-clop of hooves on pavement, the chatter of riders reciting their courses under their breath, and the sharp calls of trainers giving last-minute instructions. The scent of freshly dragged footing, oiled leather, and the unmistakable aroma of hay and sweat hangs in the air, a familiar perfume of competition.

Rows of temporary stalls stretch into the distance, their canvas roofs fluttering in the morning breeze. Vendors line the walkways, hawking custom riding boots, gourmet horse treats, and handcrafted tack, while families and friends congregate near the rings, clutching show programs and iced coffees.

Amidst the chaos, Valley Vista Ranch stands like a beacon of organization and professionalism, occupying two full aisles of stalls, meticulously transformed into a miniature version of their home base.

Each stall features a crisp blue and white stall guard, emblazoned with the Valley Vista Ranch logo—a sleek horse soaring over the bold white lettering. The entire aisle is a perfectly coordinated masterpiece, exuding professionalism and prestige.

Beside each stall, matching blue tack trunks with polished silver nameplates bear the initials of each exhibitor, standing like soldiers in a row. Every stall receives crisp, clean bedding, laid with practiced efficiency. Cooling fans line up in perfect rows, calibrated to keep each horse steady and comfortable as temperatures rise.

Groomsmen transform three temporary stalls into spotless tack stations, aligning saddles and bridles with precision. Each piece hangs in perfect order, clearly labeled with the horse's name and rider for seamless access. Every bridle gleams under the overhead lights, reins coiled with precision, girths neatly hung below their respective saddles. The air inside smells of leather conditioner, saddle soap, and the faint scent of peppermint treats tucked into neatly labeled bins.

In one of the converted stalls, Pedro stands over a half-asleep Wally, methodically wiping down his freshly braided mane, ensuring each plait sits perfectly before Alexa's debut in the show ring. Wally, ever patient, lets out a deep sigh, ears flicking lazily forward and back.

At the head of the aisle, a massive blue and white canopy announces Valley Vista Ranch's presence in bold white letters. Beneath it, a sturdy wooden standing placard proudly reads 'Tegan Miller Performance Horses,' establishing the brand of excellence that Tegan has cultivated over the years.

Beneath the shade of the canopy, exhibitors, trainers, and family members gather—some reviewing courses on their iPads, others sipping water or coffee, waiting for their turn in the ring.

At a cozy corner of the setup, Alexa perches nervously in a chair, her tiny fingers fidgeting anxiously as Olivia stands behind her, deftly weaving her dark hair into a precise show braid.

"Where's my coat? It's my favorite coat. I can't show without it!" Alexa suddenly exclaims, leaning forward and frantically shuffling through a stack of horse magazines on the coffee table as if it might magically appear.

Olivia, without missing a beat, tightens the braid with practiced ease and tugs Alexa back upright.

"Sit still, Lexi. Your show coat is hanging next to Wally's tack in the tack room. We'll get it when I'm done, okay?" Her tone is firm but reassuring.

Alexa bites her lip, nodding, but the anxiety remains. "Okay... but—" she hesitates, her voice growing small. "What if Wally doesn't listen to me in the arena? What if he stops? Or just stands there and stares at the judge like he always does?"

Her big brown eyes wells up with tears.

Olivia, surprised for only a moment, quickly sets down the hairbrush and gently squeezes Alexa's shoulders.

"Hey. Remember what we worked on all week? You've got this. Wally knows his job, but if you're really worried..." Olivia pauses for dramatic effect, then leans down and whispers, "We can always feed him extra carrots to make sure he understands the plan."

Alexa's eyes widen with a spark of hope. "Really? You think that'll work?"

Olivia grins, snapping her fingers confidently. "Yep. That's straight from the Olivia Playbook. Works every time."

Without warning, Alexa throws her arms around Olivia in a fierce hug.

"Thanks, Olivia. I'm so glad you're here."

Olivia, momentarily stunned, awkwardly pats Alexa's back.

"Yeah, yeah, kid. Don't get all sappy on me. You're gonna mess up my masterpiece." She gently pries Alexa off, inspecting her like a final work of art. Satisfied, she smooths Alexa's shirt, tucks it in neatly, and dusts off the sleeves.

"Alright, you ready?"

Alexa nods, standing a little taller. "Ready."

They fist bump, an unspoken bond formed between them.

As they make their way to the barn aisle, they pass a dog pen tucked under the canopy, where Bentley, the barn's resident mascot, snoozes in her plush dog bed. She barely stirs, her tail thumping once against the side of her bed before settling back into sleep.

Ahead, Pedro gives Wally a final once-over, brushing off any stray dust before handing over the reins. The gelding blinks sleepily, completely unbothered by the fuss.

Alexa takes a deep breath, her small fingers wrapping around the leather reins. Olivia smirks and nudges her forward.

"Let's go win you a ribbon, kid."

Carson astride Rusty ponies Remington around the show grounds. They pass the warm-up arena with amateur riders preparing for their upcoming class with their trainers. A literal chaotic zoo of humans and horses passes by Remington; he anxiously prances next to them. Carson halts both horses and allows Remington to soak in the chaos. He tenderly strokes Remington's neck, then continues back toward the Valley Vista Ranch stalls. Oscar meets him in the aisle with a worried look on his face.

"Señor Carson. You're late. They're waiting for you."

"What? The show doesn't start for half an hour." He replies as he dismounts. Oscar shakes his head and chuckles to himself.

"I forgot—you're new to all this," he says, voice quickening. "They bumped up the start time. They announced it." He glances over his shoulder. "Olivia's with Alexa now, but they'll face disqualification if you don't show up at the arena. You're listed as her trainer."

Without waiting for a reply, he thrusts a pink, bedazzled cell phone into Carson's hand. "And... Señora Tegan told me to give you this."

Before Carson can respond, he grabs Rusty and Remington's lead ropes and strides off toward the stalls, boots striking the aisle in quick, purposeful steps.

"Go. Now, Señor Carson." He says forcefully. Carson shoves the cell phone into his pocket and heads to the warm-up ring.

Olivia coaches Alexa in the warm up arena as the other junior riders zoom past them. Alexa, scared of all the traffic, forcibly halts Wally. He trips and Alexa loses her balance and slides off with a thud to the ground. Wally stands patiently and looks down at Alexa, crying. Carson rushes into the arena, picks Alexa up, and dusts her off. Olivia holds onto Wally and blocks the other riders from getting close to Alexa.

"I fell, Mr. Carson." Alexa says, tears flowing down her face.

"Yes. And look. Wally stayed right by your side. He'll never leave you no matter what."

"Really?" She blinks her eyes and looks over to Wally.

"Yep. How about I help you back on and we get you ready?"

"Do I have to still show?"

"Not if you don't want to. But I'm guessing that you and Wally still do. But no matter what, I'll be right by you." He squeezes her hand in reassurance.

"Okay. I'll show for Wally. He does look pretty." She hugs Wally and smiles at Carson. Carson sets Alexa on Wally and they head to the show arena.

"You're late." Olivia whispers angrily to Carson.

"Still trying to figure this out. Didn't know that they could move up the times like that. Thanks for covering. You're the best." He playfully elbows Olivia. Olivia giggles and punches Carson in the shoulder.

Alexa, astride Wally, stands in a military-like halt with all the other riders in her class, anxiously awaiting the results. She looks over to Carson, Olivia, Cameron, and Nate (the misfit horse brigade) and waves. They all wave back. Carson nervously taps his foot.

"She did everything right. Right?" He asks.

"Sh!" They all glare back at Carson at the same time. He continues tapping his foot as the announcer's voice booms over the speakers.

"We have the results of class 184, Pony Equitation on the flat. We have ribbons from 8th place and up. Riders, please collect your ribbons when your name and number is called and stay in the arena for pictures with your trainer. For the rest, thank you for participating... In eighth place, we have number 32, Lucky Lou, and Tina Wilson. In seventh place, we have number 45, Ping-Pong, and Marcus Handle. In sixth place, we have number 42, Marigold, and Shane Walters. In fifth place, we have number 51, Pumpernickel and Mary Andrews. In fourth place, we have number 30, Wally and Alexa Harris..."

The misfit horse brigade roars with delight. Alexa, confused, looks over at her friends.

"Wally, Wally, Wally." They all chant. Carson and Olivia wave her to retrieve her much deserved ribbon. Tears well up in her eyes as she taps Wally with her crop, whispers the word walk, and heads over to the ribbon lady. The ribbon lady hands her a white rosette fourth place ribbon and smiles. Alexa hugs her ribbon to her chest and then walks Wally over to her team. Carson and Olivia climb over the fence and join Wally and Alexa.

"I won my first ribbon, Mr. Carson." She says gleefully. Alexa hands her ribbon to Olivia. Olivia pins the ribbon onto the side of Wally's brow band, kisses his cheek, and scratches his neck. Carson looks up at Alexa with pride.

"Yes. You did. I'm so proud of you, Alexa." He squeezes her tan jodhpur dressed leg and pats her paddock boot.

"Let's go take that picture. Come on, everyone." He says to his team. They all look at him like he's delirious.

"It's just the rider and trainer, Carson." Olivia says.

"I don't care. We're a team, so we all stand together no matter what." He replies. The kids shrug their shoulders and join Carson, Alexa, and Wally.

The misfit horse brigade eat their morning show breakfast of donuts and milk, showing off their myriad assortment of ribbons under the Valley Vista Ranch canopy. Olivia hands Carson a glazed donut. He shoves the entire donut in his mouth, chews, and then makes a silly donut filled smile back at her and the kids. The kids giggle and Olivia rolls her eyes at him.

"Gross, Carson. And... I'm not doing pushups." She playfully smiles and smacks him. Carson swallows his donut and smirks.

"We should start getting you ready for your classes." He thoughtfully says. Olivia flips through the prize list book. She sets out a kit of rhinestones and glue, pours out a dollop of glue on a sheet of paper.

"There's at least five classes before mine and they'll probably drag the arena. We have plenty of time." She takes another bite from her donut and grabs Alexa's white ribbon. Alexa walks up behind her and looks over her shoulder.

"What ya doing with my ribbon?" She reaches for the ribbon and Olivia playfully slaps her away.

"Bedazzling it. Gonna post your audacious ribbon on my Instagram page. You'll be famous."

"Really?" Alexa asks.

"Ah ha." Olivia continues glueing rhinestones onto the ribbon.

"Can I help?" She asks, picking up a rhinestone. Olivia nods her head in the affirmative.

"It's your ribbon. We gotta make it special so you'll never forget how it feels. Got it?" Olivia says.

"Got it." Alexa replies. They forge ahead bedazzling Alexa's ribbon.

"I wanna help." Cameron says, kneeling on the other side of Olivia. The girls continue in focused silence on their important project. Nate, an array of colored ribbons clipped all over the top of his breeches, saunters over to Carson, pushes his eyeglasses up, and crosses his arms.

"Girls sure are silly." He exclaims. The girls look at him with disdain.

"Shut up, Nate." They say in unison. Carson chuckles to himself.

"Woof. Woof. Woof." Bentley jumps up, stands on her hind legs, and wags her tail. Everyone turns and looks out of the canopy.

"Missy!" Cameron exclaims.

Missy, dressed in jeans, t-shirt, blonde hair braided in a ponytail underneath a blue baseball cap with the label "Valley Vista Ranch"; her arm in a sling, walks into the canopy.

"Hey there, misfits." She whispers. They all jump up and swarm around her like bees to honey. Carson backs away to give them the room.

"I won a ribbon. I'm helping Olivia bedazzle it. She's gonna post it on her Instagram page. I'm gonna be famous." Alexa blurts out in one breath. Tears of joy well up in Missy's eyes.

"That's wonderful. What about the rest of you?" She asks and looks at every one of her students.

"I won a belt full of ribbons, Missy." Nate shakes his hips. "Cinnamon likes me more and shows aren't terrible. Still hate ties." He exclaims with the authority of a tenured professor. Missy smiles at him, then looks at Cameron.

"What about you, Cameron?" She asks.

"I haven't won a ribbon yet, but I got through my course and remembered all my jumps. I hope to do better tomorrow." Cameron replies.

"Awesome! I wouldn't expect anything less from you." Missy holds out her good arm in a fist. Cameron, worried, looks at Carson for reassurance. He nods his head 'yes'. She fist bumps with Missy and they both make an exploding bomb sound and giggle.

"I show later, but I hope to qualify for nationals this weekend. Max and I have been working real hard. Mr. task master over there doesn't put up with any of my—"

"Good." Missy quickly cuts off Olivia. She looks over at Carson.

"Hi, I'm Missy Harrison. Nice to meet you." She offers Carson her good hand. They shake like two old colleagues with mutual admiration and respect.

"Carson Peterson. Nice to meet you. Tegan will be so happy to know you're here. Do you want me to take you to her?" He asks.

"No need. I'm not here long. Just wanted to see my misfits, and of course, little Bentley." She replies. She heads to Bentley's dog pen, crouches, and unlocks the door. Bentley bolts out and jumps onto Missy's thighs and embellishes her with happy dog kisses.

"Hey, girl. How ya doing?" She asks as she pets Bentley with her good arm. Bentley licks her face and whimpers, expressing her loss of her best friend. Missy's eyes well up with regret.

"Don't worry, Bentley. I'm here now. You want to go for a walk?" Bentley wags her tail and barks in response. Missy clips Bentley's leash onto her collar and stands. Buzz. Buzz. Buzz. Missy notices Carson's pocket vibrate.

"You gonna answer that?" She points to his pocket.

"Oh. Yeah." Carson reaches into his pocket and stares at the screen of his bright pink iPhone, confused. Olivia swipes his phone away from him and answers.

"Yea...Olivia. He's here... Okay, I'll tell him." Olivia hangs up, inspects the phone, and hands it back to him.

"Nice phone. Pink bedazzled suits you, Carson." She says sarcastically. He raises his eyebrows.

"And?" He asks.

"Tegan needs you to show Ranger. Like now." She says in her normal bored teenage tone.

"Why?" He asks. Olivia shrugs her shoulders. Carson, frustrated, grabs his helmet.

"Can you start your flat work warm up without me? I'll get back before you need to warm up jumping." He asks, harried by the situation.

"Don't worry. I can help her until you get back," Missy says.

"I'll set the jumps if you're late," Cameron interjects. Alexa wraps her arms around Olivia's waist. "We'll all help. We 'misfits' stay together, no matter what. Right?" Alexa beams with joy at Carson. Carson, overwhelmed by his team, claps his hands together.

"Okay, everyone. Let's all help Olivia get ready for her classes. I'll be back in time, but I'm going to count on all of you to play your part. Huddle. Hands in." He directs. Everyone, including Missy, places their hand in the circle.

"One, two, three." He counts out.

"Misfits!" They all shout as they raise their hands to the sky in unison.

The hunter's warm-up arena hums with energy, horses moving in synchronized chaos, their hooves thudding against the soft footing as trainers shout last-minute instructions over the low hum of the show grounds.

Carson moves with quiet determination, his helmet tucked under one arm, jaw set. He coils every muscle, anticipating the competition—until the obnoxious vibration in his back pocket reminds him he still owns a bedazzled pink cell phone.

Buzz. Buzz. Buzz.

His fingers tighten into a fist. He yanks it out, exhaling sharply.

Neon pink. Rhinestones shaped into a jumping horse. A joke. Tegan's joke. Now, every time the damn thing buzzed, chirped, or even existed, he swore he could hear her laughing somewhere in the distance.

With a sharp exhale, he silences it and shoves it back into his pocket.

A few feet away, Tegan stands beside Ranger, the gray Westphalian flicking an ear lazily beneath her touch. She's focused on her own phone, mid-call—until she sees Carson.

Her eyes land on the pink phone, still half-visible in his pocket.

She bites her lip, trying to suppress a grin, but the amusement is undeniable.

Then—she outright snorts.

Carson shoots her a deadpan look.

And that's when Jake appears.

Dressed in designer jeans, snakeskin boots, and a button-down left open just enough to scream 'overcompensating,' he's too close—leaning in, speaking low, his breath practically grazing Tegan's skin.

Carson's eyes darken.

Jake nudges Tegan's elbow, whispers something just for her.

Tegan flinches—just slightly, but enough.

Carson sees it. And so does Jake.

Jake cocks his head, eyes flashing with satisfaction. He glances at Carson, his smirk growing like a cat toying with a mouse.

Tegan snaps her phone shut abruptly.

Carson marches up and presses the pink monstrosity back into her hands.

"This is yours." His voice is flat, but the heat in his gaze betrays his restraint.

Tegan grins, tilting her head, her fingers brushing his as she takes it. The contact—brief, fleeting—sends a jolt of something through both of them.

"Nah, pink really suits you." She teases, her voice a little softer now, a little breathier.

For a moment, Carson forgets about Jake, about the horse show, about everything except the way her eyes linger on his.

Then—Jake clears his throat. Loudly.

"Glad you could make yourself available, Carson," he drawls, voice coated in arrogance.

Carson drags his gaze away from Tegan, jaw locking.

"Take your time. Really. Don't mind us—we're just trying to do business for our clients." Jake adds, his smirk stretching just enough to make it clear this isn't about business at all.

Carson forces his hands to stay loose at his sides, but his stomach clenches.

He waits for Tegan to say something. To shut Jake down.

But she doesn't.

She just shifts her weight, looking frustrated and uncomfortable, caught between them like she knows exactly what's happening but refuses to acknowledge it.

Finally, she exhales, tucking a loose strand of hair behind her ear.

"Shelly just decided she wants to sell Ranger," she says quickly, voice tight, like she's pushing through an already fraying patience. "And she wants top dollar. I need you to show him to generate interest. Can you do that for me?"

Carson stares at her, the sting of disappointment mixing with irritation.

"Sell Ranger? Why?"

Jake laughs under his breath.

"None of your business, buddy." His smirk turns sharp. "Just ride the horse like a good boy and let the adults conduct business."

Carson's fingers tighten around the reins. His shoulders coil.

Jake wants a reaction. He wants Carson to snap, to give him an excuse to lord something over him.

And Carson? He wants to tell Jake exactly where he can shove his designer boots.

But Tegan takes a step forward, placing herself between them, her voice lower now, almost pleading.

"Please? I'm way behind and haven't worked on my horses for tonight's Grand Prix."

Carson meets her eyes.

And damn it, even when she's exasperated, frustrated, caught in the middle of this ridiculous game—she still gets to him.

He exhales sharply, jaw ticking.

"Fine. Just this once." His voice is measured, but clipped. "But I'm a trainer, Tegan. Not a sales lackey."

Tegan nods quickly, looking almost relieved.

Carson takes Ranger's reins and leads him toward the mounting block.

Jake watches, arms crossed, the glint of jealousy flashing briefly across his face.

Carson swings into the saddle with effortless ease, collecting the reins like it's second nature. Tegan watches him settle into the tack, arms crossed, chewing on the inside of her cheek. She says it's business. But Carson can feel something else shifting beneath the surface. She cares. More than she's willing to admit.

"Set the jumps for Carson, Jake."

Jake visibly stiffens. "But I'll ruin my—"

Tegan turns on her heel, already walking off.

"You want this deal or not? Your choice."

Jake's mouth opens—then snaps shut.

Carson can't help but smirk as he gathers Ranger's reins and trots toward the first warm-up fence. Jake, his ego bruised and his perfectly curated outfit about to get dusted, glares after them.

This wasn't over. Not by a long shot.

"This year's winner of class number 633, the $3,000 USHJA National Hunter Derby is number 535, Ranger Z, owned by Shelly Windham and ridden by Carson Peterson."

A row of women hoot and holler with Shelly in front, waving and pointing frantically at Carson and Ranger. Carson mounted on Ranger forces a smile, waves back to the ladies, and accepts his first place blue ribbon and medal. The ribbon lady fastens a red, yellow, and blue rosette neck ribbon just in front of Ranger's withers. The show manager, followed by Shelly, enters the arena carrying a bronze trophy of a horse jumping over a fence. They all line up in front of Ranger and Carson and take pictures; Shelly holding the trophy, smiling like she's won the Kentucky Derby.

Carson dismounts Ranger, hands the reins to Shelly, and quickly leaves the arena. He passes Jake, shaking hands and accepting a check from Ranger's new owners. He shakes his head and continues to the jumper's warm-up ring.

Olivia, in a sitting trot, leg yields Max to the rail as Carson enters the arena. She notices Carson and pilots Max toward him and halts.

"Looks like he's listening real well." Carson says.

"Yea. I didn't realize how important flat work could be. All the other horses are going nuts and me and Max, just another day in the park." She responds, overdoing her confidence, her eyes wide with fear. Carson, oblivious to Olivia's emotions, walks over to the warm-up jump.

"Great. Have they opened the arena for the course walk?" He asks.

"Not yet. Missy and the gang went down to check."

"I'll check as well. That way, I can memorize the course sheet for your classes." He says. Olivia pulls out her phone and clicks on her photos. She shows them to Carson.

"Already got 'em. Luckily, the speed round is the same as the two-bell." Carson studies the photos.

"That's real nifty, Olivia. Let's use the meter speed round as a warmup. No full throttle, okay? It's your time to get a sense of how the course rides. Then we'll tune you up for the meter ten two bell and speed round. Ready to pop over some jumps?" He hands her back her cell phone. Olivia nods her head and bites her upper lip.

"Carson?"

"Yea?"

"Do you really think I can qualify for nationals in the meter ten? What if I don't? I'll be a complete failure. I'll lose my sponsors—"

"Olivia. I believe you and Max can qualify for nationals at any height. But it doesn't matter what I believe. You have to believe it. What's important is that you're there for Max. You do that, and he'll come through for you. Just focus on that, okay?" Carson squeezes Olivia's boot leg. Alexa runs up the hill into the arena, panting from exertion; Missy, Cameron, and Nate follow in behind her.

"The course is open for walking. The jumps are huge, Olivia. Bigger than me. Can I walk the course with you guys? I've never walked a course before." Olivia looks at Carson, scared. Carson bends over to talk to Alexa.

"I have a very important mission for you, Alexa. Can you watch over Max while me and Olivia walk the course?" Carson smiles at Olivia reassuringly.

"But I want to be with Olivia." Alexa obstinately replies. Olivia dismounts Max and hands the reins to Alexa and takes her hand.

"There's no one else I would trust Max with. Please help me, Alexa." Alexa stands tall like a soldier ready for battle.

"I'll guard him with my life. We all will." Alexa looks over to her companions and Missy; they all nod their heads 'yes' and form a line on each side of Max and Alexa.

Carson and Olivia enter the Equidome; Olivia stops in her tracks and stares like a deer in headlights frozen from fear.

"They sure are big." She whispers with misgivings.

"They're just like the ones at home. Actually, they're smaller. Remember... You've been schooling Max easily over a meter twenty." He replies. He slaps her on the shoulder as if she's a horse scared to cross a lake.

"Let's walk the course." He says as he heads to the first jump.

"Right," Olivia says, clenching both fists as she follows close behind.

They move from the wide oxer toward the first fence of the triple combination. Together, they stop beside the line: a vertical, followed by an oxer, then another vertical leading into a sharp right turn toward the last obstacle—a solitary black-and-white fence standing at the edge of the arena. He studies the sequence in silence, fingers brushing his chin as his eyes trace the path. After a long moment, he turns to Olivia.

"Hmm...The triple is a one stride to a two stride. Kinda tricky, but you can handle it. Now Max has a big stride, so bring him back after the oxer leading up to this triple and go just right of center to the first vertical of the combination. Don't release too much over the oxer or Max won't be able to fit in the two strides to the vertical." Carson turns and looks over the rest of the course.

"The rest of the course seems pretty straightforward. It's the oxer leading up to this triple that's going to determine the placings. Don't worry, you and Max have a solid relationship, so if you come in the way I told you, it'll be in the bag. Trust me, the rest of the field is going to come in too hot from the oxer and knock down a rail. Got it?" He nods his head and smiles. Olivia looks over the triple combination, the rest of the course, and then back to Carson and smiles with the determination of a seasoned veteran.

"Got it." She says.

"Okay, then. Let's go jump some sticks." Carson and Olivia fist bump, make an explosion sound, and exit the arena.

The misfit horse brigade enjoy their afternoon catered meal of hot dogs, hamburgers, chips, cookies, grilled vegetables, and potato salad under the canopy. They proudly displayed their ribbons on a string under the canopy. Olivia shows off her second place medal and trophy to Missy.

"Congratulations, Olivia. Reserve Champion and qualifying for nationals at the meter ten. That's an accomplishment." Missy wraps her good arm around Olivia's waist and gives her an affectionate squeeze.

"Carson was right. Almost everyone came in too hot from the oxer to the triple combination and knocked down a rail. Me and Max got through it just fine. Could've won the two bell, but I didn't want to take the inside turn. Wanted to save Max for the rest of the weekend. And did you see Shannon's turn? She almost came off and I bet you that her horse is lame. I wouldn't do that to my Max." she excitedly says. She looks over and raises her hot dog to Carson and takes a bite. He winks back.

"Proud of you. That's a mark of a true horse person to put the needs of the horse over a blue ribbon. You learned a valuable lesson today." Carson walks over to Missy and Olivia and looks at Olivia's medal. Olivia raises her iPhone in front of her and her medal in the other hand, and takes a selfie of the three of them. She types on her screen and posts to her Instagram account.

"That should make the sponsors happy. And... Get this. I have an audition for the equestrian series I was telling you about. Maybe we could film at Valley Vista Ranch." She says with an air of teenage arrogance. Carson shakes his head in disproval.

"Is that what you really want?" Carson earnestly asks. Olivia shrugs her shoulders.

"Don't know. But a girl's gotta have options. Don't you think? Not to shock you, Carson. But horses aren't everything. There is a whole world out there, and I want to explore every part of it," she candidly replies.

"Okay. Okay. I give up." He smiles back and raises his hands, relenting to her teenage whims.

Tegan bursts into the tent, a blur of energy and purpose; her eyes locked on Olivia as if nothing else in the world exists.

"Way to go, Olivia!" she exclaims, her voice breathless with excitement. "I saw your last round from the stands. Not taking the inside turn was the right choice.

Always put the horse before the win. And... I heard through the grapevine that Shannon's horse is lame. They're out the rest of the weekend—maybe the rest of the season."

The news carries an edge, a mix of sympathy and the calculated awareness of what it means for Olivia's rankings. Olivia arches a perfectly sculpted brow, barely containing her satisfaction.

Tegan's gaze shifts to the rest of the Misfits and Carson.

"The rest of you should be proud of your accomplishments today." She looks at Cameron, who is still pouting over her lack of ribbons. "Cameron, I know you wanted a ribbon. But finishing the course is just as good. The ribbons will come. I promise."

She beams at them, radiating her usual confidence and warmth.

"I got tickets for tonight's Grand Prix. I hope you can stay and support me, Mirabella Mia, and Luke 631. Should be exciting. The horses feel good, and—"

Then—her entire world stops.

Her breath catches mid-sentence.

"Missy?"

The name falls from her lips like a whispered prayer, full of disbelief, longing, and something dangerously close to heartbreak.

The entire tent vanishes into the periphery. The buzz of conversation, the laughter, the shuffling of hooves—it all fades.

All she sees is Missy.

Missy fidgets, her fingers tightening on Bentley's leash, her knuckles turning white.

"Hey, Teegs." Her voice is flat, controlled—but her eyes betray her. Wide. Guarded. Frightened.

Tegan takes a step forward, as if drawn by an invisible tether.

"You're here." It's not just an observation; it's everything.

Missy shrinks under the weight of Tegan's gaze.

"I just... wanted to see my Misfits. And Bentley."

The words sound forced, hollow, like an excuse rather than the truth.

Tegan nods, swallowing the lump in her throat, desperate to keep this fragile moment from breaking apart.

"Of course... You know, Remi is here." Her voice is gentle, hopeful, pleading. "Carson's been working with him. He's doing great. Wanna see him?"

Missy's entire body tenses. Her eyes widen, and for a moment, raw panic flashes across her face.

Tegan sees it—the fear, the grief, the ghost of a life Missy is trying to outrun.

Missy steps back.

"Maybe some other time." The words come fast, breathless, shaky. "Gotta go. Mom's waiting. Kept her waiting too long. Thanks for taking care of Bentley. See you soon."

She grabs Bentley's leash like it's a lifeline and bolts, her movements stiff, unnatural, like she's forcing herself to walk instead of run.

Tegan snaps into action, her body moving before her brain can process it.

She lunges forward, ready to chase after her, to fix this, to make her stay—to do something—

A firm grip closes around her arm.

She whips around. Carson.

His touch is steady, grounding, his voice quiet but commanding.

"Let her go, Tegan."

Tegan's chest heaves, her pulse pounding against her ribs.

"But—"

Carson shakes his head.

"She came. That's a start."

Tegan's bottom lip trembles. The dam breaks.

Tears flood her eyes, spill over, hot and unrelenting. Her body shakes, her breath coming in short, uneven bursts. Carson doesn't hesitate. He pulls her in, his arms solid and warm, steadying her as she crumbles.

She presses her forehead against his chest, gripping his shirt like it's the only thing keeping her upright.

For a moment, it's just them. The sound of her quiet sobs, Carson's hand rubbing slow, soothing circles against her back.

Then—

A voice cuts through the weight of the moment.

"Well, this is different."

Tegan jerks back, wiping her eyes as she spins toward the voice.

Nate. The kid is holding a cookie in one hand, halfway to his mouth, watching the entire exchange with a mixture of curiosity and mild disgust.

Then, as if to hammer in the awkwardness, he shoves the cookie in his mouth, crumbs cascading onto his show shirt in an absolutely atrocious display of table manners.

Tegan lets out a wet, half-laugh, half-sob, shaking her head as she wipes her face.

"Who wants to help me walk Remington?" she asks, her voice only slightly wobbly.

The kids immediately raise their hands, eager for any chance to be involved.

Olivia, stunned by the uncharacteristic show of emotion, quickly masks her surprise and clears her throat.

"I'll get Max." She straightens her gloves. "It'll be good to stretch his legs after all his hard work."

Carson glances toward Rusty, who strides into the tent as if summoned by some unspoken call.

"Rusty and I will lead the way. Sound like a plan, Misfits?"

He pats Rusty's neck, feeding him a cube.

Tegan takes a deep breath, looking at Carson one last time—silent gratitude in her gaze.

Then she nods, turning to follow him toward Remington's stall, the misfit horse brigade falling into step behind her.

Behind them, the tent falls quiet.

A space once filled with ghosts, now carrying the echoes of something else—something fragile, something unfinished.

And somewhere outside the tent, Missy keeps walking, trying to outrun a past that refuses to let her go.

JUST ANOTHER GRAND PRIX

O scar gives Tegan a leg up onto Luke 631 and removes the warming blanket from his haunches. Oscar taps Tegan's leg and gives her a nod. Tegan trots off with Luke 631 to warm him up. Tegan, oblivious to the spectators (composed of a myriad of barns including Valley Vista Ranch) outside the warm-up arena, canters Luke in a perfectly relaxed frame. Oscar sets a three foot vertical with a trot pole in front. Tegan easily trots over the fence and halts in a perfectly straight line. She pats Luke 631 on the neck and gives Oscar a thumbs up. He quickly raises the fence and places a red flag on the standard.

Carson and the misfit horse brigade stand outside the arena. Carson, transfixed with Tegan, does not notice Cathy Turner approach him and wave Olivia over. Cathy Turner, ever the socialite, dressed in a floor length denim dress cinched with a horse shoe buckled belt with matching cowboy boots and taupe shawl leans against Carson. Carson edges away from her and continues staring out at the warm-up arena.

"Beautiful night, isn't it?" Cathy purrs in a thicker than usual English accent. Carson quickly acknowledges her presence and then resumes watching Tegan like he's watching the Super Bowl.

"Yep." He replies. Tegan and Luke 631 knock down a pole of an oxer. Luke gives a big buck in anger. Tegan halts him and backs him up a couple of steps, then resumes her canter.

"Maybe I should help them." Carson says, concerned. Cathy squeezes his forearm.

"Wouldn't do that if I were you. No one works with Tegan except Oscar. Used to be her father and Oscar. But since his passing, it's just Oscar. You'd jinx them, darling. Why don't you come to my table to watch? I have Cristal chilling and some caviar. It's absolutely divine." She looks up at him and bats her eyes.

"I promised the misfits that we'd all watch together. What you say, guys? Should we get going?" He looks at them, desperate to be saved from the infamous Cathy Turner.

"Sure, Mr. Carson. Can we get a lollipop first?" Alexa interjects, unaware of the situation. Carson looks at Cathy and shrugs his shoulder.

"Duty calls." He says.

"Suit yourself." Cathy rolls her eyes and departs in a state of acrimony. Nate pushes his eyeglasses up his nose.

"What a vile woman." He says with a fake English accent. Carson elbows him and the rest of the misfits giggle.

"Let's go gang." Carson takes Alexa's hand and they head off to their seats in the Equidome.

Lights shine down from the ceiling of the Equidome, creating a circus like atmosphere. Rows of spectators line the stands in a hushed silence while the clinging of silverware and champagne flutes emanates from elaborately decorated six-person tables encircling the outer edge of the arena within spitting distance of the momentous obstacles that create the course for this year's 1.45-1.50 meter $50,000 Opening Legis Grand Prix. Alexa, sitting between Carson and Olivia, points her lollipop at a red and white 1.45 meter high and wide oxer with a liverpool (water feature) underneath it.

"Is Ms. Tegan really gonna jump that, Mr. Carson?" She asks with wide eyes.

"Yep, and all the other jumps as well. Isn't it exciting? Your coach has two horses in the Grand Prix."

"Yea. And it's Mirabella Mia's debut. Seems like a tough course. I hope that mare can get through it. Luke's an old pro. They'll probably sell them by the end of this weekend. Anyway, gotta run. Hold my seat, Lexi." Alexa nods her head as Olivia heads to the exit.

"She's selling Luke 631? And where's Olivia off to? She'll miss the opening ceremonies." Carson asks.

"Why do you think Jake is here? He never comes to a horse show unless there's a horse sale involved. And Olivia is being Olivia. She'll be back whenever." Cameron replies with wisdom beyond her years. She points to Cathy Turner's table. Carson looks over to see Cathy Turner seated beside Jake and his wealthy clients. Jake notices Carson's gaze from the cheap seats, snickers, and raises his glass of Cristal to him. The tractors finish dragging the arena and exit. The microphone clicks on and the announcer's voice booms over the dome.

"Welcome ladies and gentlemen, to the $50,000 Opening Legis Grand Prix. Tonight we have a field of thirty-six horse and rider combinations from all over the west coast and some international guests as well vying for not only the chance at prize money but this Grand Prix is a qualifier for the $250,000 Longine Grand Prix to be held in Las Vegas at the end of the year. But before we begin, please join me in welcoming our own Olivia Mayer as she leads us in the National Anthem."

Olivia, microphone in hand, enters the arena and waves at the crowd. The spectators all stand; Carson removes his cowboy hat and places it on his chest. He smiles and shakes his head at Olivia. Olivia winks back and sings. Her pitch perfect vocals, like a songbird, echo throughout the dome. Olivia finishes the anthem in a flourish. She bows to enthusiastic applause, exits the arena as the first horse and rider combination enters.

"And we're off. The first to go in the $50,000 Opening Legis Grand Prix is Micheal Ward and California Dreaming, a 14-year-old gelding by Classic Dream. Fresh off their Nation's Cup win, let's see how they make their way on this new course designed by Captain Mark Shuwell. Eighty seconds is the time allowed for the first round of thirteen questions, sixteen jumps in total."

Micheal walks his horse around the jumps and allows his horse to take inspect the pale pink four pole vertical jump with a lonely plank panel lying vicariously on the top cups. He taps his helmet and the bell rings. He canters his horse in a circle then heads to the first jump - the 1.45 meter red and white oxer with the liverpool underneath. Alexa closes her eyes and buries her head in Carson's shoulder.

"Did he make it, Mr. Carson?" Alexa asks.

"Yes. Why don't you watch the rest?" Carson replies. He pulls her off his shoulder, and she sits back in her chair and begrudgingly watches the rest.

"Michael was able to maneuver the tricky double to double combination, but it was the lonely plank panel of the pale pink vertical that delivered the four faults. A remarkably fast time of seventy-seven seconds which could make him the fastest four fault. But unfortunately, he will not be progressing to the jump off." The announcer declares. The crowd sighs in disappointment. A couple more horse and rider combinations maneuver the course without going clear. Alexa gasps when the third horse and rider combination has a bad distance and crash through a blue and white oxer in the middle of a triple combination.

"The horse belly flopped, Mr. Carson. This is worse than a horror movie. Can we go home?" Alexa whimpers.

"Don't be such a crybaby, Alexa." Nate chastises. Cameron smacks him upside the head.

"Be nice, Nate. Or I'll tell your mom." Cameron puffs her chest in defense of Alexa.

"Go ahead." He sticks his tongue out at her, grabs his soda, takes a loud gulp, and burps.

"Gross." Cameron replies. She points at Nate and makes a pig face at Alexa. Both girls giggle. Olivia rushes to her seat carrying a tray of nachos, popcorn, sodas, and lollipops. She hands the tray to Carson and sits next to Alexa. Alexa grabs the lollipop.

"What'd I miss?" She asks.

"Oh, the usual female melodrama." Nate sarcastically replies.

"Shut up, Nate." Cameron and Alexa whip their heads like a viper at him. He shrinks back in his seat and stuffs nachos in his face.

"Checked the order of go and Tegan is fifth with Luke and twentieth-seventh with Mirabella." Carson calmly says ignoring the misfit shenanigans.

"Didn't know you could sing like that." Carson raises his eyebrows.

"There's a lot of things you don't know about me, Mr. Carson." Olivia sarcastically replies.

"No really, Olivia. That was magnificent. You're truly talented. I can understand why horses aren't a priority to you. If I had that kind of talent—"

"You wouldn't be with horses?" Olivia asks incredulously.

"I'm not saying that, but the horse-life is a hard life. Unforgiving and you won't get rich training horses if that's your goal. But, I can't imagine doing anything else. Just can't." Carson simply says as he looks out to the arena. Tegan enters with a singular, determined look on her face.

"Next to go is Olympic Gold Medalist, Tegan Miller and Luke 631, a 12-year-old Dutch Warmblood stallion by The Twain. They recently won the Longines Grand Prix in Wellington at the end of last year. Let's see what they can do today."

Tegan and Luke 631 walk over to the jumps. She stops at the pale pink vertical and allows Luke to inspect it. She pats his neck, trots to the center of the arena, halts, and salutes to the judge. The bell rings and she canters off to the first jump.

Luke 631 easily handles the oxer and they head off at blinding speed to the rest of the course. They head to the first line of a vertical to an oxer and hit it perfectly in four strides turning to another vertical on their way to the first combination - a large puissance looking wall of bricks, six strides to a one stride of an oxer to a vertical. Carson grasps Alexa's hand in apprehension.

"You're hurting my hand, Mr. Carson." Alexa teases.

"Sorry." He quickly releases her hand and clutches his jeans instead. Tegan pilots Luke 631 over the combination and heads to the pale pink vertical with the lonely plank panel. Luke 631 shakes his head, but Tegan quickly kicks him to send him forward and gives him a big release over the jump. Luke 631 clears the jump and bucks on the other side. Tegan urges him forward to the remainder of the course. They head to the last of the difficult combinations affectionately called the double to the double - a one stride, then six strides to a two stride, four jumps in total testing the horses' ride ability and ability to compress after a long six strides between the first and second combination. Tegan, with the skills of an Olympic champion, easily maneuvers over the question. She canters to the last three jumps and finishes by jumping a pale green oxer and galloping through the timers. She looks up at the scoreboard and pumps her fist at her achievement. The crowd roars with delight. Carson jumps up from his seat and pumps his fists. The misfit brigade look at one another, laugh, and continue eating their snacks graciously provided by Olivia. Olivia feverishly takes films and pictures with her iPhone and posts on her Instagram account.

"Tegan Miller has done it! We have our first clear round of the evening with a blistering time of seventy-five seconds. We'll see her later in the evening on her second mount. Could there be two Tegan Miller horses in the jump off? Stay tuned, ladies and gentlemen." The announcer exclaims as sirens blow, signaling the clear round. Tegan halts Luke 631, looks up to the misfit horse brigade, pauses at Carson, and waves. The misfits stand in unison and yell, to the dismay of Jake and his guests.

"Tegan! Tegan! Tegan!" Tegan smiles and trots out of the arena with Luke. Olivia takes more pictures and a selfie of her and Alexa. She stands and grabs her Ariat backpack.

"Who wants to go shopping?" She asks.

"We're watching the Grand Prix," Carson says, frustrated.

"Come on. Tegan doesn't come back for at least a half hour. We could go watch her warm up Mirabella Mia after. Please." Olivia pleads. The three girls all bat their eyes at Carson and Nate. Carson looks at Nate.

"I'm not saying anything." Nate jams a lollipop in his mouth.

"Okay. But we're coming right back and watching Tegan warm up. Should be good for all of you to watch her prep a green horse." Carson says, trying to convince himself.

"Let's go, Misfits." Olivia commands. The three girls exit the stands before Carson and Nate rise from their seats.

"There's nothing more powerful than the call of the credit card." Nate says with pundit conviction. "I guess it's just us men, Carson."

"Right. Let's go check on Tegan and Mirabella." Carson raises his eyebrows and replies.

Olivia and the girls return to the warm up arena carrying bags of tack and riding apparel. The girls stand next to Rusty, Carson, and Nate. Rusty nickers at the girls. His ears instantly perk up at the entrance of Tegan and Mirabella Mia. Mirabella Mia, head and tail straight up to the sky, eyes wide, whinnies in distress at her new surroundings. Rusty nickers back to her and her eyes soften and she settles, still slightly agitated. Tegan pats her on the neck for extra reassurance. The girls proudly show each other and Carson their myriad of tack purchases, causing the packages to rustle spooking Mirabella. Mirabella performs an animated dressage piaffe in place - Carson looks at Olivia. Tegan settles her again and brings her to a lofty forward trot, followed by a lively canter. Mirabella Mia performs the rest of her warm up as if she's in a Grand Prix Dressage arena to the amazement of the gathered crowd. Jake and his clients gather at the far end of the arena engaged in a spirited whisper, gesturing at Tegan and Mirabella Mia.

"Let's take our shopping to the tack room, girls. Don't want to spook Mirabella again." Olivia says as she takes Alexa's hand.

"We'll be right back, Mr. Carson." Alexa playfully says. Carson smiles at Alexa, looks over to Olivia and mouths the word "thanks." She nods and leaves them.

Oscar sets up a trot pole in front of a sub three foot vertical. Tegan brings Mirabella Mia to the fence, and she easily clears it. Oscar and Tegan perform their ritualistic sign language and he raises the fence and moves the pole in. Jake's clients gasps as Tegan and Mirabella Mia clear the vertical by over a foot. Tegan waves at Oscar and he converts the vertical into an oxer and raises it again. Mirabella Mia again clears the oxer by over a foot and lands like she's on a bed of clouds and comes down to trot. Tegan pats Mirabella's neck and smiles at Oscar. They're ready. Tegan gazes at Carson and smiles euphorically. Carson knowingly looks back at her in awe.

"Next to go is Olympic Gold Medalist, Tegan Miller and Mirabella Mia, an eight-year-old mare by Bella Mia and Zaragosa. This is Mirabella Mia's first attempt at the Grand Prix level. She successfully competed at the meter thirty level, winning Nationals last year. A home bred horse known for her scopey jump; let's see if she can compete at the Grand Prix level." Tegan enters the arena with Mirabella Mia. Mirabella Mia rears, afraid of the spectators and vastness of the decorative jumps, perfectly placed shrubbery, and floral arrangements. Tegan urges her forward. Mirabella resists and runs backwards and lets out a panicked whinny, shaking her head as if to say, 'no, this is too much'. Tegan looks back at Oscar, standing at the gated entrance. Rusty trots up to Oscar and whinnies back to Mirabella. Mirabella Mia turns and faces Rusty, who shakes his head at her and nickers. Mirabella Mia chews on her bit, drops her head, and nickers back to Rusty. Tegan smiles at Rusty and pats Mirabella on the neck. She salutes to the judges; the bell rings, and they canter off towards the red and white oxer.

"I think Rusty's in love." Nate says.

"Shh. We're watching." Olivia says as she holds Alexa's hand.

"Does Mirabella love Rusty, Mr. Carson?" Alexa asks. Carson removes his cowboy hat and scratches his head in concern.

"I don't know about that, but there is definitely a bond between them. Rusty has done a lot of amazing things throughout his life, but I've never seen him so engaged with a mare. Didn't know he had it in him." Carson chuckles to himself.

Tegan and Mirabella Mia clear the red and white oxer by over a foot and canter off at blistering speed. They clear each fence by over a foot; the crowd gasps at Mirabella's athletic abilities. They head to the last demanding combination (the double to the double). Mirabella Mia answers the question with razor-like agility, as if she's competed in hundreds of Grand Prix. They round the corner towards the last three jumps. She finishes the course, jumping the pale green oxer like it's a seven-foot puissance wall. Tegan looks up to the clock and drops her head in disappointment - 80.25 on the clock.

"What a spectacular display of athleticism! Unfortunately, Mirabella Mia decided that flying was much more fun than competing and just missed the time allowed. She will not be joining us for the jump off. But what a show, ladies and gentlemen. We've just witnessed the beginning of a spectacular career for Mirabella Mia and Tegan Miller." The announcer exclaims.

Tegan halts Mirabella Mia, the audience bearing witness to history, give them a standing ovation. Tegan waves at the spectators, feeds Mirabella Mia a sugar cube, and pats her on the neck. The misfit horse brigade chant, "Mia! Mia! Mia!" Tegan taps Mia behind her shoulder and Mia bows. The crowd roars with delight. Tegan looks up to Carson, winks, and leads Mirabella Mia out of the arena. He throws his head back and roars with laughter.

"Show off." He whispers to himself.

A soft glow of light emanates from lanterns hanging from the four corners of the ceiling of the Valley Vista Ranch show canopy. A rainbow display of ribbons decorate the front and sides of the canopy with Alexa's bedazzled fourth place ribbon prominently displayed in the center. Members of Valley Vista Ranch barn collect throughout the canopy enjoying wine, champagne, an assortment of cheese and crackers, and cookies and cakes. Carson sits in the corner with his loyal and rambunctious misfit horse brigade. Tegan's Grand Prix first place trophy, ribbon, and prizes occupy a distinguished berth on the coffee table in the middle of the makeshift party room. Tegan, still dressed in her show clothes sans show jacket, raises her glass of champagne up in the air.

"I just want to thank everyone for all their hard work and dedication for this first day of the show. It gives me such pride to see all of you out there working hard to achieve your goals. Olivia, qualifying for nationals in the meter ten jumpers... Alexa getting her first of many ribbons... Cameron finishing her course... Susan getting first in the three foot three hunters... The list goes on and on. Most importantly, we came out here as a family and supported one another. Thank you to our grooms, Oscar and Pedro. I couldn't do this or any show without you. And finally, I would like to welcome and thank our new trainer, Carson Peterson. Your work with the horses and students has not gone unnoticed. So here's to all of you, my Valley Vista Ranch Family." She drinks from her glass.

The clients and students exclaim in unison, "Valley Vista Ranch" and imbibe their drinks. Tegan sets her glass on the table, smiles, and heads to her favorite misfits, but an inebriated Jake blocks her. He places his hands on her shoulders as if they are best friends and leans into her personal space.

"I have great news, Teegs. They want to buy both of them." He says. Tegan forcefully removes his hands from her shoulders.

"You're drunk, Jake."

"Yep. But that's not the point, Teegs. I got us a great deal. Just give me the go ahead and I'll close it.".

"What are you talking about?" She asks, annoyed.

"Luke 631 and Mirabella Mia, of course. They want them both." Jake folds his arms, content with his work for the day. He sways back and forth and then steadies himself.

"Not for sale." Tegan responds. She tries to get by him, but he obstructs her departure.

"What do you mean 'not for sale'? I busted my ass putting this deal together."

"Seriously? Eating and getting drunk with the clients. In front of the children. Jake, I've agreed to let you come back to Valley Vista Ranch. Don't make me regret it. This discussion is over." She pushes him aside and walks over to the misfit horse brigade. Jake rushes after her, stumbling over himself. Oscar and Pedro block his progression and Oscar shoves him back.

"You're leaving... Now." Oscar declares in a low voice, fuming with anger. Jake raises his hands in submission.

"Okay. Okay. Just trying to do my job. You know... I own half of Luke. I have a— "

Oscar and Pedro look at one another, seize Jake by each arm, and escort him out of the tent.

Alexa stretches her arms above her head and yawns. "I'm tired."

"So am I. We should all get going. We have an early start tomorrow. Especially you, Cameron. You're first up and I can feel a ribbon coming." Olivia responds.

"Really? Then I should get going too. C'mon Nate, my mom said you could stay with us," Cameron says. They all get up to leave as Tegan approaches.

"Have you guys seen Carson?" She asks.

"You know, Carson. Parties aren't his thing. He went to go check on the horses." Olivia confidently responds as the teenage authority of all things, Carson.

"We're all heading out. Do you need anything?" Olivia asks.

"No. I probably should go check on the horses too. See you in the morning. Sleep tight, misfits." She affectionately says. She exits the tent and the misfits giggle.

"That's not all she's going to check on." Nate sarcastically replies. Olivia elbows him.

"Stop it, Nate. Let's go, misfits." She commands. They depart the tent in an excited hushed huddle of daily show gossip and predictions about tomorrow's show.

Tegan strolls down the aisle, taking stock of all the Valley Vista Ranch horses. She stops at Mirabella Mia's stall, makes a kissing sound, and Mirabella's head pops through the stall door and nickers. Tegan rubs Mirabella's forehead. She then lays her cheek on Mirabella's forehead, closes her eyes, wraps her arms around Mia's muzzle, and just breathes.

The hospital room is suffocatingly sterile, filled with the soft hum of machines and the steady beeping of a heart monitor. The fluorescent lights cast an unforgiving glow over Mirabella's frail frame, making her appear almost translucent against the stark white sheets.

She is a whisper of the woman she once was—her once-strong, vibrant body now a fragile shell draped in a thin hospital gown. The plastic tubes delivering oxygen into her nose seem too large, too intrusive for someone so small. Her cheekbones are sharp beneath pale, papery skin, and the IV in her hand stands out against veins that seem too delicate, too exhausted to continue this fight.

Beside her, Tegan, just nine years old, sleeps curled up in her show attire. Hours spent in the stiff hospital chair wrinkled Tegan's white breeches slightly before she finally crawled into the narrow bed with her mother. A single untamed strand of raven hair falls across her face.

Mirabella wakes with a soft groan; the simple act of opening her eyes is an effort. She shifts slightly, ignoring the sharp pull of pain that radiates through her body, and gently brushes the stray lock of hair from Tegan's face.

Tegan stirs, blinking sleepily before her bright emerald eyes land on her mother. Mirabella smiles weakly.

"Hello, beautiful." Her voice is barely above a whisper, breathy and labored.

Tegan immediately perks up, rubbing the sleep from her eyes.

"Hi, Mommy!" she chirps, her voice filled with the unshakable optimism of a child. "Are you coming home today?"

Mirabella's smile falters just for a moment.

She won't lie to her daughter. But she won't tell her the truth either.

"Soon, mi amor." She quickly shifts the conversation, grasping at anything that doesn't involve goodbyes. "How was the show?"

Tegan's face lights up instantly, the question successfully pulling her back into the excitement of the day.

"I won, Mommy!" she exclaims, sitting up fully. "I did everything you told me, and I got the top score in Training Level Test Three! Me and Hershey Bar were high-point champions!"

Mirabella's smile strengthens.

"That's my girl."

"Daddy took a video with the camera! You have to see it."

"I can't wait."

She means it.

But even as the words leave her lips, a stabbing pain rips through her chest, stealing her breath. Her eyes roll back for a second as she gasps, fingers tightening in the bedsheets.

Tegan sees it immediately.

"Mommy?" Her voice trembles.

Mirabella forces her features to smooth out, blinking away the tears of pain, unwilling to let her daughter see the truth. She meets Tegan's wide, worried eyes and smiles softly, reaching up with weak, trembling fingers to cup her cheek.

"I'm okay, mija. Just a little tired."

Tegan doesn't look convinced, but she doesn't press.

Instead, she takes her mother's hand in both of hers, cradling it carefully as if afraid she'll break. Mirabella's heart aches at the sight. Her daughter should never have to be this careful with her.

She inhales slowly, regaining control, and gently squeezes Tegan's hands.

"So tell me, mija. What's next?"

Tegan grins, eager to share.

"I'm gonna be a Grand Prix show jumper, a dressage rider, and a rodeo queen! Daddy says I can do anything if I work hard enough." She puffs up proudly. "The Olympics, Momma! What do you think?"

Mirabella laughs softly—weak, but genuine.

"Just like your father." Her voice is barely audible, more to herself than to Tegan.

Tegan's brows knit together.

"What, Momma?" Mirabella shakes her head slightly, smiling at her daughter as if she's trying to memorize every feature, every dimple, every speck of green in her eyes.

She reaches up, her fingers feather-light as she tucks Tegan's hair behind her ear.

"Nothing, mi amor. I just want you to be happy."

Tegan nods quickly.

"I am, Mommy! I love riding! And I love Hershey! And I love you!"

Mirabella's eyes shine, though she blinks rapidly, as if trying to keep her tears from falling.

"Horses are a gift from God, Tegan."

Tegan nods seriously, as if she already knows. Mirabella's voice grows even softer, barely above a breath.

"What would make me happy is knowing you develop a relationship with a horse that brings out the best of both of you. Juntos."

Tegan nods enthusiastically.

"Together."

Mirabella's smile is full of something bittersweet.

"That's what truly matters. Entiendes?"

Tegan grins.

"Sí, Momma."

Mirabella nods, satisfied, and pulls her daughter close. Tegan melts into her, inhaling the scent of lavender and something faintly metallic from the hospital.

Mirabella presses a lingering kiss on the top of her head.

A single tear slips down her cheek. She releases Tegan quickly, wiping her eyes before her daughter can see. Her breath hitches, exhaustion pressing heavily against her chest.

She tries to hide it. But Tegan sees. And she knows.

"Mommy?"

Mirabella forces a reassuring smile.

"I'm just tired, mija. Can you do something for me?"

Tegan nods, eager to help.

"Go get your father for me. I want to talk to him."

Tegan frowns slightly, but nods.

"Okay, Mommy."

She hops off the bed, smoothing her breeches. She pauses at the door, glancing back.

Mirabella is still watching her. Eyes filled with an almost desperate kind of longing.

Tegan smiles, completely unaware of the moment's gravity.

"I love you, Mommy."

Mirabella's smile trembles, her voice breaking.

"I love you too, mija."

Tegan skips out the door. The hospital room falls silent. Mirabella closes her eyes.

A single tear escapes, sliding down her pale cheek.

The heart monitor beeps.

Once.

Twice.

Then—

Flatline.

Tegan opens her eyes and looks at Mirabella Mia. She kisses Mia's muzzle and scratches her cheek.

"I love you, Momma." She looks again at Mirabella Mia and walks toward the lighted arena.

The arena rests in silence, broken only by the rhythmic crunch of hooves pressing into soft sand. Sunlight has slipped beyond the horizon, leaving a lavender dusk brushed with fading strokes of amber. The vast sky holds its breath—waiting.

Carson stands in the center of the ring, lunge whip in hand, his focus unwavering as he watches Remington. The striking black-faced gelding paws the ground playfully, ears flicking forward and back, deliberately ignoring him. Carson smirks, recognizing the mischief in the horse's stance.

"Alright, big guy, let's dance."

He steps toward Remington's haunches, gently urging him to shift. Remington lifts his head, eyes sharp with curiosity. He turns his nose toward Carson but remains firmly planted. Carson chuckles under his breath. He doesn't push. He doesn't demand. Instead, he does what he's always done—he gives. A moment. A breath. A chance for trust to build. He backs away, slow and deliberate, and holds out his palm. Remington hesitates, considering. Then, ever so carefully, he steps forward. Carson grins, rewarding him with a soft pat and a treat. They repeat the process. Step, reward. Step, reward. And then—something clicks. Remington follows him without hesitation. Carson turns right; Remington mirrors him. Carson turns left; Remington shadows his every move. When Carson halts, Remington stops just beside him, ears pricked, waiting. The bond is forming. Not one of dominance, but of partnership. Of trust. Carson exhales, pressing his forehead briefly against the gelding's.

"You miss her, don't you?" he murmurs.

Remington nudges him in response, as if to say: "You have no idea."

Carson knows. Missy has been running from herself, from the very thing that made her heart beat. And in training Remington, Carson can feel the longing she left behind. The way the horse searches for her, even now, even in the hands of another.

But she'll be back. Carson saw it in her eyes today—the flicker of something she wasn't ready to name yet, but it was there. He gives Remington one last pat and leads him toward the gate where Tegan and Rusty are waiting.

She's silent as she watches him, something unreadable in her expression. Together, they walk toward the barn, the quiet stretching between them. Not awkward, not uncomfortable—just full.

Rusty doesn't need to be led. He simply pushes his stall door open with his nose, enters, and begins pulling lazily at the flake of hay waiting for him. Carson guides Remington into his stall and secures the latch. The stallion nickers softly before lowering his head to eat, his breathing deep and content. Carson watches him for a long moment, the warmth of satisfaction settling deep in his chest.

Then—Tegan's hand is in his. He doesn't remember reaching for it, but somehow, it fits so naturally in his grasp. Her fingers are strong, yet delicate, calloused in places from years of reins and work, but soft where it matters. They walk in step, hands entwined, toward the empty canopy.

She breaks the silence first.

"Good work today." Her voice is soft, but firm. Carson glances at her, squeezing her hand lightly.

"You too."

A beat of silence.

Then—

"You're training Remington for Missy, aren't you?"

It's not a question. Carson nods, already knowing she sees right through him.

"Yeah."

She exhales, something caught between relief and sorrow.

"She'll be back," he adds, his voice sure. Tegan swallows, looking away. She wants to believe him. Needs to believe him. Because if Missy comes back, maybe all isn't lost after all. Maybe—just maybe—the things that matter don't have to slip away forever. Carson stops walking and turns to face her. He reaches out, fingers brushing against her cheek, tucking a stray wisp of hair behind her ear. His touch is warm, grounding, steady. Tegan closes her eyes for a brief second, leaning into it without thinking. When she opens them, Carson's gaze is already waiting, already searching.

She inhales sharply, unsure, caught between wanting and resisting.

"I will never sell Mirabella Mia or Luke 631."

Her voice is fierce, unshakable, like a vow whispered into the universe itself.

Carson smiles—not because he doubted her, but because he recognizes the fire in her. The same fire that pulled him to her in the beginning. He leans in slowly, giving her every chance to pull away.

She doesn't.

And then—his lips meet hers. It's gentle at first, hesitant, a soft question rather than a demand. But the moment she responds—arms wrapping around his neck, pressing closer—everything else disappears. The night presses in around them, wrapping them in the quiet hush of crickets and the distant nickering of horses. The stars above blink like silent witnesses, watching as fate unfolds. Carson pulls her closer, his hands settling at the curve of her waist, memorizing the way she feels against him.

For what feels like an eternity and no time at all, they lose themselves in the moment.

Then, as if sensing the dangerous edge of something too intense, Carson is the one to pull away first. His forehead rests lightly against hers, their breaths mingling in the cool night air. He smiles lazily, like a man who just found something he didn't know he'd been looking for.

"I better get going," he murmurs, reluctant.

Tegan is still catching her breath, still trying to piece together what just happened—what it means.

She steps back, blinking, gathering herself.

"Yeah. Early day tomorrow."

Carson hesitates, then takes a step backward, giving her space. He watches as she turns and walks away; her figure disappearing into the night, her hair catching the starlight like a whisper of something ethereal.

"Goodnight, Tegan."

The wind nearly carries his words away. He turns and strides toward his trailer, pulse pounding, the memory of her still burning against his skin.

Fate grips him.

Maybe this path always waited for them.

A Winning Weekend

T he Mexican tavern pulses with life, its stucco walls painted in warm sunset tones—deep reds, golden yellows, and earthy oranges. Inside, countless bottles of tequila and mezcal line the bar, and the scent of lime and salt lingers in the air. Laughter and conversation bounce off the walls, a mixture of Spanish and English blending into the melody of the night.

Outside, on the open-air patio, the real magic unfolds.

String lights zigzag overhead, casting a golden glow over tables draped in festive red, green, and white tablecloths. The air is thick with the scent of carne asada sizzling on the grill, fresh tortillas warming over an open flame, and the unmistakable sweetness of cinnamon from churros frying nearby.

A live band plays a lively mix of cumbia and salsa, their instruments blending seamlessly with the laughter and clinking of glasses. The worn wooden dance floor, scuffed from generations of celebratory feet, invites anyone with rhythm in their soul to move.

Tonight, the Valley Vista Ranch crew takes over one of the longest tables, pitchers of beer and baskets of chips and salsa scattered between them.

At the head of the table, Oscar, already a few drinks in, rises to his feet, his expression smug and celebratory.

He lifts his mug high, beer nearly sloshing over the edge.

"To Señora Tegan!" he bellows, commanding the attention of their group. "Thank you for making this weekend one of the most fun and profitable weekends this old Mexican has ever had the honor of attending."

Laughter ripples through the table.

Oscar turns to Tegan, his usually mischievous expression softening for just a moment.

"Watching you win on Luke 631 and debut Mirabella Mia with such success—it brought back memories of the old days. Of your father." His voice dips, just slightly, with the weight of nostalgia.

He shakes it off and grins.

"So everyone, raise your glasses—to Señora Tegan, to Valley Vista Ranch, and to its incredible horses. ¡Salud!"

He downs his entire beer in one long gulp, then slams the mug onto the table with a triumphant thud.

He points at the rest of the table, challenging them to do the same.

Laughter erupts as everyone takes a more reasonable sip of their drinks.

Tegan laughs, shaking her head, but when she turns back to Carson, she gently squeezes his forearm—a fleeting but meaningful touch.

Banter, Beer, and Bad Decisions

Carson meets her gaze, searching.

"Thank you," she whispers, her voice barely audible over the music.

Carson tilts his head.

"For what?"

"For standing by me—through the chaos, when Ranger sold, when another horse came in, when Jake was... Jake." She sighs and rubs her temple. "I know it may have felt transactional, but I hope you see Valley Vista Ranch as more than just deals and money."

Carson takes a long sip of his beer before responding.

"I know. But Jake—Oscar doesn't understand him. Hell, I don't understand him."

Tegan shrugs, tearing apart a tortilla chip with unnecessary aggression.

"He was there when my father died. There were bills—so many bills. The mortgage was due, the horses needed care, and the idea of losing Valley Vista Ranch... I made decisions I wouldn't make now." She hesitates, then exhales. "Jake was a part of those decisions. He's not all bad. He just... has different priorities."

Carson leans back in his chair, considering.

"I get it. But there will come a day when his priorities go against the very core of what Valley Vista Ranch means to you. You know that."

Tegan looks away, but not before Carson catches the flicker of doubt in her eyes.

"Yes. But Carson, I feel like I owe him one more chance. Call me naïve, but I believe in second chances."

She shrugs, grabbing another nacho, but before she can pop it into her mouth, Carson leans in, his lips brushing against her ear.

His voice is low, filled with something unspoken.

"That's what I love about you."

Tegan's breath catches.

She turns toward him, their faces inches apart, the air between them charged with something undeniable.

Then—

"What's going on over here?"

Oscar's booming voice slices through the moment.

Tegan jerks back, laughter bubbling up despite herself. Oscar grins like the Cheshire Cat.

"You owe me, Señora Tegan."

She tilts her head.

"What?... Now?"

Oscar nods emphatically and extends his hand.

With a dramatic sigh, Tegan takes it, letting him pull her to her feet. Ever the gentleman, Oscar guides her toward the dance floor, winking at the DJ.

The music shifts. Horns blare. The unmistakable voice of Celia Cruz bursts through the speakers. Tegan's entire face lights up.

"Azúcar!" the crowd roars in unison, honoring the legendary queen of salsa.

Tegan laughs, tilting her head back in delighted remembrance.

And then—she dances.

Oscar leads her into multiple spins, her floral-embroidered top lifting to reveal the curve of her waist, hugging her body-hugging jeans and ankle cowboy boots. Her long raven hair whips around with each turn, moving like a living thing, catching the golden glow of the string of lights.

The other dancers slow their own movements to watch her.

But none more than Carson. His eyes never leave her, drinking in every movement, every sway, every unrestrained moment of joy. He barely notices the tap on his shoulder.

"Car?"

Bethany and Janet stand before him, grinning.

He turns, snapped out of his daze and stands.

"What are you guys doing here?" He deflects.

"I came about a horse. Bethany showed Winnie in a couple of classes. Did well, I might add. And of course I couldn't let another day go by without checking on my old buddy, Car."

Janet punches Carson in the arm in the time-honored repartee between long-time friends. Carson mockingly rubs his shoulder and gestures to two chairs, and they all sit.

Janet looks out at the dance floor and arches a brow.

"Well, well, well. Carson Peterson, love-struck fool. I never thought I'd live to see the day."

Carson groans, running a hand through his hair.

Bethany gasps dramatically.

"Wait—are you blushing? Oh my God, Janet, look at this."

Janet leans in, gasping mockingly.

"I never thought I'd witness a miracle. Fancy me a matchmaker to the unflappable Carson Peterson."

Carson grumbles into his beer.

"You two are insufferable."

Bethany nudges him playfully.

"Oh, c'mon. Spill. What's she like?"

They both stare at him, waiting, expectant. Carson takes a long drink, then exhales.

"She's... amazing. She's fierce. I've never met anyone like her. I can't stop thinking about her. Rusty loves her."

Janet and Bethany exchange a victorious high-five. Janet leans back, satisfied.

"That's all I needed to know."

Bethany grins.

"He's a goner."

Carson rolls his eyes, but his gaze drifts back to Tegan.

He doesn't know what this is.

But he knows one thing for certain—it's only the beginning.

Oscar spins Tegan and then dips her as the song finishes. The audience claps to the song and to the tour de force dancing of Oscar and Tegan. Tegan throws her arms around Oscar and he picks her up off the dance floor. He gently sets her down and delivers his typical sage advice.

"Don't forget who you are, Señora. Where you come from." He squeezes both her hands and gives her a brotherly kiss on the cheek.

"I won't. You won't let me." She takes his arm and warmly shoves him with her shoulder. He guides her off the dance floor to their table.

"Looks like Señor Carson has some guests. I will leave you to it." He lets go of her hand and heads to the other side of the table. Janet stands and extends her hand out to Tegan. Tegan ignores her hand and hugs her.

"Janet. It's so good to see you. I'm so glad you're here. I've been meaning to call you and thank you for sending Carson my way." She fervently says.

"It was hard to part with good ol' Car here, but I'm glad that you've put him to good use." Janet playfully elbows Carson. Tegan glances over to Carson, who nods his head toward a wide-eyed speechless Bethany. Tegan smiles and gives Bethany her full attention.

"Hi, I'm Tegan Miller. You're Bethany, right? Carson has told me so much about you." Tegan extends her hand out to Bethany. Bethany just stares back at her like a frozen statue. Janet elbows her. She blinks, takes Tegan's hand, and shakes it.

"You're Tegan Miller. Olympic... Gold... Medalist... I'm shaking your hand." She states the obvious.

"Why don't we all sit?" Carson interjects to save Bethany from further humiliation. They all sit and Tegan fills her glass with beer. She takes a sip.

"Bethany. I'm a horse crazy girl, just like you. Okay?" She takes Bethany's hand and squeezes it.

"Okay. But will you sign my baseball cap, anyway? I brought a marker." Bethany takes off her hat revealing bright pink hair and pulls a felt marker out of her jean pocket. She stealthily slides the items to Tegan. Tegan obligingly signs the baseball cap and hands it back to Bethany.

"Thank you, Tegan. I've always wanted to meet you. I've seen all of your videos. The way you won the Gold Medal at the Olympics is burnt into my mind. I want to ride like you someday. Maybe I'll have a horse like Paratrooper." Bethany admires her baseball cap and then places it back on her wild pink hair.

"Tell me about Winston." Tegan asks like a doctor taking a patient's history.

"Winston? He can jump the moon, but Car was adamant about taking my time with him. I was mad at first, but it's done wonders for his confidence. We won the green jumpers' division this weekend." Bethany proudly responds.

"Congratulations. I would love to meet him and see you ride. Please bring Winston to Valley Vista Ranch anytime. You could meet Paratrooper if you'd like. And you too, Janet. I haven't seen you in way too long. It would be good for Carson and Rusty to have some old friends stop by," Tegan says.

"Really? We would love that. Won't we, Janet." Bethany looks pleadingly at Janet.

"Sounds good to me. Would love Car to look at my new barrel racer if that's okay with you, Teegs?"

"Would love to have you guys. Just call me and we'll arrange it."

"Well. We better get going. Want to miss that traffic heading back... Carson." Janet and Bethany stand. Carson stands and Bethany jumps into his arms and whispers in his ear.

"I really like her, Car. Can't wait to see you and Rusty again. Love you." She holds on as though Carson is being shipped to war overseas. Carson gently unfolds her arms and plays with her pink hair. She playfully slaps his hand away.

"Pink... Keep up the good work with Winston. I'm proud of you." Bethany steps back and Janet bear hugs Carson and whispers in his ear.

"Don't screw this up." She slaps him on the shoulder and then quickly exits with Bethany. Carson looks over to Tegan, shrugs his shoulders, and sits.

"You just made Bethany's year. Thank you." He says. Tegan looks off into the distance in contemplation.

"I used to be that dreamy-eyed girl. So much simpler back then. No worries except for riding and getting better. No mortgage payments. Clients. Responsibilities. Just being a kid chasing big dreams." She shakes her head, takes a drink from her beer, and looks intently at Carson.

"We need to talk." She says in an authoritative tone. He stands, walks toward her, and extends his hand.

"Dance with me."

"Carson, I don't—"

"Please." He takes her hand and escorts her to the dance floor. A country song finishes as they enter the dance floor. He embraces her and the song "In Your Eyes" by Peter Gabriel plays over the speakers. He smiles and guides her in a slow two-step like dance. Tegan's emerald eyes glisten under the string of lights. Their eyes meet.

"Valley Vista Ranch means everything to me. I can't afford to lose my focus. So many people are counting on me. I don't know if I can give you what you want. What do you want?"

"I just want to dance, Tegan." Tegan pulls herself out of Carson's embrace and stands, arms folded.

"Seriously, Carson. Now that you're a part of Valley Vista Ranch, I don't want to lose that like I lost Missy. Like I lost..." A bittersweet smile crosses Carson's face, knowing and feeling her loss and fear.

"I'm not going anywhere. I'm just happy to be a part of Valley Vista Ranch, a part of your life. Don't need much, just don't want to lose this either. Day by day is all I ask, all I want." Tegan nods her head in agreement and they resume dancing. She places her head on his shoulder, closes her eyes, and loses herself in the music.

MISSY'S BACK?

An old engine rumbles through the morning air as Tegan pulls up to the office entrance in her beloved 1972 red-and-white Chevy C20 pickup. She calls her Bess—a truck that's weathered years of dust, dirt roads, and long drives across ranch land. The two-tone exterior still holds its classic charm, though sun and time have softened the red and dulled the white. Inside, the cab breathes with the scent of worn leather, motor oil, and the faint, lingering trace of her father's aftershave—a ghost she carries with her.

Tegan and her dad spent countless hours side by side under the hood, rebuilding Bess from the inside out. They reassembled the engine with calloused hands, swapped out shocks with grit and grease, replaced the brakes, and polished the chrome until it shone. Bess became more than a truck—she became their shared project, a machine forged in love, sweat, and memory.

She kills the ignition, slides out of the driver's seat, and stretches—her arms lifting toward the sky, taking in the early morning sunlight filtering through the leaves, casting long golden streaks across the gravel drive.

She turns back and pats the hood affectionately, the metal warm under her palm.

"Good morning, Bess. How's my beautiful old girl?" she murmurs. "It's gonna be a great day. Sun is shining, students to teach, horses to train. Things are finally coming together."

She smiles, but there's an ache in it, a whisper of longing for the man who had once stood next to her, hands grease-streaked, sleeves rolled up, teaching her how to listen to the hum of the engine like it was a heartbeat.

Click. Click. Click.

Seventeen-year-old Tegan bangs her head against the steering wheel.

"Not again!" she groans.

She yanks down the window, leans out, and hollers.

"Dad!"

Across the yard, Hank Miller is astride Bob, his ever-faithful old Quarter Horse.

Hearing his daughter's cry, he trots up, then swings down from the saddle with effortless ease. Bob stands patiently as Hank ties the reins to the saddle horn, reaching into his pocket for a sugar cube.

"Here you go, buddy." Hank scratches Bob's neck, chuckling when the gelding lets out a soft nicker before wandering off to graze. Tegan leans dramatically against the seat, her boots tapping against the floorboard.

"Stupid truck won't start again."

Hank smirks, knowing full well what's coming.

"Stupid, huh? Well, let's take a look at her."

Tegan huffs.

"I'm gonna be late! Can't I just take Oscar's truck?"

Hank arches a brow, his tone firm but patient.

"Now, kiddo."

Tegan groans, yanks open the door, and stomps to the front of the truck, crossing her arms tightly over her chest. Hank lifts the hood, inspecting the engine with an expert's eye.

"Engine looks good... must be the battery." He glances at her. "Did you leave the light on again, Tegan?"

Tegan shuffles her feet, avoiding his gaze.

"I... don't think so."

Hank smirks knowingly.

"This wouldn't be an issue if we just got a new truck, you know."

"New is not always better, kiddo." He leans against the truck, wiping his hands on his jeans. "Good ol' Bess has been part of this family since before you were born. You just gotta treat her with some respect."

Tegan scoffs.

"Whatever, Dad."

Hank turns to her then, serious. His gaze locks onto hers, and the teasing fades into something deeper, more meaningful.

"Promise me you'll always take care of her."

Tegan stills. The weight of his words sinks in, cutting through her frustration.

She looks up at him—her father, solid as ever, the same man who steadied her when she tripped and skinned her knees, who hoisted her onto her first pony with a laugh, who guided her small hands over Bess's steering wheel and said, *"Now, feel the road."*

Her shoulders drop. She exhales, arms falling to her sides, a familiar warmth tugging at her chest.

"Okay, Dad. I promise." She pauses, a small smile creeping in. "I probably left the light on."

Hank's face breaks into that boyish grin of his, the kind that made everything feel okay.

"Good. I'll get Oscar to give her a jump."

He whistles, and Bob's ears flick toward him. The old gelding trots over, and Hank swings effortlessly into the saddle, tipping his hat toward Tegan.

"Try to be more careful, kiddo. Bess is family."

With that, he canters off toward the barn, leaving Tegan standing there.

She watches him go, then turns back to the truck.

With a sigh, she hops up onto the hood, lying back against the metal, staring up at the sky. For a long moment, she just breathes.

Then she rests a hand against the hood and whispers.

"I guess it's just you and me for a while."

And from that day forward, she kept her promise.

Carson rides up to the truck mounted on his trusted steed, Rusty, coffee and a bag of bagels in tow. He dismounts and offers the morning sustenance to Tegan.

"Good morning, Tegan." He chuckles. Tegan quickly drops her arms and straightens her shirt.

"You're here." She states the obvious and accepts the bagel and coffee. She shoves the bagel in her mouth to avoid stating another embarrassing comment.

"Thought I'd get an early start to the day. Caught another beautiful Valley Vista Ranch sunrise with Rusty and Remington." He says. She nods and smiles and turns her head towards her office and notices Missy's truck. She looks back at Carson, eyes widened in excitement and trepidation.

"She's mucking stalls and grooming horses." Carson says. Tegan rushes like a thoroughbred on a race track towards her office. Carson shakes his head and follows her.

"Tegan, wait." He exclaims.

"We need to put her on a training program as soon as possible. I've made notes on my iPad. I thought I would start her on one of the lesson horses. Then—"

"She's not ready. She doesn't want to ride." Tegan opens the office door; it screeches in protest and enters. She heads to her desk and pulls out her iPad. She clicks on the screen and scans her notes.

"What? That's crazy. Of course she wants to ride. She just doesn't know it yet. The sooner we get her on a horse, the better." She sits at her desk and clicks on her schedule.

"I have a busy day today, but I can start her training after four. Yes. That'll work. I'll put her on Hemingway."

"I don't think that's a good idea, Tegan." Carson softly says.

"You don't think it's a good idea! What? Now you're an expert on all things, Missy. I've been training her since she was in jodhpurs! How dare you tell me how— "

Tegan stops suddenly, eyes blazoned in anger as Missy enters.

"Hey, Teegs."

"Hey, kiddo. It's good to have you back. Carson and I were just talking about—"

"About that, Teegs. Is it okay if I shadow Carson?" She gathers all her courage, but her voice comes out barely above a whisper.

"But I have a program..."

Tegan points to her iPad.

"Teegs, please. I need..."

Missy looks pleadingly into Tegan's eyes. Tegan hugs her iPad and then shoves the iPad into the back of her pants.

"Of course, whatever you need, Missy. I should get to morning lessons. Don't want to be late." She glares at Carson, meekly smiles at Missy, and rushes out the door, leaving her coffee and half-eaten bagel on her desk.

"Sorry, Carson. I didn't mean to cause trouble."

"You didn't. That wasn't about you." He affectionately smiles at Missy.

"Ready?"

"Sure. What's first?" She asks with trepidation. Carson winks at her.

"Follow me."

Carson and Missy walk up to an arena filled with cones, barrels, poles, and a big, multicolored circus-like ball. Missy apprehensively looks at Carson, halting like a frightened horse outside the arena.

"What's all this?" She asks. Carson smiles, places his thumb and index finger between his lips, and whistles. Rusty gallops into the arena and makes a beeline to the multicolored ball. He grabs the ball, throws it up into the air, and catches it between his front legs upon landing. Carson heads to Rusty and scratches his neck.

"Show off. You know this ball is for Remington." Carson chides. Rusty be-grudgingly kicks his beloved ball to Carson. Carson sets the ball aside and feeds Rusty a sugar cube.

"We talked about this. I need you to show Missy here the ropes." Carson points to Missy. Rusty trots over to Missy and nickers. Missy cautiously walks into the arena and stands next to Rusty. Rusty wraps his head around her torso in a reassuring hug. A tear filled Missy hugs Rusty back.

"Looks like I'm leaving you in expert hands." Carson says. "I have a lesson to teach in a few, so I'll check on you guys later."

"I told you I didn't want to ride." Missy adamantly says.

"Whether you ride Rusty is between you and Rusty. I only ask you to listen to him. He's a skilled teacher." Carson chuckles to himself and heads out of the arena.

"But there's no bridle! No saddle!" She exclaims, frustrated. Carson continues out of the arena and waves with his back towards them. Missy stomps her foot and then turns and faces Rusty.

"Well, Rusty. I guess it's just you and me. So sage horse, what ya got?" She rolls her eyes. Rusty trots away from her to the first obstacle of cones and performs a perfect serpentine around each cone, finishing in a perfect square halt at the end. He performs a turn on the haunches and faces her, shaking his head up and down in a challenge.

"You've got to be kidding me." She says. She mimics the trot and heads down the obstacle. Midway through, Missy knocks down a cone. She finishes the course, halts and turns, facing the direction she came from. Rusty snorts and trots away from her.

"What?" she asks, frustrated. Rusty picks up the knocked down cone and places it back into position. He trots back to her and nudges her with his muzzle to continue. Her eyes widen in disbelief at Rusty's critique. Embarrassed, Missy performs the serpentine mindful not to disturb Rusty's precious cones. She finishes the task and smiles triumphantly, raising her arms up in the air. Rusty canters toward her and playfully halts in front of her, spraying her with footing. Missy giggles like a child with her new best friend and wipes the footing off her clothing.

They continue in unison, with Rusty leading the way through their exercises around the cones. He picks up a canter and heads to the poles. Missy dutifully follows and canters like a child at play over the poles. Rusty halts and spins on his haunches. Missy emulates his behavior and spins. She throws her arms up into the air in absolute glee. Dizzy, Missy falls on her butt. She tosses her head back, laughing hysterically. Rusty walks over to her, lowers his head, and nuzzles her cheek. She hugs Rusty's neck and closes her eyes, tears streaming down her face.

"I haven't had this much fun in such a long time. I forgot why I loved this so much. Thank you, Rusty... You are a skilled teacher." She looks up at him in reverence and affection. She nimbly stands and dusts her breaches off. Rusty shakes the dust off his coat, and bows. Missy cocks her head and shrugs her shoulders.

"Why not?" She asks herself. She mounts Rusty, grabs his mane, and pats his withers. Rusty gently stands and pricks his ears back towards her, patiently awaiting her command.

"Be gentle. Okay, buddy?" She gently presses her calves against his sides and relaxes her hips. Rusty pricks his ears forward and walks on. She moves with his four beat rhythm and carefully guides him to the cones. They perform the serpentine exercise and she halts him at the other end.

"Not bad. Wanna try it at the trot?" She turns him on the haunches and proceeds down the exercise in a trot, halting at the other end. She lets go of Rusty's mane and pumps her fist.

"Yes!" she exclaims. Rusty turns his head and nibbles her boot, as if sharing the victory. Letting go of his mane, she rests her hands on her thighs, shoulders loose, fully at ease. A soft click from her cheek sends them trotting forward again. They glide around the arena, leg yielding left, then right. A quiet smile lifts her lips.

"You sure are one of the best horses I've ever ridden. I'm surprised Carson let me ride you." She says. Rusty halts and snorts. She scratches his neck.

"Sorry, Rusty. I'm surprised you let me ride you." She laughs. Rusty nickers and shakes his head 'yes'. Missy looks out of the arena over to the resplendent green pastures replete with horses grazing underneath trees dancing in the breeze in harmony with the birdsong and other wildlife. She looks up to the cloudless sky, allowing the sunbeams to kiss her cheeks. A tear of remembrance flows down her face.

"I love it here." She whispers as she wipes her face and pats Rusty's neck. She grasps his mane.

"Let's try some canter. Canter, Rusty." She commands.

Rusty strikes off in a slow lopey canter, head low to the ground. Missy relaxes her hips and lower back and hips easily flow to his rhythm - they move as one unit around the arena. She urges him to go forward, and he eagerly complies. Missy turns him towards the poles and releases her arms out to the side like a bird in flight. They canter the poles like partners who've been together for years.

Carson enters the arena astride Remington, carrying a hack-a-more over his shoulder. He halts him just inside the arena to observe Missy canter Rusty over the poles. He smiles to himself and pats Remington's neck. With a determined look on her face, Missy grabs Rusty's mane and maneuvers around the first barrel like a seasoned pro. They gallop off to the second barrel and smoothly round it and head back towards Carson and Remington. She easily halts him in front of Carson and hugs and kisses Rusty. Rusty lowers his body and Missy dismounts. Missy walks over to Carson - a triumphant smile on her face.

"He's a Casanova, isn't he? You give him that much attention; I don't think he'll let me back on." Carson winks at Missy and they both laugh. Missy points to the hack-a-more.

"What's that for?" She asks.

"I was hoping you'd help me take Remington around the property. The hack-a-more is for you and Rusty. Wasn't expecting you to go bareback and without a bridle for the next exercise." He says. Missy, unsure, backs away.

"You don't have to. I just thought that you'd might like to join me. And Remington would benefit from a trail ride. Two birds, one hack-a-more, so to speak." Rusty walks over to Missy and nudges her with his muzzle.

"Rusty thinks you're ready. I wouldn't insult him if I were you." Carson chides.

"Okay. Okay. You two sure are manipulative." Missy replies sarcastically. Missy walks over to Carson and collects the hack-a-more. Hack-a-more in place, they head out of the arena into the pastures - the heart of Valley Vista Ranch. Side-by-side they remain silent as they traverse the hills and valleys. Missy is first to break the silence with a burning question.

"How did you know that I'd get on Rusty?" She asks.

"I didn't. I just hoped that you might. And... Rusty is a smooth operator for getting what he wants." He responds.

"He sure is." Missy giggles. "He's such an amazing horse."

"He is. But to me, he's more than an amazing horse. He's more than a friend or even a family member. He's a part of me and I'm a part of him."

"Do you think Remington could be like Rusty?" Missy desperately gazes into Carson's eyes for an easy way out of her pain.

"No. And I wouldn't want him to be. You see, Missy, each horse, like humans, is an individual being with specific needs and personality traits. The point is to understand and accept them for who they are. The more you give of yourself to any horse, the more you'll receive. Trust me... Do you think Paratrooper is anything like Rusty? Nope. But to me, he's the most amazing horse on this property. Even Rusty thinks so. And that's because of Tegan. There's a part of her in that horse and a part of Chewy in her. Understand?" He halts Remington. Missy halts Rusty. Carson looks at Missy.

"I don't think I could ever get back on Remington, Carson." Missy sadly admits.

"Doesn't matter. What's important is that you and Remington repair the pain between the two of you. You need to forgive him and yourself for what happened." Carson gently smiles at Missy and lets her ponder his comments. They continue on in silence down the valley.

Tegan astride Paratrooper gallops over the hill. She guides him over a log. He easily handles the log and shakes his head, excited to be back with his partner in crime. They head to the edge of Miller's pond. She dismounts Chewy, kisses his cheek, and sits in the grass. Chewy nickers, drops his head, and partakes in the cool water beside his beloved friend. Tegan gazes across the pond at the butterflies fluttering over the Monet-esque water lilies and tall leaves of grass. A solitary tear of memory rolls down her cheek.

"You sure loved this pond. Every big moment in our lives started here... I miss you and mom so much... Missy's back. Well, kind of. She doesn't want to have anything to do with me. Don't blame her. It was my fault... 'You're not doing it right, kiddo'... I don't know what I'm doing, Dad. I'm so lost... Carson. He's amazing. I want him in my life, but what if he wants what you wanted... I've worked so hard to get Valley Vista Ranch back. I can't go back to worrying about the mortgage every day. I just can't." She buries her face in her hands. Chewy walks over and rests his chin on Tegan's shoulder. She caresses his cheek in response.

"Don't worry, Chewy. I'm okay." She says. Over the horizon, she notices two figures shaded by the sun approaching her direction. She quickly stands to get a better view of the riders. As they approach, she realizes that it's Carson and Missy. Missy astride Rusty, no less. Her heart leaps with joy.

"She's riding." She whispers. Missy and Carson halt in front of Tegan.

"Hey, Missy." Tegan says.

"Hey." Missy responds like a total stranger. An awkward silence envelopes the air. Missy, concerned with what to do next, looks over at Carson for guidance.

"I'll give you ladies some privacy." Carson tips his cowboy hat and canters off with Remington.

"Carson!" Missy exclaims in annoyance. Carson waves his hand with his back towards them.

"I hate it when he does that." They both proclaim in frustration. They look at each other and giggle at their mutual Carson revelation.

"Join me?" Tegan asks. Missy nods her head and dismounts Rusty. Rusty nickers and heads over to Chewy; they groom each other. Tegan and Missy sit along the edge of the pond in silence, eyes fixed on the abundance of life within and beside the pond.

"My father loved this pond. "

Tegan sighs and tosses a pebble into the pond. A cascade of ripples flow from the impact, sending the butterflies in flight hovering over the lilies.

"When I was a little girl, he told me that this pond was magical and that I could always come here for answers if I listened closely with all my heart. 'Just throw a pebble in, kiddo, and watch the ripples.' Kind of wishing well-truth sayer, I guess. Till this day, I believe it. So much so that I spread my dad's ashes here, hoping he would speak to me. Silly, I know. But I made all my important decisions here." Missy looks over at Tegan.

"You miss him."

"Every day." Tegan responds without hesitation.

"He always knew what to do. What to say. Me. Not so much... I'm sorry about what happened with Remington. I should have— "

"It was an accident." Missy states, surprised at the surety of her answer. Tegan wraps her arm around Missy's shoulder and pulls her in close. Missy tilts her head onto Tegan's shoulder, tears streaming down her face.

"I've gone over what happened with Remi again and again. Blamed myself for what happened. Blamed you. Blamed Remi. I'm tired of feeling this way. I'm scared that Remington won't forgive me and that... Never mind. I just can't, Tegan."

"Listen to me. I don't care if you don't want to ride Remington or if you never want to jump again."

"Really. But what about our plan?" She asks, unconvinced.

"If there is anything that life with horses has taught me is that plans change all the time, Missy. And I've come to realize that I'm okay with that. I've been so worried about having a plan for everything. Everything being in order. Every day set from morning till sunset. I lost sight of what really matters to me. These small moments with you, with the horses. So... I just hope that you stay here at Valley Vista Ranch and find joy again with horses. You're the best rider I've seen in a long time. Remember that, okay?" Tegan squeezes Missy's shoulder and kisses the side of her head.

"You really think I'm that good?" Missy asks in disbelief.

"Yep. But it doesn't matter if I believe it. You have to, kiddo." Tegan stands and whistles over to Chewy. Chewy trots over to Tegan while Rusty continues grazing.

"I better get back. You're welcome to join me, but I think you should spend some time at the magical pond." Tegan winks and smiles mischievously at Missy, mounts Chewy, and canters off. Missy sits back down, grabs a pebble, and tosses it into the pond. She smiles to herself and whispers.

"Ripples."

GOOD EVENING

A blanket of stars spills across the sky, casting a silver glow over the barn roof as Carson moves quietly down the aisles, boots brushing against hay-strewn concrete. The evening hush settles deep—lessons wrapped, lights dimmed, horses lost in the rhythm of dinner. The only sounds are the soft rustle of flakes in feeders and the occasional satisfied snort.

Carson turns into the Misfit Horse Brigade aisle, the most colorful stretch of the barn. Each stall bursts with personality—triumphs and tender moments captured in mismatched displays. Olivia and Max's stall beams with pride. Ribbons of every color dangle from hooks. Live-action shots of Max clearing jumps midair frame one side, while printed selfies with Olivia's grinning face line the other. Gold glitter spells out "Team Max" above the water bucket, and a giant bedazzled red heart shines on the stall door.

He chuckles softly and moves on.

Midway down the row, a fourth-place ribbon shimmers under a strip of battery-powered fairy lights. A hand-drawn crayon masterpiece hangs beneath it—Alexa's scrawled vision of Wally mid-jump, his legs uneven, his tail wild and a beaming stick figure with pigtails on his back. Taped neatly beside it, the words "For Mr. Carson" stop him. He leans in, opens the card, and reads:

Dear Mr. Carson,

Thank you for teaching me and Wally.

You and Wally are my best friends.

I hope to ride like you someday.

Love, your best friend,

Alexa

P.S. Please feed Wally some cookies. He likes them a lot. They're in my tack box. You can feed some to Rusty too.

Carson blinks, lips pressing into a quiet smile. He folds the card gently, presses it against his chest, and lets the moment settle in his bones. Then he heads to Alexa's tack box, opens the lid, and finds a zip-top bag marked "Wally's Cookies–Hands Off!" with a heart drawn in pink marker.

He kisses at Wally. The chunky gelding lifts his hay-dusted muzzle, ears pricked, and lets out a soft nicker that rumbles in his throat. Carson offers the treat, and Wally snatches it eagerly, crumbs spraying, eyes shining.

Carson chuckles, slips a few more cookies into his pocket, and turns toward Rusty's stall, the warmth of the card still tucked close to his chest.

Impatient for his friend's company, Rusty unlatches his stall door and heads over to Carson. He turns down the Misfit Horse Brigade aisle and acknowledges the whinnies and nickers of his fellow four legged barn mates. He inhales; cookies are in his best friend's pocket. Mission accepted. Rusty quickens his pace and approaches Carson. He nips at Carson's pocket and Carson hands him a couple of cookies. Mission accomplished. Rusty nickers in approval to the tasty morsel. Carson takes a bite of the remaining cookie and feeds the rest to Rusty.

"Not bad. A little much on the molasses, don't you think?" Carson chuckles and pats Rusty's forehead. They move down the aisle, inspecting each stall and tending to every horse with exacting care, following Valley Vista Ranch's standards to the letter. Rusty paws the ground and snorts at a misplaced pair of bell boots and hair brushes on the aisle floor. Carson obediently places the boots and brushes on the shelf in their proper place.

"You're getting more like her by the day, buddy," Carson rebukes. Rusty vehemently shakes his head 'yes.' Carson laughs and they continue towards Mirabella Mia's stall. Rusty pauses at Mirabella's stall. He squares off in front of the stall, signaling to Carson that he'd like a moment alone with his beloved mare. Inside, Mirabella lies asleep with her legs neatly tucked underneath her torso, nose caressing the ground, appearing as if she were the last of the mythical unicorns sans the sacred horn. Carson leaves his friend to fawn over Mirabella and makes his way toward Remington's stall.

Nestled underneath a blanket lies Missy asleep on a makeshift cot beside Remington's stall. Beads of sweat form on Missy's forehead as she squirms from a nightmare. Remington pokes his head out of his stall and nuzzles Missy's cheek to soothe her. She sighs and relaxes back to a REM induced sleep.

"Love you, Remi." She whispers and a child-like smile reminiscent of her horse obsessed days with her Remington appears on her face. Remington nickers in response, hopeful that his friend will come back to him. Carson caresses Remington's forehead.

"Give her time, Remi. She still loves you." Carson whispers. Carson adjusts the horse blanket covering Missy and leaves her. He walks to the end of the aisle and turns off the lights.

"Good night." He whispers and continues to the cabin on foot to the symphonic melody of crickets and bird call - the glimmer of the stars guiding his way.

Lights shine through the cabin windows. The sound of a truck engine disrupts Carson's slumber. He leaps out of bed dressed only in boxers. Fear captures his countenance as he hurriedly throws on a pair of socks, jeans, t-shirt, and boots. Have one of the horses colicked? He just did a night check an hour ago. Didn't he? Rusty. Remington. A multitude of thoughts flood through his mind. Deep breath. He'll know soon enough what issue he must face and fix. Running a hand through his hair, he grabs his cowboy hat from the hook on the wall. Charging toward the front door, he knocks over a lamp in his haste.

Tegan's truck barrels down the road towards the cabin. The truck lights bounce up and down as the tires maneuver the creases of the dirt road. She looks in her rear-view mirror - a sleepless green eyed reflection with wild loose hair stares back at her. She looks back down the road towards the cabin. The lights of the cabin turn on. Her heart skips a beat. She slams the brakes just outside the cabin; the truck lunges forward in protest, spreading a cloud full of dust. She leaps out of the truck, barefoot, in a formfitting white cotton tank top and baggy yoga style pajama pants, and runs toward the base of the stairs. She halts at the sight of Carson standing on the porch, gazing hungrily down at her. Her heart quickens. They stare at one another for several heartbeats. His gaze captures how the moonlight creates a silhouette of her body, accenting her nipples through her white tank top. She blinks first; her breath caught in her throat.

"You were right. Right about Missy." She says breathlessly.

"So were you." He responds and smiles, his heart full of love. She runs up the stairs and leaps into his arms, feverishly kissing him. He responds, wrapping his arms around her, stroking her hair and back. He carries her into the cabin.

Tegan's gaze lingers on Carson's strong, sculpted frame as she lifts his cowboy hat from his head, setting it gently on the chair beside the bed. The room is cast in the soft glow of the ceiling fan's dim light, accentuating the warm, familiar space. Though still modest in decoration, the room holds pieces of their shared history—a king-sized wooden four-poster bed dressed in crisp white linens, a single hand-stitched pillow featuring a horse's head edged with delicate leather fringe, and her father's old trunk resting at the foot of the bed, its secrets safely locked away. A recent addition now sits on the oak nightstand—a framed picture of Carson and Rusty, a quiet testament to the life they've built together.

With a slow, lingering touch, she slides her hands under his shirt, lifting it over his head. The fabric slips to the floor like a whisper. Her fingers trace along his chest, feeling the warmth of his skin, the steady rise and fall of his breath. He exhales, his lips curling into a quiet smile before he leans down to meet her in a deep, unhurried kiss. The world outside fades away as they lose themselves in each other.

Carson eases back, his eyes shining with something deeper than desire—something unspoken but understood. "My turn," he murmurs, his voice hushed and full of promise.

He trails his fingers along her shoulders, taking his time as he lifts her tank top away, revealing the delicate curves of her form. He cups her face, pressing soft kisses along her jawline before moving to her neck, savoring every inch of her. His hands travel downward, their movements slow, reverent, as he pulls her close. Lifting her into his arms, he carries her to the bed, their bodies fitting together as though they had been made for this moment.

As they move in perfect rhythm, Tegan's heart swells with something more powerful than passion—it is love, deep and unwavering. Carson knows her, every part of her, just as she knows him. Yet still, she continues to explore, tracing the lines of his body, memorizing him all over again. Her fingers brush against a faint scar on his thigh—a reminder of his past, a story she silently honors. He lets out a quiet sigh, his body responding to her every touch, every kiss.

Their connection builds like a slow-burning fire, until at last, they find themselves lost in the rush of it all. As their breathing slows, Carson rolls onto his side, reaching for her. His fingers find a stray strand of hair, tucking it tenderly behind her ear before his hand lingers against her cheek. He studies her with quiet intensity, then presses a soft kiss to her lips, lingering as though he never wants to let go.

She furrows her brow and suddenly sits up, swings her legs over the side of the bed. She reaches for her tank top and other undergarments and hurriedly dresses. Her thoroughbred-like instincts take over.

"I... I should probably," she stutters.

"Stay, Tegan." Carson whispers. She looks back at him, flushed.

"But... Everyone..." she says desperately. He extends his hand out to her.

"Stay." He repeats with a determined smile. She closes her eyes and silently laughs at herself - still the frightened straight-laced school girl. She accepts his hand and lies back next to him. He wraps his arms and legs around her, enveloping her body with his. The weight of his body creates a calming effect and her body relaxes. She closes her eyes and drifts into a much needed tranquil slumber.

Good Morning

T he smell of coffee arouses Missy from her dormancy. She blinks her eyes and strains to focus on the countenance of an annoyed Mexican head groom and barn manager. Missy yawns and sits up. She accepts the coffee from Oscar and takes a sip.

"Thank you." She says groggily, stretching her neck side to side, working out the kinks from the night before. Oscar grunts and hands her the pitch fork.

"Señora Tegan is running late. You muck and then help with the horses. Schooling day, today. Start with Maserati." Oscar says.

"But I'm only riding Rusty for now." She replies, eyes widened in fear. Oscar folds his arms and glares at her with the unmistakable 'You're doing, not complaining' look.

"Okay. Okay! Give me a few— "

"Ahora, Missy. Ahora!" Oscar grunts again, turns, and heads back to the crossties, bellowing orders to the other groomsmen. Missy jumps off the make-shift cot, folds the horse blanket, and pokes her head into Remington's stall. Remington nickers and walks towards her.

"Hey, buddy. Gotta clean your stall. And everyone else's." She places the halter over his ears, clips on the lead rope, and leads him out of his stall. She looks into Rusty's stall, empty.

"Hmm... Where's Rusty? Probably checking on the herd. Let's get moving before Oscar comes back. He's definitely not a morning person." She rolls her eyes and giggles, pets Remington's neck as they head down the aisle like old friends on a morning stroll.

Lying together, it seemed natural for him to cradle her head on his chest. They fit well together. He interlaces his hand with hers and draws it to his lips. Tegan yawns, blinks the sleepiness from her eyes, and looks up at Carson.

"Good morning." She whispers. They kiss again, and Carson gently lifts Tegan off him. He sits up and dresses.

"Hungry?" He asks. She nods her head 'yes.' He smiles and walks toward the kitchen.

"Good. Breakfast will be ready in ten to fifteen minutes."

"What you making?" She asks.

"A surprise." He winks, then heads back to the kitchen. She grunts in playful annoyance and leaps off the bed.

"I'm gonna take a shower." She yells out to Carson.

"Okay."

She towels off her hair, wraps the towel around her torso, wipes the fog off the mirror, and stares at the image of herself.

"What are you doing, Tegan?" she mutters, eyes locking with the concerned reflection staring back. Shaking off the thought, she gathers her hair and braids it quickly, tying it off with a scrunchie in one swift motion.

Stepping out of the bathroom, Tegan swings open the closet door. Carson's wardrobe greets her—cowboy shirts and English riding gear lined up with casual precision. Fingers brush over a soft plaid button-down and a worn pair of jeans, as if trying to hold on to the warmth of the night before.

She searches through the shelves, methodical and focused, until her eyes land on a neatly folded stack tucked into the far corner—her own riding attire. A sigh of relief escapes her lips.

"Thank God you're anal." She chuckles to herself. She quickly dresses and takes a deep breath in and smiles.

"Pancakes." She sighs to herself and walks towards the kitchen.

The symphonic sounds of cutlery and pans fill the air with the familiar sounds of morning breakfast. Tegan pauses in the hallway at a family picture of herself and her mom and dad astride their beloved mounts smiling for the photographer - Oscar. Tegan leans her head against the frame and closes her eyes.

"Who's ready for more pancakes?" Sings Hank Miller, draped in a well worn white apron with the words "World's Greatest Chef" inscribed in black cursive on the chest. A seven-year-old Tegan seated at a four seat round oak table top, dressed in riding clothes, hair in braided pigtails, raises her hand and sings.

"Me, Daddy!" Hank Miller flips a pancake up in the air with great panache and catches it behind his back on a plain white plate. Tegan joyfully claps in response.

"Again, Daddy!" She begs.

"Your wish is my command." Another pancake sails through the air and lands behind his back, perfectly stacked on top of the first one. He places the plate in front of Tegan like she is a guest in a five star Michelin restaurant.

"For you, Madam." He says and kisses Tegan on her forehead. Tegan hungrily snatches the jar of peanut butter off the table and smears a layer on top of her pancakes and then drizzles home made maple syrup on top. She dives into her concoction with the flourish of Hank Miller's daughter. She looks up at her father with peanut butter and maple syrup stained lips.

"That's my girl!" He laughs and continues cooking the bacon and sausages.

Mirabella sighs with displeasure and fills her daughter's glass with milk.

"Don't encourage her, Hank." She says. Tegan raises her plate to her mother.

"Try it, Mommy." She says with a wicked grin on her face. Mirabella makes a face and shakes her head.

"I'd rather have my empanada." Mirabella replies.

"C'mon, Mommy. How do you know if you don't like it if you haven't even tried it? You always say that we should be open to new things. Right?" Tegan cuts off a piece of her pancake and hands her fork to her mother. Mirabella cocks her head and then unwillingly obliges her daughter. She chews and then swallows under the curious gaze of her husband and daughter.

"What ya think?" Tegan and Hank ask at the same time. Mirabella takes a drink from her daughter's milk.

"Not bad, but I'll never understand why Americans eat desert for breakfast, especially my wild American daughter. Such a sweet tooth. I'll stick to my empanada." Mirabella kisses her daughter's forehead and sits next to her. Hank places a plate of bacon and sausages on the table and sits next to Mirabella. Hank takes Mirabella's hand, kisses it. The family of three resumes their breakfast in an idyllic silence. Mirabella looks over at Hank and winks.

"Who's going to help me turn out the horses this morning?" She asks.

"Me. Me. Me." Tegan excitedly responds.

"Good. We better get going. Finish up your pancake concoction. The horses have waited long enough."

Tegan gobbles up her breakfast and leaps out of her chair.

"Ready!" she exclaims. Mirabella and Hank laugh at their daughter's exuberance. Mirabella finishes her coffee and stands, swaying from the dizziness. She grasps the table to steady herself.

"You okay, honey." Hanks says with a worried expression on his face. Mirabella, pale from the exertion, weakly smiles back at Hank in reassurance.

"I'm fine. Just a little tired from yesterday. Come on, mi amor, the horses are waiting."

"K, Mommy." Tegan runs over to her father and jumps into his arms. She kisses his cheek.

"Bye, Daddy." Tegan canters out of the room like a young colt.

"Breakfast is ready!" Carson yells from the kitchen. Tegan takes one last look at her family picture, straightens her shirt, fixes her braid, and walks into the kitchen. The table overflows with a spread of accoutrements—pancakes, sausages, bacon, toast, eggs, bagels, and fresh fruit crowd every inch of space.

"Hungry?" He asks. Carson, dressed in Hank's old apron, places a pitcher of juice onto the table. Tegan jabs her fork into the pancakes and drops them onto her plate.

"Peanut butter?" She asks, reaching for the maple syrup.

"Sorry. But I have strawberry jam."

"No worries." She smiles to herself and blissfully slathers the maple syrup onto her pancakes. She raises her coffee cup to Carson, and like clockwork, he tops her cup. He removes his apron, folds it neatly over the oven door handle, and sits next to her.

"I wasn't sure what to make, so— "

"It's perfect." She replies, tapping her fingers on the table with a concerned look on her face. Carson gently places his hand over hers.

"They'll be fine." He smiles and loads his dish with eggs, sausages, and toast.

"It's just that I'm never— ." She shakes her head, "You're right. Everything should be fine. Between Oscar, Pedro, Jake, and Missy, they should be able to hold down the fort for a little while. Thank God, it's schooling day." She takes a hurried drink from her coffee to cover her trepidation.

"Olivia is coming after school to help school some horses. She wants to learn how to ride Remington and Bubbles." Carson says mater-o-factly. Tegan raises an eyebrow.

"Really? Not sure Missy is going to be okay with anyone other than you on Remi. And Bubbles... Well, not sure that's a good idea either."

"It'll be fine. Olivia has been doing a lot of groundwork with Bubbles and maybe Olivia will motivate Missy to get back in the saddle with Remi." Carson winks.

"Oh. I get it. Your master plan." She giggles.

"Yep. Missy has gained a lot of confidence with Rusty, so I thought we could give her a little nudge with Olivia. Can't hurt."

"Why, Mr. Carson, I didn't know you were such a manipulator." Tegan seductively chides.

"It was Rusty's idea."

"Not surprised. That horse has a way with the females. I can't keep Mirabella Mia away from him." Tegan giggles.

"Yeah, I know. I've never seen him act like that. And trust me, he's been around a lot of mares. Can you imagine a foal out of those two?" Carson shakes his head in disbelief.

"Actually, I can, and I have thought about it a lot. Rusty and Mirabella's foal. That would be remarkable." She says with child-like awe.

"But I thought Mirabella was your up and coming."

"She is, but we could always do an embryo transfer. We have suitable mares and facilities. I can make a couple of phone calls. It would be like the old days. Would make a lot of heads turn and create a scandal that would make my dad proud." She giggles and resumes her breakfast as if this was a normal topic of conversation. Carson, jaw dropped, clasps Tegan's hand.

"You'd really do it?"

"Sure. But only if you and Rusty agreed. Valley Vista Ranch could do with a little more Rusty in it." She smiles and gazes deeply into Carson's eyes.

"You've reminded me why I do all of this, why all this matters. Carson.... I love you."

"I love you, too." Carson envelopes Tegan in his arms and passionately kisses her.

Oscar finishes tacking up Maserati as Missy rounds the corner. He wipes off Maserati's nostrils with a rag. Maserati's ears perk up at the sound of Missy's footsteps.

"Hey, Masi." Missy coos as she rubs his neck. He nickers to her touch.

"Where's Rusty?" She asks.

"Where do you think? That crazy stallion is probably messing around with Mirabella. He's going to get kicked in the head if he doesn't mind himself." Oscar shakes his head.

"I was hoping... Never mind. Let's go, Maserati." Oscar hands her the reins. Her hands shake as she reaches for the reins; she pets Maserati's neck to cover up her fear. She closes her eyes, inhales deeply, and proceeds down the barn aisle. Lucky, the curious klutz that he is, pokes his head out the stall door, knocking down a rake placed beside his stall door. The rake crashes to the floor. BANG! Maserati whinnies and rears in fear, dragging Missy along with him.

"Masi!" Missy screams. Maserati runs backward, crashing into the edge of the stall door. Tears stream down Missy's face as she struggles to get Maserati under control. Without hesitation, Oscar removes the reins from Missy's hands and settles the horse down. He masterfully places him in the cross tie and gently massages his neck, whispering in his ear. Maserati's eyes soften and he drops his head. Oscar feeds him a sugar cube.

"You okay, Missy?" Oscar asks. Missy stands frozen like she's seen Medusa's head, blood drained from her face.

"Missy?" Oscar repeats, concerned. Missy looks back at him with dead eyes.

"I... I just... can't." Missy turns and runs away from Oscar.

"Missy!" He yells to get Missy's attention.

"Mierde!" Oscar grabs his phone. He grunts at the sound of Tegan's voice mail greeting.

"Señora, Tegan! Where are you? Missy no bueno. Come now!" He shoves the phone into the back pocket of his beat up wrangler jeans and whistles twice. Rusty gallops into the aisle and halts in front of Oscar. Oscar feeds him a cookie and pats him on the neck.

"Señor Carson. Now, Rusty!" He says. Rusty bolts out of the aisle towards the cabin, creating a dust cloud behind him.

Carson dips the maple syrup-stained-pancake-crumb dish into the sudsy water, washes off the remnants with a sponge, rinses, and hands it over to Tegan. Tegan dutifully dries the dish with a towel and places it in the cupboard. Side by side, they continue the ritual in silence, like an old married couple. A coffee cup. A fork. All breakfast items enter this assembly line of love with the mundane goal of clean kitchen cutlery. No more. No less. Carson leans over and kisses Tegan's cheek. Tegan playfully flicks the sudsy water at Carson, hitting him squarely on the nose, creating a Cyrano de Bergerac appearance.

"Bull's eye! I must say, Mr. Carson, I do like this alteration." She says in a cheeky British accent.

"Very funny." He responds. Tegan lovingly wipes the suds off his face and kisses him. Carson smiles down at Tegan, entranced.

"Those eyes." He whispers. He leans down again, but the familiar sound of galloping hooves suddenly interrupts him.

"Rusty?" Carson concerned looks out the kitchen window. Rusty, in a full gallop, approaches the footsteps of the cabin. He halts, whinnies, and shakes his head.

"Something's wrong." Carson says. Tegan's face blanches.

"Missy. What did I do? I should've— "

"Don't. It's not worth it." They rush to the door.

"I'll take Rusty. You take the truck." He says. Without hesitation, Carson leaps onto Rusty and gallops off. Tegan runs to her truck, rips the door open, and shoves her body into the seat. She looks over at her cell phone. A myriad of missed phone calls, texts, and voice mails cover the screen.

"Dammit." She jams the key into the ignition and skids the tires on the dirt as she backs up. She shoves the gearshift into drive and slams her foot on the gas pedal. Her cell phone buzzes. It's Oscar. She raises the cell phone to her ear, driving like a madwoman.

"I'm coming." She calmly says and hangs up the phone.

Oscar paces in front of the office swearing in Spanish. He always hated confrontations, and he knew how Señora Tegan gets when one of her family was in trouble.

'She should be here.' He looks up and then paces again. 'She's never late. Never. That iPad would never allow it. Things were so much simpler in the old days. Less horses. Less people. Less money. The money is good, but...'

He grunts to himself and continues his stress induced reflection of the current state of affairs.

'She's having an affair with that gringo, Señor Carson. I Like him, but he's put her all out of sorts. She is happier more than ever since Hank died.'

The sound of Tegan's truck barreling down the road jolts him out of his thoughts. She halts her truck like she's in a reining competition; a pool of dust flies forward. She leaps out of the truck and runs like an Olympic sprinter towards Oscar.

"What happened? Where is she? What happened?" Anxiety pours out of her as she catches her breath.

"Remington's stall. Señor Carson is with her. She was going to ride Maserati— "

"What the hell, Oscar! What were you thinking? She's not ready!" She yells in anger.

"What was I supposed to do? You weren't here! Señor Carson not here! Nobody here!" Oscar yells back. He folds his arms across his chest and stares at her. They stand face to face as if in a dual, a dual of mental strength.

"I don't have time for this. I have to fix this," Tegan grunts in anger. She walks toward the stalls. Oscar grabs her arm.

"No, Señora." Their faces inches apart, Oscar stares her down. Still infuriated with the situation, she relents, however, trusting her friend of many years.

"What horses need to be ridden?" She asks. Oscar gently smiles and places his arm around her shoulder.

"Follow me, Señora." They walk together towards the cross ties filled with horses.

Missy, wrapped up in a ball in front of Remington's stall, knees tucked into her chest, sobs into her forearms, her entire body shaking. Carson halts Rusty at the entrance of the aisle. Remington, concerned, whinnies at Rusty. Rusty nickers back, aware of his friend's distress. Carson dismounts and cautiously approaches Missy as if she were an abused stallion. Missy looks up at Carson with her tear-stained liquid blue eyes and winces.

"Go away." She says shakily. Carson pauses allowing Rusty to approach Missy. Rusty bows his head and gently nuzzles Missy's tear-stained face. Missy places her hands on Rusty's cheeks and exhales. Carson approaches Missy again and sits next to her. Missy lets go of Rusty and buries her face in her hands.

"I can't do this." She says in a choked up whisper. Carson puts his arm around her shoulder, looks up at Rusty, and nods. Rusty nickers and walks away. Missy softly sobs into his chest. He squeezes her shoulder in reassurance. She sits up, wipes her face, and looks straight ahead towards nothing.

"Masi spooked, and I panicked like a beginner who's never been around horses. I'm just so tired of being scared. I don't know who I am anymore, Carson." She says. Carson stands up, grabs Remington's halter, lead rope, and dressage whip, and enters his stall. Remington responds with a nicker, happy to be removed from the stressful situation.

"Carson?" Missy looks up at him, bewildered and annoyed. He comes out with Remington.

"Remi needs a walk. You coming?" He asks nonchalantly.

"Remi needs... Jesus, Carson! I'm not okay!" She glares up at him.

"I know. Let's go for a walk." He replies. He heads down the aisle with Remington. Missy, angry, scrambles to her feet, and rushes to Carson's side. The party of three heads out the aisle towards Miller's pond.

Carson unlatches the lead rope from Remington's halter. He pats Remington on the neck and Remington walks to the pond and casually drinks with no care in the world. He sits in the tall grass next to Missy, who stares off into the distance in thoughtful contemplation. An almost church-like atmosphere encapsulates the pond with bird-song like a choir, horses congregating like parishioners, sunlight glistening off the water, creating a mist-like holy shimmer, with Missy and Carson silently bearing witness.

"We all need our own Miller's Pond," Carson says softly. Missy breaks her trance and looks up at Carson.

"What do you mean?" She asks.

"A place filled with hope. With truth. With peace." He smiles and looks back at her.

"You know, I quit riding."

"What? No, you didn't." Missy's eyes widen in disbelief.

"Yep. For almost two years. Was in a show in Germany. Grand Prix. Olympic qualifier. So long ago, but sometimes it feels like yesterday... I had just finished the jump off. Was a clear round. In the money. Was on my horse, Lexington, waiting for the final riders to finish. A waiter popped a champagne cork. Lex want crazy and I landed on my thigh, shattering my femur. Bone fragments nicked my femoral artery. That's was it. I should've been dead right there. Hours of surgery. I was lying in the hospital bed, my entire leg in a cast, not knowing if I'd walk again. Once I got out of the hospital, I sold Lex and never looked back. Didn't even look at a horse for over a year. But the nightmares were always there."

"What changed?"

"Nothing really. I moved from job to job. Finally ended up at a ranch in Montana. An old cowboy took pity on me and started showing me stuff. I was limping pretty bad back then. Next thing I knew, I was a ranch hand. Herding cattle. Mending fences. That old cowboy saw something that I didn't see in myself. You see, horses are in my blood, Missy. And I think they're in your blood, too. So it doesn't matter if you jump or don't jump, but your life is with horses. All you need now is to make peace with that, and move forward. If you don't, what happened with Remington will always haunt you. Trust me, I know."

"Do you think I'll ever jump again?" She asks.

"I don't know. Only you can answer that. But I'll be by your side no matter what. So will Tegan."

Carson gets up and whistles. Rusty, on cue, gallops toward him and halts by the pond next to Remington. He hands the lead rope and dressage whip to Missy, walks over to Rusty, and mounts him.

"Seriously?" Missy stomps her foot, annoyed. Carson chuckles.

"You two need some alone time. Besides, Tegan will kill me if I don't get back. You know how she can get," Carson winks. Missy knowingly nods her head. Carson rubs Rusty's neck and looks back at Missy with fatherly concern and affection.

"You can't move on, Missy, unless you forgive him and forgive yourself." He clicks his lips and he and Rusty canter back to the barn. Missy, unsure of what to do next, sits on the outer edge of the pond across from Remington. She loses herself in a meditative trance watching Remington graze. He flickers his ears as flies playfully tickle him. With whip-like precision, he swats the flies away from his belly. A silky glow envelopes his frame as the high sun shines down on his majestic body. Missy sighs at his beauty. Remington's ears perk up; he raises his head, and gazes at Missy. Their eyes meet and Remington nickers. Missy smiles back at him, her heart pulsating in remembrance of their bond. Remington walks over to his best friend and lays his chin on her head. Missy giggles.

"Remi, you know your head weighs more than my entire body." She pats him on his muzzle. He removes his weighted muzzle from her head and they spend a moment in each other's presence. Missy slowly stands with the whip in her hand, leaving the lead rope on the ground. She turns and faces him; his full attention on her. She walks toward him with the whip held low, gesturing toward the ground. He responds obediently, taking steps backwards.

"Good boy." Missy sighs in relief. She directs the whip towards his haunches and he moves his haunches away from the whip in a perfect circle around her, pivoting on his front legs.

"That's it, Remi!" she exclaims. She pulls out a cookie and shows it to him. He nickers and walks toward her, relieving her of the cookie. Missy pats Remington's forehead and giggles like a little girl with her first pony. She continues working with Remington until they become a pair of dancers in perfect harmony with one another. He mirrors every movement in complete relaxation. She drops the whip, turns her back to him, and walks away. He obediently follows her as if a lead rope tethered them. She stops suddenly and exhales.

"I love you, Remi." She whispers. Remington wraps his head around her torso and they both close their eyes in forgiveness.

Tegan pilots Lucky over a grid of jumps, measuring over three feet as Carson astride Maserati looks on. They easily clear a final wide oxer of the grid, front knees perfectly tucked underneath his chest in a perfect bascule, and canter away. She halts him, pats him on the neck, and feeds him a sugar cube. Lucky in his characteristic Bambi-like fashion trips over himself as Tegan walks him over to Carson. Tegan knowingly looks over to Carson and they both laugh at Lucky's continued foibles with his legs.

"At least he can jump. Maybe he'll learn to walk some day." Tegan giggles as she halts Lucky next to Maserati. A smile appears on Carson's face as he gazes toward the pasture. Missy and Remington walk sans lead rope side-by-side back to Remington's stall in a hushed whisper, wiping away the trauma of today's incident along with the past. Tegan follows Carson's gaze and takes in the moment with him.

"She's gonna be fine. Not sure if she'll ride or even jump him." Carson says.

"Don't care. I just want her to be happy." Tegan sighs and looks over at Carson. "Lucky was the last schooling for today. You done?"

"Not yet," Carson replies with a mischievous grin on his face.

"What are you up to, Mr. Carson?" She retorts.

"You'll see. Meet me back here with Rusty in half an hour." Carson clicks his lips and canters off with Maserati clearing a three plus feet oxer before heading to the grid of jumps. Tegan looks after him and shakes her head, chuckling to herself.

"Let's go for a trail ride, Lucky." She commands. She gently squeezes Lucky with her calves and they head out of the arena towards the green filled rolling hills of the pasture.

WESTERN BARN?

The sun dips behind the rolling hills of Valley Vista Ranch, igniting the sky in a blaze of deep orange, crimson red, and molten gold. Light pours through the arms of towering oaks that ring the Hank Miller Oval, painting the ground in streaks of fire and shadow. Long silhouettes stretch across the dirt—dirt that remembers every hoofbeat, every victory, every fall.

Wind whispers through the grandstands, stirring dust that once clung to chaps and boots. Though the Oval now shapes champions of show jumping and hunter rings, its soul belongs to the rodeo. This arena—scarred and sacred—once thundered with the wild energy of bucking broncs, echoed with the sharp pivots of cutting horses, and roared with the cheers of crowds swept up in the grit and glory of the ride.

At the heart of that history stood Hank Miller, reins in hand, astride his legendary quarter horse, Bob—the pair etched forever into the story this ground still breathes.

No one could touch them. No matter how many champions rode into this ring—whether it be bull riders from Texas, trick ropers from Arizona, or barrel racers from Oklahoma—they all left humbled by Hank and Bob.

No one ever exchanged any prize money. The Brown Jug, an old whiskey jug turned trophy, chipped, scratched, and filled with the history of the West, was the only award. But that didn't matter.

The real prize was bragging rights—the honor of having bested Hank Miller on his own turf.

Not a single man or woman ever did.

Even as Hank grew older, even as Bob's once-black mane turned silver, they remained undefeated.

Now, with Hank Miller gone and Bob nothing more than a whispered legend in the wind, the Brown Jug Challenge had returned.

Would the Miller name remain untouchable?

Or would a new champion rise?

The Oval is alive again. Not with fancy warm bloods or crisp white breeches, but with the roaring laughter of cowboys, the rhythmic twang of a country song from a radio in the distance, and the unmistakable tension of a challenge.

Tegan enters the arena bareback, astride Rusty, his flaxen mane woven into ten long western braids down his neck. Her own raven hair hangs in two loose plaits, the weight of her father's well-worn cowboy hat resting atop her head. The hat was too big, smelled of saddle oil and Hank's old aftershave, and made her feel like she was exactly where she belonged.

She halts Rusty just outside the barrels and takes in the sight before her.

Carson stands at the center of the arena, flanked by Olivia and Janet. Olivia perched atop Bubbles, her face full of excitement, while Janet, ever the competitor, sits confidently on her new palomino mare, Sista.

And there, sitting proud on the table in front of Carson, rests the infamous Brown Jug.

Oscar astride his trusty chocolate and white paint mare quarter horse, Caliente trots up to Tegan, taps his cowboy hat in a "challenge" known only between the two of them since they were children, smiles, and enters the arena. Tegan grunts, clicks her teeth, and gallops by Oscar.

"Not this time, old man!" She exclaims. She continues galloping up to Carson and slide-halts inches away from him, spraying footing all over him. He wipes his face and knowingly chuckles.

"You've been busy, Mr. Carson." Tegan says sarcastically, a wry smile appears on her face. Carson sets the Brown Jug down, walks over to Rusty, and pats him on the neck.

"Traitor." He playfully whispers. Rusty snorts and shakes his head "yes." They all laugh in unison. Tegan looks over at Olivia, raises an eyebrow.

"Why, Olivia, I didn't know you were interested in barrel racing, and on Bubbles? How long has this been going on, you two?" Carson and Olivia look at each other. Olivia giggles.

"Bubbles and I got bored with jumping so Car— "

"Never mind. I wasn't born yesterday. So. Mr. Carson. What are the ground rules? How we gonna do this?" Tegan retorts.

"The Brown Jug is up for grabs in this inaugural barrel race. Each pair will start outside the arena and go around each barrel and then gallop outside the arena. You only get one run and the fastest clean round wins. You might want to rethink your saddle choice, Tegan."

"I'm fine. I chase the barrels better bareback. You in?" She asks.

"I was gonna judge and time."

"Nope. You'll ride Bubbles bareback last. Olivia will go first."

An audience of groomsmen, stable men, farriers, and Dr. White gather outside the arena. In low rumbles, the men exchange bets. Missy walks up to the gate and nudges Pedro.

"What's going on?"

"Brown Jug challenge. You wanna place a bet?" Pedro asks. Missy looks into the arena at the pairings. Her eyes lock on Tegan. Tegan smiles and winks back at her.

"Twenty on Tegan and Rusty." She removes a twenty-dollar bill from her front pocket and hands it to Pedro. Pedro stacks the twenty over the stash of bills and fastens the pot with a rubber band. They both lean up against the rail in anticipation of the "Brown Jug Challenge". Who will win?

Tegan looks outside the arena and spots Dr. White and waves him in.

"Dr. White will judge and time. Let's see if you're a real cowboy, Mr. Carson. You in?" She raises an eyebrow in a challenge. Olivia's eyes widen and Janet sniggers.

"I think someone got his number." She sarcastically says to Oscar. Oscar grunts in response as Caliente paws the ground in boredom.

"Are we doing this or not?" Oscar snorts in frustration and trots towards the gate. Tegan, Olivia, and Janet follow suit. Carson shrugs his shoulders, grabs the Brown Jug, and heads toward the gate. He hands Dr. White the Brown Jug, stopwatch, and whistle and exits the arena.

Olivia lines up outside the gate. Bubbles gives her an affectionate buck and prances in place. Dr. White whistles and Olivia and Bubbles gallop towards the first barrel. They easily round the barrel and head towards the second, easily clearing that barrel at a blistering pace. Tegan looks at Carson with a proud smile on her face.

"I knew he had an amazing turning radius, but I didn't realize that he was this good." She exclaims. Olivia heads to the last barrel with a determined look on her face. She rounds the barrel a little too tight and Bubbles clips it with his haunches. The barrel tumbles over. The audience groans, but Olivia continues at her fierce pace and they cross the line. Dr. White clicks the stopwatch with the flamboyance of an orchestra conductor.

"16.8 seconds!" Dr. White exclaims. "If only she'd been clean!" Olivia slows Bubbles down and halts him. Bubbles shakes his head and jumps up and down like a toddler throwing a tantrum. Olivia strokes the base of his neck with her knuckles and whispers.

"It's okay, Bubs. My fault. Didn't place you right. We'll get 'em next time." Bubbles calms down and affectionately nips at the front of her boot. She feeds him a cookie. Carson approaches as she dismounts.

"Amazing first run, Olivia."

"Didn't place him right on the last barrel, that's why he clipped it with his haunches."

"Yep. But you've learned a lot from that run. And it was under 17 seconds, which is good enough for NFR. He likes to cut in, so you gotta go to the last barrel a little wider. Great job staying centered. You didn't lean into any of the turns like the last time. Cool him off and walk him before I go. Don't want him to get stiff." Carson pats Bubbles on the neck and heads back to the gate.

Janet pats her mare on the neck and readies herself for her run. Carson approaches. Janet grunts in protest.

"Don't worry, Car. I won't forget. And don't ease up for me. You hear me." She looks at him with a sisterly protest.

"Wouldn't dream of it. That Jug is mine." He winks and pats her leg.

"Have a good run." He says. She snorts back at him. Dr. White blows the whistle, and they're off, effortlessly rounding each barrel like it was a cone in perfect precision. They go a little wide on the final barrel, but Janet sends her mare forward all the way to the gate. Dr. White clicks the stopwatch.

"16.6 and clean! We have a new leader, folks!" Dr. White exclaims. The audience roars with approval. Janet halts her mare, pats her neck, and feeds her a cookie.

"Good job, Sista! Such a good girl!" Janet hugs Sista and trots back to the gate to watch the remaining riders.

Oscar steadies Caliente in anticipation of the whistle. Dr. White blows the whistle. Caliente, ears pinned back bolts to the first barrel - the audience gasps at her ferocity. She approaches the second barrel, turns too quickly. Oscar tries to move his foot out of the way, but ends up clipping the barrel with his boot, sending it down to the ground.

"¡Mierda!" He exclaims. Caliente, furious, throws a bronc sized buck, wasting precious time on the final barrel.

"¡Adelante!" He screams. They round the final barrel and Caliente bucks and shakes her head all the way to the finish line.

"16.9! Crazy fast, folks, considering the dance show at the end!" Dr. White exclaims. The audience laughs at Caliente's antics.

"Cali! Cali! Cali!" They cheer. Oscar heads back into the arena, removes his hat and bows with Caliente, and then asks her to rear on cue. The audience roars with delight. He pats her neck and trots her out of the arena, head held high. He stops next to Tegan.

"Not bad, ole man." She squeezes his shoulder.

"Taught by the best, Señora. Just need some more runs and there's no stopping us."

He tips his hat.

"Beat the Gringo, Señora. The Brown Jug must stay with a Miller." He says with meaning.

Tegan nods her head in deep understanding of Oscar's words. A Miller has never relinquished the Brown Jug to an outsider. Never. She leans forward and whispers in Rusty's ear.

"I need this one, Rusty. You know dad's watching." She kisses his neck. Rusty stomps his right front leg in response. They're ready. The whistle blows. They're off to the first barrel, so smooth it's as though they're in slow motion. Every beat is perfect. Every move is in perfect harmony. Missy looks on with tears of admiration flowing down her face. The audience is in complete silence, mesmerized by the display before their eyes. Before anyone can blink, Rusty and Tegan cross the finish line. Dr. White stops the watch.

"16.2! A new Valley Vista Ranch record!" Dr. White exclaims. The audience hoot and holler in admiration.

"Rusty! Rusty! Rusty!" They chant. Tegan dismounts and removes the hack-a-more.

"Go Rusty. You deserve this." She kisses his muzzle. Rusty trots into the arena by himself and bows to the adulation of the audience. Tegan walks over to Carson and Bubbles. Carson looks at her in disbelief. She pats Bubbles' neck and looks up to Carson with a wry smile reminiscent of her father.

"I didn't know." Carson whispers.

"I maybe a show jumper, but I'm also Hank Miller's daughter. And no one takes the Brown Jug from a Miller." She blows Carson a kiss, places her fingers between her lips and whistles. Rusty trots out of the arena and stands next to Tegan - chest puffed out with pride.

"Good luck." She whispers and walks away with Rusty. Carson shakes his head and chuckles to himself.

"Outwitted again by a Miller." He pats Bubbles' neck. "Let's see what we can do, buddy." Bubbles, wide eyed, looks back at Carson, and snorts. The whistle blows. They head to the first barrel at blistering speed, matching Tegan's and Rusty's pace. They round the barrel and head to the second. Around the second barrel, Bubbles pins back his ears and tries to cut the corner. Carson steadies him and they clear the second barrel. Bubbles shakes his head, upset at Carson's correction, costing them valuable time. They head to the last barrel. Bubbles picks up speed. The audience gasps at the laser like precision of Carson's turn. Will he make up enough time to beat Tegan and Rusty? Bubbles' ears fly forward as they gallop toward the finish line. Dr. White clicks the stopwatch and stares at it in disbelief. A murmur runs through the crowd like a dance of the bumblebees in front of their queen bee. All eyes are on Dr. White.

"This year's winner of the Brown Jug is... Tegan Miller and Rusty!" Dr. White walks over to Tegan and Rusty and hands her the Brown Jug and pats Rusty's neck. The audience roars with delight and chant, "Miller! Miller! Miller!" Tegan raises the Brown Jug above her head, and Rusty bows to the crowd's delight.

"Okay, folks. That's it for the Brown Jug challenge. See you at Morrisons." Dr. White announces. Oscar whistles and the crowd of stable and groomsmen disperse to finish the chores of the day. Olivia runs up to Dr. White with a stern look on her face.

"Tell us, Dr. White." She demands. Ever the vet, he runs his hands down Rusty's legs.

"Rusty won. That's all you need to know, Olivia." He winks at Tegan and she nods her head in approval.

"Give it up, Olivia. You'll never get it out of Dr. White." She knowingly smiles. "See you at Morrisons, Dr. White. First round is on me."

"Gonna check the other horses and I'll see you there. Olivia." He taps his hat and walks towards the stables.

"Dr. White! Wait! I wanna help!" Olivia hurries after him. Carson trots Bubbles up to Tegan and Rusty. Tegan hands the Brown Jug to Carson.

"Dr. White would never let the Brown Jug leave a Miller." Tegan says.

"But..." Carson protests.

"You won fair and square. The last gallop to the finish line. Me and Rusty know it. Bubbles. A barrel racer. Who would've thought? Dad would be proud." She winks at Carson. Carson smiles and tips his hat to Rusty.

"You put up a good fight, ole buddy." He feeds Rusty a sugar cube and looks at Tegan.

"Gonna cool down Bubbles and then head to Morrisons." Carson slaps Bubbles' neck with appreciation and feeds him a sugar cube.

"Let's go, Bubbs!" They head to the pasture, leaving Tegan with Rusty.

"I've gotta couple of things to take care of. See you there." She calls out after Carson. She sees the silhouette of Carson wave back to her as he and Bubbles walk away. Tegan dismounts Rusty and removes the hack-o-more. Rusty nuzzles Tegan and then gallops towards the stables, whinnying to Mirabella.

"Horses." She chuckles to herself and heads towards her office.

A large hauler carrying four horses pulls up towards the office. The air breaks release as the hauler stops and parks. A large man, mid-thirties, army green trucker cap covering black hair sprinkled with grey, dressed in a tan uniform with a badge on the right side of his of shirt pocket bearing the name, Fred, exits the vehicle. He looks around as Tegan and Oscar approach.

"Can I help you?" Tegan asks, confused. The echos of horses' whinny emanate from the trailer. Oscar approaches the trailer, peers in, and looks back at Tegan.

"Four horses, Señora. Well bred. Look European." He looks over to the hauler. The hauler scratches his head and walks over to Tegan and offers his hand. They shake.

"My name is Fred Daniels. These horses just came out of quarantine. I was told to bring them here, mam. Here are the papers." He walks over to Tegan.

"Fred, who—?" She asks. She looks over the papers and hands them back to Fred.

"There must have been a mistake. These horses are not mine. Please take them back." She responds.

"Ms. Miller, this is my last stop, so I can't take them back. The order specifically says that the final destination for these horses is Valley Vista Ranch. I was told that someone would accept these horses upon arrival. Please have someone remove these horses from my trailer so that I can go home to my family." He responds, frustrated, folding his arms across his chest.

A beam of lights glow from a black Maserati Grand Tourismo pulling up next to the trailer. Dust scatters as the Maserati comes to a stop. Jake steps out and stops suddenly when he sees Oscar with his hands on his hips, in a wide stance, in anger and Tegan glaring at him.

"Hey guys. Thought you'd be— "

"Enough, Jake. Why are these horses here?" Tegan places her hands on her hips, mimicking Oscar.

"I made this deal. Great deal, Tegan. All you have to do is train up these horses and I'll sell them. Loads of money. You'll see," Jake explains unconvincingly.

"We're not a sale barn, Jake, and I don't have time to train horses. Take these horses back where you got them." Tegan angrily commands.

"But, Tegan. I told... " Jake says desperately.

A dark-haired wealthy looking European woman in her thirties dressed in designer jeans, tall boots, and navy blue sweater over a finely white pressed shirt adorned with small tasteful gold hoops and diamond encrusted horseshoe necklace steps out of the car.

"Jake? What's going on?" she asks, her German accent laced with confusion. Stepping toward him, she watches as he shifts his weight from foot to foot, like a guilty child caught with crumbs on his face. Her gaze flicks to Tegan and Oscar, silently asking for backup.

"Hello, I'm Tegan Miller, head trainer and owner of Valley Vista Ranch. How can I help you?" Tegan, aware of the situation, offers the confused lady her hand.

"I'm sorry. I was told that... Jake?" She finally realizes that Jake is not who he's claimed to be.

"I see. I'll remove my horses immediately. Sorry for the trouble." She graciously says, glaring at Jake.

"Please don't. You can keep your horses here until you find a different situation. I'll make some phone calls to some reputable sale barns in the area." Tegan quickly responds.

"You are too kind. I'm new to the area, just arrived from Germany, and I was told of this facility. I was hoping to have my horses trained here. They're young prospects that I was hoping to sell in the States. They have excellent bloodlines. My family farm in Germany is looking to expand out of Europe, and I was told that there was interest in the States. Interest at a partnership at Valley Vista Ranch."

"I see. Valley Vista Ranch is not a sales facility. We sell horses that are bred on property, but we're mostly a training facility. I'll make sure that your horses are well cared for and trained until you get yourself situated, Miss ?"

"Schneider. Helen Schneider. It's a pleasure to meet you. I promise to pay whatever you need for the inconvenience." She shakes Tegan's hand and smiles.

"Not a problem. Welcome to Valley Vista Ranch." Tegan shakes her hand and smiles back. She looks over at Oscar.

"Helen, Oscar is our stable manager. He'll find a place for your horses. Oscar, would you mind-?" Tegan asks, trying not to lose her composure. He grunts his disapproval and heads to the trailer.

"If you would follow me. I have some paperwork I need you to fill out and sign." Tegan gestures toward her office.

"Of course. Jake, I never want to see you again. Please make sure he doesn't go near my horses." Helen glares at Jake, turns her back to him, and follows Tegan to the office.

"Dammit. Oscar, wait." Jake runs after Oscar. Oscar stops and looks menacingly at him.

"Leave now, before I get angry, Jake. And don't come back." Oscar walks by Jake and pushes him over with his shoulder.

MORRISON'S PART 2

Though June has just begun, Morrison's bursts with patriotic pride, already charging full force toward the Fourth of July. Red, white, and blue streamers weave across the ceiling, crisscrossing like a net, ready to capture the night's laughter and memories. Balloons sway in the corners, tethered to chairs and posts, while miniature American flags jut from behind ketchup bottles, claiming their ground with festive flair.

Vintage wartime posters line the walls, their colors faded but their presence still demanding attention. Uncle Sam glares from one side, finger aimed straight at the room, his infamous "I Want You" declaration pulsing with urgency. Across from him, Rosie the Riveter throws back her shoulders and flexes, her "We Can Do It" speech bubble punching through the air with unwavering resolve. Red, white, and blue bunting wraps around the bar, while mason jars crowd the wooden counter, each one cradling tiny sparklers ready to ignite the night when the moment comes.

The jukebox hums softly in the background, but for now, the real centerpiece of Morrison's isn't its decorations—it's the table in the middle of the room.

At its head sits Oscar, grinning like a king presiding over his court. In front of him, the table is overflowing with pitchers of beer, frosted glasses of lemonade, baskets of chips, and bowls of salsa. But most importantly, in the center of it all sits the infamous Brown Jug.

Chipped. Scratched. Timeworn.

It's seen more victories than any gleaming championship trophy ever could. Close inspection reveals names covering the jug's surface, carved in the shaky, proud lettering of those who came before.

Bob's name dominates the jug, etched deep and often. So does every horse Hank Miller ever owned, along with a few brave challengers who came close but never took it home.

Tonight, they will add one more name.

William Morrison, the bar's proprietor and longtime family friend, strides over carrying two massive trays of piping hot pizza. He sets the food down beside the Brown Jug and wipes his hands on his apron.

"Alright," he says, gesturing to the jug, "whose name is getting carved into history this year?"

Without hesitation, Tegan and Carson say in perfect unison—

"Rusty!"

Their voices overlap, their eyes meet, and a slow, knowing grin spreads across both their faces. A low groan comes from Olivia. She folds her arms and slumps back in her chair, eyes rolling so hard they might get stuck.

"Ugh, seriously? We all know Bubbles was the real winner," she says, arching an eyebrow at Dr. White, daring him to contradict her.

Dr. White barely pauses mid-bite before responding.

"Stop with the conspiracies, Olivia. My call stands. Rusty won." He takes another massive bite of pizza, chewing in satisfaction. Conversation closed.

Olivia lets out a dramatic sigh, grabs the Brown Jug, and kisses it for her Instagram story.

"Olivia!" Missy gasps.

"What? Cowgirl is so IG." Olivia flashes a peace sign at her phone, angling herself just right for maximum engagement.

Missy shakes her head, but Tegan just smirks.

"Let her be, Missy," she says with a wink. "So, Olivia, you're a cowgirl now?"

"Yep." Olivia tosses her hair over her shoulder, taking one last selfie before placing the jug back in the center of the table.

Carson leans forward, narrowing his eyes.

"What about Max?"

Olivia waves him off like it's a minor inconvenience.

"I can do both," she says matter-of-factly. "And Bubbles is getting tons of engagement on my page. My sponsors love it."

Carson looks like he physically cannot process teenage logic.

"I thought you were overworked and underpaid?" he counters.

"You worry too much, Carson," she says with a sweet, infuriating smile. "And you always say we should try new riding styles to become better riders. So... what's the problem?"

Janet snorts, shaking her head.

"I'd give it up, Car. She had you beat at 'Cowgirl is so IG.'"

Carson sighs in defeat, raising his hands. Olivia grins victoriously.

Tegan raises her beer.

"Let's all raise a glass to Rusty, Bubbles, Caliente, and Sista. To great horses."

Everyone lifts their drinks.

"To great horses!"

Glasses clink. Laughter fills the room as they drink to the legends, past and present.

Then Janet pushes back her chair, saunters to the jukebox, and drops a quarter in.

As the first chords of 'Sweet Home Alabama' strum through the speakers, she turns on her heel, winking at Carson.

"Let's shake it, buddy."

Carson downs the rest of his beer, wipes his mouth on his sleeve, and stands.

"I'd be honored."

He glances back at Tegan and Missy, winks, and heads to the dance floor with Janet.

Olivia lets out a squeal.

"This song is so lit! Let's go, Pedro."

Before Pedro can protest, Olivia yanks him up and drags him to the dance floor.

Pedro, wide-eyed, looks back at Oscar.

"Don't break him, Olivia." Oscar calls after them with a chuckle. "I need him at work mañana."

Missy and Tegan laugh in unison.

"Poor Pedro," they say at the same time.

As the music plays and the dance floor fills, Missy takes a deep breath, gripping the edge of the table. She nudges Tegan.

"Can we talk?"

Tegan turns, catching the nervous tremble in her voice. She gently takes Missy's hand and squeezes.

"Sure. What's up?"

Missy's chest rises and plummets. Her hands are clammy.

She swallows, then closes her eyes and blurts it out in one breath—

"I want to train on Remington. I want to jump again."

Tegan doesn't hesitate.

"Okay."

Missy stares.

"Okay?"

Tegan leans back, watching Carson and Janet line dance.

"That Janet sure can dance."

Missy jerks her head.

"What?! 'Okay'? Janet sure can dance?! That's all you have to say?"

Tegan smiles to herself.

"Yep. You're ready. Remington's ready. You'll start tomorrow."

Missy gapes.

Tegan casually grabs another slice of pizza, takes a huge bite, and points at the last piece.

"Stop overthinking. Eat." she says, her mouth full.

Missy lets out a huff but obeys, grabbing the slice and taking a dramatic bite.

Tegan nods approvingly. They sit in companionable silence, the music thumping around them, tapping their feet to the beat.

The song ends and everyone on the dance floor cheers. Carson hugs Janet and escorts her back to the table, with Olivia and Pedro following closely behind. Janet grabs her purse and jacket.

"Gotta run. Early start tomorrow. Olivia? I can drop you off. You ready?" Olivia takes a selfie of her and Pedro and looks at Janet.

"Sure. You can give me some pointers on how to be a real cowgirl. The outfits are..." she says excitedly.

"So IG. I know." Janet rolls her eyes and looks at Carson and Tegan.

"Catch you later. Hold down the fort for me. I'll be back to train for Vegas." She waves her hand "bye" and heads to the door with Olivia.

Dr. White finishes his drink and stands.

"I better get going, too. I'll see ya tomorrow, Tegan. We can discuss Mirabella Mia's procedure then. We harvested Rusty's semen, and it is ready. Carson." He tips his hat and heads to the exit.

"Good night, Dr. White. See you tomorrow. And thanks again!" Tegan rubs her hands together in excitement. She looks over at a shocked Missy.

"What?" she says with a smirk.

"You're breeding Mirabella? I thought—"

"Don't worry, Missy. We're using a surrogate broodmare. It's completely safe, and Rusty thinks it's a great idea." She smiles at Carson and Oscar.

"Oh, does he now? I leave for a bit and now we're breeding again. I thought you were done with breeding; that Remington was the last." Missy shakes her head in mock disapproval.

"Don't you act all surprised, kiddo. You've been bugging me forever about re-starting the breeding program. I know what your next question is gonna be."

"Why not? We need more Remingtons and a Remington and Mirabella cross would be insane. C'mon, Teegs! It would—"

"It's a maybe for now. Okay?" Tegan responds, to end the discussion. Missy fist pumps and mouths the word "yes". Carson hands Tegan her jacket.

"You ladies, ready?" He asks. Tegan accepts the jacket from Carson, and they head to the door. Tegan looks back at Pedro and Oscar.

"You guys coming?" She asks. Pedro helps a slightly inebriated Oscar stand, and they both stumble.

"We'll be right behind you." Pedro grunts. Tegan shakes her head and progresses to the door with Missy and Carson.

"You're gonna have to talk to Rusty. He's going to be heartbroken." Carson says with a smile. Tegan laughs at the hidden joke.

"What? Rusty will understand. He'll understand." Missy says unconvincingly.

"You don't know Rusty." Carson and Tegan say in unison and laugh.

"We'll have a family meeting. Me. Rusty. Remington. You'll convince him, right Carson?" Missy pleads. Carson looks over at Tegan and winks.

"I don't know, Missy. You're asking a lot. Rusty can be—"

"I'll do anything. Just convince him, okay?"

"Anything? Sounds enticing. What do you think, Tegan?" Carson holds back a laugh.

"I think it's a great idea. But, mark my words, Missy, you don't know what you're dealing with when you sign up with Mr. Carson Peterson." She bursts out laughing.

"Laugh all you want, Teegs, but me and Remi will show all of you. I don't care what it takes." Missy says with that old, determined spark in her eye.

"I bet you both will." Carson acknowledges Missy's determination and puts his arm around her shoulder and squeezes. They head towards Tegan's truck good ole Bess, waiting like she's heard everything.

Jake stumbles toward them, clearly inebriated. Carson moves forward to protect Tegan and Missy. Tegan gently grabs his forearm and looks at him. He knowingly stops and Tegan proceeds toward Jake. Jake stops square and crosses his arms.

"Look what we have here - a happy family." He slurs. Tegan looks him up and down and cuts to the point.

"What do you want?"

"What do I want? What do I want? My cut. My cut, Tegan." He demands.

"You're drunk, Jake. There is no cut. I owe you nothing."

"Nothing! There would be no Valley Vista Ranch without me. No horses. No clients. The debt. I made it go away."

"Go home, Jake." She says in disgust. He rushes towards her, grabs her shoulders to steady himself.

"Please, Teegs. We had something special, right? Great horses, great riders. We did it all! I made one little mistake. One little mistake. Don't throw it all away." He says, as if pleading for redemption and forgiveness all at once. She looks at his hands on her shoulders, and he removes them and quickly shoves them into his pockets.

"It was special." He whispers, rewriting history in his drunken head. Tegan's eyes soften with pity and she manages as much tenderness that she could muster in the situation.

"Go home." She says.

"Come on, Teegs." Jake desperately says. He reaches out towards her again. Carson steps forward and blocks him. Jake shakes with anger and points his drunken finger at Carson.

"What the... You've known this jackass for three seconds, sleep with him, and now he's calling all the shots!" He screams. Missy's eyes well up in fear. She looks towards Carson.

"Enough, Jake. Sleep it off." Carson walks toward Jake. Bam! Jake punches him in the jaw. Carson stumbles backwards and falls to the ground. Jake stands over him.

"Who do you think you are? I rebuilt Valley Vista Ranch with my own hands!" He kicks Carson in the ribs. Carson groans in pain.

"Carson!" Tegan and Missy yell in unison. Missy buries her face in her hands and starts crying in distress. Tegan protectively holds and consoles Missy, shielding her from further violence like a momma bear protecting her cub. Carson instinctively rolls away from Jake, stands up, clenches his fists and readies himself for a fight. He looks at Tegan and she looks back at him with tearful eyes and shakes her head "no." He steps back and unclenches his fist and protectively places his hand on his ribs.

Out of nowhere, Oscar tackles Jake and wrestles him to the floor, pinning his shoulders with his knees. He violently swings his fists in a blind fury at Jake's face, pummeling him like a piece of meat.

"Pendejo, drunken, piece of mierda! I should have gotten rid of you years ago!" He yells as he chokes Jake. Jake's face turns beet red as he desperately gasps for air; his body spasms from exertion. Carson and Pedro forcefully drag Oscar off Jake.

"He's not worth it, Oscar." Carson calmly says.

"He stole from Valley Vista Ranch. For years! You don't think we knew. Bidding up the client's horses, taking a larger cut. Teaching students on the side and not paying for ring use. We all knew what you were doing!" Oscar lunges at Jake again. They're barely able to hold him back from years of pent up rage. Carson looks directly into Oscar's eyes and places his hand on his shoulder.

"Not worth it." He says. Oscar coughs out his anger with labored breath and then relents. He knowingly looks at Tegan. He taps his hat out of respect.

"Señora. Hasta, mañana." He says with tenderness and years of affection, and with a rueful smile, stumbles away with Pedro.

Jake groans as he rolls to his side in agony. Carson offers his hand to help him up. Jake slaps it away, spits out a bloody tooth. His bloodshot eyes glare at Tegan.

"You'll pay for this." Jake stumbles up to his knees and then feet and limps away.

OSCAR

H ank pulls up to the county jail, the weight of the situation pressing against his chest like a boulder he can't shove off. The building looms before him, a relic of another time. A foreboding structure of aged red brick and unyielding stone, its two massive round columns stand in the center like silent sentinels, casting long shadows under the yellow glare of the streetlights. The iron-barred windows above gleam faintly in the dim evening light, giving the entire place an air of cold indifference.

Hank exhales a long, exhausted sigh and shifts his truck, Bess, into park. The gear shift sticks, resisting the motion, almost as if the truck herself was warning him against going inside.

"Everything's gonna be fine, Bess," Hank mutters, though even he doesn't believe it. His fingers gently stroke the worn steering wheel, a habit born from years of seeking comfort in the old truck.

He pushes the door open, stepping onto the gravel lot, the crunch beneath his boots the only sound in the heavy summer air. Before he can take another step, a familiar figure emerges from the entrance—Officer Trip Calloway.

Trip has the face that's seen too much—lined from stress, tanned from years under the California sun. His uniform is crisp but well-worn, khaki slacks with a faded light blue stripe down the side, a matching button-down shirt tucked neatly over a white undershirt. His black belt, loaded holster, and polished boots give him an air of authority, but tonight, his expression is anything but official.

His dark brown eyes meet Hank's, filled with something between regret and resignation.

"Hey, Trip," Hank greets, his voice rough from worry.

Trip shakes his hand, but there's no warmth in the grip.

"He's in the can, Hank," Trip says, his voice low and grim. "Drunk. Beaten pretty bad."

Hank's stomach twists.

"I tried to get there as soon as I could, but..." Trip shakes his head, placing his hands on his hips. "It's bad."

Hank looks past him toward the barred entrance, where a single light flickers above the rusted iron door. The scent of old tobacco, sweat, and stale coffee wafts from inside, mixing with something else—hopelessness.

"They're pressing charges," Trip continues, rubbing a hand over his jaw. "Bail's set at ten grand. And he's gonna need a lawyer, Hank."

Hank drags a hand down his face, feeling the exhaustion settle into his bones.

"Damn it."

He stares at the cracks in the pavement, trying to swallow his frustration, his guilt, his growing anger—but mostly, the overwhelming sense of responsibility.

"Can I see him?" he finally asks.

Trip hesitates, then nods.

"Yeah. But listen to me, Hank—" His voice drops, turning serious. "I can't make this one disappear. Not this time."

Hank nods, already knowing the truth.

"I know, Trip."

They share a long look, two men who've cleaned up messes before—this one, maybe the worst yet.

Trip exhales sharply and claps Hank on the back. "Alright, then. Let's go."

Without another word, they walk toward the heavy iron doors, where trouble—and an uncertain future—waits on the other side.

Oscar, aged 28, sits across the steel grey table, head bowed in shame. He looks up to Hank, revealing a war-torn face battered and bruised with one eye swollen shut and a bloodied split lip.

"I couldn't let him get away with it, Señor." Oscar wipes his one good tear-stained eye with his bruised black, purple, and blue swollen hand and then places it on the table. He looks past Hank and shakes with emotion.

"I know. I would have done the same. It doesn't matter now. I'll take care of everything." Hank responds.

"Just let me rot in here, Señor. Your family needs you." Oscar pleads. Hank smirks, looks directly into Oscar's eyes.

"You're a part of the Miller family and we take care of own. Remember that." He replies. Hank taps the table and stands up with stoic confidence. He places his hand on Oscar's shoulder and squeezes.

"I'll be back in a couple of days to take you home, Oscar. A couple of days." He says. Oscar looks up at him with grateful eyes.

"Thank you, Señor." Oscar responds.

"De nada. Remember. A couple of days. Four tops." He winks at Oscar and leaves the room.

Hank pulls up to the arena and parks. He looks out to the arena and takes a moment to collect his thoughts and courage for the task at hand. Tegan, aged 25, dressed in Wrangler jeans embellished with a leather Argentinian belt with a beaded flag, plaid long-sleeved cowgirl shirt, tan well worn Laredo cowgirl boots, with her long wild dark hair tucked under her cowboy hat raises her whip at four-year-old, Bob's Mystery (aka Rusty). He rears onto his hinds legs and joyfully shakes his head and whinnies. Tegan laughs.

"Good boy, BM! I knew you could do it!" She exclaims in delight. Bob's Mystery prances in place with his chest puffed out, proud of his accomplishment. He then gallops towards Tegan, bumps her with his muzzle, and runs away snorting with glee.

"You little devil!" Tegan laughs. She drops her whip and chases after him. They play a childhood game of "tag" which develops into an exotic dance of best friends mimicking one another. Tegan eventually gets close enough, grabs Bob's Mystery's mane and mounts his back. They gallop off together around the ring. Tegan and Bob's Mystery become a singular blur of speed. They head down the center of the arena and halt in a dragging stop, spraying sand behind them. Tegan pats Bob's Mystery's shoulder and dismounts. Bob's Mystery nuzzles her jean pocket. She giggles in response to his request.

"Okay. Okay. You have such a sweet tooth, BM!" She feeds him a sugar cube. Tegan wraps her arms around Bob's Mystery, and he responds by circling his head around her torso. They take a moment to take in each other's presence and just breathe. They unwind their embrace and head to the arena gate, where Hank stands watching them with a stern look on his face.

"He's really coming along, kiddo." He says.

"He's perfect, Dad. Just perfect. I can't wait to start the circuit with him. I think we're ready." She responds, patting him on the neck.

"What about Chewy? You have a full schedule in the fall." He says skeptically.

"I can do both. I got it all worked out. On the off weekends, I'll travel with BM. It'll be great." She says with conviction. Hank climbs over the fence and gently caresses Bob's Mystery's neck. He shoves his hand back into his pocket, trying to hide the emotional shake of his hand.

"Dad?" Tegan asks, concerned.

"I need you to load BM into the trailer." He says.

"Why? What's going on?" She protectively steps in front of Bob's Mystery.

"Oscar's in trouble. He needs our help." He responds.

"Oscar's always in trouble. What does it have to do with BM?" Her voice shakes with emotion.

"They're pressing charges, Kiddo. Oscar needs a lawyer. They set bail— "

"You're not selling my horse!" Tegan screams. Bob's Mystery terrified, spins on his hind legs and bolts away from them.

"BM! Come back!" She heads after him and Hank grabs her forearm.

"Let him go, Tegan."

"You can't do this, Dad. He's my horse. I trained him since he was a foal. I developed him. He's my horse!"

"Oscar needs— "

"I don't give a damn about Oscar! He's always in trouble. He's always drunk, picking a fight. We're always saving his... You do this, I'm outta here." She turns and walks away, tears streaming down her face.

Tegan sits next to Bob's Mystery, who's lying down with his muzzle resting on the arena sand. His tail nonchalantly flicks away a fly from his haunches like any other day, fully knowing it's not. She strokes his back and gently cries.

"I love you, BM." she whispers. Bob's Mystery nickers his version of "I love you" back to her. She wipes her eyes as her father approaches her with his eyes glistening from constrained emotion. He sits across from them with his legs crossed.

"You ready to talk now, kiddo?" He tentatively asks.

"I don't know if I can be here without BM, Dad. Him and Chewy are my everything. The best of Valley Vista Ranch. The best of me." She whispers.

"Me neither. Don't forget, I bred him for you. He was my dream horse for this ranch, for you. Bob will never forgive me. It breaks my heart to do this but— "

"I know, Dad. Oscar is family, and we don't abandon family. But I don't know if I can ever forgive him." She states.

"I don't expect you to. All I ask is that you give him a chance. I know you can't see it now, but Oscar will be there when it counts. He would do anything for his family. Trust me." He replies. Tegan nods in agreement, gets up, dusts herself off.

"I'll get the halter." She says.

"I can take care of it, kiddo." He gets up to help.

"No, Dad. He's my horse. I'll take care of it." She walks off, leaving Hank with Bob's Mystery.

"Sorry, BM. I'll make sure you find a good home. I promise." He forces the words out of his mouth. Bob's Mystery stands, walks over to Hank, and wraps his head around Hank's torso in forgiveness.

Tegan watches sans emotion as the trailer loaded with her beloved, Bob's Mystery, head down the road towards his new home. She drops her head in sadness and walks towards Paratrooper's stall.

Country music plays on the radio as Hank and Oscar drive up the hill towards Valley Vista Ranch. Oscar fidgets in his seat, nervous about the impending confrontation with Tegan. He tries humming to the music to calm his nerves. Hank raises an eyebrow and looks over at Oscar.

"Spill it, Oscar." He demands.

"Maybe I should leave, Señor Hank. It won't be good for me to be here." He says hurriedly.

"You're staying and that's that. We'll get through this together. That man had no right beating that horse. I would have done the same thing. I've already called animal services on him. Hopefully, that will dissuade him from pursuing charges. He won't want people to know what really happened," Hank responds with a mischievous grin.

"You called the press?" Oscar asks incredulously.

"You bet I did. My reporter friend, Will, is heading out to that infernal place as we speak to 'interview' him about the events. I might even file a countersuit on your behalf. That'll teach him to mess with the men of Valley Vista Ranch."

"You think it'll work?" Oscar asks hopefully.

"I honestly don't know, but I'm willing to try anything to get this monkey off our back. Fingers crossed, this will be yesterday's news by the end of the week. Trip says he's already changed his story several times, and the DA is losing faith in him, and isn't too keen about pursuing this case." Hank says in his typical confident manner. Oscar looks out the window and sighs in relief. They continue down the tree covered entrance in silence. Hank turns off the music.

"Oscar?" Hank breaks the silence.

"Si, Señor Hank?" He asks.

"I need you to promise me that you'll always look after my daughter. She might not want to admit it now, but she'll need all the help she can get when I'm gone. I haven't made Valley Vista Ranch easy for her with all my 'ideas'. Promise me?" He looks over at Oscar. Oscar solemnly nods his head, yes.

"Good. Good." Hank replies. Hank turns the corner and Oscar sees the Valley Vista Ranch Office approaching them.

"How's Señora, Tegan?" Oscar tentatively asks.

"How do you think she is? Not too happy about BM. I would stay away from Tegan for a while until she cools down. Okay?" Hank looks directly at him. Oscar hesitates for a moment to argue and then relents.

"Okay, Señor." He responds.

"Good." Hank says. He pulls up to the office and parks Bess. Exiting the truck, they found Tegan waiting. Tegan walks up to her father and physically turns her back to Oscar, ignoring him..

"The horses are back from pasture and fed. I've gotten through morning training and I'm going to work on Chewy and some of the baby horses. Please make sure the horses are ready for me, Dad." Tegan commands.

"Señora Tegan, I'll— "

Oscar fumbles with his words. Tegan quickly snaps her head with the precision of a black mamba at him and glares at him with complete, unforgiving hatred in her eyes.

"Never talk to me again." She storms back into the office.

"I warned you, Oscar. Give her time. She'll come around." He says, trying to convince himself as well.

"Will you ever tell her what happened, Señor?" Oscar asks.

"I don't think it matters right now, Oscar. Let's get to work." He replies. They both head to the stalls with Oscar's head hanging low in sadness.

MISSY'S COMEBACK

"**W**ake up, kiddo!" Tegan, bareback on Rusty sans bridle, holds two thermoses filled with coffee, one in each hand. The sun shines on her silhouette, giving her the appearance of a goddess astride the famed winged mythical divine horse, Pegasus. Missy lying on a make-shift cot next to Remington's stall, yawns and squints at the sun in her eyes as she tries to look up at Tegan. Confused at her whereabouts, Missy blinks her eyes, trying to focus. She shoves her blonde hair under a baseball cap, the long, shredded braid trailing out and tangled with bits of hay. Remington nickers a good morning and nuzzles her face. She smiles, remembering where she's at, yawns again, and sits up.

"What time is it?" She yawns, removing a piece of hay from her braid.

"Five-thirty. Get a move on. You don't want to miss the 6 a.m. lesson. Hank Miller Oval in a half hour with Remi. Don't be late."

"What? Lesson?" Missy, obviously confused, asks. Rusty, annoyed, snorts at her and paws the ground. Tegan giggles, rubs Rusty's neck, and hands Missy her coffee, clicks her lips and trots away.

"Twenty-five minutes, Missy." She retorts.

Missy trots up next to Tegan, just outside the arena. Remington eyes widened, tosses his head in response to the view in the arena. Polls cover the ground like an ocean filled with splintered wood from a war torn sunken ship. The Misfit Horse Brigade lines up on horseback, forming a flawless military row before their instructor.

"That's a lot of lumber." Missy comments with misgivings.

"Yep. Should be a lot of fun. Let's go. Don't want to be late." Tegan chuckles. She heads into the arena; Rusty whinnies upon entering. Missy begrudgingly follows her. They line up with the other members of the MHB, ready for their morning drills.

"Good morning, riders." Caron says. They all reply good morning in unison. Alexa shyly raises her hand.

"Yes, Alexa?" He asks.

"What happened to the jumps, Mr. Carson?" Alexa asks. Carson looks at Tegan, smiles, then addresses the rest of the group.

"Today, we focus on one thing—communication," Carson says, his voice steady as he scans the row of junior riders. "Every course asks questions. The more complex those questions, the faster they come, the harder the course becomes to ride clean. That's the challenge."

He steps toward the first set of poles laid out in the arena, gesturing with purpose. "If you want to reach the higher levels—if you want to ride like Tegan—you have to sharpen your communication with every horse you sit on. Not just in the saddle, but in the barn, on the ground, in every interaction."

He turns to face them again, tone sharpening with conviction. "Your goal is to build a connection so clear, so precise, that it looks like you and your horse share one mind. That's what separates good riders from great ones. Doesn't matter if you're jumping, cutting, reining, or riding dressage—the principle's the same."

Carson motions to the series of poles set in a challenging pattern. "Each one of these asks a different question. Your job is to answer through rhythm, balance, timing—and trust. If your horse second-guesses you, even for a moment, you've already lost the conversation."

He walks the line of riders slowly, letting his words settle in. "You don't just ride exercises—you shape the way your horse thinks. Ride with intention. Communicate clearly. That's the secret to getting better."

Carson stops. Folds his arms. Waits. The arena hangs in silence, thick with focus.

"Poles are for babies, Carson. Boring. Max and I need a challenge." Olivia adamantly says.

"Really? Then the Miller shuffle should be no problem for you." Tegan responds.

"Huh?" Olivia confused.

"Watch and learn, kiddo." Tegan scratches Rusty's neck.

"Let's show them how it's done, Rusty!" She smiles and clicks her lips.

Rusty's ears dart forward in response to Tegan and they trot towards a line of eight polls. Tegan and Rusty easily trot over the first three poles and then stop perfectly on top of the fourth pole with his forehand in front of the pole and his haunches behind it. Tegan leg yields Rusty to the right, moving his body in a perfectly horizontal line. She halts just outside the poles and stands in a perfect square halt for three seconds. Tegan and Rusty execute a turn on the haunches with his body now parallel to the poles. They reign back five steps back between the poles and turn on the haunches to face the same direction they entered the pole series. Tegan and Rusty trot the remaining poles and halt into a perfect square after the last pole. Tegan scratches Rusty's neck and giggles.

"Let's bring it home, BM." Rusty raises his head and nickers. Tegan and Rusty reign back and walk over the poles backwards. They halt in a perfect square after the last pole. Tegan and Rusty perform a turn on the forehand and face the line of students. Tegan taps her hat and Rusty bows. They rejoin the students in formation.

"Who's next?" Tegan nonchalantly asks.

"Did that just happen?" Nate asks incredulously.

"Yep." Carson replies. "Not so boring now, is it?" He chuckles in response to the look on his student's faces. Olivia waves her iPhone.

"You gotta let me post this, Teegs. It'll go viral. Rusty will be an insta star. I'll even make him his own page." Olivia pleads.

"Nope. This is just between Rusty and the MHB. Don't want him to get a big head, do ya?" Tegan replies. Rusty shakes his big head in response and everyone laughs.

"Since you're so interested in this viral thing, you're next, Olivia." Carson says. The MHB laughs even harder.

"What did I say?" Carson, confused at their reaction, shakes his head.

"Never mind, Carson. Okay, Olivia. Let's see what you can do." Tegan commands. Olivia looks over in apprehension at Missy. Missy gives her a thumbs up.

"You got this, Olivia!" She exclaims, a little too eagerly. She looks over at Tegan.

"Face plant or Buck?" She asks.

"She'll probably try to rush through and force it. Lumber will fly and maybe a buck or two. It'll teach her to listen. I hope," Tegan smirks as she responds.

Olivia kicks Max forward and rushes to the poles. They're able to trot the first three poles, but Max kicks the fourth pole when Olivia abruptly asks him to halt. Lumber flies and Max bucks in frustration, almost unseating Olivia. Olivia rights herself and stops Max over the fifth pole. She looks over to Carson; he walks over to her and pets Max's neck.

"I rushed it, didn't I? Didn't wait for him." She says owning her mistake.

"Yep. Great work."

"Huh?" She raises her eyebrow in disbelief at his compliment.

"The mark of genuine progress is understanding and admitting one's mistake. Doing that brings you one step closer to getting to the next level." He pats Max's neck again.

"Let's let Max calm down and we'll try again. Sound good?" He smiles that charming boyish proud smile reminiscent of Hank Miller. Olivia smiles back and nods her head "yes."

"Thanks, Carson." She pats Max's neck and heads back to the line.

"Okay. That was a good start. We're all going to walk through this line one by one with our eyes closed. I will lead you through it. Don't worry if your horse hits a pole. I just want you to feel every step your horse takes. Who wants to go first?" Carson asks.

Crickets. The MHB all look at one another, hoping someone will volunteer. They all finally, including Tegan, look at Missy.

"Okay. Okay. I'll go first." Missy acquiesces. Carson excitedly claps his hands together and heads towards Missy. He takes Remington's reins and guides Missy over the poles.

"Eyes closed?" He asks.

"Yes." Missy grunts in frustration. He continues leading them down the poles. Missy yawns and drops her chin to her chest in boredom. Carson smirks and suddenly halts them over the fifth pole. Missy, unprepared for the halt, jerks slightly forward. Embarrassed, she quickly corrects herself and straightens her body in a perfectly seated posture to the sounds of giggles emanating from the MHB.

"What pole are we halted over?" Carson asks.

"What?" Missy, eyes still closed, asks bewildered.

"What pole are we halted over, Missy?" Carson repeats.

"I mean... You can't be serious. How should I know?" She replies defiantly.

"Open your eyes." He responds. Missy opens her eyes and looks down at the fifth pole. She looks at Carson, ashamed.

"Sorry, Carson. I just haven't slept and— "

"No excuses. Just do better next time. Okay? I need you to set the example for the rest of the kids. This is a chance for you and Remington to create your own language. Trust me."

"I do and I'll do better." She says with conviction.

"I know." He smiles, taps her boot, and walks back to the students.

"Who's next?" Carson asks. The entire line of the MHB raises their hands.

Missy removes another jewel embellished bridle from a solid brass horseshoe cleaning hook and polishes the Neue Schule brass loose ring horse's bit. She finishes, holds it up to the light, inspecting her work. The brass bit and jewels glisten under the light. Tegan enters, and she hands her the finished bridle. Tegan hangs it up on a brass horseshoe bridle hook labeled "Max - Dressage Bridle".

"Great work this morning." Tegan says.

"Really? I thought I was a wreck." Missy giggles.

"But you went back out and fixed it. That's what's important. Going back to the basics. I'm so proud of the solid foundation you are lying with Remington."

"He's such a trier, isn't he? He's always looking to connect with me and so quick to forgive me. I've never felt such a bond with a horse." She smiles and hands Tegan another bridle.

"That's how I feel about True. Well, not at first. I didn't even want to ride him." Tegan reminisces.

"Really? But I thought— "

"Yep. I thought my dad was crazy. I was so furious and thought my riding career was over before it began. And boy did I have to earn True's trust. I had to work for every inch of that horse. Ate so much dirt trying to get to know him and gain his trust. It's like he knew and was determined that I become the rider that I am today before he would bond with me. You see, Missy, the best horses are often the most difficult. That's what separates the average to good rider from the great rider - the willingness, the patience, the persistence to be in the moment, to be one with the horse. Horses don't have a clock, and the longer you cling to human time and expectations, the more often you will fail. It took my experience with True to fully appreciate that. My hope for you is that Remington will teach you the same thing. It's one of the most important lessons in horsemanship, and in life, if you ask me." Tegan looks at Missy with motherly affection and smiles.

"That's why you didn't push me?" Missy's, tears in her eyes, asks in disbelief. Tegan places her hand on top of Missy's and gently squeezes it.

"Almost done? I need some help with Lucky and Mirabella Mia." Tegan asks.

"Just two more." Missy points to the remaining two bridles hanging on the rack.

"Good. I'll meet you at the oval. I'll be on Mirabella. Tack lunge Lucky before you get on."

"Got it. He's still in a rubber bit, right?"

"You're training him. Your choice." Tegan winks and exits.

THE EXODUS

Tegan gallops Mirabella Mia towards a triple combination. She rocks Mirabella Mia back onto her haunches and easily jumps the 1.50 meter oxer, and deftly manages the rest of the combination, creating a perfect bascule over the final vertical. She canters to the final hanging plank vertical and jumps again with a perfect bascule, lands, and gently brings her down to a trot. Tegan runs her hand down Mirabella Mia's neck in gratitude as Missy walks in with Lucky on a long reign.

"She looks amazing, Teegs." Missy acknowledges with a bit of envy.

"I know, right? Her jumping form has come so far since the last show—so much more efficient and relaxed. She's just incredible. Haven't felt this kind of connection with a horse since Chewy, and in some ways, the bond with Mirabella runs even deeper. Used to dread riding mares, but now there's real excitement about every ride. Thoughts of her fill my dreams. She's simply amazing, and getting back into the show ring with her can't come soon enough." She exclaims with child-like glee.

"You're such a silly horse girl." Missy chides.

"Yep. And proud of it!" Tegan retorts, and feeds Mirabella Mia a sugar cube. Mirabella Mia greedily accepts the treat and affectionately licks Tegan's brown leather Deniro tall boot.

"What's on the menu for Lucky?" She asks.

"Mostly flatwork to check how his 'Bambi' legs are. Some poles and if he isn't a complete klutz, I was thinking of doing a small course. Nothing too demanding. Just work his legs and brain a little."

"Sounds like a brilliant plan to me. I'm gonna cool this beauty down while you warm up and then head back in. Want me to lower the jumps?" Tegan replies.

"Nah. It'll be awhile before I jump him, if I do. I was gonna bring them down anyway for this afternoon. You know the jumps won't set themselves." She looks slyly at Tegan and they both laugh.

Tegan lengthens her reins and nudges Mirabella into a relaxed, free walk along the edge of the fence. Missy walks Lucky towards the poles in a long reign and lets him figure out his foot placement. Tegan smiles in approval. They continue with their horses in a meditative dance of horse and rider; all four beings are content and in the moment of the day.

"Woof! Woof! Woof!" Bentley barks as she runs towards the arena. Lucky, startled by the commotion, darts to the side and snorts. Tegan halts Mirabella Mia and looks towards the commotion as well. Bentley runs into the arena, stops in front of Missy and Lucky, and continues barking. Tegan walks up beside Missy with Mirabella and they all stare at this little ball of energy. Bentley sits and howls at the sky.

"What's wrong, Bentley?" Missy asks. Bentley barks again, stands, and runs back to the gate. Missy looks at Tegan, concerned.

"Something is really wrong. Bentley knows better than to run into the arena when we're working." Missy says.

"I know." Tegan replies.

"Remington?" they both say in unison.

"He's out in the pasture with Rusty the last time I checked. It's his day off and you know how much he loves hanging with Rusty, so I just left him there." Missy says apologetically.

"It can't be that. I trust Rusty. He would be the first one here if there was something wrong with Remi. Look!" Tegan points out of the arena at a male figure running towards the gate.

Oscar, drenched in sweat, enters the arena. He removes his cowboy hat and wipes his face with his forearm.

"Señora! That pendejo, gringo! They're leaving. I tried to stop them. Ten horses. They're leaving!" Oscar exclaims and points toward the stalls.

"Catch your breath, and tell me exactly what's going on," Tegan responds.

"Jake. He's stealing your clients, Señora! There's a trailer at the stalls. They're leaving!" He exclaims. Tegan takes a deep breath and dismounts Mirabella Mia and hands the reins to Oscar.

"Can you take Mirabella, Oscar? I will look into what's going on. Where's Carson?"

"He's training Bubbles. He's almost done. Should I get him?" He asks.

"I can come with you, Teegs." Missy says.

"No. Finish training Lucky and get the arena ready for this afternoon's sessions. Oscar, please get Carson as soon as you're done with Mirabella. I will need both of you. Understand?" She looks at him with a look reminiscent of her father. He nods his head in full understanding of the situation.

"Si, Señora. We will be there quickly. I promise." He says. Tegan caresses Mirabella's neck and then rushes out of the arena with Bentley following closely behind.

Jake leads Max, dressed in a leather sheepskin shipping halter and navy blue Pessoa shipping boots, towards a foreboding black and chrome Peterbilt 389 semi truck attached to a commercial ten horse trailer. Linda, mid forty's dressed in jeans, collared white floral blouse, and brown paddock boots; an older version of her daughter walks on the other side of Max with a rigid and determined step. Olivia walks along her side in complete distress at the situation.

"Please, mom. I don't want to leave." Olivia tearfully grabs her mother's arm. "Don't do this. This is my family, my home."

"Olivia, we talked about this. You're not progressing fast enough. We're moving with the other horses and that's final."

"No, we're not!" Olivia walks over to Max and grabs the lead rope from Jake's hands.

"Stay away from my horse. Max is staying." Olivia turns Max around and heads back to the stalls.

"Olivia! Come back here!" Olivia's mom demands. Olivia stops for a moment and then continues with Max toward the stables, passing Tegan. She pauses and looks at Tegan with tears running down her face.

"Don't let them make me and Max leave." She says, hands shaking and softly holding back a sob from coming out of her throat.

"I won't. I promise. Can you help Missy get the horses ready for afternoon lessons? I need Oscar and Carson. Understand?" She gently smiles and squeezes her shaking hand. Olivia squeezes Tegan's hand and looks at her with the maturity of a professional horsewoman.

"Yes. I'll make sure everything is ready. Thanks, Teegs." Olivia continues down the aisle towards Max's stall. Tegan heads toward the Peterbilt semi-truck where a crew continues loading horses and Jake is in a heated conversation with Olivia's mom.

"I found you that horse, Linda! You said Olivia was fine with leaving. I need—" Jake looks up at Tegan.

"Don't even think about stopping me. I have a right to my clients." Jake shrieks. Tegan completely ignores him and turns to Olivia's mom.

"What has he promised you?" Tegan calmly asks.

"Free boarding and that Olivia will be jumping 1.30m by the end of the year. He already has her lined up with a couple of mini-Grand Prix in the next couple of months. And none of that foolish cowboy stuff. My husband and I did not take out a second mortgage so our daughter could be a 'buckle bunny!'" She exclaims. Jake smirks and laughs under his breath. Tegan takes a deep breath and looks at Olivia's mom with the maturity and determination of a marine general.

"I've specifically designed a riding program for each of our students here at Valley Vista Ranch to achieve their goals in a safe and effective long-lasting way, to not only be great riders, but great horsemen and women as well. I'm totally committed to helping Olivia achieve whatever goal she wants." She glances at Jake and continues.

"Jake has been one of our instructors here, but he doesn't have what it takes to get your daughter to the next level. I do. I know what it takes." She replies.

"Having my daughter ride a crazy thoroughbred around stupid barrels, putting her in a group of misfits that can't ride, and having that man teach her over poles! He's wasting her horse and her talent." Linda points to Carson as he walks up with Oscar and stands on one side of Tegan while Oscar stands on the other side like two soldiers beside their commander. A group of Jake's lady riders led by Cathy Turner gather behind Jake in a showdown reminiscent of an old Western.

"This place has gone downhill, and you know it, Tegan. We're sick and tired of all your antics. I know you're an Olympian, but making us pay premium rates for substandard lessons. I should be jumping 1.10m and I should have gotten a lot more for Ranger. And the rodeo? Seriously, Tegan, if your father— "

Sally grabs Cathy's arm to stop her from completing her rude and obnoxious comment. Tegan blinks away tears and stares back at the ladies.

"My life's work honors my father, Hank Miller, and everything he built. This ranch stands for education—yours and your horses'. The staff here aren't just employees; they're family. Disrespecting them disrespects me, this ranch, and my father's legacy. If this place doesn't meet your expectations, you're free to leave. No one will hold you back. But understand this—no matter what Jake claims, you and your horses won't find the same level of care, commitment, or heart anywhere else."

She locks eyes with Olivia's mom, unwavering.

"As for teaching your daughter to ride a crazed thoroughbred around stupid barrels, my father founded Valley Vista Ranch on natural horsemanship in any discipline. I was a stupid barrel racer and I still do pole work with all my horses, no matter what level they are at. That 'cowboy' foundation has made me the horsewoman I am today. As for 'that man', Carson is one of the best horsemen I've ever encountered and I'm honored to have him as one of our trainers. And Olivia will be a better rider, a better horsewoman, a better woman because of him. But it is your choice, Linda. You tell your daughter she has to leave." She looks at Carson and Oscar, trying to hide how crushed she is by the situation.

"Can you please help them load the rest of the horses? I need to prep for afternoon lessons." Her eyes shine brightly as she turns to head to the Hank Miller oval. Carson and Oscar walk over to the trailer and help load the horses in complete silence, leaving Jake and his 'women' in shock and disbelief.

The lamp flickers in the dark as a lonely beacon sitting on Tegan's desk. It conveys the feeling in Tegan's heart - the feeling of being completely alone against an insurmountable problem. Horses and students have left, removing the much needed stabling and training fees. She turned and walked away from the commercial trailer before counting how many; it was just too devastating. Jake had surgically removed a good portion of her income that she had painstakingly built over the years in one night.

Tegan picks up the myriad of bills and inputs them into her iPad. She reads the financial statements produced by her accounting software QuickBooks and shakes her head, knowing that the expenses are not paying themselves. Frustrated, she sets it on the desk and leans back on her rusty old office chair. It squeaks a protest as she turns to face her wall of pictures. She looks up at the black-and-white picture of her father and tears stream down her face.

"I thought everything was finally coming together. Missy coming back, Carson coming into my life, Oscar creating one of the best grooming facilities in the nation, Mirabella Mia becoming the magical horse I dreamed she would be. Valley Vista Ranch was finally becoming a world class training facility just like I promised you it would be. All that hard work." She wipes the tears from her face and continues her self recrimination.

"You told me—don't trust Jake. Don't hire him. But I ignored you. Thought I knew better. Thought I could control the risk, change the outcome, fix everything. All the upgrades—the new stables, the breeding barn, the imports flown in from every corner of the world—and for what? A pile of debt so high I can't even see daylight. I've dragged Valley Vista Ranch to the edge. Again. You kept this place alive through droughts, downturns, betrayal. You made it look easy. Was it? Or did you just hide it better? Because right now? It's too much. I'm drowning in it, and you're not here to pull me out." Overcome with sadness and stress, Tegan places her head on the desk and quietly sobs.

A light knock on the door brings her back to her senses, and she quickly wipes the tears from her face.

"Come in." She says. The door opens revealing an exhausted Oscar. He takes off his hat, wipes his face with his bandanna, and sits on the couch. He looks at Tegan and meekly smiles.

"How many?" She apprehensively asks.

"Nine, Señora. Señorita, Olivia and Max are staying with us. Señora Linda offers her apologies and hopes to talk to you about Olivia's training." He responds. He looks past her at the pictures on the wall.

"It's bad, Señora?"

"Si, Oscar. We have two, maybe three, months before we run out of money." He grimaces and looks at Tegan with concern.

"I know what you're thinking—I shouldn't have invested in the surrogate. Maybe it was a crazy idea, but—" she blurts out.

"You mistake me. I was thinking there was no way I would let Jake get us into trouble. I won't let it happen, Señora." He walks over to her and pulls out a manila envelope, and places it on the table.

"What's this?" She asks, confused.

"Abre lo." His eyes light up and a whimsical smile crosses his face. Tegan opens the manilla envelop revealing a myriad of hundred-dollar bills wrapped in a mustard colored currency strap. She looks up at him in utter disbelief.

"I can't. This is your life savings." She says.

"It's my money, Señora, and my investment. I believe in Valley Vista Ranch. I believe in you. You have been my family and will always by my family." He says earnestly. Tegan's eyes well up as she stands.

"My father said you'd always be there for me. Back then, I didn't believe him—I was too angry. I'm sorry, hermano." She steps toward Oscar and wraps him in a hug. He pulls her close in return.

"Everything will be okay, hermana." He squeezes her and kisses the top of her head. She shakes in his embrace and softly sobs, overwhelmed by the day's events. He fiercely holds her, determined to take her troubles away.

"I won't let anything happen to you or Valley Vista Ranch. I promise." He says in his ever brotherly protective tone. She closes her eyes and sighs in relief that she's no longer alone. Her father sent her the answer a long time ago. Oscar will always be her family.

"Thank you, Oscar." She releases him from the embrace and offers him her hand.

"Partners." She smiles. He looks at her, confused.

"¿Estás segura?" He asks.

"Yes. I should have done it a long time ago. You are the heart of this operation. You are what makes Valley Vista Ranch, Valley Vista Ranch. Dad would have wanted this. I'm sure of it." She confidently says.

"Partners." He vigorously shakes her hand.

The door swiftly opens as Carson charges through the door.

"I put my truck up for sale and I have some savings. You're not losing Valley Vista Ranch. I'll do whatever it takes." Carson stops short in response to seeing Oscar smiling brightly with Tegan. He spans the room and his eyes catch the mountain of money on the table. He looks back at Tegan, confused. Tegan looks back at Carson and giggles. She walks over to Carson, gently places her hand on his cheek, and looks into his eyes.

"I would like you to meet my new partner, Oscar Garcia." She smiles, removes her hand from his face, and turns to face Oscar. Carson walks over to Oscar and extends his hand.

"Of course. Congratulations, Oscar." He vigorously shakes Oscar's hand and a boyish smile crosses his face.

"I didn't know you were so well-heeled." He elbows Oscar in jest. Oscar grunts in protest.

"I'll see to los caballos. Buenas Noches, Señora. Señor." Embarrassed, he puts his hat back on and leaves in haste.

"You embarrassed him, Carson." Tegan chastises.

"I was just admiring his fiscal responsibility. If I had been so keen on money— " Tegan embraces and hungrily kisses him. He responds with a soft groan and kisses her back. He runs his hands lovingly down her back and draws her closer to him. She runs her hands through his hair and explores the rest of his body.

The door swiftly opens again and Missy and Olivia scramble through the door.

"Tegan, we figured out— "

Missy starts. Olivia yelps at the sight of Tegan and Carson in a passionate embrace.

"Oh...My...G" Missy shuts Olivia's mouth with her hand. Tegan and Carson jump away from each other in response to the intrusion and Tegan dashes behind the desk and straightens her hair.

"Yes?" she asks, like nothing has transpired. A disheveled Carson chuckles under his breath. Tegan glares at him with disapproval and then buries her hands in her face in complete embarrassment.

"I need to get a lock for that door." She mutters matter of fact. They all look at each other and burst into laughter. Olivia dramatically falls to her knees and pounds the floor with her fist, and lets out a roar of laughter.

"That's enough, Olivia." Tegan says in a mock stern voice, trying to hold back another outburst of laughter. She looks at Carson and he winks back at her.

"I'm sorry, Teegs. But there are things that you just can't unsee. It's like walking in on my parents. Forever burned into my brain. This is so way better than IG." She stops her commotion but can't hide the tears of laughter streaming down her face.

"Missy?" Olivia looks to Missy.

"I'm staying out of this one." Missy retorts. "Teegs, Olivia and I came in with a brilliant idea to save Valley Vista Ranch."

"Don't worry, Missy, Valley Vista Ranch doesn't need saving. At least not yet. Thanks to my new partner, Oscar." Tegan replies with a confident smile. Missy looks down at the heaping pile of hundred-dollar bills on the desk.

"Wow, Teegs. I guess you don't need us." She responds dejected.

"I would love to hear what you two have come up with. Spill it, kiddo." She says.

"Really?" Missy asks, trying hard to contain her excitement.

"You see, Teegs. We thought— "

"We thought Valley Vista Ranch should put on a clinic and a one day show. Each trainer could teach a discipline. You could teach show jumping. Carson could teach horsemanship. There could even be a demonstration on Rusty. Missy would do a basic course in dressage. Oscar can be, well Oscar. I would, of course, handle all the marketing. This would be great on Instagram. We could even do a reel or go live!" Olivia waves her arms in teenage abandonment, rudely cutting off Missy and blurting out the plan.

"Valley Vista Ranch is real. You don't have to— "

Carson interjects confused again at Olivia's Instagram world.

"Carson, a reel is a... Never mind. This could be huge, Teegs. I'll invite all my 'Insta' friends. We'll get the word out and you'll get a bunch of new clients." Olivia replies with the confidence of a senior marketing executive.

"It sounds interesting, Olivia, really. But chasing a 'bunch' of clients? That's not it. What matters now is a solid group—people who actually value what Valley Vista Ranch offers. The cocktail riding scene... that chapter's closed. What I want—"

She stops. The words hang there, raw and honest.

"A stable life. One built around real horsemanship and riders who care about a true partnership with their horses."

Silence follows as she stares at her friends, stunned by what just left her mouth.

"Oh, my god! I finally said it. That's what I want. Do you guys understand?" She finishes her revelation and smiles.

"The misfit horse brigade, but only bigger. I get it Teegs! And don't you worry, Missy and I got it covered." Olivia grabs Missy's hand.

"We've got a lot of work to do, Missy!" Olivia commands as she spins on her foot and canters out the door. Missy shrugs her shoulders and heads out the door in Olivia's wake.

Tegan leans back in her chair and sighs. She looks over at Carson and raises her eyebrow.

"It's not a half bad idea, Tegan. Having a clinic and horse show could really show what Valley Vista Ranch really is. The Valley Vista Ranch of your father. The Valley Vista Ranch of Oscar. The Valley Vista Ranch of you. We could go back to the basics and include all the technology, too. I've seen what you've done with this place, and I have to say that I wouldn't want to teach or be anywhere else." He smiles that effervescent boyish grin filled with confidence and hope.

"Really? You really think we could pull it off?" She entreats.

"Yep. The clients you deserve are out there, and this is our chance to get them. I'm in, Tegan." He replies. Tegan stands and runs over to Carson. She throws her arms around him.

"The Valley Vista Ranch of you and Rusty too!" She excitedly exclaims, and they continue where they left off.

THE PREPARATION

A beam of golden sunlight streams through the screen door, casting a warm glow on the organized chaos of the makeshift table overflowing with stacks of crisp entry forms, clipboards, and checklists. Tegan stands at the edge, hugging a set of forms to her chest as if grounding herself in the moment.

"I can't believe the response we've had," she breathes, her voice thick with disbelief and excitement. "We're fully booked, and we have a waitlist for every event." She exhales sharply, shaking her head. "I can't believe I'm going to say this, but Olivia was right." She grins and winks at Missy. "She really knows what she's doing. Don't let her know I said that."

"My lips are sealed." Missy nods with a smirk, pretending to zip her mouth shut.

Tegan turns to Carson and Oscar, her sharp green eyes brimming with energy. "Is everything set for tomorrow and Sunday?"

Oscar squares his shoulders, chest swelling with pride as he tips his well-worn cowboy hat back. "Sí, Señora. Each arena stands prepped and ready—Dressage, Show Jumping, Barrel Racing, and Horsemanship. Grooming stations shine, and everything's in place for the clinics."

Carson crosses his arms and leans casually against the table, a wry smile tugging at the corner of his lips. "The trainers all have their assignments, Morrison's has the food tent ready, and..." His smirk deepens. "The MHB has all the awards ready."

Tegan's eyes narrow. "What do you mean, 'the MHB have the awards ready'? What are you up to, Carson?"

Missy and Oscar both turn to Carson with a look of mutual confusion. Carson tilts his head toward the barn aisle.

"Come see for yourself. You won't be disappointed." With a wink, he strides out the door.

Tegan casts a suspicious glance at Missy.

"I thought you ordered the trophies?" she asks.

Missy winces. "Carson said he had it covered. I didn't think to ask questions."

Tegan sighs. "This should be interesting."

They follow Carson, curiosity mounting.

Carson, Rusty, and the Misfit Horse Brigade stand in front of a grey plastic folding table placed in the middle of the aisle. Carson, Rusty, and the Misfit Horse Brigade step aside, revealing a breathtaking display of handmade trophies, ribbons, and framed awards.

Tegan stares, motionless, at the table, her breath catching in her throat.

The Golden Horseshoe Awards gleam in the sunlight, each one adorned with a carefully selected photograph of a legendary horse from Valley Vista Ranch. A deep wooden plaque rests beneath each shoe, featuring a custom-engraved bridle tag with space for the winner's name.

She raises a trembling hand to her mouth, her eyes brimming with tears.

"I told you she'd hate it. We should have ordered real trophies from Trophy Depot." Nate straightens his glasses to mark his comment. Cameron elbows him hard.

"Ow. I'm just saying— " Nate continues. Tegan uncovers her mouth, looks at everyone, and smiles.

"They're perfect. So original. I love it." She exclaims. Alexa walks up beside Tegan.

"Even the ribbons? I made them and Olivia and Cameron made the horseshoe trophies." Tegan kneels down, so she's at Alexa's level.

"Especially the ribbons." She whispers. She then stands and turns to the group.

"Who's idea was this?" She asks Cameron. Cameron points at Olivia. Tegan looks at Olivia, shocked at the revelation.

"Really? This was your idea?" She asks incredulously.

"I just thought... I mean... Valley Vista Ranch is above the typical trophy display and I wanted everyone to see that. The trophies show that we do things our way. I wanted it to be special, Teegs." She responds defensively.

"Come here, Olivia." Tegan commands. Olivia walks to the other side of Tegan and stands next to her. Tegan wraps her arm around Olivia's torso and affectionately squeezes her in appreciation.

"So… Give me the walk through. I know you've been waiting patiently to do so," Tegan playfully says.

"Yeah, right. Olivia has been talking our ears off about 'her concept' of awards for centuries." Nate exclaims with the utmost of hyperbole appropriate for a boy his age. Olivia glares back at him and Cameron elbows him again.

"Stop it, Cameron. You know what I'm talking about. We talked about it yesterday— " Nate pouts.

"That's enough, Nate. Olivia, the stage is all yours." Carson replies.

"Well, you know what I say, Tegan; more is more." Olivia declares with that teenage arrogance. She continues pointing at the awards.

"I thought we would have six different awards, each symbolized with a Golden Horseshoe with the picture of the honored horse in it that the class represented." She picks up one of the gold horseshoes and hands it to Tegan.

"This is the Paratrooper award. It's for the best overall horse and rider over the two days. There's a picture of True in the center, and the winner has their name engraved on this bridle tag, which is placed on this plaque that also has a picture of True. They also get a bedazzled blue ribbon made by the fabulous Alexa. And of course, it wouldn't be Valley Vista Ranch if the horse didn't get an award as well. The winning horse gets a basket of carrots and a pound of hand made horse treats."

"I made those," Nate interjects. Olivia rolls her eyes.

"Yes. We all know how much you slaved in the kitchen making the horse treats, Nate." She responds sarcastically.

"As I was saying, each award represents one of the prized horses at Valley Vista Ranch: Remington, Rusty, Mirabella Mia, Bubbles, and Oscar." She giggles.

"I'm not a horse, Señorita." Oscar growls.

"You mine as well be. You sure think like a horse. The Oscar award represents the best grooming award because exceptional grooming is the foundation of horsemanship. Wouldn't you agree, Oscar?" Olivia looks at Oscar for affirmation. Oscar grunts and nods his head in approval - a small fatherly crack of a smile appears on his face as he looks proudly back at Olivia.

"I've also assembled a goodie bag for every participant. It will be the rage of the event." Olivia waves her arms in a flourish and points to the corner of the table. Rusty snorts and stomps his hoof on the ground. Carson pats Rusty's neck.

"I think you forgot something. Liv." Carson says with mock disapproval.

"Right. Sorry, Rusty. I didn't forget about you. I promise. Over here is the Rusty-Hank Miller award for the winner of best overall horsemanship. Rusty has agreed to be the judge of the best horseman or horsewoman. The winner of this award not only gets the Golden Horseshoe with Rusty's picture, but they also receive a second golden horseshoe with their name engraved on it to be placed on display at the entrance of Valley Vista Ranch for all to see and three free lessons with the instructor of their choice."

Tegan picks up the Rusty-Hank Miller award and her mouth drops in awe, tears streaming down her face. Rusty walks up to her, and she shows him the photo. He inspects the photo and nickers. Tegan wipes her tears and affectionately strokes Rusty's neck, remembering their time with her father. Rusty nuzzles her and then walks back to Carson. She hugs the horseshoe to her chest and looks over to Oscar.

"When was this picture taken?" She asks in a hushed whisper. She looks at the picture of her father with Rusty. The portrait shows a candid shot of Rusty on his hind legs in response to Hank's arms raised to the blue cloudless sky in front of Miller's Pond.

"You know when, Señora Tegan." Oscar says, eyes gleaming with tears reflecting the years of regret felt over the loss of their beloved father and Rusty.

"I also made one for you." Oscar picks up a nondescript brown box tied with light blue hay twine from the table and hands it to Tegan. Tegan looks at everyone and then greedily opens the box, revealing an eight by ten horseshoe frame of the priceless picture. She vehemently hugs Oscar and kisses his cheek.

"Thank you, Oscar. I love it." She says.

"Thank you for believing in me, Señora." Oscar squeezes her shoulder and smiles.

"Oscar smiles? That's a first. Hey, I'm hungry. Can we eat now?" Nate blurts out his truth in one breath. Everyone laughs. Tegan places her gift on the table and looks at everyone.

"Let's go to my place. Burgers and hot dogs are on the grill for my favorite team."

"Yay!" they all respond in unison.

"Ok, MHB. Let's put all the awards back, check the horses, and meet at Tegan's place in half an hour." Carson says. The MHB all scramble to clean up the awards table at Carson's bidding. He walks over to Tegan, hugs her, and kisses her head.

"You need me to grab some burgers and dogs?" He asks.

"Nope, everything's ready and I just texted Pedro to fire up the grill. Did you honestly think I wouldn't have dinner planned?" She giggles, mocking herself.

"Never." He laughs in response. He takes her hand and they head to the stables, with Rusty in the wake of all the hustle and bustle of the MHB and the grooms and stablemen.

The warm glow of incandescent string lights stretches above the picnic table, twinkling like fireflies against the rich hues of a deepening sunset sky. The air is thick with the scent of grilled burgers, sizzling hot dogs, and the faint sweetness of freshly cut hay. A gentle breeze rustles the tall oak trees surrounding the yard, whispering through the leaves as if joining in the revelry.

A long wooden picnic table, adorned with a blue-and-white checkered table-cloth, stands as the centerpiece of the gathering. Plates piled high with perfectly charred burgers, juicy hot dogs, and overflowing bowls of crispy chips sit alongside trays of corn on the cob dripping with butter and homemade potato salad sprinkled with paprika. The scent of freshly grilled vegetables, seasoned to perfection, wafts through the air.

To the side, an old wooden barrel serves as a makeshift drink station, buckets of ice filled with bottles of soda, lemonade, and beer nestled inside. A smaller table holds warm apple cobbler, freshly baked brownies, and a towering stack of Olivia-approved cupcakes—each meticulously decorated with edible glitter.

Laughter echoes across the yard, drowning out the soft country melodies humming from the outdoor speakers. The atmosphere is alive with the spirit of family—a family built not by blood, but by the bonds of hard work, shared dreams, and the unwavering love for horses.

Nate reaches for the pitcher of beer and Cameron quickly slaps his hand away to the laughter of Alexa and Olivia. Nate pouts in embarrassment and Carson fills his glass with another pitcher filled with lemonade and pats him on the shoulder.

"Maybe next time." Carson says sarcastically.

"I don't know what the probs is." Olivia says as she reaches for the pitcher of beer. Oscar grabs the pitcher and hands it to Pedro.

"No, Señorita Olivia." Oscar looks at her with fatherly disproval. She rolls her eyes and looks over at Tegan with a bored teenager's face.

"Whatever. I gotta pee. Pray tell, where is the privy, or are we expected to use an outhouse?" Olivia drawls with dramatic disdain, crossing her arms like she's expecting someone to actually suggest a tree out back.

Tegan lifts an eyebrow, exchanging a look with Missy that practically screams, "Please handle this before I lose my mind."

Missy sighs, standing up so fast her chair scrapes the porch floor. "I'll take you, Liv."

They head toward the house, Olivia trailing behind with exaggerated reluctance—until she gets a full view of Tegan's residence and comes to a dead stop, yanking on Missy's arm like she's seen a ghost.

"Someone dumped me in Little House on the Prairie!" Olivia gasps, wide-eyed, staring up at the towering log cabin.

Missy lets out a long-suffering groan and peels Olivia's grip off her arm. "Just because it's not mid-century modern doesn't mean it's 'Little House', Olivia. It's rustic. It has charm. Move your feet."

"I'm just saying..." Olivia gestures wildly toward the house. "I didn't think log cabin was still an option in the twenty-first century. When was this built, before electricity?"

Despite her complaints, her eyes dart around, taking in every detail.

They ascend the steps of the sprawling wrap-around porch—a vast, sun-warmed expanse of locally milled timber, sanded to a smooth sheen, yet still bearing the character of nature's knots and imperfections. The entrance pillars, carved from stone of varying hues—deep reds, cool grays, sandy browns—stand like silent sentinels, framing the home with an unapologetic, mountain-lodge grandeur. The same multicolored stones form the base of the porch and four chimneys that rise like castle towers from the house's sturdy frame.

A heavy, handmade wooden door, at least ten feet tall, stands at the entrance, adorned with custom-forged iron hinges and a massive, intricately detailed iron doorknob—a testament to Hank Miller's fabrication skills. The blackened roof tiles, slightly weathered, create a jagged skyline of peaks and dormers, making the home feel like it belongs among the rolling hills and endless sky.

The porch itself is a universe of comfort—a well-loved wooden couch with overstuffed outdoor pillows sits by the entrance, flanked by matching rocking chairs, a pair of wrought-iron side tables, and a lonely, yet inviting, handmade multicolored hammock swinging lazily in the farthest corner. It's the place where someone could easily lose an afternoon with a good book and a lazy breeze.

Missy marches toward the door, but Olivia lingers, taking it all in. It's rustic, yes. But it's also... kind of stunning.

"Don't let the book cover fool you, Liv," Missy calls over her shoulder with a wink before swinging open the heavy wooden door, which lets out a low, tired groan in protest.

Missy strides inside, but after a few paces, she realizes Olivia is no longer at her side. She turns back around... and there stands Olivia, mouth agape, spinning in slow circles, taking in the interior like she's just walked into some secret luxury lodge.

"Liv, the restroom is this way." Missy points toward the hallway to the right. Olivia doesn't move.

"I never would have guessed that this would be inside." She exhales in awe, eyes tracking every single detail. "Farmhouse chic. I love it."

Above them, the vaulted ceiling stretches nearly twenty feet high, its exposed oak beams rich against the creamy white walls. A grandiose stone fireplace, built from the same multi-colored rock as the porch pillars, climbs all the way to the peak of the ceiling, anchoring the great room with an unstoppable presence.

Framed black-and-white photographs, moments frozen in time, decorate the simple reclaimed wood mantle. Olivia's eyes catch on one of a woman in full Grand Prix dressage regalia astride a massive stallion. Another shows a much younger Tegan, wild-haired and free, riding a powerful horse bareback with nothing but a bridle. The last photo makes her stop entirely—a laughing, pigtailed Tegan being carried on the back of a much younger Oscar.

She takes a few slow steps toward the fireplace, her gaze sweeping over the deep brown leather sofas facing each other, their tarnished brass rivets giving them a vintage, well-loved look. A low reclaimed-wood ottoman sits between them, stacked with books, a ceramic coffee mug, and an iron bust of a horse's head—Paratrooper, if she had to guess.

Above, a massive iron chandelier hangs like a modern take on medieval elegance, its bulbous candle-style lights casting a golden glow.

Olivia snaps out of her trance and whips out her phone.

Before she can even open the camera, Missy moves like a viper, snatching the phone from her hands with expert precision and shoving it in her pocket.

"Respect, Liv. Tegan's home is not IG fodder."

Olivia gasps dramatically, placing a hand over her heart as if victimized.

"I wasn't going to post, honest!"

Missy narrows her eyes like she's heard that lie before.

"Right."

Olivia huffs in frustration, crossing her arms. "Fine. But you know a house like this deserves aesthetic appreciation, right?"

Missy points toward the hallway. "Restroom. Now."

"Ugh. Whatever." Olivia stomps away like a woman betrayed.

Missy watches her go, shaking her head with a smirk. The girl may be impossible, but at least she's entertaining.

Missy and Olivia sit at the picnic table in complete silence; Olivia is in a trance, staring at Tegan. Tegan looks over to Missy and Missy shrugs her shoulders in response, knowing it's better to stay out of Olivia's drama.

"So. What award do you guys want to win?" Tegan asks. A cacophony of answers fills the air.

"One at a time, guys." She responds to quell the onslaught of excitement. Nate's hand shoots up in the air like a gopher coming out of his hole for the first time in spring. Tegan smiles at Nate's eagerness.

"Nate, please share with us." She says affectionately. Nate leans forward, pushes his glasses up the bridge of his nose.

"You know we all want the Rusty-Hank award. It would be terrible if someone outside the MHB won," Nate replies with confidence.

"Really." Tegan replies with a smirk on her face.

"You know, Rusty, can be bribed but unfortunately not bought. So... You're going to have your work cut out for you trying to convince him." She looks over at Carson, who winks back, understanding Rusty's discerning behavior. Cameron angrily elbows Nate.

"No, we don't! You don't speak for all of us. I want the Oscar award. Roberto is going to be the best turned out pony out there, and I've been working on my standing wraps for weeks! Right, Oscar?" Cameron exclaims with the confidence of a seasoned groom.

"Good luck trying to lunge, Ro-BER-TO. I'll never forget the last time. You ate so much dirt!" Nate snorts. Tegan gives Nate a stern look of disproval and he shrinks back in his seat in submission. Tegan looks over to Alexa with her hand barely raised, smiles, and nods her head.

"I want the Mirabella Mia award." Alexa says, her voice barely above a whisper to hide her embarrassment.

"Why?" Tegan asks with genuine interest. Everyone leans forward in anticipation of Alexa's answer.

"If I ride like a horse as beautiful as Mirabella, then maybe I'll be great, like you and Mr. Carson, some day." She says shyly. Tears well up in Tegan's eyes at the profound simple truth coming from the seven-year-old. The MHB all look at each other, wondering who should speak next. They all look at Missy.

"You guys know I'm disqualified from the competition since I'm an instructor, but if I could win a trophy; I would want the Paratrooper award. It would be one more step towards my Olympic dream." Missy says as she takes a bite from her burger. Tegan squeezes Missy's hand and then makes eye contact with Olivia, who's staring at her.

"What, Olivia? Do I have something on my face?" Tegan asks, annoyed, which snaps Olivia out of her reverie like a gelding smacked by a crop. She blinks and her eyes widen.

"You guys! Tegan has the coolest house ever! It's like Laura Ingles married Bobby Berk! So modern on the inside with a nod to the family farm life. I love it. You definitely have to host a sleep over. Girls only, of course. And... you guys know me and Max are a shoe in for the Remington award. The other competitors should just go home. Right, Car?"

Carson chuckles and raises his glass of beer.

"Great work on pulling off this clinic. We couldn't have done it without you. Trophies don't matter, but I know that ALL of you will represent Valley Vista Ranch and make me and Tegan proud. To the MHB and Valley Vista Ranch!" He smiles and takes a drink from his beer. The rest of the cohort follow suit with Olivia adding the proverbial rolling of the eyes.

"That's such a 'Carson thing' to say." Olivia retorts. Everyone laughs at her obvious statement.

"It is!" She exclaims wide-eyed with teenage disdain.

"Oh, Olivia. Where would we be without your impeccable insights?" Carson chides. Oscar lets out a sonorous belly laugh to everyone's delight and gleeful yelps of approval fill the air.

A long day, but a good day, ends as twilight drapes over Tegan's house. Rays of sun light highlight Tegan's suntanned olive-skinned face, which lies on Carson's lap. Carson slides a stray hair from Tegan's forehead. He studies her face, memorizing every feature, every line. Tegan crinkles her freckled nose and sighs. He caresses her shoulder and looks up into the twilight filled sky. Stillness fills the air as he takes in the moment of just being in her presence. Tegan blinks, yawns, looks up to Carson and smiles. She sits up and stretches her arms above her head.

"What time is it?" she sleepily asks.

"It's almost 8 p.m." He replies and kisses her.

"Want some wine? She stands and trots inside like a thoroughbred, fully awake and alert after a brief slumber."

"Sure. I guess we're going inside." He chuckles and scrambles to follow her inside. Tegan reaches into her wine fridge and pulls out a bottle of wine. She pulls out two stemless wine glasses, uncorks a 2021 Grenache with the expertise of a sommelier, takes a sip, and hands the second one to Carson. She walks around the nine foot long granite island lit by three hand made hanging wooden lights and sits in one of the three burnt orange leather bar stools embellished with brass rivets.

"Alexa, play Peter Gabriel on Sonos." She casually says out loud and smiles beguilingly at Carson. Peter Gabriel's "In Your Eyes" plays over the speakers. Carson reluctantly sits next to her and takes a sip. He raises his glass to her.

"It's a beautiful night. Why don't we take these back outside?" He asks.

"Don't you like my house, or is this techno 'mumbo jumbo' too much? Would you rather I live in a teepee?" She teases.

"It's not that. It's just... Who is Alexa and what happened to the simple record player? We're all going to become legless/mindless slugs with of all this techno stuff. If you ask me, all you need is a clear sky, a fire, a horse, and a guitar." He responds indignantly. Tegan sets her glass down and presses her index finger on his lips.

"Dance with me." She whispers, takes his hand, leads him away from the kitchen island to the great room, and wraps her arms around his shoulders. She lays her head on his shoulder. They sway back and forth to the heavenly sound of Peter Gabriel's voice. Tegan looks up into Carson's eyes.

"I love you." She says without hesitation. He looks back at her and gently smiles.

"I love you too, Tegan Miller." He replies.

It's Clinic Time

T egan, perched confidently atop her loyal partner Chewy, lifts her coffee for a slow sip. The steam mingles with the cool, dewy air, filling her lungs with a crisp freshness that ground her. Her tan breeches hug every precise line of her leg, and her white polo—marked with her name, the five Olympic rings, and bold USA lettering—lays smooth against her frame, freshly tucked and sharp with pride.

Chewy shifts underneath her, ears twitching as if he, too, senses the rare pause in the day's rhythm. Together, they take in the morning's hum—birdsong blending with the distant clink of metal, the inaudible murmur of voices, and the occasional stomp of hooves. Peace, fleeting yet full, settles over them like a familiar blanket.

She hasn't carved out a moment like this in far too long. And yet, as warmth stirs in her chest, joy doesn't surprise her. It's the happiness that only comes from time spent with a best friend—one with four hooves and an honest heart.

Her gaze travels past Chewy's attentive ears toward the barn. Oscar moves with brisk purpose, gesturing to the grooms and stable hands as they ready the tack, prep horses, and tidy stalls for the busy day ahead. The clinic hums to life before it even begins.

Tegan pats Chewy's neck, fingers pressing into his sleek coat with affection, and gives a soft squeeze with her legs. Together, they move forward into the unfolding day.

Tegan rides by the dressage court, halts, and lets go of the reins to watch her protégé lead the dressage lesson. Missy dressed in a formal dressage coat adorned with a stock tie, white full seat breeches and patent leather jeweled encrusted dressage high boots, sits astride Mirabella Mia in a perfect square halt at the center of the dressage court in front of her students dressed in less formal schooling attire - a mic next to her mouth attached to her helmet.

"Thank you so much for participating this morning. I've seen so much improvement in your riding already, and I hope today translates to great scores in tomorrow's dressage schooling show. A couple of tips for tomorrow. Use tomorrow as a dress rehearsal for the real deal, right down to what you wear and how you prep your horse. You're not required to be in full dressage show clothes and your horse's mane doesn't have to be braided, but I would take the opportunity to present your best, especially if showing makes you nervous. As one of my mentors always says, 'The closer the rehearsal to reality, the more likely you'll be ready'." Missy looks over at Tegan and winks. Tegan nods her head and smiles back in approval.

"You will receive verbal and written comments, including a score from the judge. And you'll also have the option to run through a portion of the test after you've received comments from the judge." Missy explains.

"Questions?" She looks at her students with a smile. An older blonde and grey-haired woman dressed in a casual pink polo shirt, khaki full seat breaches, and black dressage boots astride a stunning 17 hand KWPN grey gelding raises her hand and speaks with a lofty voice.

"I loved all the information you provided, even in a group class setting. I was concerned that I wouldn't get enough attention, but I feel like I got more information today than I did in most of my individual lessons. Would you mind going over again the common mistakes a rider makes in the sitting trot?" She asks.

"Thank you for your kind words, Jessica. Valley Vista Ranch has always been about individualized attention, even in a group class setting. I've basically grown up here and the most I've learned was not only in group lessons but also in the quiet moments at the barn. Tegan would always take a moment to explain even the most mundane horse chores. I cherish that education. I've learned a lot from watching others and hearing their questions. So... with that, the most common mistake I see riders make when attempting the sitting trot is trying to sit still." Missy walks Mirabella Mia forward and starts the sitting trot gripping with her knees and bounces violently on Mirabella Mia's back. Mirabella Mia tosses her head in disapproval and swishes her tail. Missy quickly goes back down to a walk and pats Mirabella Mia's neck.

"Sorry, Mia." She whispers. She looks back at her students.

"So you can see how Mia responded to my stillness. I had no connection with her and she was obviously uncomfortable."

She resumes the sitting trot and moves seamlessly with Mia's lofty trot. Mia lifts her back in complete relaxation up into Missy's seat, and they dance together across the arena. She leans back slightly and Missy responds by effortlessly extending her trot. The students clap and Missy continues into a passage (characterized by a collected cadenced trot with elevated movement of the knees and hocks), her four legs looking like they're floating on a cloud. Missy heads back to her original position in the center of the arena and in a perfect square halt. She clicks her mic back on and says.

"It's so important to move with your horse. The movement in your body creates the stillness. You need to move through your ankles, hips, elbows, and lower back. Gripping with the knees draws the leg up, and the movement becomes stunted. When your horse goes up in the trot, your heels go down. But be careful not to move everything, especially your head. The 'bobble head' is not good for your neck and creates tension in the rest of your body. And as you saw earlier, I make sure that my horse keeps tempo. I don't slow her down. That's another mistake I see - slowing down the horse. What you need to do is the exact opposite - speed up your movement. Your hips move in double time with the trot of the horse. Does that help?" She looks up her students and they all nod their heads in unison.

"Okay, well, that wraps up today's session. Let's go out for a trail ride to cool off the horses." She heads toward the end of the arena with her students in tow.

Tegan smiles to herself, and she and Chewy head to the round pen. Built of solid oak, the round pen stands at an impressive eighty feet in diameter and six feet in height with an iron hinged eight-foot door framed with a sign engraved with the words "Bob's Playpen" on top. Tegan closes her eyes in remembrance.

Hank Miller nails another plank into a pole held by a young Oscar drenched in sweat. Tegan rides up bareback on Bob with only a rope halter, halts, hops off, and dusts off her fringed buckskin chaps with her cowboy hat.

"What ya think?" Hank asks with his typical boyish big grin on his face.

"We could've just bought one and had it all installed by now." Tegan rolls her eyes, frustrated.

"Wouldn't last, kiddo. Millers build stuff that lasts." He proudly smacks the pole. Tegan inspects the build and then looks at her father with a sly grin.

"You know what would be great, Dad?" she asks the all knowing loaded question.

"Pray enlighten us with your wisdom, dear Daughter." He responds, leaning against the pole, arms folded in full attention, meeting her with the same sly grin.

"A Eurociser. It would be a game changer for Valley Vista Ranch and the horses would benefit. I read this article yesterday and— "

"Not gonna happen, kiddo. At least not while I'm alive. We're horsemen here at Valley Vista Ranch. We don't need a cockamamie Eurociser to keep our horses fit. We ride them. Plain and simple." Hank shakes his head in disapproval.

"But Dad, all the top barns are putting in Eurocisers." She says adamantly.

"Don't care about those barns. Valley Vista Ranch is always going to be about horsemanship and not about those worthless trends. Now stop this nonsense and help me and Oscar." He replies.

"Not gonna happen, Dad." Tegan angrily responds and walks away to Bob, silently grazing in the field next to the construction. She grabs Bob's mane, mounts his back, and gallops off, leaving dust in her tracts.

Tegan giggles to herself and looks up to the sky.

"You were right, Dad. I've had that damn Eurociser rebuilt twice and still doesn't work right. It took me some time, but now I get it." She looks back to the old but still standing round pen, a little worn, but looking mostly brand new. She shakes her head and looks over at Oscar.

Oscar, dressed in a Miller Sport Horses white polo shirt with a navy blue collar, Wrangler jeans, cowboy boots, leather belt with a silver belt buckle, and hat stands at the center of the round pen with Lucky, mic attached to his shirt and transmitter clipped to his belt, like he's on a talk show. The students stand outside the round pen, next to each other, leaning against it.

"Hola, students. My name is Oscar and I will be showing you how to lunge a caballo. This is Lucky and he doesn't like to be lunged." He strokes Lucky's neck and Lucky responds by nodding his head up and down. The audience laughs at Lucky's behavior.

"So... I started this horse with verbal cues before attaching a line. Ground work is key for a productive lunge. If the horse doesn't trust you, lunging becomes impossible. Every horse is different, with different needs, but I found it helpful to put verbal cues in all our horses." Oscar turns toward Lucky and clicks his lips.

"Walk on." He says. Lucky responds by expressively walking towards the edge of the circle, head held anxiously high.

"Good boy. You see, he's a little nervous, so I make sure to always be at an angle to the horse, at his shoulders, with my lunge line not touching the ground. I ease him with the whip and wait until he calms down before asking him for anything else." He demonstrates and Lucky continues walking in a circle and slowly lowers his head in relaxation.

"Eso. That's what you want to see. Relaxed Horse. Trot, Lucky." Lucky trots, tossing his head momentarily in protest, but then lowering it.

"Good boy," Oscar reassures him and Lucky relaxes more with his nose almost touching the ground. He continues trotting him a circle for a couple minutes and Lucky flicks his ears and sighs.

"Canter." Oscar commands. Lucky picks up a lopey canter and raises his head a little to balance, but still completely relaxed. Oscar presses him forward into a gallop with his whip and Lucky lets out a playful buck. The audience laughs at Lucky's antics.

"This is good. If the horse can buck, he can jump, and Lucky is turning into a great jumper. Aren't you, boy?" Oscar explains and Lucky responds with another buck. Oscar slows him down to a canter, then down to a trot, and finally, to a walk. He pulls Lucky back towards the center of the round pen and pats him on the neck.

"I will finish Lucky by doing the same gates in the other direction. Remember, keep it simple and always be gentle with the horse. It's never of any use to over lunge a horse. All you'll have is a sore horse, or even worse, a lame horse. Your lunge should always have an intention. We'll go over more advanced techniques in the next session. Questions?" Oscar looks over the crowd and there's no response. He looks up at Tegan, smiles, and taps his hat to her. She waves back then leaves with Chewy. Oscar brings his attention back to his students.

"Bueno. Meet me at the cross ties with your horses and we'll go over the correct way to put on a polo wrap. Sound good?" He asks. The audience claps and head to the stalls to get their horses. Oscar sends Lucky out and continues lungeing.

Tegan guides Chewy toward the Hank Miller Oval, his hooves crunching over the gravel path. A group of students wait inside the arena, already mounted and shifting in their saddles, eyes turning as she approaches. She orients herself and Chewy just outside the arena; a smile of pure joy covers her face at the sight before her. Carson, dressed in full cowboy regalia with full fringed buckskin chaps, wrangler jeans, Simms button down western shirt, cowboy boots, and black Stetson hat with a mic attached to the rim, sits astride Rusty at the center of the arena. They transformed the arena into an obstacle course filled with wooden logs, a wooden bridge, barrels, poles arranged like a parking space, a lonely four-foot oxer decorated with archery targets, a blue liverpool, a plastic steer, and a pole with a rope attached to a bell on top.

Carson pats Rusty's neck, looks at the gathered crowd, winks, and legs Rusty towards the first obstacle. Rusty walks over the blue liverpool with ease and then canters toward the row of logs and jumps them. The audience cheers in approval. Carson brings Rusty back down to a trot and goes up the ramp over the bridge and down the exit ramp. They canter again and circle around each of the barrels like a highly tuned race car smoothly cornering a series of cones on a track. Carson flicks his reins at Rusty's haunches and they gallop towards the poles assembled in a U configuration marking a parking spot. They drag stop to a perfect square halt in the center of the poles. He raises his reins to the right and Rusty spins like a top on his hind legs eight times and stops again in a perfect square halt. He does the same spin to the left and stops is a perfect square halt. Carson pats Rusty's neck and they head back to the barrel, which has a lasso on top. He picks up the lasso and canters toward the steer circling the lasso above his head. He lets go of the rope and lassos the steer's neck.

The crowd cheers in delight, and they chant Rusty's name. Rusty's ears prick forward with pride as they head towards the archery targets. Carson lets go of the reins, grabs the bow from his back, and draws an arrow from the leather pouch fastened to his thigh. He aims the arrow at one target and lets it fly. The arrow hits the bullseye of one of the four targets, and the crowd roars with joy. Rusty eases into a walk as they head toward the pole with the bell. Reaching the spot, Carson halts the stallion, rises smoothly onto his back, and stretches to ring the bell overhead. Dropping back into the saddle, he cues Rusty into a lope, gliding toward the center of the arena. With a clean halt, Carson turns on his mic, ready to begin.

"Questions?" He asks with a boyish smirk on his face. The crowd roars with approval. Carson taps his hat and Rusty extends his front leg forward and bows. He looks over at Tegan, raises his eyebrow, and cocks his head to the side as if to challenge. She nods her head in affirmation and enters the arena riding Chewy bareback with a Native American styled hack-a-more. Rusty whinnies at Chewy and Chewy responds with a nicker and tosses his head.

"Who wants to see Tegan and Chewy attempt the course?" Carson asks with the same boyish smirk on his face. The crowd roars with delight and chant Chewy's name. Carson hands Tegan his bow and arrows. She attaches the satchel of arrows to her thigh and leans down and whispers into Chewy's ear. Chewy pricks his ears forward and stomps the floor, ready for the challenge. Tegan and Chewy negotiate the obstacles with ease and head to the final oxer. Tegan urges Chewy into a full gallop, drops the reins, and draws an arrow in one fluid motion. The first shot strikes the target dead center. Without hesitation, she nocks another, then another—each arrow flying with precision, each target falling in rapid succession. Slinging the bow across her back, she grabs the reins and rolls Chewy back to face the four-foot oxer.

With a grunt and a gathering of strength, Chewy launches into the air, clearing the jump with a flawless bascule, as if chasing Olympic gold all over again. The audience gasps, then erupts into applause, clapping in perfect rhythm.

Tegan swings her legs back, rises to her feet atop Chewy's back, and canters toward the bell, a blur of balance and fearless control.

"Whoa." She softly says to Chewy. He slows down to a walk and then halts underneath the bell. Tegan grabs the rope and rings the bell. She sits back down and proceeds to the center of the arena in a piaffe - a highly collected and cadenced trot. She halts next to Carson, and Chewy bows to the audience.

"Show off." Carson chides Tegan in a low whisper. He turns on his mic and looks towards his students.

"Thank you, Tegan, for the incredible demonstration of horsemanship." He says. Tegan nods her head, smiles, and waves her hand towards the students. She and Chewy then head towards the gate at the end of the arena. Chewy lifts the latch and opens the door and head out like it's a normal day at the ranch and Chewy is just another ranch horse and not an Olympic gold medal winning show jumper. Rusty whinnies his approval and the audience claps. Carson taps his hat and smiles at Tegan and Chewy with adoration.

"So, can anyone tell me what horsemanship is?" He asks his students. All the students raise their hands in unison.

Tegan guides Chewy into his stall and kisses his muzzle. He knickers back and gently lays his muzzle in her hands, and closes his eyes - their ritual since he was a foal. She closes her eyes and just stands with him, connected to his presence, embracing these small moments which sum up her happiness - a moment of joy.

"Tegan?" The haughty English accent disrupts Tegan and Chewy's tranquil moment. She opens her eyes, revealing Cathy Turner and Shelly Winters standing outside Chewy's stall. Tegan strokes Chewy's head, whispers in his ear, and heads into the aisle, closing Chewy's stall door behind her.

"It's so good to see you, Tegan. This clinic seems like a smashing success. It would be even better if the caterer was— "

"What do you want, Cathy? I have to get ready for my session." Tegan interjects as politely as possible, given the intrusion.

"There is such a history here at Valley Vista Ranch. I remember when your father would work on the horses before anyone was at the barn. I would set my alarm at 3:30 just to catch a glimpse of him working. And you would be right there by his side. Learning from the best." She reminisces.

"Thank you for the history lesson, Cathy. Now, if you'll excuse me, I really need to get ready." Tegan walks past them.

"Jake never shows up!" Cathy exclaims. Tegan stops, turns to face them, and crosses her arms.

"And the horses, it's a mess, Tegan. Please do something!" Cathy shouts.

"I'm sorry for your situation; I truly am, but I actually don't have to do anything. You're more than welcome to stay and audit the session, but this conversation is over." She says calmly, shaking her head at Cathy's consistently brazen behavior.

"Please! The horses. Can we just bring the horses here? You don't have to do anything. We'll find another place. We just have to get the horses out of there. You can't let your disdain of me harm the horses." Cathy pleads with desperation, her blue eyes welling up with tears.

"We're sorry for everything, Tegan. We shouldn't have left the way we did. Please help us." Shelly adds with a pleading tone. Tegan shifts her weight side to side, clearly uncomfortable with the confrontation, yet her eyes soften at their plight.

"Let me talk to my partner. I'll get back to you later." She replies and continues to her office.

"Partner?" Cathy asks. Shelly grabs her elbow and propels her towards the Hank Miller arena.

"That's it, Bethany. Now balance him up to the combination. Easy. Easy." Tegan says in her mic attached to her baseball hat as she guides Bethany through a one meter triple combination of two verticals and an oxer spaced two strides and three strides, respectively. Bethany steadies Winston through the combination and he lands a little on the forehand. She quickly sits up, half halts the reins, and balances him through a right turn to the final combination of two verticals separated by two strides. She finishes the combination and brings Winston down to a trot and guides him to a series of poles and then canters to the final oxer.

"Ride to the base of the jump, Bethany." Tegan directs. Bethany and Winston head towards the final oxer and easily clear it. She brings him down to a trot and halts him next to the other students in front of Tegan. Tegan smiles, walks up to Winston, and pats him on the neck.

"Good boy." She proudly says. Tegan steps back and addresses her students.

"Can anyone explain to me why I put poles in this course?" She asks as she gestures towards the twelve jumps in the arena. They all raise their hands in earnest, hoping that she'll notice one of them. She looks over at Nate and nods her head.

"To slow him down." He answers definitively.

"That's true. The poles did slow Winston down, but why would I ask that question at that moment?" She responds. All the students look around, trying to understand the question. Olivia confidently raises her hand.

"Olivia?" Tegan asks.

"You're looking for rideability. You're asking the rider if, at any moment, they can correctly communicate with their horse. Communication is key," Olivia responds.

"That is correct, Olivia. Well done. If you're not in sync with your horse, you won't be able to navigate the higher/more technical courses. I know pole work might seem boring, but it's so important to know where your horse is at every stride. It's also important that your horse understands what you're asking. Communication goes both ways. Listening and asking. Taking time with your horse, through ground work, pole work, and just being with them develops that two-way communication. If there was one thing I would hope you would take away from this session, is that consistent, clear communication creates trust. Remember that every time you run into a roadblock." She looks over at Bethany.

"Bethany, I'm so proud of the progress you've made with Winston. This part-nership has really developed, and I can see all the work you've put in. I see how much your bond has grown and I can't wait to see it mature more." Tegan taps Bethany's boot, drawing a flash of a bright smile that competes only with the burst of neon green hair peeking out from beneath her black Samshield helmet.

"Questions?" Tegan looks around her group and they all smile in silence.

"Alright then. I can't wait to see all of you at the schooling show tomorrow. No matter what happens at the show, know that I'm so proud of all of you. Let's cool down our horses and break for lunch. Morrison's have graciously agreed to cater over at the tent." She clicks off her mic and walks toward the gate where she is met by the ever present Rusty scrupulously watching the session. She opens the gate, feeds Rusty a mint, and runs her hands down his mane.

"How did I do, BM?" she whispers, hoping that her session met Rusty's approval. Rusty nickers back and affectionately bumps her side with his muzzle. She places her hand on his withers and they casually walk toward the tent - side-by-side, two colleagues and best friends.

A BANQUET FOR ALL

R ows of gingham covered round tables seating eight equestrians still wearing
their show clothes from the day's schooling show line the tent. At the end
of the tables sits a head table reminiscent of a wedding party with Tegan, Oscar,
Missy, Janet, Carson, Dr. White and the grooms and stablemen of Valley Vista
Ranch enjoying the night's festivities of awards, music, and community. The Live
Again Band, a local favorite country band, finishes their set with a lively Texas two
step. The audience applauds with approval at the band's efforts.

"Thank you. We're going to take a thirty-minute break. In the meantime, I
would like to welcome Tegan Miller, the host of tonight, to the stage to present
the final two awards. Thank you, Tegan, for including us in your first annual
clinic. We hope to be back next year and the years to come." The lead singer,
dressed like a cowboy with the well worn tan boots and jeans topped with an
embroidered western shirt and dark brown cowboy hat, gestures towards Tegan
to come to the stage. Tegan finishes her beer and marches toward the stage.

"Thank you, Steve. We're honored to have you here to share in this momentous
event. Okay. I know you've all been waiting for the final two awards of the two-day
clinic, so I'll be brief." She says. The audience chuckles at her statement.

"I promise. Anyway, my partner Oscar and I just wanted to thank all of you for
not only participating in our first annual clinic but being with us tonight as we
acknowledge the efforts of a few individuals these past couple of days. So let's get
to it. The last two awards are the Paratrooper award for best overall horse and rider
and the Rusty Hank Miller award for the best display in overall horsemanship.
The Paratrooper award holds a special place in my heart for obvious reasons,
but the recipient of this award and her horse have surprised me with how much

they've grown as a team and as individuals. I don't know what Valley Vista Ranch would be without this incredible duo - Olivia Mayer and Maximillian Roulette." The audience cheers their approval and the MHB roars with delight, chanting,

"Max! Max! Max!"

Olivia, uncharacteristically shy, stays seated like a Greek statue. Tears roll down her face in disbelief at the announcement. It can't be true. Olivia would often boast in disdain of her prowess as a show jumper to her fellow Misfits, but deep down inside, she'd always felt like an imposter. On cue, Carson gets up from the master table and escorts Olivia to the stage for her award. Tegan hands the bedazzled blue ribbon to Olivia and warmly embraces her, causing Olivia to melt into an uncontrollable teenage sob. The audience sighs at the beauty of the moment and whispers ripple through the tent like the wave at a college football game. Olivia clips the ribbon onto her breaches at her belt and then holds up the golden horseshoe to her dear friends - the Misfit Horse Brigade. They cheer and begin chanting,

"Liv, Liv, Liv!" Olivia blows a kiss and then looks at Tegan. Tegan waves her hands to quiet the MHB and whispers to Olivia.

"Would you like to say a few words?" She asks. Olivia at first shakes her head 'no', then rethinks her decision and greedily grabs the mic from Tegan's hands.

"Thank you, Max, for teaching me how to ride. Thank you, MHB, for being my family, my best friends. Thank you, Tegan, for being my coach when I didn't deserve one. And..." She wipes her tears and looks at Carson.

"Thank you, Carson, for believing in me when no one else would. I love my Valley Vista Ranch family. Thank you." She finishes her speech barely above a whisper and quickly heads back to her seat. Alexa and Cameron both wrap their arms around her and give her a hug. Nate shifts uncomfortably in his seat, then offers her a high five. Olivia giggles and slaps his hand as hard as she can.

"Ow, you would have to ruin it, Liv." He responds defensively.

"I wouldn't be Liv if I didn't." She responds sarcastically. She passes the golden horseshoe to the team for them to admire.

Carson steps off the stage, and Tegan grabs his hand. He raises his eyebrow in confusion.

"Just follow my lead." She whispers and winks with a sly grin across her face. She looks back at the audience and smiles proudly, displaying her affection for Carson.

"The last award tonight is the Rusty Hank Miller Award, honoring the best overall horsemanship," Tegan says, her voice thick with emotion. "While it means the world that my Valley Vista Ranch family named this after my father, I'd be remiss not to recognize another remarkable horseman—someone who reignited the spirit of true horsemanship here at the ranch."

She pauses, eyes shining. "Carson Peterson."

Applause breaks out, loud at first, then softens into a wave of reverent whispers that ripple through the tent. Tegan turns and hands him the microphone, her hand lingering just a moment longer than necessary. Carson shifts uneasily, running a hand through his hair as the spotlight tightens around him. The Misfit Horse Brigade giggles from their table, knowingly, as they watch their fearless leader squirm in front of a crowd that now sees what they've known all along.

"You can do it, Car!" Olivia shouts. Carson looks back at her in mock disapproval. He clears his throat and brings the mic to his mouth.

"Hello, everyone. Thank you for coming. It's been an honor to be one of Tegan's trainers at Valley Vista Ranch's first annual clinic. I hope all of you gained some insights into the power of a relationship with your horse. Relationships need to be nurtured and held sacred, and there's no one better at understanding relationships than my best friend, Rusty. So without further ado, I'm proud to have Rusty select this year's winner." Carson places his thumb and index finger in his mouth and whistles. Rusty lopes into the tent and halts in front of the stage and bows.

Carson eyes widened at Rusty's appearance; his mane and tail braided with a rainbow color of ribbons, his face and body painted with different symbols honoring the Native American heritage, and his hooves covered with glitter and bedazzled with diamond-like crystals. Rusty is definitely a member of the MHB whether Carson likes it our not. Carson looks accusingly at the Misfits and they all innocently shrug their shoulders and point to the person seated next to them. Cameron mouths the words, "He looks spectacular!" and gives two thumbs up. The rest of the audience claps and shouts out his name.

"Rusty, Rusty, Rusty!"

Rusty paws the ground for silence. The audience giggle and then settles into a proper mindful attention for Rusty. Rusty's ears perk forward to one table placed at the far right side of the first row. He walks over to the table and places his muzzle in Bethany's lap. Bethany gently caresses his forehead and looks tearfully at Carson, who returns her look with a wide smile, beaming with pride. Tegan leans over and whispers into Carson's ear.

"That's who I would have chosen." She says.

"Me too." He responds. He holds the mic to his lips again.

"Bethany Jackson and Winston are this year's winner of the Rusty Hank Miller award!" He exclaims like a proud father watching his daughter win their first medal. The audience applauds and gives her a standing ovation. Hands flying to her mouth, she sways unsteadily, the moment hitting hard. Leaning into Rusty for support, fingers gripping his mane, she lets the steady stallion guide her like a loyal service dog toward the stage. Reaching Carson, she throws her arms around his neck, and he sweeps her off her feet with a grin, lifting her into the air.

"Well done, kiddo!" He exclaims and then playfully tugs at her neon green pony tail. She slaps his hand away in mock anger - a familiar game they've shared over the years. Tegan hugs her and offers her the ribbon and golden horseshoe, and Carson quickly disposes of the mic into Tegan's hands and steps behind them.

"No pressure—but as the first winner of the Rusty Hank Miller Award, you earn three lessons," she says, a playful glint in her eye. Who do you want to train with?" She asks with a twinkle in her eye. Bethany bites her lip in contemplation and twirls her neon green ponytail around her finger. She smiles and leans into the mic.

"Well, I'm the horsewoman I am today because of Car, and I'm the show jumper I am today because of you. And I never would have mastered the standing wrap without Oscar. So... Can I have all three of you?" She beguilingly asks. Carson and Tegan look at each other and then at Oscar, who's fallen asleep in his chair. Pedro elbows him awake and whispers in his ear. Oscars raises both thumbs up, not sure of what question he's answering. The audience explodes in laughter and cheer.

"Well, that's that. You'll get all three of us. You deserve it, Bethany!" Tegan tries to suppress a giggle, but it comes out as a piggish snort. The audience laughs at her lapse in decorum and she quickly regains composure. She nods to Carson, and he knowingly escorts Bethany to her seat, with Rusty following closely behind. Tegan looks back out to the audience, filled with emotion.

"I just want to express my heart-felt thanks to all of you who participated in Valley Vista Ranch's first annual two-day clinic. It has always been a dream of mine to continue my father's legacy of horsemanship and love of competition. And fingers crossed, we'll continue this event in the years to come. Please enjoy the rest of your evening and get out on the dance floor for more live music from The Live Again Band. Good night!" She places the mic back on the stand and heads back to the head table with the audience applauding in the background.

It's late. Tegan rubs her eyes and looks at her iPad in complete, solitary concentration. Oscar sips from his coffee and coughs, reviving her from her intense trance. She blinks and looks back at him and smiles, recognizing that she's been ignoring her steadfast partner.

"Sorry, Oscar. But... You're not going to believe this. We're going to be back at full capacity by the end of the month and we have a waitlist with eight more horses." She exclaims excitedly, raising the iPad for Oscar to see. He sets his coffee cup on the desk and leans forward, pretending to see the display, but then looks down at his hands.

"I'm so happy for you, Señora. You could buy back my shares if you want to. I know how much Valley Vista Ranch means to you."

"Heck, no." She grabs his hands and squeezes. "We're partners and we're family. I need you by my side, hermano. And you know, my dad wouldn't have it any other way." She responds. A bright smile appears on Oscar's face and he takes another sip of his coffee to cover up his enthusiasm.

"There's another thing we need to discuss." She says with a look of concern.

"Yes?" He sits back and looks at her with full attention.

Carson enters with Missy in tow. They both make a beeline for coffee after the long days and nights of the two-day clinic, with each of their designated coffee cups sitting on the table, begging to be filled. Carson fills his coffee cup inscribed with, "Cowboys do it Better", and fills Missy's coffee cup labeled "Horse Crazy Girl for Life". They click mugs and take a sip. Carson turns and looks at Oscar and Tegan.

"Bubbles' abscess finally came through, thanks to Oscar's diligent poultice regimen. But Dr. White wants him on antibiotics for a week to make sure he's completely cleared. That horse always seems to have something going on with those hooves. Should we put him on a different supplement?" Carson asks.

"Not sure it'll help, but we should definitely add a probiotic to his feed. I'll call the farrier tomorrow and see if we should change his shoeing." Tegan replies. She motions them to have a seat.

"I was just about to discuss an important topic with Oscar, and we would appreciate your point of view as well. Cathy and Shelly have asked to come back to Valley Vista Ranch." She says with raised eyebrows. Missy immediately jumps out of her chair.

"No way, Teegs! Cathy Turner has been nothing but trouble at Valley Vista Ranch. And I'll never forgive what she did to me and Remi." She says vehemently. She scans the room, heat rising to her cheeks as embarrassment crashes over her.

"I'm sorry guys, but Cathy Turner and her cronies leaving Valley Vista Ranch was the best thing that happened to us." She sits back down and crosses her arms in indignation.

"So we got one vote, 'no'. What do you think, Carson?" She asks.

"I actually have to agree with Missy. I respect the history, but they go against the culture you want to create here at Valley Vista Ranch." He says calmly.

"Another vote, 'no'." She sighs. "Oscar? Thoughts?" She asks. Oscar settles back in his chair, eyes narrowing slightly as he turns the words over in his mind, silence stretching while wisdom takes its time to surface. He takes off his hat, runs his hands through his hair, places it back on his head and simply responds.

"Señor Hank would never turn away a horse. We could put them in the back pasture away from the other horses and deny them access to the arenas. I will oversee their care until they can find another arrangement." He leans back in his chair and sips from his coffee, at peace with his opinion. Tegan tilts her head and looks at Missy and Carson.

"You're right, Oscar. Valley Vista Ranch has always been about the horses. I will help with the horses." Missy sighs.

"So will I." Carson affirms.

"Well, I guess we're unanimous. I will let Cathy and Shelly know tomorrow." Tegan gets up and stretches.

"You guys go home. I'll do night check." She says.

"Good. I'm exhausted. I'll see you at home, Teegs. Good night, everyone." Missy yawns in reply, then hustles out the door.

"Come on, Bentley! The bus is departing in three minutes!" Missy yells. Bentley barks in reply, paws skittering across the pavement outside.

"Buenas noches, Señora. Hasta Mañana." Oscar tips his hat and exits before she can reply.

"You want some company?" Carson asks. Tegan takes Carson's hand, and he escorts her out the door.

Remington bucks and squeals running through the pasture with his buddy, Rusty, glued to his side. The moonlight creates an ambient light over their play time. Side-by-side, they mimic each other in an elaborate display of horse play. Tegan and Carson walk together to the fence line and watch in complete silence. Tegan sighs.

"Love watching Remington play. He's become the horse I knew he could be because of you. My father's last living legacy. Thank you, Carson." Carson wraps his arm around her torso and kisses her on the side of her head.

"You are your father's legacy. And I know that he's smiling from up above knowing that his daughter has protected it, protected Valley Vista Ranch."

She looks out at the horses and then stares up to moon and starlit sky.

"I miss him, especially during the quiet times of the day when I'm watching over the horses and all the clients and staff are gone. Those were the times when it was just me and him facing the world. He would always make a point of taking me on trail rides. Making up any excuse to be on a horse. Mending fences. Check on the broodmares. Any excuse. I would always feel annoyed by it when I was younger, but now I yearn for those days." She wipes the tears from her face and smiles wistfully at Carson. Carson takes her hand and kisses it. He whistles and Remington and Rusty trot up to them. He hops over the fence, grabs Remington's mane, and with a leap mounts his back.

"Let's go." He commands, and a sly grin materializes. Tegan huffs in mock annoyance, but quickly obliges and jumps over the fence and joins him astride her trusted friend, Rusty. They gallop out of the pasture, up and down the grass-covered hill filled with a blanket of wildflowers kissing the horses' legs as they pass by; weaving through the large oak trees dancing with the breeze that creates a staggered line towards Miller's pond. They halt at the pond and dismount. Rusty and Remington partake of the freshwater pond and then graze in a relaxed moment of tranquility amongst the birds, toads, crickets, and all the animals of nature as God had intended.

Carson looks hungrily into Tegan's emerald eyes and passionately kisses her. She responds and presses her body against him, wanting more. He caresses her breasts as his lips find her neck. She groans and guides her hands to his buttocks. He lifts her into his arms, their eyes locking, breath catching as the world around them fades. Carrying her into a quiet clearing beneath an ancient oak that has stood watch for over a century, he lowers her gently onto the grass. Under a sky strewn with stars, they continue their love, wrapped in moonlight and each other.

Tegan lies on Carson's bare chest, his arm wrapped around her waist; she softly caresses his arm.

"I wish we could stay here forever." She says as she sits up and looks down at him, her hair cascading down her shoulder, covering her olive skin and shoulder dusted with sun kissed freckles.

"We could. I'll build a lean-to right here," he says with a half-smile. Sitting up, he brushes her hair behind her shoulder and kisses the spot tenderly. After handing her shirt back, he quickly pulls on his own.

"Of course you would. 'Just give me the stars, a good horse, and a warm fire'. Isn't that your creed?" She chides.

"I just don't need a lot of stuff. Stuff just gets in the way of what's important." He playfully kisses her nose. She giggles and slaps him away.

"So if I asked you to move in with me, that would be too much 'stuff' for you." She states unemotionally as she finishes dressing. Rising to her feet, she zips up a pair of black, well-worn paddock boots and saunters shamelessly toward Rusty, leaving Carson speechless in her wake. Gripping the gelding's long mane, she swings onto his back with practiced ease. Her hand glides fondly along his neck, and he responds with an affectionate nibble at her boot. Carson dusts off his Wrangler jeans with his cowboy hat and mounts Remington. He joins Tegan and they begin their journey back to the stables through the long green grass and decorated with wildflowers in silence. The moonlight guides their path through the oak trees that stand guard along the trail.

"I didn't want to mention it in front of Missy, but I'm concerned about Jake. How he will respond to his horses coming here. I can't get out of my head how he reacted when you fired him." He says, breaking the silence.

"Jake is not worth a conversation. He's made his bed, and he's a part of my past, and that's all I care to talk about that. I want to move forward. I want to move forward with you. What do you want?" She asks. Her heart skips a beat in trepidation about his response.

"You know what I want. It's always been you and always will be, waking up by your side every morning and seeing your smile. That's what I want." He says matter-o-factly.

"Are you saying?"

"Yes. I will be a part of your stuff. All of it. Just know there will be days where I will also be a part of the earth, under the moon and stars, with my horse and a warm fire." He replies and starts humming to the stars. She considers speaking but stops herself in order to take in the moment with her beloved. They continue their path back in silence.

I'm In!

M issy and Remington gallop across the sunburnt tall grass and jump over a three and half foot old log lying on its side in perpetual slumber from its days as an oak tree providing shade to its family and friends; turning left, they continue galloping through the winding tree path lane from Miller's pond. Remington lets out a playful buck, and Missy giggles with joy as she urges her best friend towards the stables. Beams of sunlight hit her face like lasers from ray guns unveiling her blue-green eyes masked underneath her Samshield black helmet. The crisp fall morning wind whips through her honey blond braided ponytail as she stands in a two-point, lifting her seat off the saddle, giving Remington full motion underneath. Fall leaves crunch under Remington's hooves as they dance on the ground, kicking up a plentiful medley of leaves, grass, and dirt.

Their morning playful excursion ends as she brings him down to a trot next to the barn and then gently halts him. Missy swings down from the saddle and scratches Remington's neck. He responds with a deep nicker, curling his forehand around her in a tender, horse-sized embrace. Gratitude floods through her—his forgiveness wraps around her just as firmly. Their bond, once strained, now feels unbreakable. She kisses his muzzle and exhales, peace settling in her chest. Valley Vista Ranch isn't just home; it's where she belongs.

With a gentle pat, she releases Remington and turns to find Bentley beaming, her wide, Joker-like grin wrapped around a burnt yellow manila envelope. Her tail sweeps the air like a windshield wiper on high, body quivering with excitement. Beside her, Pedro stands ready with a currycomb in hand, calm and patient as always.

Missy arches a brow in question. Pedro shrugs, a knowing smirk playing on his lips.

With a reluctant sigh, she passes Remington over and crosses the yard. Bentley scampers toward Missy, entire backside wagging as if her joy has nowhere else to go.

"What's this?" She asks. Bentley sits and drops the envelope at the tips of Missy's black tall Deniro field boots and looks up affectionately, tail still wagging in anticipation. Missy scratches underneath Bentley's chin, picks up the envelope, and quickly opens it. She gasps and clutches the prized envelope to her chest.

"Let's go, Bentley!" She shouts and they run off towards Tegan's office.

Carson astride Bubbles with a western bareback pad halts Bubbles at the cross ties. He dismounts and removes the hackamore, removes the bareback pad, and pats him on the neck. Bubbles nuzzles him and nibbles his pocket quickly removing a sugar cube from Carson's hand. Carson hums along to the song "Free Bird", and feeds Bubbles another sugar cube. As he hangs the hackamore and places a leather rope halter over Bubbles' head, Bentley bolts right into his legs and circles around him, butt and tail wiggling double time to the beat of his song. He ties Bubbles to the hitching post, looks down at the commotion, and smiles.

"Hey, girl. What's the fuss about?" He asks. She rolls onto her back with her wide Joker smile, tongue hanging out in bliss. He dutifully rubs her belly. Missy soon follows her best friend and halts with a similar Joker smile, hugging her manilla envelope. Carson cocks his head with an inquisitive look.

"Spill." He demands.

"I'm in. I'm in. I'm in." She says jumping up and down with Bentley by her side, mimicking her behavior.

"Details would be nice." He smirks. She shoves the manilla envelope into his face. He pulls out the document and a wide smile appears.

"I qualified for WEF. Remi and I. In the 6-year-old jumper division. I never thought this day would come." She lunges at him and voraciously wraps her arms around his neck like a horse crazy girl receiving her first pony, almost dislodging the manilla envelope from his grasp. He steps back to rebalance himself.

"Thank you. I couldn't have done this without you." Tears run down her face. Carson, with fatherlike pride, wipes her tears away and kisses her forehead.

"You did this. I'm just the lucky guy that's been able to witness it. I tell you what, let's tell Tegan after I turn out Bubbles. I want to see the expression on her face." He responds.

"I'll do it. Bubbles and I are besties, and I want to tell Rusty before I see Teegs. I'll meet you at Teeg's office afterwards. Don't let her know. I want to be the one to tell her."

"Wouldn't dare." He chides.

"Bentley, come." She commands. Bentley obediently walks over to Missy and stands at a heel position on Missy's left side.

She snatches the lead rope from Carson and escorts Bubbles to the pasture, chatting away all her equestrian dreams to Bubbles' ever nodding and bobbing head on her right and Bentley right in step with her on her left, leaving Carson standing horseless holding her correspondence. He rolls up the envelope, chuckles to himself, and proceeds to Tegan's office.

Piles of papers stacked perfectly in a row line Tegan's desk as she scans a statement and places it back on the pile. Tegan sips from her coffee mug and hands Oscar her iPad. He looks at the screen and then hands it back to her.

"You're entering both horses? I thought Mia wasn't ready." Oscar muses, eyebrows raised with slight concern. Tegan leans back in her chair; the springs squeak in protest with the additional wait.

"She will be by next year. I have a plan. With boarding back at full capacity, we have enough money to bring both horses. I'm also applying for a couple of grants. Fingers crossed, we can use the grant money instead. But mark my words, we're going to take WEF." she confidently replies as she takes another sip and bites into her bagel.

"Of course you do. You always have a plan." He chides and gives her a brotherly nudge.

The door announces with a sonorous squeak Carson's entrance. He waltzes in with a big smile on his face, the manila envelope tightly secured in his armpit. Tegan and Oscar look at him and then look at each other. Tegan tilts her head and asks.

"What's that grin for? You look like you just won the lotto. Spill."

"Nope. Not my news to tell." He responds and fills his coffee mug with freshly brewed coffee and grabs a bagel. He sits down across from Tegan, places the envelope on his lap, and partakes in his coffee and bagel breakfast.

"What's in the envelope?" Tegan coyly asks as she reaches for it. Carson slaps her hand away, winks, and takes another sip from his coffee.

"Well, if you're not saying anything, then I've got some news. I'm registering Luke and Mia in the Grand Prix at WEF. And before you ask, she'll be ready." She announces.

"I know." Carson replies and takes a bite from his bagel.

"That's your response? C'mon, tell me what's going on, Carson." She says, frustrated.

"Nope. You'll learn soon enough."

Missy bursts in on cue as Carson finishes his reply. She looks at the envelope on Carson's lap.

"Did you tell her?" She asks.

"Somebody better tell me what's going on— "

Tegan, on the verge of losing her patience, grabs Carson's half eaten bagel and takes a bite.

"I'm in, Tegan! I'm in! Me and Remington are qualified for WEF!" Missy exclaims. Tegan jumps out of her chair and rushes over to Missy. They embrace and jump up and down like crazy horse girls that have won their first lead line class at a show. Carson stands and hands Tegan the envelope. Tegan greedily opens the envelope and reads the letter. She holds the letter to her heart and smiles at Missy with motherly pride.

"I knew you could do it." She says.

"I can't afford it, Teegs, but— "

"Don't worry about it; we'll figure it out. I'm applying for grants and you should too. We're going to take WEF by storm, Missy." She responds.

The door protests again as Olivia unexpectedly bursts in, waving a manila envelope.

"Teegs. Car. I'm in! Me and Max qualified for WEF. WEF or bust, baby!" She exclaims. The room suddenly gets as quiet as a church on a weekday.

"Aren't you supposed to be in school, Olivia?" Tegan sternly asks.

"I have study hall and this was WAY too important to wait." She responds dramatically.

"I'm not the only one, either. Come in, guys." Olivia commands. Nate and Cameron slowly walk in and ceremoniously place their envelopes on Tegan's desk, then abruptly turn and stand behind Olivia. Tegan stifles a giggle and puts on her trainer's face and tone.

"I take it you two have study hall as well?" Tegan states and nods her head with raised eyebrows, demanding a response.

"She made us do it. We were kidnapped! I thought it would be better after school, but SHE couldn't wait!" Nate adjusts his glasses, points at Olivia, and then cowers to Olivia's glare.

"Well, the news was too important to wait. And, it wasn't only my idea." Olivia looks at Cameron.

"I'm taking the fifth." Cameron whispers. Tegan, Oscar, and Carson look at each other and laugh.

"Okay. Okay. We'll call your parents to sort out these shenanigans. Go clean your tack and help the grooms with the horses." Tegan says.

"But how are we going to get there? How are we going to be ready?" Cameron whispers.

"You let me worry about that. And don't worry about being ready? Carson will make sure the MHB is more than ready." Tegan responds as she caresses Cameron's cheek.

"Hell to the yeah! Carson's bootcamp! Let's go, MHB!" Olivia commands. She extends Carson a fake salute and struts out of the office with Nate and Cameron in toe like soldiers off to battle.

They all huddle at Tegan's desk and inspect the letters. Missy pulls up a chair and sits next to Carson.

"I guess we're going to Wellington." Carson breaks the silence with an obvious statement.

"How are we going to get all the horses there? We've been to Vegas, but the last time we went out East— " Missy asks concerned.

"I know. It's been a while, but I still got my connections. First, we need to get a count of how many horses are going to make the trip. Right now, it seems like there are five horses, but it could easily turn into ten by the end of the week. I'll send out a newsletter and put up a sign-up sheet at the tack room." Tegan says as she types into her iPad.

"Six horses. I'm not going to Florida without Rusty." Carson replies.

"Right. Rusty wouldn't let us go without him. He'd probably follow us all the way to Florida if I tried to keep him here." She laughs and adds Rusty to her list.

"Once we know how many, then we can look at haulers. I have a four-horse head-to-head trailer, so I can only take four. We also need to find accommodations; I have an old friend who has a place we can stay at. It's a lot of coordination, but I know if we put our heads together, we'll figure it out." She looks around the table.

"Any thoughts?" She asks.

"I will take care of transporting the horses. Pedro has a professional hauling business and I have other cousins who can help." Oscar responds.

"I'll put together a training program for, what did Olivia call it, "Carson's bootcamp". Wanna help, Missy? I could use your input." Carson looks over to Missy.

"Sure. And, I'll work on the grant writing and fundraising. I'll ask Olivia to help. She did such an amazing job with the clinic. Raising money for the trip should be a piece of cake." Missy gets up and heads to the door.

"I'm gonna get the horses out and check in on the MHB. Can't leave those guys by themselves too long." She laughs to herself, exits, and calls out to Bentley.

"Let's go, Bentley." The pitter patter of paws follows Missy's footsteps to the barn. Oscar gets up on cue, readying himself for his day with the horses.

"I'm going to check on the horses and the grooms." He cocks his head to the side and looks up at Tegan's wall of pictures.

"It's been years since we've been out east. Father would be proud. I'm proud. Vamos a Wellington!" He raises his arms, claps, and dances out the door. Tegan giggles in remembrance of Oscar's playful nature any time they were contemplating a long trip; it was a sign of adventure, a sign of accomplishment.

"I guess it has been a while. Oscar always loved it when my dad and I would plan a trip out east. He has an entire network out there. I always thought he would stay in Wellington, but every time the trip was over, he'd pack up the gear, horses, souvenirs I don't want to mention, and head back west with us." She muses as she stands and walks over to the pictures on her wall depicting not only accomplishments, but the history of all her travels. She points to a worn out photo of a serious teenage Tegan dressed in a navy blue show coat, white breeches, black riding helmet and boots astride her caramel colored mount adorned with a red and white sash and red ribbon clipped to his bridle with her father and Oscar standing just as serious in front of her holding a silver platter.

"This was our first trip out east. Gone for months. We hit every show on the circuit up and down the coast, ending at Wellington for the Winter Equestrian Festival. I was upset because I lost to Stephanie Wilcox again, and I stormed out of the arena without taking care of my horse. My dad was not happy with me and I got such a telling. He almost scratched the rest of my classes. I begged him to let me continue showing, and he allowed me, but for the rest of the trip, I had to muck out the stalls and basically do all the grooming. Oscar broke the rules and helped me, anyway. That's Oscar, always there for me, even when I didn't deserve it."

She looks at Carson with tears in her eyes.

"I bet you didn't have all this drama in your plans. I can't expect you to go. You had a life before me. If you don't want to go, I understand." She says.

He walks over and envelops her in his arms. They kiss passionately; Carson runs his hands down towards her buttocks and lifts her onto his torso. She responds by wrapping her legs around his waist. She gazes deeply into his eyes.

"I feel like Valley Vista is home now that you're here. I wouldn't want to do this without you." She whispers, kissing his lips. He fiercely responds and deeply kisses her and holds her in a firm embrace, getting lost in her essence. She groans in pleasure and, with her hands, asks for more. The heat of passion almost overwhelms him, but he remembers their location—her office, with the MHB outside, and the unlocked door. He sighs and regains his sense of decorum and releases her legs from his body and sets her down, gently caressing her cheek.

"Where you go, I'll follow—east, west, south — it makes no difference. This is where I should be. Teaching, coaching, sharing in this incredible journey with you—it all feels right. Being part of your life is all that matters. Right now, there's no doubt... this is what lucky feels like." He takes her hand, kisses it, and they walk out of the office.

CARSON'S BOOTCAMP

B ethany takes a long sip of her Big Gulp—half Sprite, half Coca-Cola, the ice rattling inside the cup as she leans her forehead against the cracked black steering wheel of her 1970 El Camino. The deep, guttural bass of punk rock music blares through the speakers, vibrating through the worn-out leather seats. She drums her fingers against the dashboard, tapping to the rhythm, before letting out a sigh and lifting her head.

She turns onto the tree-lined road leading to Valley Vista Ranch, the once lush green canopy now transformed into a fiery display of autumn—leaves in golden yellow, burnt orange, deep red, and crisp brown shimmering under the warm afternoon sunlight. She rolls down the window, letting in the cool, earthy scent of fallen leaves and hay mixed with the distant scent of horses.

To her left, a sprawling pasture stretches along the fence line, dotted with horses lazily grazing in the crisp autumn air, their tails swishing at invisible flies. Some lift their heads as she passes, ears flicking at the sound of her engine. To her right, the imposing two-story barn comes into view—a European-inspired structure of aged gray and black wood, its weathered beams telling generational equestrian stories. Above the arched barn entrance, a black circular iron window sits like a watchful eye, casting intricate shadows on the ground below.

Her brakes protest as she slows to a stop in front of the barn, the gravel crunching under her tires. She throws the car into park, kills the engine, and shoves the driver's side door open, the old hinges groaning in defiance.

Bethany swings her legs out, unfolding from the low seat, and grabs her well-worn saddle and equestrian backpack—its contents a chaotic jumble of a helmet, crop, spurs, and other riding necessities from the passenger seat. She slings the backpack over her shoulder, balances her Big Gulp in one hand while gripping the saddle in the other, and blows an errant pink-dyed bang from her forehead before making her way toward the barn.

Dressed in a black, ripped-up Ramones t-shirt and equally distressed black jeans, she looks more ready for a mosh pit than a day at the barn—the only indication of her equestrian side being her well-worn black paddock boots.

She strides into the tack room, the familiar scent of leather, hay, and horse sweat filling her lungs. Just as she shifts her saddle against her hip, she skids to a stop, eyes widening at the surprise waiting for her—

A makeshift welcome sign, strung up with light blue hay-binding twine from the ceiling, sways slightly in the barn breeze.

"WELCOME TO THE MHB, BETHANY!"

She stares for a beat, blinking in surprise. Then, a slow, amused smirk tugs at her lips.

"I guess I'm not in Kansas anymore."

Bethany sets her saddle on a gleaming brass rack framed in polished, lacquered wood grain. Above it, a brass plaque engraved with her name catches the light. She hangs Winston's bridle on a brass horseshoe hook, his name etched with care. Leaning against the cherry oak tack island, she surveys the spotless porcelain sink, and the neatly arranged cleaning racks above it.

"You've got to be kidding me," she mutters, striding toward her personal tack locker. Swinging open the cherry oak door, she spots a bag of horse cookies tied with a ribbon, a note attached: *"For Winston."* A smile spreads across her face. She hangs her backpack on the hook inside and shuts the door with a satisfied click.

Eyes sweeping the room, she takes in the immaculate rows of bridle racks, polished blanket holders, and boot shelves that line the walls. Crossing the antique rug, decorated with galloping horses and red-coated riders, she flops onto an overstuffed leather sofa, sinking into it like a kid diving into a beanbag. Fingers laced behind her head, she gazes up at the equestrian photos circling the ceiling—each one a frozen moment in the ranch's proud history.

A soft nicker interrupts her reverie. Rusty lazily pokes his head through the open door, eyes bright, ears flicking forward.

"Rusty!" she exclaims and jumps out of her seat and rushes towards him standing outside. He wraps his head around her and she scratches behind his ears - his favorite; he yawns in appreciation.

"How ya doing, buddy? I hear that you already run the place. Not surprised. I also hear that you gotta girlfriend." She teases in a monosyllabic tone. He snorts back and nibbles her jean pocket.

"Okay. Okay. Here you go." She hands him a cookie. "Your favorite." He quickly snatches the treat from her hand.

"Where's Car and Winnie?" She asks. He head-bumps her hip and walks down the aisle toward the pasture.

"Wait for me." She trots up to him, places her hand on his withers and they head out.

Carson leans against the fence dressed in his signature cowboy hat and boots, wrangler jeans, and plaid button-down shirt, and well-worn brown leather woven belt cinched at his waistline, admiring a fully muscled and beautifully conditioned Winston grazing in the pasture. Winston's ears prick up and forward, and he raises his head at the sight of Rusty and Bethany walking up the path towards the pasture. He nickers 'hello' to both of them and lowers his head as Rusty lets himself in and walks over to Winston to graze. Bethany joins Carson at the fence and they stand in silence, enjoying the view.

"Janet dropped off Winston last night. She couldn't stop talking about you and Winnie. You know, Janet. She's coming to Florida, 'come hell or high water' to support her protégé." They both laugh at the inside joke.

"It's good to have you two here. Makes this place feel more like home, if you know what I mean." Carson sighs as he looks out to the paddock, remembering the carefree days at his ranch.

"Yeah. I felt like I entered the Palace of Versailles when I walked into that tack room. So not like the Up and Over days, but it has its charms." She nudges his shoulder in jest. He plays with her bright pink hair, harkening back to their common big brother/little sister bond. She knowingly slaps his hand away.

"You two were amazing at the clinic and show. I can't get over how amazing Winnie looks. Filled in, in all the right places. I knew I left him in good hands." Carson says in a more serious tone as he squeezes her shoulder.

"Can't believe this is real—training for WEF, standing here while Winnie watches Rusty graze like it's any other day. Horses. Only thing that makes sense in this place. They bring you back down to earth. Ground you." Missy tucks her hair behind her ears and rests her chin on her hands that are sitting against the fence.

"Look who's gotten all wise and mature. It suits you." Carson raises an eyebrow and smiles in admiration.

"Look who's gotten all settled in, rooted to this place. It suits you." Bethany retorts. Carson grunts in protest but knowingly smiles back at her.

"I guess it does." He responds as he turns and starts heading back to the barn.

"Hey. Where are you going? I just got here. Haven't had breakfast yet." She asks following him.

"Lesson in ten. Bagels and coffee are in the office. Meet me and the MHB at the Hank Miller Oval." He continues down the path, quickening his pace.

"What about Winnie?" She asks, frustrated.

"Not that kind of lesson." He responds.

"Not again. Can't take the 'Car' out of Carson." She quickens her pace to match his.

Carson coffee in one hand and a piece of paper in another stands with Bethany and the rest of the MHB, dressed in their riding attire, outside the pristinely manicured Hank Miller Oval. The ever inquisitive Nate pushes his glasses up the bridge of his nose.

"Where's the jumps?" He asks and looks accusingly at Carson. Carson takes a sip of his coffee and points to the rainbow color of poles and planks loaded on the flatbed trailer and the standards sitting next to them. He hands Bethany the piece of paper and walks away.

"You know the drill. I'll be back in an hour to inspect your work." He smirks to the groans and protests emanating from his disgruntled students. Olivia and the rest of the MHB glare at Bethany like she's complicit in the added work.

"What's going on, Bethany?" Olivia, hands on hips, demanding an explanation.

"Follow me. The sooner we get this done, the sooner we ride. Carson would always tack a piece of paper like this on a post the night before for me to set up the course before morning lessons." Bethany walks off to the poles and standards. Olivia doesn't move, and the MHB stay with her in fear of reprisal from their general.

"We have groomsmen to do this stuff. I'm going to talk to— "

"I wouldn't argue with Car about this. Trust me. I used to set up courses by myself at his barn all the time. With all of us working together, we can get this done way before an hour. And, I have to admit you learn a lot about a course when you build it yourself. Who's with me?" Bethany raises the paper to her side and the MHB one by one, excluding Olivia, line up at her side. They stand in a silence like pons on a chessboard awaiting Olivia's next move. Olivia walks over to Bethany and snatches the piece of paper from her hand.

"I'm directing. Let's go, MHB." She glowers back at Bethany.

"Whatever." Bethany rolls her eyes, realizing it's not worth it to quarrel with Olivia when there are horses to ride. They all head to the poles and standards.

Mirabella Mia tacked in a leather rope halter with the lead rope casually hanging over her withers, stands patiently in the aisle next to her stall in a perfect square halt as Carson gently grooms her silky white fur into a glisten. He places the brush on the ground and dips a rag into a sudsy bucket and rubs the remnant of a poop stain from her left haunches.

"That a girl." He whispers as he gently massages her shoulder and front leg. He grabs a blue polo wrap from the bucket hanging on her stall and begins wrapping her leg like a professional groom. Mirabella ears prick up to the sound of her beloved partner in crime, Tegan, dressed in dressage training attire - navy blue full seat breaches, tall black dressage boots with a navy blue leather embellishment at the top, white long sleeve riding shirt with lace sleeves, and a black leather belt. She fastens her blue helmet onto her head and smiles at Carson. He finishes the last polo wrap and stands alert for inspection.

"You're early." He says with mock frustration.

"If I knew how good of a groom you are, I would have kept you working for Oscar." She replies with a smirk on her face. He finishes grooming Mia with a finishing brush and pats her muscular neck.

"I probably would have taken it. Oscar is not as pretty as you, but his Old Fashion is killer." He chides back as he heads to the tack room for the saddle and bridle.

"Really. Well, I guess I missed out." She responds as she places her white dressage pad with navy blue trim and half pad on Mia's back. Carson hands her the dressage saddle and girth and holds on to the bridle as she gently places the saddle on Mia's back and adjusts the dressage pad and half pad underneath.

"Where's Missy?" He asks, concerned. Tegan smiles as she tightens the girth.

"Back at home, Missy dives into her workout before heading to the barn. She mapped out the entire training plan herself—every rep, every ride timed to the minute. I used to think I pushed hard, but that girl burns with purpose. I'm stepping back, letting her take the reins. If she needs guidance, I'll be there."

Tegan slips off the leather rope halter and swaps it for the bridle, gently guiding the Neue Schule loose ring bit into Mia's mouth before fastening the throat latch and nose guard. With practiced hands, she adjusts the brow band, then plants a soft kiss on Mia's muzzle. Lowering the stirrups, she gathers the reins and catches a handful of mane while bending her left leg to mount. Carson steps in, brushes a kiss across her cheek, and runs a hand along her lower leg.

"Ready?" He asks. She nods her head 'yes'. He gives her a leg up onto Mia's back.

"Thanks." She adjusts her seat and pats Mia's neck.

"I saw that you're already putting the MHB to work. Course prep, great idea. That's what my dad would do with me. I should have my adults do that, too. The grounds keeper would love that." She muses sarcastically. "Can't wait to see how the MHB does." He taps her leg.

"I'm heading back to check on them. Rusty should already be there." He responds.

"Of course he'd be there." She laughs. She kisses and Mia walks forward out of the aisle.

Rusty enters the arena and witnesses the onslaught of the MHB course prep; the MHB sitting back to back in exhaustion as Bethany finishes setting up the course. He wanders over and nuzzles Bethany's pocket. She obligingly feeds him a sugar cube and scratches his neck. Rusty walks over to Nate, sitting miserably next to Cameron. He nudges Nate's boot with his muzzle. Nate groans.

"I can't move, Rusty." Rusty shakes his head in response and Nate slumps even more onto Cameron's back and looks away in defiance. He stomps his hoof on the footing and rears. The MHB unwillingly stands up at attention. Olivia dusts herself off and looks at Carson's drawing and then back at the arena.

"Fences 12 a and b are a two-stride and b is an oxer, Bethany." She commands. Bethany sets the last cone down and heads to the gate, and stands with her arms crossed.

"I'm done. You guys finish it." She whistles, and Rusty turns on his haunches and canters to her. The rest of the MHB look to Olivia for guidance. She rolls her eyes.

"Whatever. Let's go, MHB." They walk over to the jumps and reluctantly finish setting the course.

Carson walks the course, inspecting the set up. He adjusts a standard and moves some poles.

"Not bad." He walks over to the MHB and leans against Rusty and pats his shoulder.

"So, what did you learn from this experience?" Carson asks.

"The groundskeeper deserves a raise." Nate blurts out without hesitation. Cameron elbows him and the rest of the students giggles.

"Ouch. I'm just saying." He replies.

"It's true that the groundskeepers, stablemen, and groomsmen should be valued for all their efforts, but what I really want to know is what is this course trying to accomplish. Anyone except Bethany." Carson responds. The MHB look at each other and then back to Carson with a blank, haven't-got-a clue expression on their faces.

"Let me show you," Carson says, grabbing Rusty's mane and vaulting onto his back without saddle or bridle. With a pat to the stallion's neck, he heads toward the first cone, starting the course at a steady walk. At the second cone, he cues for a canter. A quick left brings them to cones three and four, where they slow once more. At cone four, he picks up a counter canter—Rusty's outside leg leading as they arc around the short side of the arena with perfect balance.

At cone five, they drop into a trot and continue to the first set of trot poles. Rusty flows smoothly over them, then clears a vertical with ease. The pace drops again before the next set of poles, building into a one-stride combination from a vertical to an oxer. Carson urges him forward, and Rusty opens into a gallop for the long approach to a single oxer. After the jump, they collect into a canter, turning left at the diagonal's end to meet a line of bounce jumps.

A sharp turn sets them up for a two-stride from oxer to vertical, feeding into a three-stride bending line that leads cleanly into another oxer. Without hesitation, they flow into the mirror image on the opposite side of the arena—another two-stride, three-stride combination. The course ends with a balanced trot circle, Carson guiding Rusty with quiet precision.

Returning to the MHB, he walks Rusty calmly back, the group staring in silent awe. Swinging his leg over the withers, Carson dismounts, offers Rusty a sugar cube, and pats his neck in appreciation. He glances back at the wide-eyed group, their expressions full of wonder—as if watching the demigod of show jumping in the flesh. With a small chuckle, he points to the course.

"This course tests your understanding of the bridge between flatwork and jumping. Over there are flatwork elements such as gait transitions, counter canter, simple or flying lead changes, and shortening and lengthening of stride. Then over here, the jumping elements test your ability to turn quickly and shorten your horse's stride through a combination. Questions?" He asks. Nate makes a loud gulping noise like he's swallowed a frog and raises his hand.

"Do we have to do all of it today?" Nate asks, wary of the answer.

"Nope. Don't worry, we'll break it down into the components and by the end of the week or next, we'll put it all together. Sound good?" He claps his hands together in excitement. The MHB unwillingly nod their heads 'yes'.

"Okay, then. Saddle up and let's jump some sticks!" Carson gleefully responds and walks out of the arena with Rusty at his side.

Missy finishes cleaning Remington's bit, wraps up the bridle using the figure-eight method of fastening the cavesson around the reins and fastening it through its keeper and then wrapping the throat latch around the reins twice and fastening it through its keeper and finally storing it on its brass bridle hanger labeled Remington. She wipes her forehead and sits on the sofa in a heap, slumping down in exhaustion. She gazes around the room and smiles, satisfied with her day's work.

Bethany briskly enters the tack room covered like a Christmas tree with her tack. She dumps her saddle on the saddle rack, and horse boots in the sink and hangs her bridle on the tack cleaning hook above. She turns on the faucet and grabs a toothbrush and viciously scrubs the green smudge of hay and dirt from Winston's bit.

"What a piece of work. I can't believe her. Who does she think she is, anyway? I'm not her personal groom. She can take her tack and just shove it." Bethany mutters to herself as she continues cleaning her bridle.

"Bethany?" Missy yawns and sits up. Bethany jumps back, unaware that she is not alone in the room.

"I didn't realize you were there." She responds, ignoring the question.

"C'mon, Bethany, spill. What's Olivia done now?" She presses.

"How did you... Never mind. She tried to unload her tack on me to clean it like I'm her personal groom. She's so obnoxious and full of herself. I don't think I'll make it to WEF without punching her in the face." She responds. She takes apart her bridle and continues cleaning the leather. Missy giggles.

"I wouldn't get too bent out of shape about that. That's just Olivia's way of welcoming you to the MHB. You're lucky. She had Nate muck out all their stalls for a week when he first came."

"Seriously?" Bethany shakes her head in disproval. Missy nods her head 'yes' and walks over to the sink, opens the cabinet, and pulls out a bucket.

"Let me help." Missy grabs a tack sponge and saddle soap and begins cleaning Bethany's saddle.

"Thanks. I guess I'm just overwhelmed with all this. One moment it's just me and Carson at Up and Over ranch working horses and just getting by every day, and now I'm going to WEF and cleaning my tack with a future Olympian." Bethany sheepishly says.

"I don't know about that." Missy responds with the sincerity of a young woman full of hope, but knowledgeable about life's challenges.

"But isn't that your goal? To win a Gold Medal like Tegan and run a Grand Prix Show Barn. I never thought beyond the next day, let alone the rest of my life." Bethany reassembles her bridle and hangs it back on the hook to inspect her work.

"You might think that I have my life all together, but it was just recently that I got back into riding. I was all set on hanging up my spurs after my accident with Remi. If it wasn't for Tegan and Carson, I would've given up on riding, given up on my dream. Nothing is set in stone, and life always seems to throw you a curve ball when you least expect it. But it's the daily mundane things like cleaning tack, mucking stalls, and being around the right people that bring you to where you want or even need to be. WEF has a lot to offer all of us. Yes, I want to go to the Olympics, but that doesn't have to be your dream. Just know that we're here to help and listen as you figure it out." She affectionately elbows Bethany and smiles.

"Right now, I don't know what I want to do; I just love being around horses. I could be happy just riding and grooming horses." Bethany responds.

"Well then. Hand me the conditioner, fellow groomsmen." She demands in a lofty voice, mimicking Olivia. They both giggle as they finish up.

"I can't believe that I'm staying with Tegan and Carson. My first night and Carson is making his famous brisket. I know I should be thankful, but it would be easier if you were there." Bethany looks pleadingly at Missy.

"You'll be fine. Early morning workout before lessons beckons me to turn in. I'll do the night check and then head back to the cabin. I'll come by tomorrow. Promise." Missy squeezes Bethany's forearm with affection and then turns off the light and they head out.

JAKE

Jake pulls into the gravel lot of the arena, his gold 2000 Honda Accord wheezing as it rolls to a stop. The car, battered by time and too many long drives to nowhere, rattles as he kills the engine. A cigarette dangles from the corner of his mouth, the smoke curling around his face like a restless ghost. He takes a long drag, letting the nicotine burn through the nerves buzzing in his chest. His fingers tap against the steering wheel, the same anxious rhythm he always falls into before a performance.

With a sigh, he crushes the cigarette into the already overflowing ashtray, smearing the embers into the mess of past failures. He leans back against the headrest, staring at his reflection in the rearview mirror.

A young man in his mid-twenties stares back at him—olive-skinned, hazel eyes shadowed with exhaustion, his dark brown hair slightly disheveled, a goatee he keeps neatly trimmed to maintain some semblance of control. He reaches up, running his fingers over the sharp edges of his jaw, smoothing out his goatee as if that alone could make him look the part.

"You got this." The words leave his lips, but even he doesn't believe them.

His stomach tightens as he reaches for the dog-eared, coffee-stained script lying in the passenger seat. He flips it open, the familiar scent of ink and desperation rising from the pages. Page thirty-three. His one line, highlighted in yellow, stares back at him like a taunt.

"I'm with Cole. I was born in the saddle and I'll die in the saddle."

He recites it again and again, shifting the weight of the words, testing their strength. Confidence. Arrogance. Defiance. Each time, the line falls flat—a hollow echo of the way he wants it to sound.

Why does it sound so damn fake?

His jaw tightens. His pulse pounds in his ears. He rubs a hand down his face, dragging the tension from his temples. He'd done this before. Plenty of times. But this time is different. This time, it's not just about the line—it's about proving that he still belongs in this world.

Jake closes his eyes, takes a deep, shuddering breath, and forces the fear down. "Let's go."

His voice is gravel, forced steel, as he shoves the door open and steps into the crisp air.

The scent of dust and horses fills his lungs as he pulls the weathered black driver's seat forward, reaching for the only thing that's ever felt like home—his handcrafted western saddle. The leather is worn, but pristine, the tooling carved with the precision of a man who understands the weight of tradition. This saddle is his legacy. The only thing that ever made him feel like he belonged.

Hefting it onto his shoulder, he squares his jaw and heads toward the arena.

Whatever happens next, he'll be ready. He has to be.

Jake struts into the arena filled with eight men drenched in sweat (looking miserable from the morning's exertion) mounted precariously on their horses in front of an obstacle course of logs, poles, fences, mechanical bulls, and cones. He sniggers to himself and heads to the table where three men and a woman sit with clipboards and a stack of head shots.

"Jake Moore." He says as he presents himself in full cowboy regalia - Stetson hat, boots, Wrangler jeans, and a tan Simms long sleeve button-down shirt. The woman begrudgingly hands the man to her right, Jake's headshot.

"You're late." The man replies. Jake knowingly remains silent. There's no point in arguing with the man that he had been called only thirty minutes ago about this audition. The man hands the headshot to the director and leans back in his chair with disdain. The grey-haired director places his reading glasses on the bridge of his nose and quickly peruses the headshot. He takes off his glasses and points them at Jake.

"I need someone who can actually ride, unlike the catastrophe I witnessed earlier. Is that you, or are you going to waste my time as well?" He asks.

"No, sir. I've been riding since I was a kid and been on most of the professional circuits. I own a riding facility, buy and sell horses, and break young colts. If it has four legs, I can ride it." He puffs up his chest. The director huffs and leans back in his chair, looks over to the line of men slouched in their saddles, shakes his head, and crosses his arms.

"The men back there can barely sit a horse. Let's see if you can do any better. Get him a horse, Ryan." He commands, annoyed at the day's previous auditions. The man next to him instantly jumps out of his chair and whistles over to the horse wranglers.

"Follow me." He says to Jake. Jake obliges, and they walk over to the line of men and horses. After a bit of confusion, and animated exchange of words, a man auditioning dismounts his horse and departs, throwing the reins at the horse wrangler spooking the horse; and it violently backs up and rears, almost taking the horse wrangler off his feet. The horse wrangler yanks the horse back and smacks him with the reins. The horse stands still, wide-eyed with fright. Jake walks over to the horse, places his saddle next to his leg, gently massages the horse's neck, and whispers in his ear. The horse's eyes soften and he nuzzles Jake's shoulder. Jake smiles and hands him a treat that was buried, forgotten, in his pocket.

"What's his name?" Jake asks. The bow legged horse wrangler shrugs his "Frankenstein-like" shoulders, damaged from many falls and kicks and motions his wrinkled hand at the horse.

"He's a horse. Are you gonna get on or not?" He replies. Jake quickly removes the sweat encrusted saddle, adjusts the wool saddle pad, and places his saddle on the horse's back. He mounts the horse after tightening the cinch and pats the horse's neck. He walks the horse to get a feeling of how it moves. The director coughs sharply, signaling his displeasure. Jake cues his horse into a lope and guides him through the course with effortless synchronicity, moving as if they've trained together for years. Eyes narrowing, the director and colleagues lean forward, drawn in by the smooth display of horsemanship. He grabs Jake's headshot, flips it between his fingers, and jots notes on a clipboard. Leaning toward his assistant, he whispers something low. The assistant nods and strides toward Jake.

Jake halts, grins, and pats his horse's neck with pride. The gelding nickers softly, ears flicking back in quiet approval.

"Not bad. The director wants to make sure you're the real thing. Can you do what you just did on this horse, on any other horse?" He asks.

"Sure." Jake confidently replies. The assistant nods his head and goes over to the horse wrangler who brings Jake another horse - not just another horse, but a beautiful palomino with a glistening golden coat and white mane perfectly braided in a basket weave and white stripe down the front of its face. Jake dismounts and removes his saddle.

"Uh. Uh. You're riding this one bareback and don't think for one second that I'm legging you up." The horse wrangler hands him the new horse and takes the saddled horse back to the other side of the arena. Jake looks after the wrangler, aware that he might never see his saddle again, and decides to 'let the chips fall where they may' and instead focuses on nailing the audition. He grabs the horse's mane, pulls himself onto the horse's withers, and swings his leg over. The horse lets out a sizable buck, but Jake stays firmly in his seat. He pats the horse's neck and trots. The horse tries to bolt, but Jake quickly pulls on one rein and spins him to a stop and gently walks him backwards. The horse shakes his head in defiance and kicks out with his rear hind. Jake ignores his antics and patiently waits for the horse to settle. After a few moments, the horse lowers his head and Jake urges the horse to the course. Mid-way through the course, Jake slows the horse down to a walk and then halts.

"Let's show these guys what you can do, buddy." He whispers. He spins the horse to the right eight times and stops in a perfect square halt, and then spins the horse to the left eight times and stops in a perfect square halt. The other men clap as the horse spins and hoot and howler like they're at a rodeo. Continuing on course, Jake finishes with a powerful gallop toward the table where the director and his colleagues sit. With a sharp cue, he drag-stops the horse just inches from their polished shoes, a spray of sand fanning across the ground. Flashing a grin, he tips his hat to the gentlemen and lady.

"I'm with Cole. I was born in the saddle and I'll die in the saddle." He delivers the line in a gruff voice. The assistant frantically applauds the performance and the other men and woman behind the table glare at the assistant to stop. He quickly ceases his applause and picks up his clipboard and pretends to take notes. Jake smiles and gazes unswervingly at the director and pats the horse's neck.

"Nice horse." He says.

"I know. He's mine. That'll be all. We'll get back to you by the end of the week." The director replies. He looks at his assistant. "Make sure Jim gives this cowboy back his saddle." The assistant nods his head, gets up and walks over to Jake. Jake dismounts and they walk back to the other horses. A man at the audition, who could be mistaken as Brad Pitt's twin still astride a horse, dressed in 'Hollywood's' Gucci version of cowboy attire, tips his hat at Jake.

"You sure can ride, buddy." He declares with genuine admiration. Jake gives him a once over and tilts his head.

"I know." He replies. Jim, the horse wrangler, pats him on his shoulder and hands him his saddle.

"I believe this belongs to you," Jim chuckles, and walks out of the arena. Jake smiles back, heaves his saddle onto his shoulder and struts out like a cowboy who's just won his first all around cowboy buckle.

Jake's studio apartment is an exercise in contradiction—minimalist yet refined, sparse but intentionally curated. A single Japanese paper lantern, ivory with faint wisps of calligraphy, sways slightly over a handmade maple dining table, its wood grain catching the glow of the warm light. The space radiates intention, each piece of high-quality furniture placed with purpose over flair. A black leather Barcelona chair anchors the corner beside a mahogany bookshelf, which showcases well-worn screenplays, weathered classics, and a single dusty rodeo trophy nestled in the shadows at the back.

A faint haze of cigar smoke from the night before lingers, blending with the subtle spice of expensive cologne. The jazz from his vintage record player hums low, the sultry tones of Miles Davis' Kind of Blue filling the room like a slow-burning candle. Jake stands at the edge of the table, tracing his fingers over the maple surface, before picking up his cell phone for the fifth time in the last twenty minutes. He checks again—fully charged, no missed calls.

With an exasperated sigh, he sets the phone back down and leans back in his chair, tilting his Riedel wine glass toward the only decoration on his otherwise bare walls—an authentic, autographed portrait of Al Pacino as The Godfather.

Pacino's intense stare meets his own.

"What do you think, Al? My shot or not?" Jake murmurs, taking a slow sip of his Caymus Cabernet, savoring the bold taste before rolling it over his tongue. It was his favorite bottle, a guilty pleasure he rarely indulged in.

Then, suddenly—his phone vibrates violently against the table, shattering the quiet anticipation in the room.

His stomach twists. For a brief second, he hesitates, staring at it, willing himself to play it cool. He doesn't want to seem too eager. Letting it vibrate once...twice...he finally snatches it up and answers in his most nonchalant tone.

"Hello, what's up, Mike?" His voice is steady, but there's a boyish hope beneath the facade.

Mike's voice on the other end is quick, matter-of-fact. Jake listens, nodding, grinning at first.

"Yeah, I know. I nailed the audition. The other guys could barely sit a horse, and I delivered the line exactly how we rehearsed."

Then his expression shifts. His forehead creases. His fingers rake through his thick, dark hair.

"What?"

A beat.

"They're going with the 'Brad Pitt-looking guy?'" His voice sharpens with disbelief. "That's bull—! I don't care what the studio wants! The director LOVED me! And that guy? He can't ride! You should've seen what he was wearing—fake Gucci cowboy crap. I nailed it, Mike. I NAILED IT!"

His fist slams against the table, rattling his half-empty wine bottle.

Mike keeps talking, trying to smooth things over, but Jake isn't hearing it. He clenches his jaw, his knuckles white as they grip the phone.

"No. Not gonna do it. I'm done with stunt riding. Tell the director to shove the—"

A pause.

"How much?"

Jake exhales, leans back in his chair, his jaw tightening. He pinches the bridge of his nose, eyes closed, weighing the inevitable.

"Let me think about it. I'll call ya later."

He hangs up, then flings the phone toward the couch—but at the last second, he catches himself. He can't afford another broken phone. Instead, he slams it down onto the table, staring at it as if it had betrayed him.

His gaze shifts to the bottle of wine. Without hesitation, he grabs it, empties the remaining contents into his glass, and gulps it down in three angry swallows. He wipes his goatee with the back of his hand, his chest rising and falling with frustration.

Then the phone vibrates again.

Jake glares at it before snatching it up.

"What?" His voice is raw, impatient. He listens, rubs his temple, then exhales sharply.

"I'm at home. Today? It's my day off." His head tilts back against the chair, staring at the ceiling. "Whatever. My fee is still fifteen percent. I'll be there in an hour."

He slams the phone back onto the table, shoves his chair back, and pushes himself up too fast. His head spins for a second, forcing him to grip the edge of the table to steady himself.

He mutters a curse under his breath and, without a second thought, starts stripping off his clothes as he heads for the shower. A trail of his leather jacket, t-shirt, and jeans litters the polished wood floors as he disappears into the steam-filled bathroom.

Jake steers his gold, slightly rusted 2000 Honda Accord down a narrow, tree-lined lane, the towering oaks and maples forming a canopy of flickering sunlight across his windshield. On either side of the gravel road, open fields stretch toward the horizon, dotted with foals of every shade—chestnut, bay, palomino, black, and gray—kicking up their heels in playful abandon.

As his car rumbles past, the foals stop abruptly, ears pricked in curious fascination. Then, as if accepting the challenge, they bolt into a spirited gallop, matching his speed. Their manes and tails whip wildly in the wind, hooves pounding the earth in a rhythmic drumbeat. Jake exhales a chuckle, taking a long drag from his cigarette, the smoke curling lazily out of the open window as he presses the accelerator.

Ahead, the unmistakable arching wooden sign of Valley Vista Ranch looms overhead, the name burned into the rich mahogany planks, weathered by time and legacy. He coasts to a stop beside a meticulously crafted round pen, its wood grain smooth, solid, and hand-hewn—a rare sight in a world of mass production. Jake sees the pen's artistic and functional construction as proof of these people's commitment to horsemanship.

And yet, Jake remains skeptical.

As he slides out of the car, a younger Oscar stands near the round pen, his gaze locked on the quiet mastery unfolding before him.

Inside the pen, Hank Miller rides a young, raw-boned gelding, his seat deep and quiet, his hands feather-light on the reins. The horse moves in a slow, easy lope, his muzzle nearly brushing the dirt, completely tuned in to Hank's subtle cues. A flexible metal stick with a blue flag sways in Hank's hand, barely more than a whisper against the breeze, yet the young gelding responds to every soft flick of the flag. Hank touches it to the horse's hindquarters, then his shoulder, then his poll—desensitizing him, shaping him, communicating without a word.

Jake watches, unimpressed but intrigued.

The horse he's looking for is a modern sport horse, something bred for scope, power, and precision. He needs a horse that's been in a jump chute since birth, one with papers, lineage, and a track record. This? This looks like something out of a cowboy's playbook.

Still, he doesn't disrupt the session—at least, not until Oscar notices him and strides over.

Oscar tilts his head, his dark eyes shrewd, already reading Jake in a way that makes him feel oddly exposed. He never trusted smooth-talking trainers who came sniffing around for horses with their tailored jeans and practiced charm.

"Can I help you, Señor?" Oscar asks, his deep, accented voice carrying the weight of quiet authority.

Jake flicks his cigarette to the ground and grinds it under his boot. "Jake Moore. I'm here to check out one of your show jumpers for a client of mine. I was told there was a nice one here." He stretches out his hand, but Oscar doesn't take it right away—just looks him over like he's deciding whether Jake is worth his time.

Oscar finally shakes his hand. Firm. Calculated. A test.

Before Oscar can respond, Hank's voice rings out from the round pen.

"Bring him over."

It's not a suggestion—it's an order.

Oscar gestures for Jake to follow as they head toward the pen. Jake watches Hank wrap up his session with the gelding, never breaking stride as he dismounts, loosens the cinch, and walks toward the gate. The horse follows him without a halter, completely at ease, reading Hank's body language with an unshakable trust.

Hank swings the gate open, his signature boyish grin etched onto his face.

"Here he is." He pats the gelding's neck proudly.

Jake frowns.

"This?" He raises a skeptical brow, looking over at Oscar like this is some kind of joke.

The horse is young. Too young. And doesn't look a damn thing like a jumper.

"I believe there's been a misunderstanding," Jake says flatly. "That young horse looks like he'd make a nice cutting horse, but I need a 'bulletproof' young show jumper. Something my client can grow with."

Hank doesn't flinch. He doesn't even blink.

"Yep," he says casually. "Charlie will do the deed."

Jake barks out a short laugh, shaking his head. "I have a hard time believing that 'Charlie' can jump anything. He doesn't even look like a show jumper. What breed is he anyway?"

Hank scratches his jaw, unfazed. "Oh, he's a little bit of this and a little bit of that." He grins at Oscar, a private joke between them. "Here at Valley Vista, we train all our young horses in every discipline. A good horse is a good horse—papers don't make 'em jump, training does. And as you can see, Charlie's bombproof."

Oscar watches Jake carefully. Jake doesn't trust this. Everything about this place feels too... nostalgic, too "old school" for his taste. The industry has changed—science, breeding, and selective conditioning have replaced instinct, gut, and natural feel. And yet, something about Hank Miller doesn't feel like a fraud.

Jake scoffs. "But don't take my word for it," Hank adds. "He's plenty warmed up. I'll have Tegan jump him for you."

Jake pauses mid-breath.

Tegan Miller.

He stiffens. "Tegan Miller is here? I thought she was still in Europe."

"Nope." Oscar smirks knowingly. "She's home now, working all the horses."

Jake exhales through his nose, weighing his next move.

Hank doesn't give him the chance to object.

"Follow me," he says simply, leading Charlie toward the show jumping arena.

Jake hesitates. Then, against his better judgment, he follows.

Oscar lingers behind for a moment, watching Jake's retreating figure with an all-knowing smirk.

"You're already losing, gringo," Oscar mutters to himself before falling in step behind them.

Tegan guides Paratrooper (aka True, aka Chewy) through a grid of bounce jumps and then turns left and slices a square oxer and finishes by easily clearing a five foot vertical. She brings him down to a trot and then releases the reins and pats Chewy's neck as he comes down to a walk. He nibbles at her boot heel and she quickly feeds him a sugar cube. She notices her father and Oscar coming towards her with a handsome young man she doesn't recognize. She quickens Chewy's pace, hoping that her father has finally agreed to allow her to hire an assistant trainer and import European broodmares and stallions. Her chest falls as she notices Charlie walking next to her father - another sale trial. She dismounts Chewy, loosens his girth, and kisses his cheek. Her dad smiles and hands her Charlie's reins as he takes Chewy's. Chewy nuzzles Hank's pocket, and he obligingly feeds him a sugar cube. She looks over at Jake and they lock eyes. She looks away and pats Charlie's neck.

"You interested in Charlie? He's a good horse. Dad bred him and I trained him." She says.

"To be honest. Not sure it's a fit." He replies, not able to take his eyes off her.

"I know he's not your typical European show jumper stock, but he's the best young horse for the AO level I've seen in a long time." She replies.

"Home bred. Not sure I'd agree with that, but I drove all the way out here, so let's have a look." He crosses his arms and leans against the fence. Tegan looks over to her father and winks. She pats Charlie's neck and walks over to the mounting block and sits astride Charlie. Oscar follows her and lowers the fences to around three-feet in height. She picks up a canter and quickly maneuvers Charlie over the grid and then turns toward the three-foot oxer and slices it exactly like she did with Chewy, but then quickly turns inside the vertical and rolls back to the same square oxer and slices it the opposite direction. Jake jumps to his feet in full attention and exclaims.

"He's unlike anything I've seen." He looks over at Hank.

"Not bad, huh? Guess I know a little somethin' about breedin'. But if you're lookin' to talk numbers, deal with my daughter." Hank pats him on the shoulder and walks away with Chewy as Jake continues watching Tegan school Charlie over fences.

Jake watches Tegan hose down Charlie in the wash rack as Oscar puts away her tack. She grabs the scraper and gently removes the excess water from Charlie's coat, working from his shoulders towards his croup. She finishes with a towel and quickly places ice boots on the cannon bone of all four legs. Jake walks up with her with a cocky actor demeanor, which quickly diminishes when she looks at him with her emerald eyes.

"What ya think?" She asks with her arms folded across her stomach.

"You've done a great job with him, but I'm not sure he's what I'm looking for." He replies, trying to not sound too interested.

"Your loss. I have a trainer coming at four who's interested, so I guess you can show yourself out." She replies as she heads back to the tack room. He quickly walks toward Tegan.

"Wait. I'm interested. How much you asking?"

"A buck fifty." She says.

"You've got to be kidding me. He's not even been to an 'A-rated' show yet," He argues. She turns back and stands square in front of him without breaking her gaze.

"I never kid about the value of our horses. Charlie is one of our top horses trained by my dad and myself. You won't find another horse who has his scope and will also willingly pack around any amateur rider over a meter plus course. As for him not being shown at an 'A-rated' show. That's on purpose. Once I show and win (and I will), his price will soar over two hundred. So, in my humble opinion, you're getting him at a bargain. So, cowboy, what'll it be? Do we have a deal?" She puts out her hand and looks directly at Jake. Jake looks over to Charlie, who's half

246

asleep in the crossties, and then loses himself as he gazes into Tegan's emerald eyes. He takes her hand and shakes it.

"You drive a hard bargain, Ms. Miller, but Charlie will make a great addition to my training facility." He looks around at the barn and notices all the manual tools and hand made stalls. Nice, but a little outdated and quaint.

"Please follow me and I'll get you all the paperwork." She interrupts his thoughts and starts walking to the tack room. He follows closely behind her. She enters the tack room and goes to a wooden file cabinet behind a handcrafted, well-worn oak desk. She pulls out a manila folder from the cabinet and grabs a pen from a steel horseshoe cup filled with writing implements on her desk and hands the items to Jake. He opens the folder and looks over the bill of sale, breeding info, and detailed feeding and training schedule. He takes a check from his back pocket and fills in the amount and hands it to Tegan.

"Ever thought about getting into the import business? I'll handle the buying, you train, and we sell. Through my work in acting and stunt gigs, I've built strong connections in the entertainment industry. A lot of 'Hollywood' money is hunting for the next great horse. We'd make a killing—and you could put the profits into updating this place." He waves his hands around the tack room. Tegan raises an eyebrow, interested but skeptical.

"I have plenty of connections in Europe and was hoping for a mix of imports and homegrown, but dad's set in his ways. Home grown is the 'Valley Vista Way'. Hopefully, someday, he'll come around. Until then, it was nice doing business with you." She hands him a receipt and walks out of the office with Jake following closely behind. She pauses, and he suddenly grabs her shoulders to avoid colliding with her. For a moment, their lips are but an inch apart. Tegan sighs, looks deeply into his eyes, and then fidgets, embarrassed by her behavior. He quickly releases her, and she steps back.

"If you leave me your card, I can have Oscar bring Charlie over to your facility later today." She says, avoiding eye contact.

"Yeah. Have him come after five. I should be done with lessons by then." He pulls out a card and hands it to her. She looks at his headshot on the front and info on the back, smirks, and shoves it into her back pocket.

"I better get going. Don't want to keep the horses waiting. I hope to do business with you again. You have my card." He walks passed her and waves leaving her standing in the aisleway. She takes out his card and looks more intently at his head shot.

Oscar drives a 2012 white Dodge 3500 Ram dually with a Valley Vista Ranch logo painted on the driver's side door carrying a sleeping Charlie in a horse trailer hitched behind under an overhang of a sign 'Heritage Ranch' and then turns right past a barn and pulls to the side of an arena decorated with professional jumps. Oscar exits the truck and walks to the outside of the arena and leans against the fence. Jake, astride a magnificent bay gelding with four white socks, jumps over a four-foot oxer and gallops off to a set of triple fences with two strides between them. He easily completes the jumps and continues to the final vertical and clears it. He brings the horse to a trot and then to a walk and pats the horse's neck. Oscar coughs and Jake looks up and quickly dismounts. He walks with the horse toward the fence.

"You're early." He says, concerned. "I need to take care of Monty before— "

"I'll wait." He replies in a stern voice. A stand off ensues for a minute; Jake looks around, then quickly disappears into the barn with Monty trotting behind him. He reappears after a few moments with a hurried look on his face.

"How was your trip?" His attempt at small talk falls flat with Oscar as he grunts and walks away and opens the trailer door. He whistles and Charlie walks out wearing a rope halter with the lead dangling over his withers. Oscar hands the lead rope to Jake.

"Thanks, Oscar. Let me buy you a beer later at— "

"Jake! What the hell is Monty doing fully tacked in the cross ties covered in sweat?" A fiery red faced woman, petite but built like a tank, dressed in professional riding attire and a red baseball cap with the logo Heritage Ranch stamped on front covering her long blonde braid, marches toward him with her steel-blue eyes gleaming with anger. She halts in front of Oscar, kicking up a cloud of dust around her boots. Her gaze shifts to the logo on his truck door, eyes narrowing with recognition. Embarrassment creeps in as she blinks and rubs her hands together, trying to recover from the outburst.

"I'm sorry. I've just come from my last lesson. Can I help you?" She asks.

"I'm just delivering the horse, Señora." Oscar replies.

"I apologize. I wasn't aware of any horse delivery. I'm Patricia Martin, owner and head trainer of Heritage Ranch." She says as she turns to confront Jake.

"Trish. I left you a voice mail. I found this amazing horse for Heather." Jake says, avoiding eye contact with Oscar. Patricia rolls her eyes, shakes her head and looks at Oscar.

"Thank you for coming all this way. How much do I owe you for the haul?" She pulls out her wallet.

"Don't worry, Señora. Just take care of Charlie and we'll be square. He's a good horse." Oscar pats Charlie's neck, smiles, and holds out his hand. Patricia vigorously shakes his hand with both of hers like they've been friends for a long time.

"Thank you— " She asks.

"Oscar."

"Thank you, Oscar. Please know we'll take excellent care of Charlie, and let Tegan and Hank know I look forward to doing business with them again. They're always welcome here at Heritage." She smiles back. Oscar tips his hat, looks at Charlie one last time with a little sadness, and then sternly looks at Jake before entering the truck. He turns the ignition and heads out, leaving Charlie in his rear-view mirror.

"Never go behind my back to purchase a horse for my clients again." Patricia says fiercely, standing with her hands on her hips elevating her diminished height by a couple of inches.

"Heather called me Trish." He replies defiantly.

"I don't care. You run all horse purchases through me before completing a deal." She demands.

"You'll get your percentage." He says.

"That's not the point and you know it. You do not represent Heritage Ranch. Don't make me regret hiring you, Jake." Patricia grabs the lead rope from Jake.

"Go take care of Monty and finish mucking the stalls." She walks off in a huff with Charlie by her side, leaving Jake in a dust of dirt.

THE CARAVAN

Hank Miller forcefully blinks his eyes to keep from dozing as he passes the blue 'Florida Welcomes You' sign bearing white letters and a yellow sun at the letter 'O' forged between two stone pillars. Rain drops create a steady drumbeat on the windshield of Bess, the rhythm quickening, obscuring his view. He quickly turns on the wipers and looks over to his daughter, who's in a blissful state of slumber. He smiles with pride and then speaks in a prayer-like whisper.

"Wish you could see her, Mira. She's accomplished so much more than I could have dreamed. And you know me, the big dreamer. Olympic Gold Medalist. But she's so much more than that. She's more talented than the two of us put together. Such a strong woman. Just like you. I'm in awe of her every day, but I'm scared for her too. She still gets really nervous before each event. Puts so much pressure on herself. Has to be perfect. Not sure she's going to be happy in this life. Not by herself. I couldn't have done this life without you, without her. God, I miss you.." He looks over at Tegan, who crinkles her nose in agitation and mumbles in her sleep.

"You'd know what to do. What to say." He pats Tegan's thigh just above her knee to reassure her. She sighs and buries her face in her elbow. He continues looking at his daughter and almost misses the exit. He jerks the truck over to the right lane and the trailer pulls the truck sideways, disrupting her sleep. Startled, she suddenly sits up and looks out the window.

"What's wrong?" She asks.

"Nothin', kiddo. Just almost forgot to take the exit. Everything's fine." He coughs and sheepishly smiles at Tegan.

"I can take over if you need to rest." She responds, her eyebrow raised in concern.

"Nope. I'm good. We're almost there, anyway. Go back to sleep. I'll wake you when we get there. Big things are going to happen at WEF. I can feel it." He gleams with his boyish smile.

"You always say that, Dad. There's so many exhibitors - more than the Olympics. And some of them have multiple horses. The class is huge, and it's just me and Chewy." She says.

"I can feel it, kiddo. Go to sleep and let me take care of the rest." He taps her knee and places his attention on the road. She protests and then realizes that it's no use when Hank Miller gets his mind set on something. She leans her head against the window and immediately goes back to sleep.

"Wake up, Teegs." Missy says as they drive past the blue 'Florida Welcomes You' sign. Tegan stretches her arms above her head and yawns as she looks at the sign.

"I guess we're almost there. I was just dreaming of the last WEF trip I made with dad. Remember that trip?" She smiles and looks at Missy.

"How could I forget? You were so mad at me for dying my hair pink and purple." Missy laughs.

"Admit it. You looked ridiculous." She retorts.

"I was just ahead of my time. Now, everyone is doing it. Bethany has a new hair color every week! Hank was the only one who defended me. Hank understood." She responds and they both knowingly laugh.

"My dad would let you get away with anything. Me. No way. He'd be on my case if my hair net wasn't perfect. 'You gotta do it right, kiddo. You're an Olympic Gold medalist now.'" She says in a gruff voice.

"God, I miss him." Tegan continues as she looks out the window, watching the myriad of palm trees wave 'hello' to her in the breeze.

"Me too." Missy whispers as she continues driving the I-10 towards Tallahassee. Missy checks the side-view mirror and sees Carson's truck casually traveling behind them and wistfully smiles.

"Hank would have a hoot knowing that Rusty is heading to WEF with us. Don't you think?" Missy says to lighten the mood.

"You bet he would. I can see him now, pulling off to the nearest rodeo to give it one more go with BM. He'd disappear and then come back at dinner, winning the entire purse." Tegan exclaims with delight.

"Yeah. And he'd plop that purse and buckle on the table, puff his chest and declare 'That's how it's done, folks.'" Missy chimes in and they both laugh at the joke.

Tegan looks longingly in her side-view mirror, hoping to glimpse Carson. She shakes her head at her foolishness and looks at Missy.

"You okay until Ocala?" She asks, concerned.

"Yep. It'll be nice to stop for a couple of days before heading to Wellington. I'm surprised we're not staying longer." She replies, fishing for an answer.

"I want us to focus on WEF. We'll catch Ocala on our way back. That way, the horses will be at their freshest. Don't want the horses to be burned out before we get there, especially since this is their maiden voyage." She responds in an educating tone.

"That makes sense. I keep forgetting how long it's been since we last did a cross-country trip. It's tiring and sometimes I think that we'll never get there, but there's nothing like the open road and witnessing the real America pass you by with each little town's story right there in front of you. And... the company's not so bad either." Missy sticks her tongue out at Tegan, drawing laughter from them both. With a quick signal, she shifts into the right lane, merging toward the I-75 ramp to Gainesville. Her eyes catch the highway sign, and a sudden wave of emotion bucks through her like Remington in a mood. She blinks hard, fighting back the sting of tears.

"I'm so excited to be on this trip with you, Teegs. No matter what happens at WEF, thanks for not giving up on me." She barely gets the words out and her voice cracks with emotion.

"No matter what, I will always be proud of you. Means the world to me that you and Remi are together again. And... I bet dad is smiling from above." She replies. Missy reaches out her hand and Tegan clasps it, and then quickly withdraws her hand and mischievously looks at Missy.

"Ready?" she wittingly asks. Tegan turns on the radio and they both sing to Beyonce's Single Ladies.

'Bam! Bam! Bam!' Rusty's hoof stomps demanding music in his quarters.

"Not again!" Bethany says, exasperated. She looks over at Carson and he shrugs his shoulders.

'Bam! Bam! Bam!' A repeat of his demand reverberates towards the front cabin and then suddenly Winston joins the declaration with the pounding of his hoof.

"Et Tu, Winnie? Okay!" Bethany declares as she dutifully rewinds the cassette tape in the dashboard and hits play - the first chords of 'Sweet Home Alabama' echoes in the cabin and trailer attached behind fitted with speakers years ago. Rusty and Winston both nicker their approval and resume eating their hay. Bethany rolls her eyes and looks out the window.

"Teach Rusty a new favorite song." She mutters and sighs in relief as they pass by the 'Florida Welcomes You' sign. Bentley sits up on her lap and voraciously licks Bethany's face.

"Not you too? You like this song?" She says, mystified by Bentley's behavior.

"You probably just miss your momma. Not too long until we get to Ocala and you'll have all the doggy treats and belly scratches you want from Momma Missy." She kisses and scratches Bentley's ears. Carson taps his left foot and begins belting out the song with a boyish smile on his face.

"I give up." Bethany laughs and joins the chorus and bobs her head in synchrony with the music. The songs ends and Bethany quickly clicks the radio button and lowers the volume, hoping that the local country station will suffice for the remainder of the trip.

"Janet's already at Ocala with Sista. She says she's here to support me, but you and I know why she's really here." She nonchalantly says.

"Don't you start. Janet's been pestering me all month about entering with Rusty. I already promised that I would coach her, but I'm on this trip for Tegan and the MHB," He replies and turns up the volume. Bethany turns off the radio and faces him.

"Just think of all the money you and Rusty could win. You could get your own place again. Up and Over Ranch part two." She insists.

"I've got a good thing going on with Tegan and I'm not ruining it with 'cowboying'." He replies.

"I love Tegan. I truly do. She's opened so many doors for me, and I wouldn't even be on this trip if it wasn't for her. But I know you, Car. You'll never be truly happy at a show barn. Can't take the cowboy out of Carson." She looks at Carson with sisterly affection and concern.

"I love her, Bethany." He simply says as he pats her hand and turns the radio back on.

"Wake up, kiddo. We're here." Hank says as he turns left off Pierson Road into the exhibitor entrance of Wellington International. He grimaces and grabs his left arm as he turns the wheel of Bess. Tegan grumbles in protest, blinks her eyes open, and looks out the window. The backstage chaos of the Winter Equestrian Festival looms in front of her with grooms unloading horses from trailers, exhibitors from around the world either setting up their tack rooms and stalls or mounted on their horses heading to the International Arena to acclimate their horses. Tegan bolts straight up in her seat and straightens her weathered blue USA baseball cap.

"We're late, Dad. I need to get Chewy acclimated to the grounds and the arena by now. Expectations are sky high and..." She fires an accusing glance his way, frustration flashing in her eyes.

"Don't worry. The Grand Prix isn't until Saturday and the warm up classes don't start for a couple days. You and Chewy will be more than ready by then. I bet you he's probably asleep in the trailer, anyway." He looks back and smiles with a diminished twinkle in his eyes and gently squeezes her hand. He parks the truck and backs the horse trailer into their designated spot.

"I'll check on Chewy and help Oscar unload the horses." Tegan kisses her father's cheek like a hen pecking grain from the ground and jumps out of the truck before her father can respond. Hank chuckles to himself and reaches to open the door. His arm spasms and he gasps in pain. He reaches into his shirt pocket and takes out a pill and swallows, leaning his head back against the headrest.

'Knock. Knock. Knock.'

"Señor, Hank?" Oscar taps the window with a concerned look on his face. Hank opens his eyes and quickly opens the door. He stumbles out and his knees buckle underneath him and he almost falls. Oscar grabs Hank's upper arm and steadies him until he's able to stand on his own. Hank pulls out a handkerchief and fiercely coughs into it, his entire body convulsing and his knees buckle again. Oscar quickly wraps his arm around Hank's torso and places Hank's arm around his shoulder. He walks Hank down an empty aisle and sits him on a bale of hay. Hank smiles and shoves the handkerchief into his front pocket. He takes a couple of deep breaths and looks up at Oscar.

"You need to go to the hospital, Señor." Oscar demands. Hank vehemently shakes his head 'no' and stands erect like General Patton, placing his hands on his hips.

"Let's check on the horses." He commands, and he walks off, leaving Oscar in his wake. Oscar hurries to his side and walks with him in silence.

"Don't let her know." Hank's eyes glisten as he looks at his trusted friend. Oscar looks down at the floor at a loss for words and nods his head 'yes.' They continue down the aisle in silence.

Carson veers onto NW Hwy 225A, the truck's tires crunching against the freshly graveled road as he approaches the grand, tree-lined driveway of Seaton Hills. The majestic live oaks arch overhead, their twisted limbs draped in Spanish moss, forming a cathedral of green that stretches endlessly down the winding lane. Sunlight filters through the dense canopy, casting long golden streaks across the immaculate black wooden fencing enclosing rolling pastures of lush, emerald-green grass.

To Carson's left, a sprawling 120x250-foot covered riding arena looms into view—its handcrafted European timber beams supporting an intricately designed roof that allows for perfect ventilation and light exposure. The footing is pristine, an imported blend of premium GGT fibers and silica sand, creating the ultimate stage for high-performance horses. Inside, a full course of Grand Prix-level show jumps stands ready, each pole and standard painted in the regal colors of famous European events.

Carson lifts a brow, his curiosity piqued. He glances at Bethany, who is now practically crawling over the dashboard, eyes wide in disbelief. In her attempt to get a better look, she nearly squashes Bentley, who lets out a grumble of protest and headbutts her in retaliation.

"I thought Valley Vista was swanky," Bethany mutters, sitting back and smoothing her hands over Bentley's coat in apology. "What is this place? When Tegan said we were stopping at a friend's place in Ocala for a couple of nights, I didn't realize she meant the royal equestrian estate of the Duke of Wellington."

As they continue up the drive, Carson spots Tegan's trailer already parked in front of a striking two-story stone-built barn. The barn itself is pure old-world luxury—its facade constructed of hand-cut European limestone, its towering oak-and-iron doors imported from England gleaming under the late afternoon sun. Intricately forged iron chandeliers hang from the aisle's vaulted ceiling, casting a warm glow over the meticulously laid stone pavers.

Just outside, Tegan is unloading the horses, her movements casual and practiced, while a tall, golden-haired man in his forties, dressed in tan breeches, a blue-and-white checked country shirt, and polished mahogany tall boots, stands beside her. His attire—classic English country equestrian—radiates a posh but effortless refinement. He exudes the air of a man who belongs to centuries-old fox hunting traditions, yet carries himself with the ease of a lifelong horseman.

Carson watches as the man embraces Tegan with a gesture that is both familiar and affectionate. Then, sensing their arrival, the man turns toward Carson's truck, a charming smile playing at his lips. He waves them over, his movements smooth and assured.

Carson, reluctant to move, grips the steering wheel a little tighter. Bentley, always impatient, bounds onto his lap and licks his face enthusiastically, demanding they get on with it.

Bethany, catching his hesitation, smirks. "He seems nice. Just give me the signal, and me and Rusty'll come rescue you." She punches his shoulder, then hops out of the truck to help with the horses.

Carson exhales, reaches for his worn cowboy hat resting on the dashboard, and places it on his head. He adjusts the brim, as if settling into his own armor, then climbs out.

Bentley, sensing freedom, launches herself from the truck and makes a beeline for Tegan, her tiny hind end wagging so furiously it nearly sends her sideways. Tegan kneels to greet her, scratching behind her ears before handing her a treat.

"She's already making herself at home," Carson remarks as he approaches.

Tegan smiles and gestures toward the elegant Englishman beside her.

"Carson, may I introduce you to my dear friend, Leslie Seaton? We go way back. I spent summers at his father's facility just outside Oxford as a working student. Learned everything I needed to know about show jumping, international competition, and—"

Leslie cuts her off with a warm, rich laugh, his accent crisply British but touched with the warmth of familiarity.

"She's being modest, mate. Teegs rode circles around everyone—including me. She'd hop on anything with four legs and make it look easy. Even taught one of our donkeys how to jump!" He winks at Carson. "We just polished her up like a piece of the Queen's silver."

Tegan rolls her eyes, but the fondness between them is evident.

Leslie extends his hand. "Pleasure to make your acquaintance, Carson. Teegs won't shut up about you."

Carson shakes his hand, noting the firm but effortless grip—the mark of a horseman who's handled more than his fair share of reins. "Nice place you got here."

On cue, the trailer doors swing open, and Carson instinctively places his fingers between his lips and whistles.

Rusty trots out, ears pricked, his movements effortless and powerful. He halts squarely at Carson's side, nodding his head like a seasoned showman acknowledging his audience.

Tegan giggles and steps toward him. Rusty, recognizing an old friend, wraps his neck around her torso in an affectionate embrace.

Leslie studies Rusty with a discerning eye, his lips curling into an appreciative smile.

"And this," he muses, "must be the incomparable BM."

Rusty shifts his gaze to Leslie, nostrils flaring with curiosity.

Leslie reaches into his breeches pocket and produces a peppermint, holding it between his fingers.

Rusty, always the opportunist, immediately sidles over and plucks it from his palm, crunching in satisfaction.

"Teegs spent entire summers telling me about you, old chap," Leslie murmurs, stroking Rusty's forehead with practiced ease. "An honor to make your acquaintance."

Rusty, pleased with himself, nudges Leslie's pocket, searching for more.

Leslie laughs. "Oh, you are a clever one, aren't you?"

With a final affectionate pat, Leslie straightens and gestures toward the estate atop the hill.

"Right, I'll leave you all to settle in. Shall we meet for tea on the veranda in an hour?"

He turns gracefully on his heel, heading up a winding cobblestone path toward the stately ten-thousand-square-foot estate. The French limestone exterior catches the late afternoon sun, casting a golden glow over the grounds.

Massive arched French doors lead to an expansive veranda, complete with a summer kitchen, elegant outdoor dining, and a double-sided fireplace. Beyond the perfectly manicured gardens, an exquisite infinity pool glistens, enclosed by transparent glass walls that seem to merge with the horizon.

Carson, taking in the sheer grandeur of the estate, feels his shoulders stiffen. His life had always been trailers, open land, and miles of hard-worn leather. This? This was something else entirely.

Rusty nudges his side, grounding him back to reality.

Carson exhales, offering his arm to Tegan in mock chivalry.

"Shall we get settled, milady?" he teases, a smirk tugging at the corner of his lips.

Tegan, catching the unease in his eyes, gently takes his hand and kisses it.

"Just another barn with a bunch of sticks, Carson."

Her voice is soothing, certain.

And somehow, he almost believes her.

With Rusty trailing behind, they head toward the barn, stepping deeper into a world Carson isn't sure he wants to be a part of- but is willing to try.

Bethany brushes the hay off her jeans as she climbs the stone steps up to the veranda revealing an assortment of linen-covered tables embellished with finely sculptured sandwiches and cakes, a tray of English teapots and cups, and a cart containing an espresso machine with coffee cups next to an ice filled steel horse trough brimming with a cornucopia of soda. Bethany grabs a Coke and continues toward Carson, seated next to Tegan and Missy. She sits next to Carson, and a butler dressed in a hand tailored light grey suit and tie relieves her of her soda can and pours the remaining contents into a glass.

"Your drink, miss. I remain at your disposal, should anything else take your fancy." The butler says. Bethany's eyes widen and she looks over to Tegan and Missy for guidance. Missy clandestinely points towards the sandwich and cake table.

"Sandwich and cake, please?" She responds, not knowing exactly what she ordered. The butler nods his head and walks over to the table and pulls out hand carved silver tongs and fills a china plate with a myriad of sandwiches and cakes. He places the plate onto the table and then takes the linen napkin and gently lies it on her nap.

"Would that be all, miss?" He asks, genuinely concerned for her comfort.

"Sure. My name is Bethany." She responds, unsure of the question.

"Very well, Miss Bethany. I'll leave you to it." He looks at everyone, nods, and walks back into the estate.

"Are we still in the US?" Bethany asks, clearly disturbed by the setting.

"Leslie likes to bring a bit of England with him. He gets awfully homesick when he's in the States and Richard has been with him since he was a little boy," Tegan nonchalantly responds as she plops a sandwich into her mouth.

"What, is he like, a duke or something?" She jokingly asks.

"Actually, he's a viscount." Tegan responds.

"Are you kidding me? I'm in front of royalty!" She looks over at Carson.

"We're definitely way beyond Up and Over." She says as she grabs a cake and shoves it in her mouth.

Carson fidgets in his seat, clearly uncomfortable with the setting. He picks up a sandwich, twirls it between his fingers and then places it on his plate. He settles on a glass of lemonade and imbibes the entire contents in one gulp. The French doors open and Leslie enters the veranda bearing the countenance of casual royalty dressed in jeans, burgundy polo shirt, brown loafers and matching leather belt. He fills his plate with sandwiches and cakes and pours himself a cup of tea. He saunters towards the table and indifferently sits next to Bethany, who stares at him, mouth gaping.

"You're a viscount." She says. He smiles at the recrimination.

"Yes... I am," He replies and winks at Tegan.

"How did that happen?" She asks, genuinely interested.

"I inherited the title from my grandfather; my mother was his only heir, so the title passed down to me." He responds.

"Do you have a castle?" She presses further, hoping to get as much information as possible. Carson gives her a stern look of which she completely ignores.

"Yes. But enough about me; I want to know about you, Carson. I hear that you're a genuine cowboy. Is that true?" He leans forward in full attention, like he's finally come across the 'Ark of the Covenant.'

Carson fills his glass with more lemonade and takes a drink to delay his response.

"I did a little 'cowboying' in the past, but now I spend my time training horses and humans at Valley Vista Ranch with Tegan." He raises his glass to Tegan in admiration and then drains the remaining contents. Bethany rolls her eyes and throws her arms up in disgust.

"Ugh. Do I have to do everything here? Car, stop being a turd. His trophy case is a virtual history lesson in 'cowboying' if I say so myself. And— "

"Do tell." Leslie interjects with enthusiasm, clasping his hands together like a little boy about to receive his Christmas present.

"Riders from around the world used to come to Up and Over just to get a moment to learn Car's 'cowboying' ways. He's a— ."

"Bethany." Carson interjects. She raises her chin with pride and jabs another cake from her plate and with a full mouth mumbles.

"I don't know why he won't do Silver Spurs." She grabs Carson's sandwich and shoves it into her mouth.

"Silver?" Leslie probes.

"Spurs. It's one of the top rodeos in the nation. Me and Car would go before Vegas NFR, almost every year. You probably didn't know about that, right Teegs?" Bethany grabs a crystal goblet filled with jam and uses her knife to spread the jam on her scone. She inspects her scone and then stuffs her mouth. Leslie looks at Carson and asks.

"I would love to see this rodeo. Are you entered?"

"No. I promised to help my friend Janet with barrel racing." He replies curtly.

"What he isn't telling you is that Janet wanted to do team roping with him and Rusty." Bethany blurts out in between cakes and Coke Cola.

"Really?" Tegan asks as she squeezes his arm.

"I'm focused on you and the MHB and WEF," He replies and glares at Bethany.

"But we're not at WEF. You should do this rodeo. Leslie and I would love to be your fans. It would be a delightful diversion for me. Please, Carson." Tegan pleads as she bats her emerald eyes at him.

"I wouldn't try to resist those eyes, old chap. And besides, it would be a pleasant respite for me as well-watching a genuine cowboy in his element." Leslie snickers and hands Bethany one of his cakes like she's his best friend. Looking at a grinning Leslie and then at Tegan, Carson realizes he cannot say 'no'.

"I'll do it if Rusty agrees. If you'll excuse me, I'm going to check on the horses." He stands and leaves the table before anyone can respond. Leslie looks at the ladies, befuddled.

"He does that." They say in unison, to which they all laugh at the knowledge that the cowboy has relented to their wishes.

NOT MY FIRST RODEO

L eslie, seated on the passenger side of his immaculate 2024 black crystal Bentley Flying Spur, casually lowers the tinted window as the mammoth entrance to Silver Spurs Arena comes into view. The peach-colored 33,000-square-foot indoor facility, adorned with a bold green and white sign proudly bearing its name, looms ahead, its impressive stature a testament to the long, storied history of rodeo in Osceola County.

His driver pulls smoothly into the VIP entrance, the car barely making a sound as it rolls to a stop. With practiced efficiency, the driver immediately steps out, rounds the car, and opens the back passenger door, revealing an exquisite cream-colored custom-designed interior with subtle aluminum accents.

Missy, wide-eyed and clearly enjoying the moment, lets out a giggle as Leslie graciously extends his hand to help her out of the sedan. She takes it, stepping onto the pavement with an air of excitement.

"I can't believe I'm stepping out of a Bentley without my Bentley," she quips, glancing down as if half-expecting to see her dog bounding out behind her.

Leslie chuckles, his posh British accent tinged with amusement. "I promise to take your Bentley out for a spin when we get back." He winks, adjusting the cuffs of his tailored navy sport coat before smoothly turning to open the door for Tegan and Bethany.

Bethany looks visibly uncomfortable, shifting from foot to foot as if the mere concept of sitting in a luxury sky box for an entire rodeo is physically suffocating. She eyes Leslie warily as he gestures toward the entrance.

"Shall we head to our seats? I've acquired a sky box for our comfort." He beams with the satisfaction of a man who spares no expense for creature comforts.

Bethany grimaces, already feeling trapped. She clears her throat, trying to come up with a plausible excuse before deciding to abandon all subtlety.

"Yeah, uh, you guys enjoy your fancy balcony or whatever. I'm gonna help Car and Janet." She flashes them a quick, forced grin and practically bolts through the double doors, her well-worn paddock boots clunking loudly against the polished floor like a woman on a mission.

Leslie watches her departure with an amused smirk, shaking his head. "Charming girl. Such grace."

Tegan, suppressing a laugh, takes his offered arm without hesitation. "Bethany is about as comfortable in a skybox as a cat in a bathtub."

Leslie nods knowingly. "Ah, yes. The 'free spirit' type. Best to let them roam."

Missy, still giddy, loops her arm through Leslie's other and sighs happily. "I just want to be a fan today. It feels nice not to be thinking about training schedules or vet bills."

Tegan nods in agreement. "Same here. It's been a long time since I've just sat back and enjoyed a good rodeo. Thank you for taking such good care of us, Les." She gives his arm a reassuring squeeze.

Leslie pats her hand affectionately as he leads them toward the grand entrance. "Ladies, I wouldn't have it any other way."

As they step through the entrance, the grand scope of the Silver Spurs Arena unfolds before them. The air hums with excitement, the scent of leather, dust, and fried food mixing in that unmistakable rodeo perfume.

Silver Spurs is the beating heart of rodeo east of the Mississippi, annually ranked among the top 50 PRCA-sanctioned events. Its history dates back to a humble gathering of Osceola County ranchers in the early 1940s, when the sport was born from necessity, not spectacle. The first official rodeo, held in 1944, was a fundraiser for the war effort, where the price of admission was simply the purchase of a war bond.

They may have torn down the original arena in 1999, but its legacy remains, now boasting 8,300 seats, a state-of-the-art sound system, and twelve luxury skyboxes—one of which, of course, belongs to Leslie Seaton.

Leslie, ever the connoisseur of fine experiences, glides through the crowd with ease, guiding his guests past the bustling vendors selling rodeo hats, leather goods, and fresh funnel cakes dripping in powdered sugar.

They ascend a private set of stairs to the skybox level, the noise of the crowd dulling slightly as they step into a well-appointed, glass-enclosed suite. Plush leather chairs, a fully stocked bar, and a catered spread of hors d'oeuvres greet them, a stark contrast to the dust and grit of the arena below.

Missy, spinning in place to take it all in, gasps. "Oh wow. This is so much better than the nosebleeds."

Tegan, smirking, takes a seat near the edge, her eyes drawn immediately to the arena floor. The broncs are already loading into the chutes, their muscles rippling under the floodlights as cowboys adjust their gear.

Leslie, unfazed by the commotion, pours himself a drink and leans back, watching with a satisfied expression.

"Now then," he says smoothly, "shall we enjoy the show?"

They sit as the announcer begins the bronc event.

"Bring us the first matchup, Scotty Turner, all the way from Iowa. Look at this, twentieth in the world, matched up against Crazy Sue. Crazy it is. For the first numbers in this flight. Seventy-six points. Not the best start, but we're definitely in the midst of some great riding tonight." The announcer continues as the first bronc rider jumps off the bronc and two other horsemen wrangle the bronc out of the arena.

Leslie's eyes widen as he sips his champagne in front of the glass window. He walks toward Missy and Tegan seated on an overstuffed cream sofa, watching the event on a seventy-five inch television.

"Aren't you ladies going to join me?" He asks.

"I'll head out when Carson enters the chute. I'm starved." Missy replies. She reaches for a cracker and places a piece of salami and manchego cheese on top and then adds a dried Turkish apricot to finish her snack. She plops it into her mouth and smiles.

"Well then, educate me on this sport. What is a good score and how does one attain it?" He sits next to Missy and starts assembling his hors d'oeuvres.

"There's one hundred points - fifty goes to the rider, and fifty goes to the bronc. See how the saddle bronc rider keeps one hand on the rein and the other in the air?" She points to the television and Leslie obediently nods his head.

"Well, the judges will look at the bronc riders' control of the bronc, his spurring action, and if he's able to keep his toes pointed outward. If at any time his free arm touches the bronc or himself, he's disqualified. The rider tries to be as fluid as the bronc's bucking spurring from the points of the horse's shoulders to the back of the saddle for eight seconds. A smooth rhythmic ride will get you a better score than a wild, uncontrolled effort." She responds, sounding like a seasoned rodeo aficionado.

Tegan stands abruptly and strides to the window, her eyes scanning the arena below with an intensity that betrays her calm exterior.

"Carson's next to the chute," she murmurs, almost to herself.

Missy and Leslie exchange a glance before hurriedly finishing their hors d'oeuvres and joining her at the glass. Below them, Carson swings a leg over Wicked Dreams, a notorious bronc with a buck off rate of 94%. The announcer's voice booms through the speakers, adding to the electrified atmosphere.

"Next up, ladies and gentlemen, is Carson Peterson, all the way from California! Been a while since we've seen this cowboy in the chutes, but it's always a treat to watch a former World Champion ride. This is one of those fearsome animals from chute gate number one—Wicked Dreams out of Kissimmee, Florida. Watch this, folks. We're in for something special!"

The chute gate swings open, and Wicked Dreams explodes forward, his powerful muscles rippling beneath his dappled coat. Carson moves with the bronc, a fluid extension of the beast itself, every movement controlled yet effortless, like a dance performed at the edge of chaos.

The crowd gasps. Then cheers.

"It's poetry in motion, folks! Look at that form! Carson Peterson is making the most of every second on Wicked Dreams! This is a masterclass in bronc riding!"

The eight-second buzzer blares through the stadium. The pickup rider gallops alongside, and with a natural grace, Carson times his jump perfectly, dismounting mid-stride onto the other cowboy's horse. He tips his hat, waves to the roaring crowd—then looks up.

His gaze locks onto Tegan's.

He grins. Points. Blows her a kiss.

Tegan's breath catches. Instinctively, without thinking, she blows one back.

"Are you seeing what I'm seeing, folks? I'm hearing word that none other than Olympic gold medalist Tegan Miller, daughter of our own Hank Miller, is in the house! And looks like she's here supporting her man, Carson Peterson!"

The jumbotron catches her reaction, flashing her image across the stadium, and the audience erupts. She gives a playful wave, cheeks burning with something that isn't quite embarrassment—something deeper. More dangerous.

Carson gives one final tip of his hat before disappearing down the alleyway.

Leslie, watching from the side, is stone still, his usual suave expression replaced by something unreadable. He lets out a long breath, following Tegan as she turns from the window and heads back into the plush inner sanctuary of the skybox. He sinks into the leather sofa, staring blankly ahead.

"I didn't know he could ride like that," he finally mutters, shaking his head in disbelief. "I am in the presence of equestrian royalty. A World Champion Rodeo Cowboy. An Olympic Gold Medalist. What a pair the two of you make."

He refills his Dom Perignon, taking a longer-than-necessary sip.

Tegan chuckles, though her expression remains distant, as if her heart is still in that arena. "Carson is full of surprises," she says, swirling the champagne in her glass. "I didn't even know he was a World Champion. But that's just Carson. No bragging. No fanfare. He speaks through his actions."

"A rare breed," Leslie muses. But there's something in his tone. Something... hesitant.

Missy, sensing the shift, rises quickly and grabs her coat. "I'm gonna check on Carson, help Janet get ready for barrels. You guys coming?"

Tegan shakes her head. "Tell Janet to kill it out there. I'll watch from here."

Missy nods and heads for the exit, casting one last knowing glance at Leslie before slipping out.

Silence stretches between Tegan and Leslie. The sounds of the rodeo outside become muffled by the thick glass, the distant cheers and pounding hooves now a distant hum. Leslie sits back, arms crossed, fingers tapping against his forearm.

Finally, he speaks.

"Splendid, T. But that's not what I want to know, and you bloody well know it."

Tegan smirks, twirling her glass between her fingers. "What could you ever mean?"

Leslie leans forward, fixing her with a piercing stare. "Tegan. I will not allow you to leave this suite until we address the rather large, glaring pachyderm in the room."

She exhales through her nose. Places her drink down. Looks him dead in the eye.

"I love him."

Leslie's brow twitches, just slightly. His polished exterior cracks, just for a moment.

"I love him," she repeats, softer this time. Her hands cover his. She squeezes, then lets go.

Leslie's jaw clenches. He stares down at his own hands, as if trying to form a response that won't betray what he's truly thinking.

He doesn't get the chance.

"I just don't want you to get hurt again," he whispers, almost to himself. Then he looks up, and there it is—the memory, the history, Argentina. The polo player.

"Need I remind you of Buenos Aires?" he adds quietly.

Tegan flinches. Her fingers curl around the edge of the sofa. The wound is old, but not forgotten.

"That was different." Her voice is firm, but she avoids his gaze.

"Was it?" Leslie tilts his head, voice gentle but unrelenting. "Tegan, love, you fall hard. You always have. And when you fall, you expect the other person to catch you."

She swallows hard, forcing herself to meet his eyes.

"I was young, Les. I had no clue what I wanted. Who I was." She takes a shaky breath. "I'm still figuring it out, but with Carson..." She closes her eyes for a moment, then opens them. "With Carson, I feel calm. I feel—steady. For the first time, I'm not trying to outrun my father's shadow. Or my past. Or myself."

Leslie watches her, his expression unreadable. Then, finally, he exhales and nods.

Tegan, desperate to shift the conversation, forces a grin and nods toward the door Missy disappeared through.

"Speaking of falling hard, can we talk about Missy? I mean, she's really come a long way, hasn't she?"

Leslie narrows his eyes, catching the deflection immediately. "Oh no, darling. Don't think for a second you're getting out of this discussion so easily."

Tegan shrugs dramatically. "I'm just saying! It wasn't long ago she wouldn't even step into a barn, and now look at her. WEF, a whole new chapter ahead. I think she's gonna kill it."

Leslie purses his lips, watching her closely. "Ah yes, very smooth. Change the subject to the prodigal student."

Tegan sips her drink, feigning innocence. "I'm just making conversation."

"And I'm just making sure you don't break your heart over a cowboy who doesn't belong in your world," Leslie retorts.

Tegan's expression hardens. "Don't belong?"

Leslie softens slightly but doesn't back down. "You know what I mean. He's rough edges and reckless charm. He's—"

"The best man I've ever met."

That gives Leslie pause.

Silence stretches between them again, but this time, it's different. A shift. A new understanding.

Leslie finally sighs, running a hand through his golden hair. "Alright, T. I surrender. But just promise me one thing."

Tegan arches a brow. "What's that?"

"That if he breaks your heart, you'll let me buy you an ungodly amount of champagne and tell you I told you so."

Tegan laughs, tension melting from her shoulders. "Deal."

Leslie clinks his flute against hers, then gestures to the window.

"Now, enlighten me—how does one race a barrel?"

Tegan giggles and points down to the arena- three steel white barrels with a red stripe at the center arranged in a triangular pattern.

"You don't race the barrel, silly. You race around the barrels. The fastest horse and rider pair, without knocking down a barrel, wins." She replies.

Organized chaos. A bevy of horse and rider combinations warmup behind the entrance alley as the first barrel racer adjusts her cowboy hat before heading down the alley to make her run. Her cream-colored quarter horse canters sideways and rears as she enters the alley. The announcer clicks on the microphone as the first pair enters the arena.

"We have Emily Minter starting us off. She made a list minute switch to her older mare, Chango. Let's see how this pair fairs on this run. First barrel nice and smooth. Second. Got some trouble there. Looks like her hind legs went out from under her in the deep footing and she couldn't make the turn. Oh, no. Barrel down. She continues to the third nice and smooth and finishes with a 22.5 because of that five second penalty. Too bad for Emily. That run was fast, but she's out of contention. A slight error has proven costly for our first rider. "

Bethany adjusts Sista's turquoise splint boots, backs away and gives Janet a thumbs up. Janet dressed in a pink button-down shirt, cream straw cowboy hat that heightens her bright orange hair tucked underneath, and Wrangler jeans and cowboy boots to finish her Western assemblage. Sista's golden braided mane glistens under the lights. She closes her eyes and takes a deep breath, and then opens them as Missy arrives.

"How's the footing riding?" She asks Missy.

"Looks pretty good. Little deep at barrel two, but the straight is smooth." Missy responds. Janet looks at Carson and smiles.

"Any final thoughts, chief?" She asks. Her voice cracks, betraying her nerves.

"You got this, Janet. Remember, Sista does not respond to whipping. It's actually a waste of time. And make sure that you're at a full gallop before you split the beams. What's your pattern?" He responds as he adjusts Sista's turquoise beaded breastplate. Sista nuzzles him and he pats her neck.

"Left, right, right." She responds her focus on the alley.

"Good. You're next." He says, taps his hat, and walks to the side. Bethany and Missy follow Carson.

Janet, holding the reins high and loose in each hand, gets Sista into a full gallop as she heads down the alley towards her run.

"And here comes Janet Newman. New to rodeo with her five-year-old mare, Sista. Beautiful horse, but let's see what this little mare can do. First barrel, clean. This mare loves to turn. Looking like a good run. Barrel two is even faster. Look at that little mare go. She keeps this up; we might have a new leader. Barrel three. Lightning. She comes home, and it's a 16.5. The fastest run of the rodeo! Out of nowhere, Janet Newman has laid down the gauntlet. Hailey Morgan has her work cut out for her if she wants to hold on to her title. What a great day for rodeo!" The announcer chuckles into the microphone and the audience roars with approval.

Janet vigorously smacks Sista's neck with approval and smiles as she pulls up on the reins as she exits the arena. She slows down to a walk and Carson, Bethany, and Missy mob her chanting her name. She dismounts, hands Carson the reins, and kisses Sista's cheek.

"Sista was on fire. All I had to do was sit there, and she took care of the rest. No whipping needed. I just rose my hands up and let go. Woo hoo. Love me, my Pali girl!" Janet exclaims.

"I couldn't get over that second barrel. Everyone else was dumping it, and you guys took that turn like it was nothing." Bethany says as she quickly removes Sista's saddle.

"Well done, Janet. That was a great run. Your relationship with Sista is something special. The two of you could easily beat me and Rusty. Don't let him know that." He smiles and knowingly winks at Janet. She laughs and checks Sista's legs as she removes the protective boots.

"Where is my boy, Rusty? You'd think he'd be strutting his stuff all around this rodeo." She asks.

"He's eating his well deserved dinner of oats and hay. He was so determined to win team roping after he saw his arch nemesis, Boots, do his run. We were out so fast; Gary almost missed his mark. But you know, Rusty. He hates losing." He remarks.

"Just Rusty? Black? Kettle? Need I remind you of why Boots is Rusty's arch nemesis." Janet chides.

"Let's hose off Sista and get those ice boots on." Carson says. He hands Missy the reins and struts off to Rusty's temporary paddock to avoid further conversation.

"Who's Boots?" Missy asks.

"Short story long; Boots is the one of a very select few horses that's beaten Rusty. Follow me and I'll give you the complete story." Janet laughs. They both head to the wash racks as the next barrel racer starts her run.

Carson unlatches the trailer and Rusty saunters out with Sista in tow as the sun crests over the horizon in front of Leslie's Tudor barn. He places a rope halter and lead on Sista and hands her to Bethany. Bethany pets Sista's muzzle and heads to the barn, chattering away with Sista and Rusty on either side. Ahead, Leslie opens the door to his Bentley for Janet and she leaps out and greedily takes his arm. The two head off to his estate house, jabbering away like they've been best friends for decades, leaving Missy and Tegan in their wake. Missy shrugs her shoulders and heads off by herself into the chalet.

Tegan walks towards Carson, her eyes gleaming with affection. He slides her hair away from her forehead, revealing her emerald eyes, and kisses her. She gently groans and kisses him back, running her hands through his hair. Her hands wander down his back and she envelopes his hand in hers. She looks intensely into his hazel eyes.

"Follow me." She commands. He eagerly follows her to the barn where they encounter Mia and Luke saddled and ready for an excursion. Tegan caresses Mia's forehead and Mia knickers back her approval.

"It's a great night for a ride, if you're not too tired." She says with a raised eyebrow.

"Wouldn't miss it." He responds and guides Luke to the mounting block, following Tegan and Mia.

Both mounted, they head out.

They pass through a twilight row of Bottle Palm trees covering a trail path towards a shaded wood just beyond the arena. Fireflies emit a mythical glow highlighting the unruly undergrowth of wild grass and flowers. Black mangroves, cypresses, and buttonwood trees adorn the wood and provide ample coverage as Tegan and Carson head towards the middle of a clearing in a comfortable silence. An English styled picnic rug brimming with chips, potato salad, a cooler, Kentucky Fried Chicken, and Rice Krispie Treats, lies in paradoxical contrast to Leslie's fine linen, china, crystal, and cutlery behind an unlit fire pit of stones within the clearing. Tegan hastily dismounts and leads Mia toward the grass, tying her reins to the saddle. She pats her neck and Mia responds with a grateful nicker and lowers her head to graze. Tegan kneels in front of the fire pit, arranges the pile of firewood and kindle, and lights the fire with a set of matches set in front of the fire pit. She gently blows on the kindle, giving it life with a healthy glow and pulse of flames.

The fire heightens the shine from Carson's 'All Around Cowboy' belt buckle as he walks toward Tegan, seated filling the wine glasses with foamy cold beer from the Yeti cooler. He picks up an orphaned stick, kindles the fire and sits cross-legged next to Tegan, who offers him the glass. He chuckles as he inspects the fine crystal filled with the local lager and greedily inhales the contents. She obligingly refills the glass and they both tap their glasses in a celebratory fashion.

"Leslie?" He inquires with a bit a sarcasm.

"Actually, it was Richard. He wanted to add a little 'class' to our celebration. And when Richard gets involved, you don't say 'no'." She responds.

Carson takes another drink and sets down his glass; he searches Tegan's face, caressing her cheek and drawing a wayward strand from her eye, tucking it behind her ear. He looks at her with longing like it was the first time they dared to touch each other in love, the power of their connection undeniable.

"Hungry?" she asks and knowingly smiles as she reaches toward the plates in front of her to hand Carson a plate. He begrudgingly accepts the plate and fills it with potato salad and three pieces of chicken - a thigh and two legs.

"I almost didn't recognize you at the rodeo. You seemed at home there. Like. I don't know. Like. You belong there." She says, half nervous of the revelation.

"I've been a cowboy most of my life. So I guess rodeo will always be a part of me. And, yes, I feel at home when I rodeo. But don't you worry, pretty lady, this cowboy knows where his heart is." He winks and takes a big bite of his chicken leg. Tegan looks at the changing amber colors of the fire and takes in Carson's honest, heartfelt words. She gets up suddenly and heads in an indeterminate path towards a line of trees.

"Where are you going?" He asks as he attempts to stand.

"Just a little surprise for my handsome prizewinning cowboy." She giddily responds like a child and waves him to sit back down.

"I'll be right back." Her voices echos from the treelined path. With a raised eyebrow, he resumes the feast laid out before him.

Tegan eventually emerges bearing a red ribboned case in her arms like a templar bearing a hand fashioned sword. She lays the case next to Carson.

"Open it." She commands. Carson obediently removes the red ribbon, casts it aside, and clicks the brass fasteners, revealing a brand new round shoulder mahogany tri-burst colored Gibson J-45 guitar. He looks up to her, smiling in adoration, knowing that the gift meant more to him than she'd ever know.

"I was going to wait til' WEF, but I thought... No better time than the present. Right?" She shrugs her shoulders and grabs a Rice Krispie treat; she points at the guitar.

"Bethany helped me pick it out. Told me you used to play all the time at your barn after barn chores when it was just you, the starlit sky, and the horses. Pretty good at it, too. So... I was hoping...Sing for me... Please?"

She pleads, looking up at him. Running his fingers over the guitar, adjusting the tuning pegs with care, he strums again, coaxing a richer sound. A low hum escapes his lips before the familiar notes of *Tennessee Whiskey* pour from the strings. Locking eyes with Tegan, his gaze heavy with a lifetime of pent-up passion, he sings.

Used to spend my nights out in a bar room
Liquor was the only love I've known
But you rescued me from reachin' for the bottom
And brought me back from being too far gone
You're as smooth as
Tennessee Whiskey
You're as sweet
As strawberry wine...

He continues serenading her and his raspy tenor voice resonates with the long years of loneliness they both have endured by choices made in the past, but now removed with choices made in the present.

WEF

Wellington's cold snap is more than a simple drop in temperature—it's a shockwave. The air, razor-sharp and bitter, wraps itself around the show grounds, carrying with it delicate lace-like snowflakes that vanish on contact. Under the arena floodlights, the crystalline specks create an almost surreal effect, swirling around horse and rider like an enchantment.

But for the competitors in Ring 8, this is no fairy tale.

The cold has put an edge into every horse—nerves fray, tension thickens, the arena a powder keg waiting for a spark.

And Max is that spark.

Olivia canters a circle, feeling the electricity coiling beneath her saddle. Max pins his ears, kicks out, his muscles bunching like a loaded spring. A flurry of snowflakes lands on his gleaming bay coat, and he twitches violently, his tail lashing like a whip.

"Easy, boy," Olivia murmurs, giving his heaving neck a firm pat.

But Max is past listening.

She adjusts her seat, lining him up for a meter-high vertical. The second she so much as hinted at asking, Max explodes forward.

Too fast.

Too late to stop him.

BAM!

Max plows straight through the jump, splintering poles, toppling standards, sending a wave of flying debris across the arena. The impact sends a tremor up Olivia's spine, her grip faltering just as Max launches into a blind buck.

For a split second, she hangs in the air—weightless.

Then she hits the ground, feet first, skidding in the dirt as Max wheels away with a defiant squeal, tail flagged high.

Olivia lunges for the reins—misses.

Max is loose.

The gelding bolts, head snapping side to side, reveling in his newfound freedom. He whips into a gallop, circling the ring like a rodeo bronc, dirt spraying from beneath his powerful hooves.

Oscar moves fast. With an almost unnatural ease, he cuts across Max's trajectory; his sharp instincts anticipate every evasive maneuver. Max fights, hooves digging deep, but Oscar doesn't flinch. One firm step, one deft hand on the reins, and Max is his.

The gelding snorts in protest, but Oscar only pats his neck, murmuring low.

Missy is already at Olivia's side.

"You good?" she asks, offering Olivia her fallen crop.

Olivia dusts off her breeches, forcing a tight-lipped smile. "Nothing a little retail therapy couldn't fix." Her laugh is hollow, betraying the shakiness in her fingers as she adjusts her helmet.

Max hasn't seen snow before.

Or maybe... she hasn't seen this Max before.

Oscar hands back the reins. Olivia takes them, but hesitates.

"I'll fix the fence, Señorita Missy," Oscar calls over his shoulder.

Missy nods her thanks, gaze still locked on Olivia.

"I can get on him."

The MHB have gathered, staring wide-eyed, their expressions like troops watching their leader fall in battle.

Bethany shifts in her saddle, forcing a weak smile and a half-hearted thumbs-up.

Olivia inhales sharply.

"I'll get back on."

"Why don't you trot him in a circle while I work with Bethany."

Bethany pales. "What?" Missy waves her over. Bethany glances nervously at the others, takes a steadying breath, and picks up a trot. Olivia peels away, taking Max to the far end of the ring.

But the night has only just begun.

Missy lowers the jump, adding a trot pole in front to keep Winston focused. Bethany adjusts her grip, guiding him forward with a hesitant nudge.

They approach the fence—then Winston stops.

Or launches, rather.

He hurls himself into the air, clearing the standards like a 1.60m jumper.

Bethany barely has time to process before they land—and Winston explodes.

A buck. A violent, spine-jarring buck. Bethany hits the ground hard.

And then—all hell breaks loose.

Winston tears off, his panicked whinny splitting the air.

His wild flight sends the other horses into a frenzy.

Robbie rears.

Cinnamon kicks out.

Nate and Cameron hit the dirt, their ponies galloping after Winston. Within seconds, the arena erupts into a full-blown stampede. Olivia quickly dismounts Max and holds him steady, eyes wide with fear.

Grooms swarm outside the fence, halters and lead ropes clutched uselessly in their hands, awaiting guidance from a leader that hasn't emerged.

Then—

Thunder.

Two riders storm into the ring.

Carson and Rusty from the right.

Tegan and Sista from the left.

They split the stampede, diving headfirst into the chaos.

Winston lowers his head and charges. Straight at Rusty.

Carson halts.

Rusty rears, slicing the air with his hooves—but Winston doesn't stop.

Carson's hand snaps to his lasso.

One fluid motion—

The loop flies. Catches.

Rusty digs his hooves deep, muscles straining, as Carson ties off the rope and backs him up. Winston bucks hard, thrashing against restraint—then freezes.

Carson eases forward, hand brushing Winston's dampened neck.

Tegan, meanwhile, is all motion. She and Sista cut Cinnamon and Robbie off, forcing them into a controlled circle.

Missy sweeps in, grabbing their reins, calming them with steady hands.

The grooms move fast, wrangling what remains of the chaos.

And then—

Silence. The dust settles.

The only sound left is panting—human and equine alike.

Carson slides off Rusty, leading Winston back to Bethany. He hands over the reins, giving her shoulder a firm squeeze.

Bethany nods, eyes shining.

The MHB cluster near the mounting block, their gazes flitting nervously between Carson and Tegan, still mounted, still watching. Uncertainty hangs heavy in the air; their collective breath, visible in the frigid night, embodies their doubts.

Cameron shifts in her saddle, knuckles white against the reins. Then, hesitantly, she raises her hand.

"Mr. Carson? Can we go back to the barn? We're... I'm scared."

Her voice is small, yet it echoes through the silence. Her lip trembles, her cheeks blotched pink from cold and fear, the snowflakes softly dissolving against her skin.

Tegan's eyes flick to Carson, concern deep in her emerald gaze.

He nods, and Tegan guides Sista to the gate, waiting.

Carson doesn't answer right away. Instead, he studies Cameron, really looking at her, before finally offering a small, knowing smile.

"I think Robbie would love a trail ride with his friends, don't you?"

Robbie, as if on cue, nuzzles Cameron's jacket, tugging at the fabric. A little reminder—he's here. He's not afraid. He's with her.

Cameron sniffs, straightens slightly. "I guess so."

She glances at the others. One by one, they nod, tentatively at first, then with growing confidence.

"Let's go for a trail ride, then," Carson says. "And after, how about some burgers and hot chocolate?"

That gets a few grins.

"Mount up, MHB."

With quiet determination, the team climbs back into their saddles, falling into a nose-to-tail line behind Tegan, while Carson and Rusty bring up the rear. They move out of the arena, hooves crunching against the frost-kissed path.

Olivia and Bethany fall in beside Carson, a tense silence settling between them.

Olivia shoots Bethany a look, lips barely moving. "Talk to him."

Bethany glares. Shakes her head. Looks away. Carson chuckles, sensing the storm before it comes. He pats Rusty's rump.

"Spill it, kiddo."

Bethany lets out a frustrated breath, casting Olivia one last glare before hanging her head in defeat. Tears brim in her eyes, but she bites them back.

Carson doesn't push. He simply clicks his cheek to Rusty and veers toward an open field.

"Follow me."

The MHB hesitates, then follows.

Carson swings off Rusty, tying off the reins. The others do the same, leaving the horses to graze. Carson walks to the center of the field, the moonlight stretching his shadow long across the frostbitten grass. Tegan stands beside him, arms folded, waiting.

Then he gestures.

"Sit."

Slowly, reluctantly, the MHB drop into the cold grass, forming a half-circle around him.

Bethany avoids his gaze.

"I ate dirt, Car." Her voice cracks. "Nate and Cameron ate dirt. Winston's never been out of state. It's snowing. This was a mistake."

Cameron blurts, "What if I don't remember my course?"

Nate mutters, "What if Cinnamon doesn't listen to me?"

Olivia throws up her hands. "Why are we here, Carson? The horses aren't happy. What if we embarrass ourselves?" A thick silence follows. The wind whispers through the trees, the cold biting at exposed skin.

Finally, Carson sits too, arms draped over his knees.

"Where are we?" he asks simply.

The MHB exchange glances, confused.

Olivia huffs. "We're freezing our butts off in a field."

Carson smirks. "Exactly."

He gestures around them. "Same grass. Same footing. Same sky. The only thing different is your mind."

They blink at him.

"Your horse isn't worried about 'what if.' No overthinking. No watching the crowd or chasing ribbons. Just standing there, waiting for you. He feels what's in your hands, what's in your heart. Doubt weighs heavy on him. Fear shows up plain as day. But bring even a little heart — even if you're scared — and you'll find him right there with you. Every time."

He lets the words hang in the air.

"So tell me, what are you bringing here?"

Silence.

Then—

Cameron whispers, voice small but steady, "We don't want to disappoint Ms. Tegan."

Tegan inhales sharply, the weight of their words settling deep in her chest.

She adjusts her USA baseball cap, running her fingers over the worn brim. Then, softly—

"You think I'm never scared?"

Cameron nods.

Tegan lets out a breath, eyes distant. She hadn't told this story in years.

"When I was younger, I used to act out at shows. If I was anxious, I made sure everyone knew it. I'd slam rails. Get into arguments with my dad. And he'd just... watch."

She stares out across the darkened field, as if seeing it all over again.

"Then, one day, I had an awful ride. I was shaking, frustrated. I was making excuses—blaming the course, the footing, my horse. My dad said nothing. Just told me to go for a walk."

She smiles to herself, bittersweet.

"We walked forever. I remember being mad about it. But then, he just... stopped. Right in the middle of the woods."

She pauses, her throat tightening.

"He picked up a leaf. Turned it over in his hands. And then he looked at me—really looked at me—and said, 'If you take a moment to listen, to be still, nature will teach you everything you need to know.'"

She exhales.

"He told me fear was just noise. That if I focused on gratitude—if I could find awe in every moment—I'd never have a reason to be afraid."

She looks up, eyes shining.

"I still think about that. Every time I step into the ring. Every time I'm scared. And when I don't know what I'm doing, or why I'm here, I choose gratitude. Because I get to do what I love. Because I have you guys. And because fear..."

She smiles.

"Fear is just a story you tell yourself."

For a long moment, no one speaks. Then—Carson stands. Opens his arms. Tegan does too.

And suddenly, the MHB surge forward, wrapping them both in a crushing embrace.

Someone sniffs. Someone laughs through tears.

Finally, Nate mumbles against Carson's jacket—

"I'm hungry."

Laughter bursts through the tension, shattering it like ice.

Carson grins, ruffling Nate's hair.

"Burgers and hot chocolate, then."

The MHB cheer, the last of their doubts melting into the night.

They mount up, lighter now, stronger now.

And together, they ride home.

"Are we at Disney World?" Cameron exclaims as she twirls around the opulent Italian marble flooring of the foyer furnished with a crystal chandelier and Italian marble fireplace on one side and a spiraling staircase beautifully marked by Tuscan iron railings. On the other side, a door leading to a movie theater and an entryway to the kitchen complete the rotund. Leslie appears through the kitchen.

"Greetings, fellow equestrians. The burgers and chips and hot cocoa are awaiting you."

"Yay!" they all exclaim at the same time and they all head into the kitchen except Bethany. She looks around the foyer and heads to the door.

"I'm out. Heading back." She exclaims.

"Hold on, spice girl. Let me pack you a 'go pack' before you head back." Leslie says.

"Fine. But pack something for Oscar as well." She commands.

"I offered Oscar a room, but Oscar is, well, Oscar, and your wish is my command, milady."

He quips as he guides Bethany into the kitchen. Tegan takes Carson's hand and heads to the kitchen. Carson holds firm in the center of the foyer.

"You want to head back, don't you?" She whispers. He nods and kisses her hand.

"I'll take Bethany with me and we'll do night check. I won't be long." He says as he looks deeply into her eyes. He kisses her forehead and they enter the kitchen.

The night life at a typical horse show is a virtual carnival with Wellington's Winter Equestrian Festival setting a new standard; Latin music booms throughout the aisles as grooms proceed through their duties of horse care - intricate horse braids with gold and silver metallic rubber bands accent the horse's crown filled mane, finely tuned clip sculptures accenting the horses' haunches, horse hooves polished with multiple grades of sandpaper and oil all to create 'the perfect show horse'. Hammers and drills create an underlying beat along with the music as groomsmen convert stalls into tack rooms and lounge areas and hang strings of lights along the stalls to create a festive environment for the junior equestrian exhibitors.

And then there is Rusty sauntering through the aisles several paces in front of Carson and Bethany, completing his night check, a duty he takes with the utmost seriousness. He passes Oscar's newly assembled stall/grooming station and pauses. Oscar obediently walks over to Rusty and feeds him a cookie. Rusty muzzles Oscar's side and he reluctantly feeds him another cookie and pats his cheek. Rusty, now satisfied, continues his patrol down the aisle. Oscar looks down the aisle and notices Carson and Bethany feeding carrots to the horses and checking their water buckets. Oscar finishes rolling a white polo wrap, places it on the shelf with the other professionally wrapped polos, and intercepts Carson and Bethany.

"It's good to see you both, but why are you here?" He asks, concerned. Bethany and Carson knowingly look at one another.

"Love Leslie, but I needed to get away from the luxury accommodations and just hang with the horses. You mind?" She asks as she grabs a rake and cleans the aisle before Oscar can answer. Carson smiles and clicks his lips and Rusty trots back to him, standing next to his side.

"Thought I would go for a walk with Rusty underneath the stars before the craziness begins." He responds.

"I'll join you." Oscar quickly hangs his rag on the tack hook and they walk down the aisle out towards the grounds.

The snow diminishes, and the sky clears revealing a blanket of stars hanging in a pitch black sky. The glistening northern star guides the trio along the horse path as they pass competitor barns. Oscar waves at another groom, who is busily finishing up cleaning and polishing bridles.

"¿Qué onda, Oscar?" He yells with delight.

"Nada, todo tranquilo." Oscar responds as they pass by.

"Bueno, Nos vemos!" He replies and waves with his soapy rag and then continues to work on his final bridle of the night. Oscar, Carson, and Rusty maintain the same direction and then veer back to the left around the lungeing arena. Rusty trots into the arena and bucks and spins, kicking up dirt everywhere. Oscar and Carson lean against the fence and take in Rusty's festive mood in silence. Rusty walks to the end of the arena with his nose skimming the ground and suddenly paws the sand; bends his knees, bringing his body to the ground for a much needed roll. He happily rolls from one side to the other, creating the horse version of a snow angle covering his entire body with sand. He pauses for a moment and lies on his side in peaceful bliss. Carson and Oscar knowingly look at each other and smile.

"If it were up to Rusty, he'd spend the night out here. Don't say I'd blame him."

"Si, Señor Carson. Rusty understands the good life much more than we do. No?" Oscar responds. Carson shrugs his shoulders and smiles. "I don't know if that's true anymore. I'm pretty sure I'm figuring it out."

"You certain?" Oscar raises an eyebrow and asks.

"Yes." Carson's face reveals more than his response.

"Follow me." Oscar moves off the fence and heads back to their barn aisle. Carson whistles and Rusty extends his forelegs in front of his body, quickly stands, shakes the sand off his body, and gallops out the arena and trots up to Carson. They catch up to Oscar and head back.

Rusty enters his stall and Oscar and Carson walk back to the tack room. Oscar enters a converted stall; makeshift quarters with a cot to sleep, a lantern and army duffle on top of a folding table next to the cot, a hot plate, coffee maker, a small fridge plugged into the wall, and two lawn chairs. Oscar opens a tack box and removes two mugs, hands one to Carson and fills both with coffee. They tap their mugs and sit in the lawn chairs.

"Señor Carson." Oscar says in his thick accent, carrying a mix of gravity and brotherly warmth. "We need to talk."

Carson raises an eyebrow. "Something wrong, Oscar?"

"No, nothing wrong. Something...important." Oscar fidgets in his chair, produces a worn leather box buried deep in his black Stormy Kramer steelhead wool vest and places it on a 'milk crate' table between them, his calloused fingers brushing its surface.

"This," Oscar betrays years of pent up emotion, "belonged to Señor Hank. He gave it to me a long time ago, after Dona Mirabella passed. He said, 'Oscar, this is the ring that started my family, and I'm entrusting it to you. One day, give it to someone who will keep that family alive'." Oscar's eyes grew misty as he continued, "I remember the day he handed it to me. It was after a long day of working the ranch. We were sitting by the fire, and he had this faraway look in his eyes. He told me about the love he shared with Dona Mirabella, how this ring was a symbol of the life they built together - the life at the ranch, their dreams. He said, 'Tegan deserves someone who will cherish her as much as I cherished her mother. Oscar, when the time comes, you'll know who that man is. You'll see it in his actions, not just his words.'"

Carson's breath hitched. "Oscar are you saying..."

Oscar nodded, his eyes glistening. "I've watched you, Señor Carson. You bring something here that has been missing since Señor Hank. Stability. Heart. You're good for the ranch. You're good for Tegan. And she... mi hermana, is good for you."

Carson stares at the box, the weight of the moment settling on him. "Oscar, this is..." He hesitates, searching for the right words, but cannot adequately express himself.

"This is a big deal. Are you sure?"

"Si." Oscar opens the box, revealing a simple yet elegant gold ring, its surface worn but timeless. "I know you will honor this. And I know Tegan will say yes."

Carson slowly exhales, his hand hovering over the box before finally taking it. The cool metal of the ring felt heavy, not with burden but with a legacy.

"Thank you, Oscar," he says, his voice thick with emotion. "This means the world to me. I'll do right by Hank, by his legacy. And by Tegan."

Oscar claps a hand on Carson's shoulder. "I know you will. Now go. Make your plan. But maybe not with the horses watching. They gossip too much."

Carson chuckles, the tension breaking like the morning mist. "I'll keep that in mind, but you can't keep anything from— "

"Rusty." Oscar finishes his sentence. "Rusty is not a horse, Señor Carson. Doesn't count." He smiles and takes one last drink from his coffee. Carson hands Oscar his mug and walks out the door.

Carson stops at Rusty's stall and holds the ring up to the light. It glows underneath the stall lights, a reflection of hope and new beginnings. He slips the box into his pocket and turns to Rusty.

"Well, old friend, I guess we've got some planning to do." Rusty nickers softly, as if in agreement, and Carson smiles, his heart full as he envisions the future he is about to create.

JUMPING OFF

Equestrians dressed in their professional show white attire are giving the false air of confidence amongst the chaos of young 6-year-old horses vying for the championship. This championship most likely leads to national team placements and endorsements which would be life changing for any equestrian and, most notably, Missy Harrison. The future of horse sport is in full display in the warm-up ring.

The warm-up ring is a powder keg of tension, with anxious riders weaving between young, excitable horses. Hooves churn the footing into a cloud of dust, and the air buzzes with the clipped commands of trainers and the occasional shout of frustration. Missy eases Remington into a careful trot, her heart already racing. The dark bay stallion moves with electric energy, his every stride coiled like a spring with power. Across the crowded ring, another rider's horse cuts too close, spooking the already alert Remi.

"Whoa, easy Remi." Missy calls, but it was too late. Remington throws his head, rearing high, striking at the air. His body twists sharply, pitching Missy sideways as she clings desperately to the reins. Her heart leaps into her throat, and for a split second, she thought she might tumble to the ground. Somehow, she stays aboard, but her breath comes fast and shallow, her knuckles white.

"Missy! Over here!" Tegan's voice rings out, cutting through the chaos like a lifeline. Tegan stands by the rail, hands on her hips, her sharp green eyes locked on the duo. Her calm presence is a grounding force. Missy brings Remington around, her grip on the reigns still too tight. Tegan steps into the ring, her boots crunching the dirt, and motions for Missy to halt. Missy obeys, her chest heaving.

"I don't know, Teegs," she confesses, her voice trembling. "I can't- he's just too much today." Tegan gives her a long, steady look. "No, Missy, he's not too much for you. But he can feel your nerves. You've got to trust him. Right now, you're fighting yourself as much as you're fighting him."

Missy nods but can't stop her fingers from trembling against the reins. "It's just- what if he— "

"You can't think about 'what if,'" Tegan interrupted gently, stepping closer to Remington. She lays a firm hand on the stallion's neck, her calm energy rippling through him. He nickers and drops his head slightly, responding to her touch.

"Here's what we're going to do," Tegan says, meeting Missy's eyes. She points to a nearby vertical, standing at an imposing 1.35 meters, well above the height of the course. "You're going to jump this. Just once. It's bigger than anything in your round, but if you can handle this, the rest will feel easy."

Missy's stomach tightens. "That's — Tegan, that's bigger than— "

"It's not about the height," Tegan says firmly, holding her gaze. "It's about the trust. You trust him to get you over, and he trusts you to guide him. You've done this before, Missy. Do it now."

Missy exhales shakily, nodding as she turns Remington toward the jump. The world narrows to just her and the vertical. Her heart thuds loudly, but she focuses on Tegan's words, letting them drown out the rest of the noise. Missy urges Remington forward. The gelding's ears flick forward, locking on the jump. Two strides. One. Take off. The air seems to hold them as they soar over the fence, Remington's knees tucked high and tight. They land smoothly, his stride steady and confident.

"Yes. That's it, Missy!" Tegan claps her hands, her grin wide. "See? He's ready, and so are you."

Missy lets out a breath she hadn't realized she was holding, leaning down to pat Remington's neck. "Good boy, Remi." She whispers, her smile growing.

"Now go jump some sticks." Tegan says, pointing toward the in-gate. "Get out there and show them what you've got."

Missy turns Remington toward the exit, her heart lighter, her nerves dissolving with every step. She can do this. They CAN do this.

The crowd erupts as Missy and Remington clear the last jump, the timer flashing 40.00 seconds. The announcer's voice booms over the speakers, cutting through the cheers.

"Ladies and gentlemen, we have a new course record! Missy Harrison and Remington, fault-free in 40 seconds! What a dynamic duo! I can't wait to see what the future holds for this incredible pair!"

Missy slows Remington to a walk, her breath catching in her chest as the realization of their win washes over her. The Misfit Horse Brigade leaps to their feet in the stands, chanting at the top of their lungs.

"Remi! Remi! Remi!"

She turns in the saddle, waving to them, a wide grin breaking across her face. Beneath her, Remington tosses his head and snorts, feeding off the crowd's energy as his ears flick toward the applause.

The ribbon presenter steps into the arena, holding a large blue rosette and a championship sheet embroidered with the event's name. Missy guides Remington forward, her heart swelling as the presenter pins the ribbon to his bridle. Another helper drapes the blue-and-white sheet over Remington's torso, the fabric gleaming in the sun.

Missy glances toward Tegan at the rail. Tegan's green eyes shine with unshed tears, and her hands cover her mouth, unable to contain the pride on her face. Missy tips her helmet in Tegan's direction, the simple gesture saying more than words ever could.

The announcer's voice booms again. "Let's celebrate this exceptional round! Please welcome Missy Harrison and Remington for their well-earned victory gallop!"

Missy presses her legs into Remington's sides, and he surges into a canter, his stride confident and buoyant. Behind them, the other competitors join in, their mounts adorned with ribbons of their own. Cheers echo through the arena, and the Misfit Horse Brigade chants louder than ever.

"Remi! Remi! Remi!"

Missy's grin never falters as she waves to the crowd, her heart full. She feels an unshakable connection to her horse, a bond built on trust and determination. As they round the arena, she takes in the faces of the cheering spectators, the joy of the moment filling her to the brim. Finally, she slows Remington to a trot, completing their lap, and guides him toward the exit.

Oscar waits by the gate, a broad smile lighting up his face. He steps forward and taps Missy's leg with affection. "Fantástico, Missy. You and Remi, the champions."

"Thanks, Oscar." Missy swings her leg over and slides down, landing softly. She turns to Remington immediately, cupping his muzzle in her hands. "You were incredible, Remi. Thank you." Her voice is soft, and she presses her forehead gently to his, feeling the warmth of his breath against her skin. Remington lets out a low nicker, leaning into her touch.

Behind her, Olivia approaches, her iPhone raised.

"Don't move, Missy! This is so IG-worthy. #ChampionMoment!" She snaps a photo, her eyes lighting up as she checks the shot. "This is going viral for sure!"

Missy chuckles, shaking her head. "Thanks, Olivia." But her expression quickly shifts, her focus narrowing. "Where's Bethany? Her class is soon."

Oscar takes the reins, stroking Remington's neck. "She's warming up in Ring 10 with Carson. Don't worry. I'll take care of your valiant Remi."

Missy gives Oscar's hand a quick squeeze. "Thanks, Oscar." She turns to the Misfit Horse Brigade, who is buzzing with energy. "Let's go cheer her on!"

The kids cheer in agreement, and they all rush toward Ring 10, their excitement contagious. Missy glances back briefly at Remington and Oscar, her heart filled with gratitude, before hurrying to support Bethany.

Oscar watches them disappear into the crowd, shaking his head fondly. He turns to Remington, patting the gelding's shoulder. "You've earned your rest, amigo," he says softly, leading the champion back toward the stables.

Ring 10 buzzes with anticipation as Bethany canters Winston into the warm-up ring. The paint gelding, with his striking chestnut patches against a white coat and a thick flaxen mane, moves with an effortless rhythm. He looks like he belongs in a western movie, not in a jumper ring, but Bethany rides him with precision and quiet confidence. Her pink-streaked hair peeks out from under her helmet, and her eyeliner and dark lipstick give her an edge that stands out against the sea of polished competitors.

Bethany is wearing one of Tegan's old show coats, a navy jacket that's slightly too small across her shoulders and hits just short of her wrists. She doesn't seem to mind—it feels like armor, and she rides like it.

As she guides Winston through a series of transitions, her confidence radiates. Each trot-to-canter shift is seamless, her hands soft and her posture perfect. Observers along the rail take notice.

"She rides like a professional," one trainer murmurs, watching her calm demeanor and instinctive connection with the quirky paint gelding.

Janet, standing near the rail with a cup of coffee, pipes up loudly.

"That's because her trainer is the best! She rides just like Carson." She jabs her cup in Carson's direction, where he stands adjusting a vertical. "See? Right there! That's him!"

Bethany, catching Janet's excited gesturing, calmly raises a hand to wave back before circling Winston to resume her warm-up. Janet, undeterred, starts frantically waving both hands, calling out, "You've got this, Beth! Show 'em what you're made of!"

Carson chuckles softly but keeps his focus on the jump he's setting. Bethany smiles faintly, her focus unwavering as she brings Winston around for another approach.

Not everyone is impressed. Near the rail, a girl with a glossy chestnut mare and an impeccably tailored show coat sneers.

"I didn't know this was a costume class," she says, her voice loud enough to carry. "And that horse—seriously? He looks like he should be herding cattle, not jumping fences."

Bethany catches the comment but doesn't break stride. Her back straightens, and she guides Winston into a smooth circle before trotting toward Carson, who is adjusting a vertical jump. Carson glances up as she approaches, his brows knitting together.

"What did she say?" he asks, his voice calm but laced with quiet intensity.

Bethany shrugs, patting Winston's neck. "Nothing. Don't worry about it. She's not important." Carson watches her for a beat, then nods, his respect for her quiet resilience clear. "Okay. Let's keep warming up."

Bethany steers Winston to the vertical and approaches with quiet determination. They clear the jump effortlessly, Winston's knees high and tidy despite his unorthodox appearance. Carson raises the fence, and they do it again, the pair moving as one.

"You're ready," Carson says simply, his in his tone.

Bethany nods, guiding Winston toward the gate. Her focus sharpens as the ring steward calls her number. She takes a deep breath, her hand brushing Winston's neck as if to ground herself. Together, they enter the arena.

Bethany and Winston ride the course like they've been doing it for years. They meet each jump with confidence; Winston's unique appearance drawing eyes but his athleticism leaving no room for doubt. They finish the first round clear and fast, earning a spot in the jump-off.

The snooty girl with the glossy chestnut mare doesn't fare as well. She approaches the triple combination with too much speed, sending the top rail of the oxer crashing to the ground. She leaves the arena with a face redder than her horse's polished coat.

In the jump-off, Bethany and Winston shave seconds off their time with tight turns and a daring inside line. They finish second, just shy of first place, but the crowd applauds enthusiastically. Winston tosses his head, his long mane flying as they leave the arena.

The Misfit Horse Brigade swarms Bethany as she exits the ring, their cheers nearly drowning out the crowd. "Bethany! Bethany!" they chant, their excitement contagious. Winston snorts and shifts beneath her, his ears flicking toward the noise.

Missy strides forward, grinning ear to ear. She raises her hand. "High five, Bethany!"

Bethany grins back and slaps Missy's hand, the crisp smack punctuating her triumph.

Olivia steps forward, already holding up her phone.

"Okay, everyone! Picture time. Let's go!" She ushers the group into a cluster around Bethany and Winston, tilting the phone to capture everyone in the frame. "Beth, I'm tagging you. We're basically besties now."

Bethany rolls her eyes, laughing. "Lucky me."

Olivia steps back, looking pleased. "Okay, Misfits, it's time for lunch and retail therapy. Let's move!" She marches off, the Brigade trailing after her like ducklings.

As the group heads off, Bethany lingers with Missy, still holding Winston's reins. Missy smirks. "Looks like you've got a new bestie."

Bethany laughs. "She's... enthusiastic, I'll give her that."

Carson approaches, patting Winston's shoulder.

"Good ride, Bethany. Cool him off, then meet me at the barn aisle. We've got hunters to prep for the afternoon."

Bethany opens her mouth to respond, but Carson is already walking away, his boots crunching on the gravel.

Missy smirks as Bethany dismounts, holding Winston's reins. "He's all business."

Bethany laughs softly, her hands trailing down Winston's neck. "Yeah, that's how Car rolls."

Missy looks at her curiously. "Ever think about doing this for a living?"

Bethany hesitates, then nods, her eyes thoughtful as she gazes at Winston. "Maybe. I always thought I'd just ride for fun, but... training? Teaching? It doesn't sound so crazy anymore."

Missy grins. "Well, if you ever want to talk about it, you know where to find me."

Bethany smiles back, her confidence surging as they walk back toward the barn together, the cheers of the Misfit Horse Brigade echoing in the distance.

SATURDAY NIGHT LIGHTS

L ights blaze across the International Arena, casting long, electric shadows over the packed grandstands. Spectators surge with energy, their voices colliding with the driving beats of a reggaeton band electrifying the far end of the ring. Music ripples through the cool Florida night, each note quickening the pulse of the crowd, setting the stage for the sport's biggest moment: the $750,000 Rolex US Equestrian Open CSI5* Grand Prix. The British announcer's voice carries through the arena, crisp and commanding.

"Good evening, ladies and gentlemen, and welcome to Saturday Night Lights at the Winter Equestrian Festival. Tonight, sixty-two of the world's finest equestrians converge to battle for victory in one of the year's most challenging and prestigious events. This is the $750,000 Rolex US Equestrian Open CSI5* Grand Prix."

Spectators and riders alike move through the ring, weaving between the towering jumps that form tonight's challenging course. The announcer continues, highlighting the key elements of the design.

"Tonight's course, built to a maximum height of 1.60 meters, features thirteen questions across fifteen jumping efforts. Riders will face a mix of power and precision, with one triple combination, a one-stride double combination, and several tricky rollback turns designed to test their mettle.

The jumps, a stunning blend of artistry and technicality, include:

- **Fence One**: A sleek black-and-gold Rolex vertical to ease horses and riders into the rhythm.

- **Fence Two**: A wide green-and-gold oxer with painted shamrocks, nodding to the weekend's St. Patrick's Day theme.

- **Fence Three A & B**: A one-stride double combination, starting with a vertical and followed by a wide oxer.

- **Fence Four**: A liver chestnut wall at 1.55 meters, solid and imposing.

- **Fence Six A, B & C**: The only triple combination of the course—a vertical to an oxer, followed by a vertical, each set with precise distances to challenge even the most seasoned competitors.

- **Fence Seven**: A bright yellow vertical set on a tight rollback turn.

- **Fence Eight**: A striking 1.60-meter triple bar oxer with poles painted in deep greens and golds.

- **Fence Nine through Eleven**: A long, curving line featuring a vertical, a two-stride oxer, and finishing with another vertical.

- **Water-Jump Twelve:** An open water jump with a 3.80m spread, with a rail in front. Riders must judge takeoff carefully to avoid faults.

- **Fence Thirteen**: A delicate black-and-white vertical, positioned near the exit gate to test horses' focus as they near the finish."

Tegan and Oscar walk the course with practiced precision, Tegan's iPad in hand as she points out key elements. The live band shifts into a new track, their beats reverberating through the arena as the crowd sways along. Tegan barely notices her focus on the technical aspects of the course.

"The triple combination will be fine for both Mirabella Mia and Luke 631," Tegan says, pausing near Fence Six. "She'll handle it naturally, but Luke needs a bit more support coming out of the oxer."

Oscar nods thoughtfully. "And the double? Looks tight."

"It is," Tegan agrees. "We'll need to collect them sharply after the oxer at Fence Two. No room for hesitation."

Oscar smiles, reflecting his confidence in her. "You've got this, hermana."

Meanwhile, on the other side of the arena, Carson leads Missy, Bethany, and the Misfit Horse Brigade through the course walk. The kids' eyes are wide as they take in the scale of the fences. The liver chestnut wall looms above them, its sheer size intimidating even the bravest among them.

"Those jumps are taller than me," Cameron exclaims, her hands on her hips. "There's no way I could ever jump that height."

"Not yet," Olivia counters, flipping her braided ponytail. "But one day, we'll all be here."

Cameron glances up at her skeptically. "Even me?"

"Especially you," Olivia says, her voice unusually firm. "You're braver than you think."

Nate shifts uncomfortably, adjusting his glasses. "I don't know. All this Grand Prix stuff sounds dangerous. I'd rather stick with numbers and become an accountant."

Bethany chuckles, nudging him playfully. "You'd be the first accountant in the Misfit Horse Brigade."

As they linger at the chestnut wall, Olivia pulls out her phone. "Okay, everyone, gather around. We need a picture."

The group clusters in front of the imposing fence, their arms draped over each other. Olivia raises her phone, snapping several shots before typing furiously. "Posting this. #FutureGrandPrixRiders #MisfitGoals."

Carson stands back, watching with a faint smile. "Anything's possible if you're willing to work hard," he says, his voice carrying just enough weight to grab their attention. "Doesn't matter where you start. What matters is that you show up every day and give it your all."

The kids nod, inspired despite the massive task ahead. Olivia holds out her hand dramatically. "Okay, let's make a vow. We're all going to show in a Grand Prix someday. Deal?"

Cameron hesitates, glancing back at the towering wall, then slowly reaches out. "Deal."

Bethany grins and joins in. "Deal."

Nate sighs heavily. "Fine. But I'm keeping accounting as a backup."

Missy places her hand on top of theirs. "You can all do it. I believe in you."

Carson steps forward, placing his hand over theirs. "Let's make it happen, Misfits."

"Misfits!" they cheer in unison, their voices ringing out against the rhythm of the reggaeton. Laughter ripples through the group as they take in the grandeur, the atmosphere buzzing with possibility.

The announcer's voice returns, signaling the end of the course walk. "Ladies and gentlemen, the moment we've all been waiting for is here. Let's welcome our competitors as we prepare for the start of the $750,000 Rolex US Equestrian Open CSI5* Grand Prix. Let the games begin!"

The band surges into a vibrant reggaeton anthem, rhythm guiding riders and spectators toward the warm-up area. Misfits follow Carson, their excitement and dreams rising into the charged night air.

The warm-up arena hums with activity, the sounds of hoofbeats and soft conversations blending with the rhythmic bass of the reggaeton band in the distance. Leslie adjusts his gloves with a flick of his wrist, sitting tall atop Landon, his 10-year-old chestnut Zangersheide gelding. Landon's gleaming copper coat reflects the arena lights, his neatly braided mane emphasizing his refined, athletic build. The gelding shifts beneath him, alert and eager, his ears flicking forward as they approach a 1.50-meter vertical Oscar has just set.

At the far end of the ring, Tegan canters Luke 631 in a large circle, her focus split between her own warm-up and watching Leslie out of the corner of her eye. Luke's long stride glides effortlessly over the footing, his tail swishing rhythmically with each stride.

Leslie straightens his helmet with a precise motion, glancing at the jump ahead. "All right, mate," he murmurs to Landon, his clipped accent underscoring his calm confidence. "Showtime."

He collects Landon into a powerful canter, the gelding's rhythm steady as they approach the vertical. With a subtle shift of his weight, Leslie cues Landon, who launches into the air, clearing the fence by a foot. They land solidly, though slightly on the forehand, and Leslie softens the reins, bringing Landon back into balance with a light half-halt.

"Well done, old chap," he says under his breath, giving Landon a quick pat on the neck. He turns the gelding toward Tegan, who slows Luke to a walk as he approaches.

"Thoughts?" Leslie asks, his tone casual but tinged with curiosity as he rolls his shoulders, loosening up from the jump.

Tegan eyes him critically, her sharp green gaze locking onto his. "The height's no issue, but you need to mind the double combination. If you over jump the first like you just did, you'll throw Landon onto his forehand, and you'll risk a rail on the second. Balance is key."

Leslie tilts his head, absorbing her feedback. "Spot on. Didn't think he'd launch quite like that." He straightens his posture, his trademark smirk tugging at the corner of his lips. "Good catch, coach."

He winks, tipping his head slightly, his tone full of playful charm. "Right then, I'm off."

Leslie adjusts his reins and nudges Landon forward, the gelding stepping out confidently toward the in-gate. "Keep your fingers crossed, won't you?" he calls over his shoulder, his grin apparent even without a backward glance.

Tegan shakes her head, a faint smile playing on her lips. "Let's hope he actually listens," she mutters, turning her attention back to Luke, whose long stride resumes its steady rhythm as they continue their own preparations.

Energy surges through the International Arena as Leslie Seaton and Landon, his 10-year-old chestnut Zangersheide gelding, rocket over the last jump. The timer flashes — double clear — and the crowd erupts, a wave of cheers crashing through the night. Over it all, a British announcer's voice booms from the speakers, driving the excitement higher.

"A masterful performance! Leslie Seaton and Landon finish double clear, securing their place in the jump-off!"

The DJ immediately cues up a victory anthem, its triumphant melody booming through the speakers and adding to the electric atmosphere. Leslie pumps a fist in celebration, his grin as bright as the arena lights. Landon prances beneath him, tossing his head as if reveling in the applause.

Leslie reins the gelding back to a walk, his eyes scanning the stands until he spots the Misfit Horse Brigade in a private box he's rented for them. The kids are on their feet, cheering wildly and waving their arms. Leslie tips his helmet toward them, eliciting an even louder ovation.

As Leslie approaches the in-gate, Tegan Miller and Luke 631, her striking black Dutch Warmblood stallion, prepare to enter the arena. Leslie reins Landon to a halt, leaning slightly toward Tegan.

"See you in the jump-off, coach," he says with a wink, his British accent adding a playful edge.

Tegan chuckles softly, adjusting her reins. "Go cool him off, Seaton. I've got this."

Leslie tips his helmet again, grinning as he steers Landon out of the arena toward the warm-up area. Tegan, ever composed, gathers Luke into a collected canter and enters the ring as the announcer's voice fills the air.

"Ladies and gentlemen, entering the arena now is Olympic Gold Medalist Tegan Miller, riding Luke 631, a Dutch Warmblood stallion owned by Valley Vista Ranch. Prepare to witness one of the sport's finest partnerships."

The DJ fades the victory anthem into a suspenseful beat, perfectly setting the stage for Tegan's round. She pats Luke's neck, murmuring a quiet word of encouragement before cantering toward the first fence.

The course begins smoothly. Luke 631 clears the early fences with power and precision, his massive stride and careful form making the challenges seem effortless. Tegan rides with her trademark calm, navigating the tight turns and combinations with ease.

As they approach Fence Nine, a rollback turn to a towering vertical, Luke's hind hooves slip on the footing. His stride falters, and Tegan instinctively tries to rebalance him. But before she can recover, Luke hesitates and slams to a stop just before the fence. The sudden halt sends Tegan forward, and she collides with the vertical, the sound of crashing poles echoing across the arena.

Spooked by the commotion, Luke bolts across the ring, his reins flapping wildly. The crowd gasps collectively; the cheers replaced with tense murmurs.

Oscar, stationed near the in-gate, reacts immediately. He sprints into the arena, his calm demeanor cutting through the chaos. "Easy, amigo," he calls, expertly intercepting Luke and taking hold of the reins. The stallion, snorting and wide-eyed, settles under Oscar's steady hand.

In the stands, Carson, Bethany, and Missy exchange a quick glance. Without a word, Carson rises, and they nod in silent understanding. He exits the box and makes his way toward the arena.

Leslie, having handed Landon off to a groom, is the first to reach Tegan. He kneels beside her, his expression one of concern and determination. "Hold still, love," he whispers, his British accent soft yet firm. "Let's not make anything worse."

Tegan winces, her hand gripping her left ankle. "It's my ankle," she manages, her voice tight with pain. "Can't put weight on it."

"Right, then," Leslie replies, his tone calm and reassuring. "We'll sort it out."

Carson arrives moments later, his stride purposeful as he kneels at Tegan's side. "I've got her," he says, taking one of her arms to help her up.

With Carson on one side and Leslie on the other, they assist Tegan to her feet. She hobbles, clearly unable to bear weight on her left foot, her face pale but composed. As they near the in-gate, she pauses, looking up toward the Misfit Horse Brigade. The children clutch the rail of their box, faces pale with worry.

"Wait," Tegan says, halting their progress. She straightens as much as she can, lifting a hand to wave toward the kids. Despite her obvious pain, she musters a small, reassuring smile.

The Brigade erupts into cheers, their relief palpable. "Tegan! Tegan!" they chant, their voices ringing through the arena.

The announcer's voice fills the air, his tone heavy with the question on everyone's mind. "Tegan Miller, showing true resilience. But now, the question is: Will she return for her second ride?"

The crowd buzzes with speculation as Carson and Leslie help Tegan out of the ring. Luke 631, now calm, follows behind, led by Oscar's steady hand. The night, once filled with triumph, hangs in tense uncertainty as the next phase of the competition looms.

The stable aisle is quiet compared to the hustle and roar of the arena. Mirabella Mia, Tegan's stunning homebred mare, stands in her stall, her coat gleaming under the soft overhead lights. Tegan leans against the doorframe, her left foot grazing the ground. Carson, Oscar, and Leslie hover nearby, their expressions a mix of concern and support.

Carson crosses his arms, his tone gentle but direct. "Can you put any weight on it?"

Tegan exhales sharply, testing the injured foot. A grimace flashes across her face, but she straightens. "A bit," she admits, her voice quieter than usual.

Without waiting for a response, she opens Mia's stall door and limps inside. Mia greets her with an affectionate nicker, the mare's warm breath brushing Tegan's face. Tegan strokes Mia's neck, the familiar texture of her coat grounding her amidst the whirlwind of pain and doubt.

Behind her, Carson, Oscar, and Leslie exchange a glance. Their worry is palpable, but none of them say a word.

"I need a moment," Tegan says softly, not turning around.

Leslie nods, his usual teasing tone subdued. "Right then, we'll give you a moment. But let me say this—it's not a competition without you and Mia." He gives her a small, reassuring smile and steps away.

Carson's face softens, and he places a hand on the doorframe. "Take your time. I'll be right outside, no matter what you decide."

Oscar shifts, leaning casually against the stall door but radiating quiet strength. "Whatever you need, hermana. If you want to tack up Mia, say the word. But you've got nothing to prove. We'll follow your lead."

Tegan turns, her lips curling into a faint, grateful smile. She mouths the words, "Thank you."

The three men exchange looks, nodding silently as they step back to give her space. The door closes softly behind her.

Tegan rests her head on Mia's strong shoulder, closing her eyes. The mare stands perfectly still, sensing her rider's need for solace. Tegan's mind drifts back to a memory she's held close all her life.

It's a warm spring afternoon at a bustling Grand Prix dressage show. The air hums with the rhythmic footfalls of horses and the murmur of spectators. A nine-year-old Tegan stands at the edge of the warm-up ring, clutching her father Hank's hand. Her mother, Mirabella, sits tall and elegant on Lorenzo, her powerful black Holsteiner stallion.

Tegan watches, wide-eyed, as her mother finishes a practice piaffe and transitions seamlessly into a perfect square halt. Mirabella exhales deeply, slumping forward for just a moment before catching herself. Her gloved hand dabs at her forehead, now damp with sweat, and she picks up the reins to walk Lorenzo on a long rein toward her family.

Hank steps forward as she nears his brows knit with concern. "Are you okay?" he asks, his voice low but firm.

Mirabella smiles faintly, straightening in the saddle. "I'm fine," she says, though her voice wavers slightly.

Hank's jaw tightens. "You don't have to do this," he says softly but insistently. "You've already done enough."

Mirabella's eyes blaze with determination. "Yes, I do," she replies, her voice steady. "Don't worry, mi amor. Lorenzo will take care of me. He always does."

Tegan, oblivious to the weight of the moment, beams at her mother with pure admiration. "You look so pretty, Momma."

Mirabella looks down at her daughter, her expression softening with emotion. She knows this will probably be the last time her daughter sees her ride. Her voice is gentle but full of love as she replies, "Thank you, mija."

She removes her jewel-encrusted dressage whip, holding it out to Tegan. "Hold my whip for me, okay?"

Tegan takes it carefully, clutching it to her chest like the most precious treasure in the world. She watches as her mother gathers Lorenzo's reins and trots out of the warm-up ring toward the dressage arena. Her figure is regal, unwavering, the epitome of strength and grace.

Tegan hugs the whip tightly, her heart swelling with pride. Her mother is her hero.

Tegan opens her eyes, the memory of her mother's determination filling her with strength. She strokes Mia's neck and whispers, "I need you to take care of me, Mia."

The mare responds by wrapping her head around Tegan's torso, pulling her close in an embrace as if to say, "I've got you." Tegan's lips tremble into a smile, and she presses her forehead to Mia's.

Moments later, her expression shifts. Gone is the uncertainty, replaced by the same fierce determination she saw in her mother's eyes all those years ago. She turns her head toward the door and calls out, "I'm ready."

The door opens immediately, and Carson and Oscar step inside without hesitation. Oscar moves toward Mia with quiet efficiency, already reaching for her tack. Carson comes to Tegan's side, his gaze steady and reassuring.

"Whatever you need," he says simply.

Oscar nods. "We've got this, hermana."

Tegan's smile grows. "Thank you," she whispers, her voice steady now.

As they work together to prepare Mia, there's no hesitation, no doubt. Just trust and quiet resolve. The team knows what's at stake, but more than that, they know they're stronger together.

The energy in the International Arena is palpable as the final rider enters. Tegan Miller and Mirabella Mia, her stunning grey homebred mare, stride confidently through the gate. The DJ transitions into a heart-pounding track, the rhythm building the tension as the announcer's voice echoes through the arena.

"Ladies and gentlemen, our last competitor tonight: Olympic Gold Medalist Tegan Miller aboard the breathtaking Mirabella Mia. Her first round was a master class in equitation, but now, the question is—can she and this extraordinary mare bring home the prize? The time to beat is an incredible 40.26 seconds, set by Leslie Seaton. Let's see what this dynamic duo can do!"

Tegan pats Mia's neck, murmuring softly, "We've got this, girl. Let's show them."

The bell rings, and Tegan gathers Mia into a collected canter before pressing her forward. They approach the first fence with precision, Mia clearing it effortlessly, her legs snapping up tightly beneath her. Tegan's posture is immaculate, her body moving fluidly with her mare's every stride.

As they round the turn to the second fence, Tegan leans forward slightly, urging Mia into a gallop. The crowd collectively holds their breath as they soar over the oxer, the arc of Mia's jump elegant and powerful. They answer each question with precision—tight rollback turns, a daring angle over the double combination, and Mia's explosive power carrying them effortlessly over the fences.

"Look at the speed!" the announcer exclaims, his voice rising in excitement. "Tegan and Mia are flying through this course as one being!"

They approach the penultimate jump, a towering vertical set on a sharp angle. Tegan takes a wicked slice, cutting the turn tighter than anyone dared. The crowd gasps as Mia lifts off at a precarious angle, her athleticism defying gravity. The poles stay up.

With only the final fence ahead, Tegan urges Mia into a flat-out gallop. The mare's powerful strides eat up the distance, and they clear the last fence cleanly. The timer flashes **39.20 seconds.**

The arena explodes into a deafening roar. The announcer's voice struggles to be heard over the crowd.

"Unbelievable! Tegan Miller and Mirabella Mia have shattered the time! Thirty-nine point two seconds! Ladies and gentlemen, your champions!"

Tegan slows Mia to a halt, her chest rising and falling as she processes what they've just accomplished. She looks around, tears streaming down her face, and covers her head with her hands as her body shakes with sobs of joy. Mia stands quietly, her ears flicking toward the thunderous applause.

The crowd rises in a standing ovation, their cheers echoing through the night. From the stands, Carson and the Misfit Horse Brigade cheer wildly, their voices rising above the rest. Leslie Seaton strides into the arena, clapping loudly as he approaches.

Leslie stops a few feet away and bows dramatically, a wide grin on his face. "You've done it, Miller. Absolutely brilliant."

He steps beside her, taking Mia's reins gently and walking them toward the exit as the crowd continues to roar. "Let's get you out of here, champ."

The atmosphere is celebratory as Tegan re-enters the arena, mounted on Mirabella Mia, who now wears a winner's sheet emblazoned with the event's logo. Tegan herself wears a ribbon across her chest, the colors gleaming under the lights. Behind her, Leslie sits astride Landon, followed by the third-place rider, both waving to the adoring crowd. The three riders circle the arena at a walk, their smiles wide as they acknowledge the cheers.

The procession halts in front of the podium, where grooms step forward to attach lead ropes to the horses. Leslie dismounts first, moving to help Tegan down from Mia's back. She places her hands on his shoulders as she slides down, her injured foot lightly grazing the ground.

The announcer's voice booms through the arena. "In third place, with a remarkable performance, we present the silver dish to Alexander Van der Meer!"

The third-place rider steps forward, receiving his award with a gracious nod.

"In second place, after an extraordinary jump-off round of 40.26 seconds, we present the silver dish to Leslie Seaton!"

Leslie accepts the dish, lifting it briefly to acknowledge the crowd before stepping back with a grin.

"And now, your champion. With an unbeatable time of 39.20 seconds, we present the first-place trophy to Tegan Miller and Mirabella Mia!"

The crowd erupts into cheers as Tegan steps onto the top of the podium. She lifts the trophy above her head in triumph, tears glistening in her eyes. Looking up to the box where Carson and the Misfit Horse Brigade cheer wildly, she blows them a kiss, her smile radiant.

Then, turning toward Oscar, she motions for him to join her on the podium. He waves her off, shaking his head and grinning, but Tegan insists, beckoning him forward with a wide, encouraging gesture. The crowd cheers louder, loving the moment.

Reluctantly, Oscar hands Mia's lead rope to another groom and steps onto the podium. Tegan hands him the trophy with a grin, stepping back and applauding him. Oscar hesitates for a moment, then raises the trophy above his head as the crowd roars with delight.

Tegan beams, clapping enthusiastically as she gives him the spotlight. "All yours, Oscar," she says warmly.

For a moment, it's not just a victory for her—it's a victory for the entire team, a testament to the bond between rider, horse, and those who believe in them.

THERE'S NO PLACE LIKE HOME

The early morning sun streams through the tall windows of Tegan Miller's master bedroom, bathing the room in a warm golden glow. The space is an exquisite blend of elegance and comfort, a room that feels like a sanctuary.

At the center stands a handmade king-sized four-post bed, its rich mahogany frame a masterpiece of craftsmanship—a treasured gift from her father. Soft cream bedding drapes the mattress, layered with plush pillows and a hand-stitched quilt woven in shades of green and gold. Muted sage walls cradle family photographs and snapshots of her barn family.

One photo stands out—a black-and-white portrait of her parents on their wedding day. Her mother, radiant in her lace gown, smiles adoringly at her father, who gazes back with the same depth of love. On the nightstand sits another framed picture, this one recent and vibrant: a candid shot of Tegan and Carson, laughing as their horses—Rusty and Paratrooper—play near Miller's Pond. The image is full of life and joy, a reflection of their bond.

On the nightstand, next to the photos, is a small vase of wildflowers and a framed note in her mother's handwriting. The words read:

"With love and unwavering determination, anything is possible."

The smell of breakfast wafts through the room, tugging Tegan from the edges of sleep. Her eyes flicker open, and a soft smile spreads across her face as she stretches her arms overhead. Her ribs ache faintly, but it's a dull reminder of her equestrian life's challenges—and rewards.

The door creaks open, and Carson steps through, crisp in his riding clothes. His navy jacket gapes halfway open, boots catching a faint gleam in the light. He balances a tray in his hands, a feast arranged with care—steaming eggs, golden pancakes flanked by a jar of peanut butter and a bottle of homemade maple syrup, vibrant slices of fresh fruit, and a protein shake swirling with froth.

"Good morning, sleepyhead," he says, setting the tray gently on her lap, his expression warm.

Tegan beams, sitting up straighter. "My favorite."

Carson picks up a napkin and drapes it elegantly over her chest. Leaning down, he presses a kiss to her forehead. "Only the best for you."

She unscrews the jar of peanut butter, spreading a generous amount over her stack of pancakes before drizzling them with syrup. "You've outdone yourself," she remarks, grinning as she slathers the mixture onto her first bite.

"You know me," Carson replies, settling onto the edge of the bed. "Always aiming to impress."

Tegan takes a blissful bite, savoring the rich combination. "Perfect," she says through a mouthful.

He watches her for a moment, his expression softening. "How're you feeling?"

"My ribs still ache a little," she admits, taking another bite. "But I'm so excited. My cast comes off today, and I can finally start riding again."

Carson chuckles, his brows raising in mock disbelief. "Miss the horses already? You see them every day."

She pouts dramatically. "You know what I mean. It's not the same."

He leans forward, brushing a stray lock of hair from her face. "You're impossible," he murmurs with a smile before leaning in to kiss her softly. For a moment, the world outside fades away.

Carson pulls back with a sigh, reluctant. "I'd stay all day if I could, but morning lessons won't teach themselves. And you know how much Oscar hates dealing with 'the ladies' by himself."

Tegan laughs. "He'll survive."

"How's Mia?" she asks, her tone growing serious.

Carson smirks. "Pole day today. She's a dream to ride, but she doesn't let me forget who her real master is."

Tegan smiles, her eyes sparkling with affection for her mare. "Thanks for holding down the fort. I couldn't do this without you."

Carson reaches for her hand, his thumb brushing gently across her knuckles. "The barn isn't the same without you. Rusty and I'll wait with bated breath for your arrival later."

He leans in for one last kiss, lingering before standing and straightening his jacket. "I'd better get going before Oscar files a formal complaint."

Tegan chuckles and waves him off. "Go. I'll see you later."

As Carson steps into the hallway, his steps slow, and he pauses. His hand slips into his pocket, retrieving a small weathered box. He holds it in his palm, staring at it as his thumb lightly traces the edges.

For a long moment, he lingers, his thoughts swirling. The sound of distant hoofbeats outside breaks his reverie. Carson exhales, slipping the box back into his pocket before heading downstairs, his boots tapping softly against the hardwood floors.

Late afternoon sun casts a warm glow over Valley Vista Ranch as Tegan's beloved 1972 red and white Chevy C20, Bess, rumbles up the long driveway. Bess gleams, polished exterior reflecting the care Tegan has poured into it over the years. The engine growls softly as she pulls into her usual spot near the barn, its sound as familiar as an old friend.

Beside her in the passenger seat, Bethany glances over with a smirk. "You sure you're ready for this?" she teases, her tone light.

Tegan grins, adjusting her baseball cap. "I've been ready since the day this cast went on."

As the engine quiets, they both hop out, Tegan's jeans catching the sun's golden light. She stretches briefly, testing her freshly healed leg. Carson is already waiting near the barn aisle, standing tall between a perfectly groomed Rusty and Mirabella Mia, both outfitted with sleek bareback pads. The horses shift eagerly, their coats gleaming in the sunlight.

Bethany pats Tegan on the shoulder. "No problem. Just thank me when I win 'groomer of the year' with Señor Oscar. If I'm late…"

Tegan chuckles knowingly. "Don't worry. Go charm him. You've got this."

Bethany flashes a playful salute and jogs off toward the grooming station, leaving Tegan alone with Carson and the horses.

Tegan approaches Carson, hands on her hips, a playful grin on her face. She lifts her healed leg with a dramatic flourish, balancing on her good leg as if performing a magic trick.

"Ta-da! Good as new," she says, twirling for effect.

Rusty stomps a hoof in approval, while Mia whinnies softly, her ears flicking forward. Carson smirks, adjusting his hat as he watches her antics. "Glad to see the dramatics haven't dulled."

He hands her the reins to Rusty. "It's a beautiful afternoon for a trail ride."

Tegan narrows her eyes suspiciously, her grin softening. "And I suppose this has nothing to do with you being sneaky?"

"Maybe," Carson replies, his grin widening.

Tegan shakes her head, mounting Rusty with Carson's steady help. He strides to the mounting block and climbs onto Mia's back with practiced ease. Together, they head out, the sound of hooves mingling with the gentle breeze.

They follow a well-worn path through the rolling hills; the barn shrinking into the distance. Warm afternoon light bathes the serene countryside, and the world around them remains still and tranquil. Tegan clicks her lips, and Rusty, ever the eager companion, pricks his ears forward and takes off into a canter.

Carson calls after her, feigning exasperation. "Seriously? You promised to take it easy!"

Tegan glances back, her eyes sparkling with mischief. "This is easy!"

Carson laughs, urging Mia into a gallop to catch up. He falls into stride beside her, and together they slow to a trot, the horses breathing deeply as they match each other's pace.

As they approach a wooded trail, the sounds of the ranch fade completely. The symphonic chatter of birds serenades them as sunlight filters through the canopy above, casting dappled shadows on the ground. The path opens into a clearing by Miller's Pond, where a stunning scene awaits.

The clearing transforms into a picturesque retreat. Someone spread a plaid picnic blanket near the water's edge, anchoring it with a wicker basket. A bottle of champagne chills in a bucket of ice, and a fire pit, ringed with smooth stones, stands ready to be lit. Nearby, an acoustic guitar rests against a makeshift cluster of hay bales.

Tegan halts Rusty, her jaw dropping in surprise. She dismounts with Carson's help, her eyes darting between him and the setup. "Somebody's been busy."

Carson feigns innocence, his expression unreadable. "I thought we should celebrate," he says cryptically.

Tegan steps closer to the picnic blanket, her gaze softening as she takes in the thoughtful details. Carson retrieves a plate of fruit and cheese from the basket, handing her a small plate before taking a seat on one of the hay bales. He pats the space beside him.

She sits, the serene atmosphere settling over her. Carson's voice is calm but deliberate. "What do you see in your future, Tegan?"

Tegan takes a bite of fruit, her mind immediately racing. "Expanding the teaching program to include all disciplines, expanding the breeding program—Leslie wants in on that—and Oscar's idea for a professional grooming program is brilliant. I—"

Carson interrupts her, gently taking her hand. His touch stills her rambling, his eyes locking onto hers with a quiet intensity.

"Tegan," he breathes, his voice steady and low. "I want all that, too. But more importantly..." He lowers himself to one knee, pulling a small antique box from his pocket. "...I want you. Will you marry me, Tegan Miller?"

Tegan's breath catches as he opens the box, revealing her mother's wedding ring. The simple yet elegant band glistens in the fading sunlight. Her hand flies to her mouth as tears spill down her cheeks.

"Yes," she whispers, her voice trembling with emotion. "A thousand times, yes."

Carson rises, sliding the ring gently onto her finger. The warmth of his hands steadies her as she looks up at him, her heart full to bursting. Without hesitation, he pulls her into his arms, their lips meeting in a kiss that is both tender and fiery. It speaks of love, passion, and the promises they've yet to make.

The world around them fades as the kiss deepens, their connection anchoring them in this perfect moment. When they finally pull apart, Tegan rests her forehead against Carson's, her smile radiant.

"I love you," he whispers.

"I love you, too," she replies, her voice filled with certainty.

The kitchen is alive with warmth and laughter. A simple yet elegant tablescape of white plates and wine glasses adorns the rustic, well-worn handcrafted wooden table.

A lasagna, its cheese bubbling and golden, sits at the center alongside a basket of freshly baked bread, a large salad, and bottles of red wine and water. The soft hum of country music plays in the background, completing the cozy atmosphere.

Tegan and Carson sit at opposite ends of the table, their smiles reflecting the joy of the moment. Missy, Bethany, and Oscar occupy the seats between them, their chatter filling the room.

"Let me see it again!" Bethany demands, leaning across the table as Tegan extends her hand to show off her engagement ring.

"It's beautiful," Missy says with a knowing smile, examining the simple but elegant band. "Is it your mom's wedding ring?"

Tegan nods, her voice soft. "It is."

She glances at Oscar, and for a moment, their eyes meet in shared understanding. Oscar's face softens, his normally stoic demeanor giving way to emotion. He pounds the table lightly with his fist, making the wine glasses tremble.

"¡Por la familia!" he exclaims, lifting his fourth glass of wine high into the air.

The others raise their glasses in unison, their voices ringing out. "Familia!"

Tegan laughs as she serves generous portions of lasagna, the smell of garlic and cheese wafting through the air. As she places a plate in front of Bethany, the younger woman's curiosity gets the better of her.

"So... how did he propose?" Bethany asks, leaning on her elbows, her eyes alight with anticipation.

Carson, cutting into his lasagna, raises an eyebrow. "That information is between me, Tegan, and the horses."

Bethany groans dramatically, setting down her fork. "Oh, come on! Tell me."

Missy nods in agreement. "You're outnumbered, Carson. Spill."

Carson sighs, clearly outmatched. "Fine. If you must know—"

The phone rings, cutting him off. The sound echoes through the kitchen, a stark contrast to the warmth of the moment. Tegan's brow furrows, and she stands.

"Let it go to voicemail," Oscar says, waving his hand dismissively. "We're celebrating."

Tegan hesitates but sits back down, her attention returning to Carson. He clears his throat and continues. "As I was saying, I took her out to—"

The phone rings again, sharper this time, demanding attention. Tegan's concern deepens. "It could be the barn," she says, standing quickly. "I'll get it."

She steps into the kitchen, leaving the table behind. The laughter fades as the others exchange uncertain glances. The sound of her muffled voice carries back as she speaks on the phone, her tone serious.

After a few minutes, Tegan returns, her expression calm but her posture tense. She forces a smile. "Finish your meal. I'll be back in an hour, if not sooner."

Before anyone can ask what's wrong, she grabs her jacket and heads toward the door. Carson pushes his chair back and follows her.

Carson reaches the door just as Tegan is slipping on her boots. "What's going on?" he asks quietly, his brow creased with worry.

Tegan glances at him, her voice low. "It's Jake. He's in trouble."

Carson steps closer, his concern deepening. "I'll come with you."

Tegan shakes her head, resting a hand lightly on his chest. "It's better if I go alone. I'll tell you everything when I get back, I promise."

He hesitates, searching her face, but eventually nods. Reaching over, he hands her the purse, his fingers brushing against hers. "Be careful," he whispers, leaning in to kiss her gently.

"I will," Tegan whispers, squeezing his hand briefly before stepping out into the cool night air. The door closes behind her, and Carson stands there for a moment, his thoughts racing. Finally, he sighs and turns back toward the table.

The room feels quieter without Tegan. Carson reclaims his seat, forcing a smile to mask his unease. Bethany, unable to hold back her curiosity, leans forward.

"What was that about?" she asks.

Carson shakes his head. "She'll tell us when she gets back."

Oscar watches him closely, then raises his glass. "To Tegan. And to whatever adventure she's off to. Let's hope it's a short one."

"Here, here," Missy says, raising her own glass.

The group toasts again, though the atmosphere has shifted slightly. They continue their meal, their laughter lighter as they wait for Tegan's return.

The fluorescent lights hum softly as Tegan stands at the counter, her arms crossed tightly against her chest. The officer processes the paperwork for Jake's release, the monotonous rhythm of his typing filling the silence. Tegan glances at her watch, frustration simmering just below the surface. She should be at home, celebrating her engagement—not bailing out her ex-employee.

Finally, the officer stands and gestures toward the holding cells. Moments later, Jake emerges, his shoulders slumped, his hands shoved into his pockets. His disheveled hair and weary eyes only deepen her frustration.

"I didn't know who else to call," Jake says, his voice low, almost apologetic.

Tegan exhales sharply, her jaw tightening. "Let's get this over with. I need to get back."

Jake hesitates, his gaze darting to the floor before looking at her. "Could we... could we talk? Just for old times' sake?"

She frowns, her tone clipped. "I was in the middle of dinner when you called Jake."

"It'll only be a few minutes," he pleads. "There's a Starbucks down the road."

Her patience wears thin, but she nods reluctantly. "Fine."

As they walk toward the exit, Jake fidgets nervously, his hands stuffed into his jacket pockets. "My car's still at the bar," he mutters.

Tegan halts, her frustration boiling over. "Get in the car."

They sit across from each other in a small booth, the soft hum of conversation and the hiss of the espresso machine creating a background buzz. Jake cradles a cup of coffee, his fingers drumming against it, while Tegan picks at a croissant, her patience wearing thin.

"So," Jake starts, his voice overly casual. "I, uh, heard you won the Grand Prix. That's a nice purse."

Tegan's lips tighten as she places the croissant down. "What do you want, Jake?"

He shifts uncomfortably, avoiding her gaze. "I need another chance. I've got a lead on some amazing horses out of Germany. Top-quality bloodlines, and I can get them for a steal. We could—"

"No," she interrupts firmly, shaking her head. Her tone leaves no room for negotiation. Reaching into her purse, she pulls out a small roll of cash and places it on the table, sliding it toward him.

Jake's eyes flick to the money, but something else catches his attention—the engagement ring on her finger. His face changes instantly. He grabs her hand, holding it up.

"You're going to marry him?" he exclaims, his voice rising with jealousy. "Unbelievable. What's he got that I don't? I did everything for you, Tegan. Everything!"

His voice grows louder as he continues, drawing glances from nearby tables. "You wouldn't even be where you are without me! You owe me!"

Tegan jerks her hand away, her eyes flashing with a mix of anger and hurt. She stands abruptly, her voice low but full of force. "Take the money, Jake. And don't call me again."

Jake stares at her, stunned and sputtering, but before he can respond, Tegan turns on her heel and strides out of the café, her dignity intact. The bell above the door jingles as it closes behind her, leaving Jake alone at the table with the roll of cash sitting in front of him.

Tegan leans against her truck, her breaths coming fast as she steadies herself. She stares out at the night sky, the cold air biting at her skin but doing little to dull the ache in her chest. After a long moment, she climbs into Bess, starts the engine, and heads back toward the life she's chosen—the one filled with love, stability, and the people who truly care for her.

Tegan steps into the kitchen, the warm glow of the overhead light wrapping her in comfort. On the island, a plate of lasagna and a glass of wine wait for her, their inviting aroma softening the weight in her chest. Carson stands at the sink, his sleeves rolled up, methodically washing the last of the dinner dishes. The hum of country music still plays faintly in the background.

He glances over his shoulder as she enters, offering her a soft smile. "Hey. You're back."

Tegan pulls out a stool at the island and sits down, letting out a long breath as she slides the plate toward her. "Where is everyone?"

Carson turns off the water, drying his hands on a dish towel. "Bethany went with Missy to do night check on the horses and then to the cabin. Those two are inseparable these days."

Tegan smiles, picking up her fork. "It's good to see Bethany clicking with someone in the barn. I love that Missy's taking on a mentor role now."

She pauses, her expression softening with nostalgia. "I remember when I first started mentoring Missy. She was all nerves, second-guessing every decision she made around the horses. I had to remind her to trust herself as much as she trusted the horses. And now, she's mentoring someone else. It's amazing to see."

Carson watches her with quiet affection, a small smile tugging at his lips. "It's good for both of them."

As Tegan eats, Carson continues. "I told Oscar about Jake."

Tegan pauses, her fork hovering over her plate. "And?"

"He wasn't happy about it," Carson admits, leaning back against the counter. "But he understood why you wanted to go alone. He just wants you to call him first thing tomorrow and fill him in."

Tegan sighs, setting her fork down. "I'll do that. Thanks for handling it."

Carson shrugs, rinsing the last plate. "It's what we do."

There's a pause as he moves to sit beside her at the island, his chair angled toward hers. The room feels still, the country music humming softly in the background.

Tegan pushes her plate slightly aside. "Jake's finally out of our lives," she says quietly. "That chapter is closed."

Carson studies her, his expression calm and patient. "What happened?"

She exhales slowly, recounting the details with measured calm: the call, the station, the meeting at Starbucks, Jake's desperate plea, and how she walked away for good. When she finishes, Carson doesn't speak immediately. Instead, he reaches across the island, taking her hand in his. His thumb brushes lightly over her knuckles as his eyes search hers.

"Are you okay?" he asks gently.

She nods, her voice soft but resolute. "Yes. I'm okay. It's done now."

He presses a kiss to her hand. "I'm proud of you."

Her lips curve into a small, grateful smile. "Thanks, Carson."

His grin grows as he tilts his head, his tone lightening. "So... you still feel like celebrating? Or has this night completely worn you out?"

A quiet giggle escapes her lips, and she shakes her head. "I think I can manage a little celebrating."

He stands, offering her his hand. "Come on, then."

Tegan takes his hand, her smile widening as she lets him lead her out of the kitchen, leaving the lasagna and wine behind. The weight of the evening lifts with every step, replaced by the quiet joy of the life they've built together.

Monday, Monday

S oft morning light spills through Tegan's curtains, casting a golden sheen across the room. Beams catch on the handmade four-poster bed, quilt tossed in the lazy patterns of sleep. Silence lingers over the house, thick and warm, the kind born from simply being alone together.

Carson lies beside Tegan, his head propped on one hand as he watches her sleep. Her breathing is soft and steady, her features serene. A gentle smile plays on his lips as he brushes a wayward strand of hair away from her face, his touch featherlight.

As if sensing his presence, Tegan stirs, her lashes fluttering open. She blinks a few times, her lips curving into a sleepy smile as her eyes meet his. "Good morning, Mr. Carson," she says, her voice warm and teasing.

He chuckles, leaning down to press a kiss to her forehead. "Good morning, Ms. Tegan."

She stretches lazily, the movement unhurried, and shifts to snuggle closer to him. "What time is it?" she asks, her voice still husky from sleep.

He glances at the clock on her nightstand. "Almost eight."

Her eyes widen, and she bolts upright, the quilt slipping down to her waist. "Eight? I've got to get up! The horses—"

Carson chuckles softly, placing a calming hand on her shoulder. "Relax. Missy and Bethany volunteered to handle turnout and the morning chores. They insisted we sleep in."

Tegan protests, her lips parting, but before she can say a word, Carson leans in and kisses her, silencing her argument. When he pulls back, her indignation has melted into a reluctant smile.

"I don't like feeling useless," she mutters, settling back against the pillows.

"You're not useless," he says firmly, tucking a loose strand of hair behind her ear. "You're just taking a well-deserved morning off. I'll check on the girls after Rusty and I inspect the paddocks."

Tegan sighs, picking up her cell phone from the nightstand. She scrolls briefly before setting it back down.

"Oscar and Dr. White are meeting with me to check on the broodmares around nine," she says. "After that, I'll meet you in the office to finalize the training schedule for the rest of the week."

Carson grins, trailing his fingers lightly over her arm. "That's my Ms. Tegan. Always thinking ahead."

She rolls her eyes but smiles, tossing the quilt aside and swinging her legs over the edge of the bed. As she stands, she stretches again, her movements languid and unhurried. At the doorway to the bathroom, she pauses, resting one hand on the frame as she glances back at him with a teasing smile.

"You coming?"

Carson doesn't hesitate, swinging his legs off the bed and getting to his feet. "You don't have to ask twice."

Her laughter echoes softly as they disappear into the bathroom together, the warmth of the morning wrapping around them.

The feed room is a well-organized symphony of motion. Missy and Bethany move in an efficient rhythm, scooping feed and supplements into empty buckets lined neatly on the counter. The sunlight filters through a small window, illuminating the labels on the bins as they work.

"Triple Crown, next bucket," Missy says, her voice steady as she scoops grain.

Bethany, holding the bucket, slides it forward and grabs another empty one. "Got it."

Their movements are almost automatic, an assembly line of precision. The occasional nicker of a horse outside breaks the faint hum of the barn only.

Suddenly, the sharp cry of a distressed horse pierces the air, shattering the tranquility. Both girls freeze, their eyes meeting.

Bethany tilts her head toward the door. "What was that?"

Missy frowns, handing Bethany the iPad tucked in the waistband of her jeans. "Here. Finish this. I'm going to check it out."

Bethany hesitates, her grip tightening on the iPad. "Call me if you need help."

Missy nods, already heading toward the barn aisle. "I will."

Missy strides toward the front of the barn, her heart pounding as the distressed cries grow louder. As she rounds the corner to the parking lot, her stomach drops. Jake is there, struggling to lead Mirabella Mia, who is rearing and resisting his grip. The trailer behind him already holds a panicked Luke 631, stomping and thrashing inside.

"Jake!" Missy yells, her voice cracking with fear. "What are you doing?"

Jake's head snaps toward her, his face twisted with frustration. "Stay out of this, Missy!" he snarls. "These horses are mine! Tegan hasn't paid me my share for them!"

Anger overtakes Missy's fear. "That's not true, and you know it! Let them go!"

Mia rears again, kicking out and loosening Jake's hold on the lead rope. With a triumphant whinny, she breaks free, galloping away with her tail high in the air. Jake spins around, swearing violently as he watches her escape.

"Stop this, Jake!" Missy pleads, stepping back instinctively. "Please, just stop!"

Jake's face hardens as he pulls a gun from the back of his jeans, aiming it directly at her. Missy freezes, her breath hitching.

"Get Mia back here," Jake growls, his voice low and threatening. "Help me get her in the trailer. Now."

Missy shakes her head vehemently, her voice trembling but firm. "No. I won't."

Meanwhile, Mirabella Mia races through the paddocks, her grey coat gleaming in the sunlight. She gallops straight toward Carson, mounted on Rusty, inspecting the fencing. Carson sees her approach, his eyes narrowing as he immediately recognizes the urgency in her movements.

He grabs her loose lead rope as she slows beside him, her sides heaving. "Easy, girl," he murmurs, quickly ponying her into an empty paddock. He unclips the rope and secures the gate.

Without hesitation, Carson spins Rusty around and presses him into a full gallop, heading back toward the barn. He steels his jaw, adrenaline spiking through his veins as Rusty hurls them forward, each stride pounding the earth beneath them.

The barn parking lot feels heavy, the tension hanging thick in the cool morning air. Jake, visibly frazzled, grips the gun in his hand as he faces Missy, who stands a few feet away, her hands trembling but her voice steady.

"Listen," Jake starts, his tone shifting to something almost pleading. "I'll cut you in on the deal. Mia alone will sell for several million. No one has to get hurt. We just need to make this happen, and it'll be over."

Missy stares at him with a mix of hatred and disbelief, her voice sharp with anger. "What's happened to you, Jake? How did you become this person?"

He falters for a moment, his grip on the gun loosening slightly. "I'm just trying to get what's mine," he mutters defensively.

"You won't get away with this," she continues, her tone resolute. "Everyone knows these horses. You can't sell them. People will recognize them in an instant."

Jake's jaw tightens as her words hit home, and for a moment, he seems lost, his eyes darting nervously. Missy's stalling works, buying just enough time.

Suddenly, the pounding of hooves breaks through the tension. Carson, astride Rusty, gallops into the parking lot. He dismounts in one smooth motion, tying Rusty's reins to the saddle horn. His voice is calm but commanding.

"Missy, go back to the barn and stay there!"

She hesitates, her eyes flicking between Carson and Jake. Carson meets her gaze, and his meaning is clear—she needs to call for help. She nods quickly and runs back toward the barn without looking back.

Carson turns to Jake, his movements deliberate and unthreatening. He holds his hands out slightly, palms up, his voice steady. "You don't want to do this, Jake."

Jake raises the gun, aiming it squarely at Carson's chest. His voice is nearly hysterical. "Don't tell me what I want! You don't know me!"

"I know you're not a murderer," Carson replies, his tone unwavering. "Put the gun down."

Jake's face twists with anger and desperation. "Tegan and I were doing fine until you came along. Everything was fine until you ruined it!"

Carson takes a slow step forward, his voice low and calm. "What's going to happen here, Jake?"

Jake shifts his stance, the gun shaking in his hand. "What's going to happen is I'm taking Luke. He's mine. I found him. I trained him. He's mine."

Carson shakes his head, his voice firm. "I can't let you do that."

Rusty stomps his hoof, snorting in agitation. The sudden noise startles Jake, who cocks the gun. His grip tightens, and his aim steadies. Time seems to freeze.

Rusty's ears pin back, and without warning, he charges. The gun fires. BANG!

Rusty collapses to the ground with a sickening thud, his body sliding slightly across the gravel. His whinny of pain cuts through the air. Both Bethany and Missy burst from the barn, their screams echoing in the lot.

"NO!" Bethany cries, her voice breaking as she runs toward Rusty.

In the trailer, Luke 631 squeals in panic, kicking violently against the door, the metal clanging with each strike.

Jake stares at Rusty's fallen body in shock. The gun slips from his hands and clatters to the ground. He falls to his knees, muttering, "What have I done?"

Carson rushes to Rusty's side, his voice steady despite the chaos. "Missy! Get Luke out of there. Now!"

Missy nods, running to the trailer, her hands shaking as she unhooks the latch. Luke bursts out, wild-eyed, but she quickly calms him, leading him away to safety.

Moments later, Tegan, Oscar, and Dr. White pull up in the truck. Dr. White jumps out with his bag, running to Rusty's side. Carson kneels beside his horse, gently stroking his neck. Rusty tries to lift his head but groans in agony.

"Easy, boy," Carson murmurs, his voice cracking. "I'm here."

Dr. White pulls out a syringe and preps it. "It's a sedative," he explains, but when he leans forward, Carson grabs his forearm.

"No," Carson says, his voice firm but trembling.

Bethany, tears streaming down her face, kneels beside Carson. "Please, Car. Rusty's in pain."

Carson hesitates, his hands gripping Dr. White's arm tightly before he finally lets go. The vet administers the sedative, his hands shaking. He feels around Rusty's chest and shoulder, his expression darkening. Sitting back, he exhales shakily.

"It's shattered, Carson," he whispers, his voice laden with sorrow. "There's nothing I can do."

Carson buries his face in his hands, his shoulders trembling. Bethany sobs beside him, clutching Rusty's mane.

Dr. White pulls out another syringe, his hands trembling uncontrollably. Bethany places a hand on his shoulder. "Doc?"

"I just need a moment," Dr. White murmurs. "I delivered him, you know. Bob's Mystery. I mean... Rusty. Just... a moment."

Tegan steps forward, her hand steady as she places it over Dr. White's. He looks at her, his eyes glassy, and after a long pause, he hands her the syringe.

Tegan kneels beside Rusty, her hands trembling as she places them gently on his cheek. Rusty shifts his head slightly, his dark eyes meeting hers. For a long moment, they stay like that, the world around them fading into silence.

"Hey, BM," Tegan whispers, her voice soft and full of love. "It's okay, boy. You've done so much for us. It's time to rest."

Rusty exhales a long, shuddering breath, his ears flicking slightly as if he's heard her every word. He looks back at her, his gaze steady and full of understanding. It's as if he knows what's coming and, in his own way, gives her permission. His eyes soften, a flicker of trust and love passing between them.

Tears stream down Tegan's face as she leans forward, pressing her forehead gently against his. "You were always the best boy. Always."

Carson, kneeling beside her, gently strokes Rusty's mane, his voice breaking as he says, "He knows, Tegan. He knows."

Tegan nods, her hands steadying as she picks up the syringe. She strokes Rusty's cheek one last time. "Goodbye, BM," she whispers, her voice trembling but filled with love.

Carson cradles Rusty's head in his lap, his voice soothing. "It's okay, boy. I'm here."

Tegan administers the injection, her hand steady despite the ache in her heart. The group surrounds Rusty, their collective love and grief palpable. His breaths grow shallow, each one slower than the last. He looks at Carson one final time, his gaze filled with trust and love, before exhaling his final breath.

Tegan drops the syringe and stands, tears streaming down her face. She turns toward Jake, who remains on his knees, staring blankly. Without a word, she strides over to him and slaps him hard across the face. He flinches but doesn't move.

"Take him," she says, her voice cold as she looks at Oscar.

Oscar steps forward, looping a rope around Jake's wrists. Jake doesn't resist, his head hanging low as the sound of sirens fills the air. The police cars pull into the lot as Tegan turns and walks away, her steps steady despite the weight in her chest.

Tears welling in her eyes, Tegan heads toward her office, disappearing into the shadows as the officers begin their work.

THE PROCESSION

T he following morning, dawn's gray and heavy, a quiet drizzle softening the
edges of the world at Valley Vista Ranch. The barn, usually bustling with
life and energy, feels subdued, as if even the horses understand the weight of the
loss.

Rusty's stall stands in the center of the barn aisle, his Western bridle hanging from a hook, a wreath of wildflowers draped tenderly across the door. His
nameplate catches the faint light, gleaming after Bethany's careful polish, her tears
slipping down unchecked as she traced every letter with trembling hands.

The air is heavy with emotion as the procession winds its way down the path
toward Miller's Pond, the site of Rusty's final resting place. Tegan, astride the elegant Mirabella Mia, and Carson, atop the loyal Paratrooper, lead the solemn line
of horse-and-rider combinations. Each rider dons Western attire—plaid shirts,
faded jeans, and well-loved cowboy hats—paying silent tribute to Rusty, the soul
of Valley Vista Ranch.

Behind them rides Missy, mounted on the spirited Remington, her posture
unusually subdued. Janet, aboard the playful Bubbles, follows closely, her expression somber. Bethany, on her steadfast paint gelding, Winston, rounds out
the lead group, with the rest of the Misfit Horse Brigade trailing behind on their
mounts. The sound of hooves is rhythmic and steady, accompanied only by the
faint rustle of leaves and the distant call of birds.

As they reach the clearing by the pond, the beauty of the site comes into
view. Oscar waits near the freshly filled grave, a mound of earth surrounded by
hand-picked polished stones he had arranged with care. Rusty's final resting place
is marked by the large oak tree that shades the area, its branches outstretched as

if offering comfort. The Percherons that had pulled Rusty to this spot now graze quietly nearby, their reins tied loosely to a fencepost.

The riders dismount, each leaving their horses to graze in the nearby pasture. Even Mia and Paratrooper seem to understand the gravity of the moment, standing still as if paying their respects. The group gathers around the grave, the silence heavy with unspoken grief.

Carson steps forward, his boots crunching softly against the dirt. His hand rests on the simple wooden marker he'd carved himself. His voice is steady, though it trembles with emotion.

"Rusty was more than a horse," he begins, his gaze sweeping over the gathered group.

"He was a partner, a protector, and my best friend. He carried me through every storm, always giving more than I could ever ask for. I'll never forget what he gave me—his heart, his strength, and his love. Goodbye, Rusty. You'll always be with me."

Carson steps back, his hands falling to his sides, and Tegan steps forward. Her voice is soft but steady, her words carrying the weight of her loss.

"Rusty wasn't just Carson's. He was all of ours. He brought us together, reminded us why we do what we do. His legacy will live on in every horse that steps through our gates, in every life he's touched. Goodbye, BM."

Carson places the wooden marker at the head of the grave. It reads simply:

Bob's Mystery
aka "Rusty"
The Heart of Valley Vista Ranch
Forever Galloping Free

One by one, each member of the group steps forward to lay a wildflower on Rusty's grave. Their movements are slow and deliberate, their gestures filled with love and reverence.

Cameron and Alexa, the youngest of the Misfit Horse Brigade, approach Carson hesitantly. Cameron holds out a handmade bracelet fashioned from beads and strands of Rusty's tail hair. "I made this for you," she mumbles.

Alexa steps forward, her small hands clutching a drawing of Carson standing triumphantly on Rusty's back, along with a bag of homemade horse cookies. "In case Rusty gets hungry in heaven," she whispers.

Carson's voice catches as he accepts their gifts.

"Thank you, both of you."

Off to the side, Missy and Bethany huddle together, heads bowed, grief radiating in tense silence. Olivia approaches, her boots crunching softly against the gravel. Her voice cuts through the air, firm but wavering.

"What's going to happen to Jake?" she asks, arms crossed. "Because I'm thinking of starting a #JusticeForRusty campaign on Instagram. People need to know the truth."

Bethany's head snaps up, eyes blazing. "Are you serious right now? This isn't about your social media. Rusty's gone."

Missy steps forward, a warning in her tone. "Olivia, not now. This isn't the time."

"I just want people to know what happened," Olivia presses. "He deserves that."

Bethany takes a step closer, voice low and dangerous. "Shut up. Just shut up—or I'll shut you up myself."

Olivia's breath catches. Tears spill over as she stammers, "I'm sorry. I didn't mean—"

Missy softens, resting a hand on her shoulder.

"I know you care. We all do. But this isn't helping. Go back to the barn, okay?"

With a nod and trembling lip, Olivia gathers the rest of the Misfits and heads off, the fire of justice still flickering behind her tearful eyes.

As the others leave, Tegan kneels by the grave, gently laying her wildflower atop the mound of earth. She strokes the marker with her fingers, her voice breaking as she whispers, "Goodbye, BM. Watch over my dad for me, will you?"

She straightens and looks at Carson, a small smile breaking through her grief.

"I'll see you back at home," she whispers. She strides toward Oscar, already astride Paratrooper, and together they guide their horses back to the barn in heavy silence.

Carson lingers by the grave, his shoulders heavy with the weight of his loss. Janet steps up beside him, cradling her arm protectively around his torso like a sister offering silent strength.

"You want to talk about it?" she asks gently. "You don't have to, but I'm here."

Carson hesitates before sinking to one knee, his face buried in his hands. His body shudders as the memories flood back, and his voice trembles as he quietly recounts the horrific events of Rusty's demise.

"I don't think I can stay here," he whispers finally. "I love Tegan more than anything, but... I'm no good to her like this."

Janet tightens her hold, her voice steady.

"I understand. More than you think." She pauses, then adds, "Do you want me to talk to Tegan?" Carson shakes his head vehemently.

"No. I'll do it. I owe her that much."

Later that evening, Carson stands in the foyer of Tegan's home, a well-worn leather duffle bag slung over his shoulder. He looks around the space they've shared, his heart heavy.

Tegan enters quietly, her steps hesitant but sure. She stops in front of him, her voice soft but firm.

"I love you, Carson. More than anything. And I know you have to go."

His eyes fill with emotion as he looks at her. "I don't want to leave," he murmurs, his voice cracking. "But..."

She stops him with a fierce hug, wrapping her arms tightly around him. When she pulls back, she kisses him, the intensity of the moment saying everything words cannot.

"Promise me," she whispers, her voice trembling. "Promise me you'll come back when you're ready."

Carson nods, his head falling against her shoulder. "I promise."

She releases him and steps back, her eyes glistening as she watches him walk to the door. Carson hesitates one last time, glancing back before stepping outside. The door closes softly, leaving Tegan standing alone in the quiet house.

Moving On

The bedroom is dark, illuminated only by the faint sliver of moonlight streaming through the curtains. Tegan lies tangled in her sheets, her body restless. Beads of sweat glisten on her forehead as she stirs, her breathing shallow. Rusty's collapse and the echoing gunshot haunt her dreams.

In her sleep, she whimpers softly, her voice thick with sadness. "Carson..."

The sharp ring of her cell phone jolts her awake. She bolts upright, her hand instinctively wiping her damp forehead. Blinking against the haze of sleep, she glances at the clock on her nightstand. The glowing numbers read 3:28 a.m.. Her phone buzzes insistently beside it.

She grabs it, answering without hesitation. "Tegan here."

She listens, her brows furrowing, and then she swings her legs over the bed. "I'll be there in five."

The headlights of Bess, her trusty 1972 Chevy C20, cut through the darkness as she pulls up to the breeding barn. The ranch is silent except for the hum of crickets and the soft rustling of leaves. Tegan quickly parks and exits the truck, jogging toward the barn with purpose.

Inside, the warm glow of the barn lights spills across the aisle. Oscar stands outside a stall, his arms crossed, his expression focused yet calm. Dr. White, with his ever-present stethoscope draped around his neck, turns to her as she approaches. He nods, a small smile creasing his face.

"She's ready," Dr. White says simply.

Tegan steps into the stall, her heart pounding with both anticipation and worry. The broodmare, a large bay with kind eyes, shifts slightly on her feet, her flanks heaving as she prepares to deliver. Months earlier, veterinarians placed

Mirabella Mia and Rusty's embryo in the mare—a hopeful pairing to carry their legacy forward. Tegan kneels beside her, fingers tracing calming circles along her neck. "You've got this, girl," she breathes. Dr. White adjusts his position, kneeling near the mare's hindquarters. "Should be any minute now," he says, his voice steady.

The moment comes quickly. With one final contraction, the foal emerges. Dr. White expertly guides the delicate form into the bedding, his practiced hands moving with care. The foal's wet, glistening coat gleams under the soft barn lights as it takes its first breath.

And then, to everyone's astonishment, the foal stands.

"She's up already," Dr. White exclaims, his voice filled with awe. "I'll be damned. I haven't seen a foal stand that quickly since..."

"Since Rusty," Tegan finishes, her voice breaking with emotion. She wipes at her eyes as the memory of Rusty flashes through her mind.

Dr. White nods, a broad smile breaking across his face. "It's a filly."

The foal steps forward, her legs still wobbly but confident, her instincts driving her toward Tegan. Her tiny, multicolored mane sticks up like a mohawk, and her white coat gleams as though kissed by moonlight. Tegan kneels, tears streaming down her cheeks as she gently wipes the placental fluid from the filly's coat. The foal nuzzles her face against Tegan's protruding belly, as if sensing the life growing inside her.

"She knows you," Dr. White murmurs, shaking his head in amazement.

Oscar, who had been silent, steps closer. "She's a beautiful mix of her parents," he says softly. "Rusty and Mia."

Dr. White glances between Tegan and Oscar. "What's her name?"

Tegan looks at Oscar, a tearful smile playing on her lips. He doesn't hesitate. "Rusta Bella."

Tegan's eyes light up. "Rusta Bella... that's perfect. And her barn name can be Rusty's Mystery." She laughs softly, the sound warm and full of love. "It's only fitting."

The three of them laugh quietly, the weight of grief momentarily replaced by hope and joy.

Tegan guides the curious foal to the broodmare, who lowers her head and nickers softly. The mare nudges her filly gently, encouraging her to nurse. Rusta Bella latches on, her tiny tail flicking as she drinks.

Dr. White watches with satisfaction, his hands resting on his hips. "Healthy mare, healthy foal. It doesn't get better than that."

Tegan turns to him in gratitude. "Thank you for coming, Doc. I know it's late."

He smiles, waving her off. "I wouldn't miss this for the world. Moments like these make it all worth it."

Tegan nods, her eyes fixed on the pair before her. "Mia's going to love her. And when the time's right, I'll bring Rusta to visit Rusty's grave."

Dr. White pats her shoulder. "He'd like that."

As the barn quiets, Tegan looks over at Oscar. "You hungry?"

Oscar chuckles, rubbing his stomach. "Starving."

"Come to the house," Tegan says, a small smile tugging at her lips. "I'll make us some breakfast."

Oscar nods, his face softening as he glances back at the peaceful scene in the stall. "It's been a good night, Tegan."

"It has," she agrees, her hand resting briefly on her belly as she looks back at the mare and foal. "Let's go."

Together, they walk out of the barn, the first hints of dawn breaking over the horizon.

Pale morning light slips through the small window, spilling across the rough floorboards of Carson's modest room. A patchwork quilt drapes a narrow bed pushed against the wall; a wooden chair leans beside a scarred table cluttered with an empty plate. Near the door, a pair of scuffed boots waits, dust clinging to cracked leather. Carson hunches over the table, wiping the last crumbs of breakfast from his plate. Beyond the walls, cattle low in the distance, their calls weaving through the soft groan of the old ranch house, waking with the day.

In front of him lies a sheet of paper, his handwriting neat and deliberate as he pens a letter to Tegan. The act is slow, deliberate, as if each word carries the weight of his heart.

My Beloved Tegan;

Life here is simple—fixing fences, herding cattle, and all the chores that come with being a cowboy. The days are long, and the work is hard, but it keeps my hands busy, even if my mind refuses to be quiet.

I think of you constantly. I miss the sound of your voice, the way your laughter fills a room, the touch of your hand when everything feels too much.

But Rusty... I can't escape him. The memories haunt me. Some days, I swear I see him out here, galloping across the fields. I close my eyes, and I'm back at that moment—the gunshot, the look in his eyes. I don't know if I'll ever stop reliving it.

Still, I promise you this: I will come back. I don't know when, but I will. I just need you to wait for me.

I love you... always,

Carson

A knock on the door pulls Carson from his thoughts. "Time to bring the cattle in from the outer pen!" a voice calls.

Carson sighs, folding the letter carefully. He slips it into an envelope, presses a kiss to the seal, and sets it aside. Pulling on his boots and hat, he straightens, the weight of his thoughts still lingering as he heads out to the day's work.

The morning mist blankets the fields of Valley Vista Ranch, the dew glistening on the grass as the sunlight begins its slow work of drying it away. The ranch is still quiet, the hum of activity yet to begin.

Tegan, dressed in a soft sweater and jeans, walks through the serene landscape with Mirabella Mia trailing behind her. They stop at Rusty's grave, nestled beneath the large oak tree near Miller's Pond. The simple wooden marker stands tall, the engraved words still crisp:

Bob's Mystery
aka "Rusty"
The Heart of Valley Vista Ranch
Forever Galloping Free

Tegan crouches, her fingers gently rearranging the polished stones surrounding the grave. Some had shifted slightly, and she moves them back into place with care. Mia nickers softly, her ears pricked forward as she looks at the grave. Tegan smiles faintly.

"Good morning, Rusty," she says softly. "I have news. Your filly was born last night. She's beautiful—so much like you. Her name is Rusta Bella. When she's weaned, I'll bring her here to meet you."

She pauses, her hand resting lightly on the marker as her other drifts to her belly. Stroking the gentle curve, she adds, "I'm going to have a baby, Rusty. And this baby will be Rusta's best friend. She'll never be alone."

Her voice catches, and she shakes her head, answering an unspoken question. "I haven't told Carson. He's written to me, but I can't bring myself to write back. Oscar thinks I should tell him about the baby, but... I want him to come back because he's ready, not because he feels obligated."

Her composure falters and tears spill down her cheeks. "I miss him, Rusty. I miss you. But I know he'll come back. He just needs time."

Mia steps closer, lowering her head to rest her chin on Tegan's shoulder. The mare's warmth and steady presence offer comfort. Tegan strokes her muzzle, the sadness in her eyes giving way to gratitude.

She sniffs, wiping her tears, and smiles faintly. "What do you say, girl? Want to play?"

Mia lifts her head and lets out a sharp whinny, trotting out into the open field with her tail flagged high. Tegan chuckles softly, standing and pressing a kiss to her hand before placing it gently on Rusty's grave.

"See ya, Rusty," she whispers.

Tegan walks to the middle of the field, where Mirabella Mia waits eagerly. The mare's sharp eyes watch her every move, her muscles quivering with anticipation. Tegan raises her hands, signaling the start of their liberty training. Mia responds instantly, circling around her in smooth, precise strides.

As the morning sun rises higher, burning away the last remnants of mist, the two move together in perfect harmony. Mia's movements are graceful and free, her mane and tail rippling like a banner in the soft breeze. Tegan's laughter rings out as she spins, sending Mia into a joyful gallop, only to call her back with a single command.

From the grave beneath the oak tree, the sight is one of pure love and joy, a reminder that even in the face of sorrow, life continues.

Tegan's smile is wide and unrestrained as Mia rears playfully, then lands softly, her head tossing as if in celebration.

"That's my girl," Tegan calls, her voice full of pride.

As the sun shines down on the ranch, the message is simple: no matter the sorrow, life moves forward. One can always find joy in the insignificant moments, even after the darkest of days.

ABOUT THE AUTHOR

Maria V. Badin is an equestrian, writer, and lifelong advocate for living close to the land. With decades worth of experience in show jumping, eventing, and dressage, she brings authenticity and heart to every story she tells. Based in California, Maria lives on her ranch with her husband, her horses True, Bubbles, and High Duty, her dog Bentley, and her cats Turbo and Indy. Her work celebrates the grit, grace, and unbreakable bond between horse and rider.

You can follow her online: @badinmaria